Piers Anthony was born in Oxford in 1934, but moved with his family to Spain in 1939 and then to the USA in 1940, after his father was expelled from Spain by the Franco regime. He became a citizen of the US in 1958 and, before devoting himself to full-time writing, worked as a technical writer for a communications company and taught English. He started publishing short stories with *Possible to Rue* for *Fantastic* in 1963, and published in SF magazines for the next decade. He has, however, concentrated more and more on writing novels.

Author of the brilliant, widely acclaimed *Cluster* series, and the superb *Incarnations of Immortality* series, he has made a name for himself as a writer of original, inventive stories whose imaginative, mind-twisting style is full of extraordinary, often poetic images and flights of cosmic fancy.

By the same author

Chthon
Omnivore
The Ring (with Robert E. Margroff)
Sos the Rope
Var the Stick
Neq the Sword
The E.S.P. Worm (with Robert E. Margroff)
Orn
Prostho Plus
Race Against Time
Rings of Ice
Triple Detente
Phthor
Ox
Steppe
Hasan
A Spell for Chameleon
Vicinity Cluster
Chaining the Lady
Kirlian Quest
Thousandstar
Viscous Circle
God of Tarot
Vision of Tarot
Faith of Tarot
Split Infinity
Blue Adept
Juxtaposition
Bio of a Space Tyrant Volume 1: Refugee
Bio of a Space Tyrant Volume 2: Mercenary
Bio of a Space Tyrant Volume 3: Politician
Bio of a Space Tyrant Volume 5: Statesman
Incarnations of Immortality 1: On a Pale Horse
Incarnations of Immortality 2: Bearing an Hour Glass
Incarnations of Immortality 3: With a Tangled Skein
Incarnations of Immortality 4: Wielding a Red Sword
Incarnations of Immortality 5: Being a Green Mother
Macroscope
Anthonology
Shade of the Tree
Ghost

PIERS ANTHONY

Bio of a Space Tyrant
Volume 4: Executive

GRAFTON BOOKS
A Division of the Collins Publishing Group

LONDON GLASGOW
TORONTO SYDNEY AUCKLAND

Grafton Books
A Division of the Collins Publishing Group
8 Grafton Street, London W1X 3LA

Published by Grafton Books 1986
Reprinted 1986, 1988

ISBN 0-586-06271-8

Printed and bound in Great Britain by
Collins, Glasgow

Set in Times

Contents

Editorial Preface

Hope Hubris was just fifty years old as he became the government of the United States of North Jupiter, by the grace of the Constitutional Convention to Balance the Budget. He had reached this pinnacle by surviving the terrors of travel in space that decimated his family, rising through the ranks of the Jupiter Navy to become a planetary hero, and through the political levels to become the first Hispanic to win the presidency, only to be denied it on a technicality. But his sister, Spirit Hubris, had been active behind the scenes, and so the victory was restored to him in a fashion never before accomplished on Jupiter.

He was called the Tyrant, but his ascension was legitimate, and he was highly popular at the outset. He was to become unpopular and then feared and hated by some, but it is today generally conceded that he did what was necessary to restore Jupiter to equilibrium financially and in other respects. Such restoration was bound to be painful initially, which was why the democracy that preceded the Tyrancy had been unable to accomplish it. Only the absolute authority of a dictator could have unravelled the complex morass of conventions and special interests that existed. But he *did* balance the budget – eventually.

Other texts have examined the myriad technical and social changes wrought by the Tyrant and analysed them for their net effect on Jupiter. This personal diary by Hubris himself covers the other side of it: the private experience of the man who made it all possible. The business of running the Tyrancy, which was actually quite detailed and complicated, he mostly skims over, mentioning that Spirit handled it. She did – and there is surely a major untold story there. Spirit was competent and disciplined in ways that Hope was not, and she evidently lacked the private social and sexual passions he possessed. Thus he could afford to dally with incidentals and even suffer a siege of madness while the Tyrancy endured.

However, a good deal of substance is also revealed here. We learn that the so-called 'Siege of Saturn' was neither impulse nor madness, nor was the disarmament that followed it. Critics have suggested that the Tyrant was appallingly lucky; now we know that he acted with reckless genius at the outset to accomplish his purposes. This is not to say that he never suffered madness, merely that it was not of the precise nature we supposed. He had after all been memory-washed; perhaps that had a long-term effect on his sanity. Certainly the way he passes off the conquest of the other nations of Jupiter as if it were a minor incident is suspect; it was, in fact, a savage and dangerous exercise of military and economic power.

But if Hope Hubris was less than the popular image made of him, he was at least honest and dedicated and gifted in special ways, and perhaps he was the only person who could have accomplished what he did. Spirit and the others had competence; Hope had magic. There was no other person who could motivate an audience the way he could, or inspire the absolute and enduring loyalty he did. When he addressed an audience, that audience swayed to his power. He could make almost any man join him, and, as is apparent here, almost any woman love him.

Herewith his version of the story, written in the months after he was deposed. This volume was written in English, needing no translation; it has been edited only for chapterization, though it must be confessed that there are portions that this particular editor would have preferred to delete.

H. M. H

1

It Has To Be

I stood in the reception area of Pineleaf Bubble, which was a tiny park made up to resemble a section of pine forest. Megan, my beloved wife, was turning away from me in tears. I had lost her – not legally or socially or physically but in that cruel but necessary separation of paths that was now upon us.

'Sir?'

It was Emerald, my former wife, now in her fashion reclaiming me. For she was Admiral Mondy, commander of the task force of the Jupiter Navy designated to enforce order, and I was the man designated by the Constitutional Convention as the government of North Jupiter. I was the Tyrant. I had to give her my first order, by that act committing myself to responsibility for the operation of the most formidable nation in the Solar System.

The Constitutional Convention had been assembled to balance the budget – a thing that had never been accomplished on any continuing basis hitherto. The planetary debt (North Jupiter is only part of the planet, but common usage tends to term it a planet, regardless) exceeded a trillion dollars and was increasing at an accelerating rate. My first commitment had to be to deal with that.

'Get me the most knowledgeable expert on the budget,' I said to Emerald's brown face in the park camera. 'I promised to balance the budget and I shall do it.'

'That would be in the civilian sector,' she said.

'I *am* the civilian sector,' I said. 'Get me the personnel I need to do my job.'

'We'll get on it, sir,' she agreed with a certain muted satisfaction. 'Meanwhile we'd better get you aboard ship.'

'Aboard ship?' I asked querulously. 'Why?'

'To guarantee your safety, sir,' she said.

I looked across at the Secret Service men who had been guarding me through my political campaign just past. 'My safety is already guaranteed.'

'No, sir,' she said. 'There is a sub homing in on your bubble.'

A sub! I knew what damage they could do and who had control of one or more. I had defeated President Tocsin and now had taken power from him, but he was not a man to allow legality to stand in his way. 'I suppose, then – '

'We have detached a destroyer to pick up you and your personnel,' Emerald said. 'But if that sub opens fire before we nullify it – '

'There are other people here!' I exclaimed. 'Innocent residents! I can't go and leave them to be – '

'When you go, the bubble will no longer be a target, sir,' Emerald said. 'Wait there and be ready for pickup in fifteen minutes.'

I saw a Secret Service man nod affirmatively. He knew this was best. I shrugged.

'Shelia,' I said. 'Coral. Ebony.'

They appeared. Shelia, so named because her father had not spelled 'Sheila' correctly, was in her wheelchair, a Saxon I had hired at age sixteen, fifteen years ago; almost half her life had been in my employ, as executive secretary. Coral, a Saturnine émigré in her mid-thirties, my personal bodyguard and still a fine-looking woman. Ebony, our gofer, Black and uneducated and surprisingly useful. I kept them with me because I trusted them, and they understood my complex needs.

'Sir, better get suited,' Emerald said.

12

'Suited?'

'That sub is firing. That will help us pinpoint it. But until we take it out – '

'But the other residents – '

'Had all better get suited,' she said grimly.

Hastily we broke out the emergency suits. The law required all bubbles to have suits for every resident, in case of accidental pressurization, as might happen if there was a leak. There were regular drills, but seldom was there really a need. The suit-alarm sounded, alerting everyone in the bubble.

However, suiting was a complicated process for Shelia, because of the wheelchair and her inoperative legs. It was possible to get her into a suit, but it would interfere with her ability to function in her chair. I felt guilty, getting into my suit while she did not.

'They are finding the range,' Emerald said, evidently reading her battle indicators. 'Proceed to confinement alert.'

That meant that each resident had to get into his or her chamber and seal it shut. This was to maintain normal pressure in individual apartments even when the bubble itself was holed.

'But I can't – ' I protested, thinking of Megan. I knew she didn't want me with her now.

'Mine,' Shelia said, propelling her chair rapidly down the hall. The Secret Service man followed, glancing around warily.

Her apartment was next to mine. She shared it with Ebony, so that the two were always handy for notes or errands. Coral's was on the other side, and she shared with my sister, Spirit, who was elsewhere today. We entered, and the Secret Service man took up his position in his suit, in the hall. Coral, I knew, was going to join Megan, to be sure she was all right. Megan had left me,

13

but her life remained precious to me and would always be so.

Shelia had a transceiver in her wheelchair. 'He is with me,' she was murmuring into it. I could hear her despite my suit, somewhat foggily.

'It's going to be close,' Emerald said. 'Those subs are almost impossible to nail down quickly when they take evasive action. We'll get it, but it will have several more shots at the bubble.'

I removed my helmet. 'If you can't get suited, I won't be, either,' I said to Shelia.

'But Hope – ' she protested. She always addressed me as 'sir' in public, but in private her feeling for me showed.

Then the first shell struck. I knew by the feel of the impact that it was a shell; my Navy experience had left me with the ability to interpret such strikes instantly. A nonexplosive, hull-piercing shell, designed to hole a ship without otherwise damaging it. Ships were valuable once the personnel were eliminated; holing could save the one while accomplishing the other.

'Oh!' Shelia exclaimed in alarm. As a lifetime civilian, she was not used to being under fire.

'They'll take out that sub in a moment,' I reassured her. 'Every time it fires, it provides another line on its position.'

Her chin firmed. 'Of course,' she agreed.

'Sir, I am in contact with Coral,' Emerald said in the tiny chair-screen. 'She tells me to "Wash his body". I'm not sure I understand.'

'It is a Saturnine expression,' I said, remembering. 'More completely, it is, "Wash his body in blood". It means – '

'Now I get it. That sub!'

'That sub,' I agreed.

'About two more shots and we'll have it zeroed in.'

14

'We've been scored on once,' I reminded her. 'Two more strikes might make the matter academic.'

'You've got to take evasive action,' she said.

'In a residential bubble? This is no spaceship, Em!'

'Be creative,' she suggested.

'Maybe – ' Shelia said faintly.

'Out with it, girl,' I snapped, knowing that her mind made up for what her legs lacked.

'If the shield were turned off briefly – '

'Done!' I exclaimed. 'Get me the Pineleaf engineer.'

She touched buttons. In a moment the man's harried face came on the little screen. I had to shove my head almost into Shelia's lap to get it into the pickup range. 'Hubris, here. I have just assumed the government of Jupiter. We are under fire, in an attempt to take me out before I can consolidate my power. We must take evasive action for a few minutes, until the Navy scrubs the enemy sub. Cut off the gee-shield as long as you dare.'

'But, Mr Hubris, that would risk – '

Emerald's face appeared in split screen. 'Do it, man. Want to get holed?'

The engineer swallowed. 'It has to be very brief because – '

'*Do it!*' Emerald and I yelled together.

For answer, the bubble lurched as the gravity of Jupiter took hold. Pineleaf, like all the towns and cities of Jupiter, was a good deal more solid than the atmosphere and would plummet to the hellish depths if not shielded from the main effect of the planet's gravity. The pressure at this level was about five bars – that is, five times the pressure of Earth's atmosphere at sea-level – which the bubbles and suits were constructed to withstand. The pressure below was much greater. Too great a drop would cause a bubble to implode – a far more certain demise

15

than depressurization. But it was the only motion we could quickly make.

We did not lose weight. This was because the bubble spun on a vertical axis, generating a centrifugal emulation of gravity. Neither did we gain weight, for we remained in free-fall. That spin continued, unaffected by the cessation of the shield. But now we were dropping.

Another shell scored. It must have been on the way even as we began our descent. Had we not moved, it might have struck dead centre and holed us. As it was, it struck at the top, and its formidable impact translated into a nudge of rotation in another direction.

Remember what happens when you nudge a spinning top? It doesn't just fall over; it precesses. There is a complex explanation for this, but the essence is that there's a lot more energy in the spin than in the nudge, so the compromise resultant motion is not in the direction of the nudge. So it was in this case. We started to rotate to the side, in addition to our normal spin and the sliding descent into deeper atmosphere. It wasn't enough to throw us around, but we did feel disoriented. Even the slightest complication of orientation can nauseate a person.

I had been trained to handle this during my time in the Navy, of course. My memory of that experience remained imperfect, because of a recent memory-wash I had been subjected to, but my reflexes remained. Shelia lacked that experience, but I think her lifetime in the wheelchair enabled her to adapt to other handicaps of motion. She clung to her wheels, preventing the chair from moving around.

Information was still coming in on the transceiver. 'Glancing hit,' Emerald said. 'Damage report?'

'Hull intact,' I said. 'Some modification of attitude, not

serious.' By 'attitude' I meant the situation of the bubble in the atmosphere, not the feelings of its residents.

'Evasion tactic successful,' she continued briskly. 'Third shell missed.' Then, after a pause: 'Coral, watch the screen.'

I knew what was coming. I jammed my head at Shelia's midsection again, to get a view of her screen. It had required three shots to pinpoint the sub; now they would take it out, ending the immediate crisis.

There was the dark blob that was the sub, highlighted on the image. A sub is a small ship that possesses a screen to absorb radiation, so that neither light nor radar reflects from it. Thus the normal methods of location aren't effective; it is invisible. But it does occlude background radiation and can be approximately located by analysis of the pattern of occlusion if it is careless enough to position itself where such a pattern manifests. For fast, specific location it is necessary to triangulate on its own emissions: such as the shells it fires. This had now been done. The sub remained invisible, but the Navy computers knew exactly where it was, and so were able to mark it on the screen.

Then the blot exploded. The screen damped down the brilliance, but still, it was impressive. A tiny nova had formed in Jupiter's atmosphere.

'We washed his body,' Emerald reported grimly. 'Cease descent.'

I had forgotten: we were still going down. The atmosphere of Jupiter is enormous, and the constant winds prevent a straight drop, but still, this was not a process we wanted to continue one moment longer than necessary. 'Engineer,' I snapped. 'Restore the shield!'

There was no response.

'His station is near the point that the shell struck,' Shelia said. 'He may have been jarred, hit his head – '

'I've got to turn on that shield!' I exclaimed.

'Stay where you are, sir!' Coral cried from the transceiver. 'I'll handle it!'

Of course, it was better for her to do it; I could not afford to go dashing off on every errand. Still, I chafed. I preferred to be a man of action.

Ebony came on. 'She says to cut the power. We don't know how much we'll need to lift back to proper position.'

'Right,' I agreed.

The light went out. Shelia and I were locked in darkness, as were the other residents, scattered through their apartments. I understood the necessity, but nonetheless felt the psychological impact. We were still falling, the pressure rising outside. How much could the hull take? Would Coral get the shield restored in time? Of course she would – but my alarm would not be quieted.

Each person, I suspect, has his own special fear. Many planetary-bubble inhabitants fear the empty reaches of deep space, and depressurization is their ultimate horror. Navy personnel, in contrast, understand space but tend to fear the horrendous pressures of the planetary environment and are appalled at the notion of implosion. I was born and raised to age fifteen on Callisto, which is termed a planet (technically a moon of Jupiter), but it had no atmosphere, no threat of pressure. Then I joined the Navy, for another fifteen years. Thus my fear aligned with that of the spaceman. Vacuum I could handle; a good suit would protect against it. But pressure – simple holing at normal level would mean an increase to five bars, and that would stifle all Navy personnel, for true space suits were not constructed to withstand that. The pressure suits would, but my conditioned reaction did not quite accept that, and, of course, those seldom-used suits are not perfectly reliable. That was why we had had to seal ourselves in our cabins; they were rated at six bars and would save us from such pressure.

But, if the bubble imploded, so would the cabins. It would take ten or more bars to implode the bubble, because it was spherical and sturdy – but when it happened, it would be virtually instant. One moment we would be alive and nervous; the next we would be crushed, more or less literally, to pulp. We were surely approaching the limit now. That notion insinuated itself right into my consciousness and knocked the props from under my courage, leaving me a coward.

Then I thought of Megan, now alone in the next chamber, and was horrified for her as well. Even if we survived this ordeal, she would not be mine. She had left me for the soundest of all her reasons: the philosophical. She accepted the necessity of what was to be termed the Tyrancy but could not support it personally. So she had freed me to do what I had to do – and left me desolate. What the fear of implosion did to my physical courage, the knowledge of my loss of Megan did to my emotional courage.

Shelia knew. She had invisible antennae that resonated to human distress, and she knew me as well as an executive secretary of fifteen years could. 'Hope – here,' she said in the darkness.

I got to my knees and leaned over her wheel and armrest. Her arms came up to enclose me, to draw my head to her bosom. She held me there and stroked my hair while I sobbed.

'It had to be, it had to be . . .' she murmured over and over. Of course, she was right; this was a necessary pass. But a necessary thing is not necessarily a pleasant thing.

Then there was illumination of a sort, and I lifted my head and looked at her face. 'Helse,' I said.

'I always come to you when you need me,' she replied.

'You always do,' I agreed.

Helse was my first love. She had been sixteen, I fifteen when we met, thirty-five years before. She had taught me love. She had died on the eve of our wedding, helping me survive. Death had changed her only in this: she had not aged from that moment. She was always sixteen, for me. Always lovely, always understanding. Always there for me, in the recess of reality.

And I was always fifteen, for her. Always the innocent, loving her and grateful for her kindness.

'If I am to die,' I said, 'this is the way I would do it.'

'It has to be,' she agreed.

I got to my feet and reached my arms down around her and lifted her out of the chair. I set her on the bed, her head on the pillow, and gently, methodically stripped her of her clothing. My subsequent experience advised me that there were women more thoroughly endowed than Helse, and I had possessed more than one of them, but none was ever better formed for my taste than she. I kissed her bare breasts, and she held my head to them. 'It has to be,' she murmured again.

I removed my suit, then undressed myself. Then I took her, and she was what she had always been for me, my ultimate delight. I kissed her, she clung to me, her face was wet with her tears or mine, and her tongue met mine as her legs lifted to wrap around mine. I bit her on her right ear as I pumped my essence into her, and she sighed and convulsed against me and relaxed at last. We lay embracing, the sweat of our exertion between us, and my delight in her body remained, though my sexual passion had passed. 'It has been so long,' I murmured in her ear.

'So long,' she agreed.

There was a sound from the chair. 'Shield coming on,' Coral announced.

We clung to each other as the bubble passed from the

free-fall of falling to the free-fall of null-gee. Technical experts say there is no distinction between them, but we more ordinary folk know that there is. We felt the change – and the enormous relief of knowing that if we had not imploded yet, we were not going to, for we would descend no farther.

'I must leave you before the light returns,' Helse told me. She took my head in her hands and kissed me once more, deeply. 'It has to be.'

'It has to be,' I agreed. I knew what happened when I forced her to overstay her leave. She could become a corpse or a skeleton – or worse. Helse's terms had to be honoured.

Quickly I got up and dressed her and myself. I lifted her to the chair. Then, in an accident of timing that was fortunate indeed, the light returned.

I blinked, and she blinked, adjusting. She was Shelia, my paralysed secretary. Her hair was mussed and her clothing was in a certain disarray, but the rigors of the bubble-situation could account for that.

She brought forth a handkerchief. 'Sir, there is a smudge on your face,' she said.

I brought my face down, and she wiped it carefully. She had done the same for me on other occasions, making sure I was presentable before a public appearance.

But this was more than that. 'Shelia,' I said. 'I – '

'You had a vision,' she said. 'I understand.'

She surely understood – but there are limits. 'It was never my intent to – '

'I know who Helse is,' she reminded me firmly.

'But – '

'She comes to you when you most need her, bringing what you need.'

'That is true. However – '

'Did you feel her legs move?'

I stiffened in a kind of shock. *Helse's legs had moved.* They had enclosed my body at the essential moment.

Shelia's legs had been paralysed since her childhood. Never since I had known her had she moved them. I knew that electro and chemical therapy had maintained their structure, but the nerves simply were not there. This was no psychological thing; it was not physically possible for her to move them, even a trifle, unless she picked them up with her hands.

Helse's arms had clasped my upper torso. Her legs had spread and lifted themselves. That could have been my fancy of the moment, of course; if I could summon her likeness from eternity, I could summon her motion.

But how had Shelia known?

I stared at her, bemused. Her eyes were bright with tears not of sorrow. 'They moved,' I agreed. Then I kissed her.

She returned the kiss, then, womanlike, chastised me. 'You're smudged again – right after I got you clean.'

With the same lipstick as before. Shelia's lipstick. But the body I had held had been Helse's.

I gave up the effort to explain or apologize. Either nothing had happened between Shelia and me, or it was something so significant as to be beyond our understanding.

But there was something else. I had separated from Megan. Never during the years of our marriage had I touched any member of my staff in any way other than proper or professional. I had touched another woman outside that number, but that had been a special situation and, I think, did not represent a dilution of my marriage. I had been faithful to Megan. But now I had broken from her – and what I had just done represented my recognition of that fact. Helse had come to me, to show me that my

22

marriage was over. I had known it intellectually, but now I knew it in my gut.

I still longed for Megan, and I knew I would always love her. But our relationship had been sundered, as it had had to be.

'It had to be,' I murmured.

'It had to be,' Shelia repeated.

'Ship has rendezvoused,' Emerald reported. 'If you will board now . . .'

I realized that I had not returned to my suit. Fortunately Emerald could not see me as I stood outside the pickup range of the transceiver. Actually, knowledge of what I had done wouldn't have fazed Emerald one whit; she too, understood me. 'On our way,' I said.

2

Beautiful Dreamer

We were aboard the flagship: Coral, Ebony, Shelia, and me. Emerald was establishing a Naval cordon around Pineleaf Bubble and all that region, to ensure that no further acts of mayhem occurred. Megan would be safe, and my daughter, Hopie. I had never discussed it with Megan, because our separation had come upon us so abruptly, but I knew Hopie would remain with her. My sister, Spirit, was in the state of Golden, where she had gone to organize the Constitutional Convention that had just put me in power; she would join me as soon as she could.

My limited personal staff was understanding and loyal, as Shelia had just demonstrated, but none of these women were politicians. I knew I needed competent advice in a hurry. Had the election been honoured, I would have assumed the presidency and designated selected officers from my party in the conventional fashion. But the election had been voided, and now I had taken power outside the normal framework of government. That made it an entirely different game, and I wasn't sure I understood the rules. I was certain to blunder and quite possibly get myself killed if I did not take precisely the correct steps, quickly.

'Sir,' Shelia said, summoning my attention. We were at the moment in an officer's dayroom, designated a temporary headquarters. Coral was taking a shower, having got grimy when squeezing into the obscure engineer's compartment, restoring the shield and reviving the unconscious engineer. Ebony was sorting through a bundle of my clothing she had had the foresight to take from my former apartment, knowing I would not return. She would see that I had a decent suit to wear for whatever occasion occurred. Shelia remained my liaison with the rest of the planet, fielding a continual hailstorm of messages and disposing of all but the most critical. When she alerted me, I snapped to.

'Admiral Emerald Mondy has the budget expert on the screen,' she said.

Oh, yes. I had asked for the most knowledgeable expert on the budget, in that manner signalling my commitment to the cause that had brought me power. That had been scarcely an hour ago, yet it seemed like days. 'I, uh, guess I'd better, um, talk to him,' I mumbled uncertainly. I had no idea what to say to the man – or woman – I had asked for.

'Hope Hubris will interview Senator Stonebridge immediately,' Shelia said smoothly.

A face came on the dayroom's large screen. I recognized it, of course; no person spends twenty years in the Jupiter political arena without becoming familiar with the prime movers of the society. Stonebridge had been a leading financier until tapped by President Kenson to be Budget Director, and in the time he had held that office, the finances of Jupiter had been disciplined. When Kenson retired, Stonebridge had run successfully for the Senate and become the leading critic of President Tocsin's financial policies. I had no doubt of his expertise; had my wits been more about me, I would have realized at the outset that he was the one to consult. I had, however, never dealt with him personally.

'Senator, you know my situation,' I said, collecting my wits so as to put on a good front.

'Yes, Mr President,' he agreed.

I grimaced. 'I'm not sure I'm president. I have assumed power outside the framework of – '

He smiled. 'If you will provide the appropriate title, then.'

I pondered the matter of a title, and my mind went blank. I spread my hands. 'I suppose you had better stick with what you have. Now I am committed to balance the budget, but I am no budgetary expert. If you will advise me how to – '

'Mr President, I can't do that.'

I was startled. 'You – ?'

'You must provide me with a context. What are your priorities? Do you plan new taxes? What stress do you place on military preparedness? On social welfare? I can make suggestions, but I have to know my mandates.'

I shook my head ruefully. 'Senator, I don't even have a government yet!'

'Perhaps you had better consult me at a later date,' he suggested delicately.

I made a gesture of submission. 'At a later date,' I agreed.

The connection broke. Then Emerald entered the day-room. 'You haven't changed, sir,' she said, like a mother addressing an errant child.

'My wife and sister aren't here,' I replied, knowing that she would understand what I meant. I had never claimed to be expert at organization; the women in my life had always run things for me. In the Navy, Emerald herself had served in that capacity.

'Sir, I don't think you can afford to wait until Spirit gets here,' Emerald said. 'I would help you if I could, but I don't know the civilian sector, and I think it would be best to keep the military sector subordinate. As it is, we have all we can do to keep the peace during the interim.'

'Keep the peace?' I asked blankly.

'There is armed rebellion in some sectors. We can only sit on it so long without your direct input. Also, the other planets are getting restive. I suggest that you get your house in order within the hour, sir.'

'But I hardly know where to start!' I wailed.

She nodded, knowing my problem. 'I think, sir, that you need a very special consultation. Take half an hour; he will put you straight.'

'*Who* will put me straight?'

She stepped into me, took my head in her hands, and kissed me. I was abruptly aware of how attractive she remained to me, despite the passage of twenty years. 'The Beautiful Dreamer,' she murmured so that only I could hear. Then she turned around and departed, leaving me stunned.

Shelia wheeled up to me. 'Are you all right, sir?'

'I – '

'You still have feeling for her? It is obvious that she still loves you.'

'All true,' I agreed. 'I retain feeling for every woman I have had, in whatever fashion, and they for me.' I touched her hand momentarily. 'But this is something else.'

'Did she give you a name, sir? I can connect – '

'You cannot connect me to this party,' I said. 'He is . . . like Helse, in one respect.'

She paused, and I could almost see the synapses connecting in her head. Shelia had made it her business to know every business and personal connection I had, so that when I asked for 'What'shisname in Ebor' she could have him on the screen in a moment without asking for clarification. Now she was sifting, computerlike, through my Naval contacts that predated her tenure, knowing that this was the most likely area of Emerald's suggestion.

Her face paled. 'Lieutenant Commander Repro?' she whispered.

'The same. The one whose dream of grandeur I implemented.'

She paused again, and I knew she was assessing the implications. She had helped me animate Helse, but that had been a special case. She could not do the same for a dead man.

It was Ebony who came to the rescue. From the collection of my things she brought out a device with five steel balls. 'If you take this into the chapel, sir,' she said, holding it out, 'I don't think God would object.'

I took the device into the chapel chamber adjoining the dayroom. This was a nondenominational place intended for prayer of whatever nature desired. Indeed I did not think God would object if I sought communication with the dead here.

I set the little structure on the table. It was a framework like a cube with five steel balls suspended by paired threads from the top beams.

The balls hung in a row, almost touching each other. When one at the end was swung into the next, the shock was transmitted through the line until the ball at the far end swung out, leaving the four others virtually stationary. Friction made it imperfect, of course, but it remained a nice demonstration of a physical principle. I had amused myself for many hours, swinging those balls by ones, twos, and threes, noting how perfectly the pattern transmitted to the far side.

This device had belonged originally to Lieutenant Commander Repro, who had used it to illustrate his thesis that every force had its impact and its reaction. He had conceived the notion of an ideal military unit, staffed by the most capable, yet unknown, officers. He was a drug addict, and the Navy had not taken him seriously. But I had become his ideal commander, because of my talent in understanding people, and with his help I had formed that ideal cadre, and in due course we had swept the pirates out of the Belt. Success hath its price in the Navy, and that price had been my retirement and his death, but the unit we had formed remained and now governed the Navy itself. That, of course, was the true root of my present power: the Navy was backing me.

I had had a rule: every member of my unit had his song. It had to be bestowed on him by the group, in the manner of the migrant workers. My song was *Worried Man Blues*; Repro's song was *Beautiful Dreamer*. He had not been beautiful physically, and perhaps not mentally; he had been wasting away from the ravages of his addiction. But his dream had been beautiful, and its legacy remained – and was now ready to expand to planetary scale. I owed what I was emotionally to Helse, and what I was politically to Megan, but I owed what I had been militarily to the Dreamer. In that sense I was his dream.

I lifted an end ball and let it go. It swung to impact on the next, and the far ball swung out. The far one swung back, knocking the near one out, not quite as far, and so on, back and forth, until the inefficiency of the system caused all five balls to be swinging gently in unison. I watched, feeling myself being mesmerized by that process.

I lifted two balls and let them go. Two swung out opposite, and back, and two near balls again, and on, until again the swings diminished into uniform motion. Then three balls, so that only two remained stationary in the centre, and the centre ball was always in motion, swinging back and forth, as it were picking up the two on one side and then the other. Fascinating!

Then I lifted two from the near side, one from the far side, and let them go simultaneously. Sure enough, one rebounded on the near side and two on the far side, their impetuses passing through each other unscathed. This always fascinated me most. Every force did have its reaction, regardless of the other forces operating.

I hummed, hearing the words clearly in my mind: *Beautiful Dreamer, wake unto me . . .*

And he was there, sitting across from me. 'You steal my song, Worry?'

'I steal your dream,' I replied. 'I cannot handle it alone. I need your guidance.'

'Where do you stand?'

'I have assumed power over Jupiter, politically. I must balance the budget. But I don't know how to start.'

'Over Jupiter!' he exclaimed. 'You have gone beyond my dream!'

'No. I merely seek to extend it. I have the power now, but not the insight.'

'The very first thing you must do is to consolidate your power,' he said. 'You have enemies; eliminate them. You have opposition; nullify it. Do not allow any challenge to your power or you will lose it.'

'But power is not my object!' I protested. 'I simply want the chance to right the wrongs that exist on the planet.'

'Power is the means, not the end,' he agreed. 'Secure it first, then get on with your ends. Just see that the means do not *become* the ends.'

It did make sense. 'But after that – I have no government, no structure to accomplish my ends.'

'One thing at a time,' he said. 'Rome was not built in a day, and Jupiter will not be revamped in a day. Declare the present institutions to remain in force until further notice, on an advisory basis. Then, piecemeal, as convenient, revise them. But always make sure your base of power is secure.'

'My base of power is the will of the people – and the Jupiter Navy,' I said.

'Then heed the will of the people – and keep your own folk in charge of the Navy.'

Suddenly it seemed so simple! Still, I doubted. 'I must have a context! I must have priorities. I need to establish mandates. I need personnel to execute these things.'

'You can promote them from the existing structures as you turn your attention to each. It will be years before your programme is complete. Have patience. As long as you maintain your purpose and your power and are not corrupted by either, you may safely pursue both. Remember' – here he lifted a ball and let it go – 'action – reaction. Take care that you understand the consequences of your actions.'

'I will,' I said.

He smiled and put his hand out to still the moving balls, and when their motion stopped, he was gone.

I sighed, missing him already. But the dead cannot be held beyond their terms. I stood, picked up the structure, and stepped back into the dayroom.

There are those who do not seem to understand my contacts with the dead. Over the years explanations have been put forward, few of which are complimentary to me. It has been said that I am crazy, or that I suffer hallucinations, or that I dose myself with mind-distorting drugs, or that I merely invent the visions to justify my actions. The most popular theory is that I am a covert epileptic and that the visions are seizures. That may be so; certainly there has never been any physical evidence of what I have experienced. Yet it seems to me that the visitations are authentic, and certainly I have benefited both emotionally and practically from the reassurance and advice they have brought me. When I was fifteen, stranded in a bubble in space, my deceased father came to me and showed our group how to survive. Thereafter, Helse came many times to me, always at my greatest need, and whether she came without physical substance or by animating a living woman, her visits were always most precious and welcome. Once Megan visited me, before I met her in person; the contacts are not necessarily limited to the dead. Now Repro, the Dreamer, had come to set me straight, and if this can be said to be a feature only of my imagination, then my imagination has a wider scope than my ordinary consciousness does. Perhaps the visits are real, and the technical term for this type of reality is epilepsy. Regardless, I would be poorer and less effective without it. In fact, I would be dead without it. So call it what you will, and call me what you will; it is the way I am. I believe that every person exists in a construct of his own reality, and if that reality includes the occasional restoration of those other people whom he loves or values, that is no bad thing.

I returned the steel balls to Ebony. 'Thank you,' I said, reaching out to tweak a strand of her glossy black hair. 'I reached him.'

'Good thing, sir,' Shelia said. 'Because all hell is breaking loose on Jupiter.'

'I am ready for it now.'

Emerald came on the dayroom screen, evidently connected by Shelia. 'Sir, there is trouble.'

'I'm sure there is,' I agreed.

'I have been removed as commander of this task force.'

Thanks to my interview with the Dreamer, I knew how to proceed. 'Get me the commanding admiral of the Jupiter Navy,' I told Shelia.

'Admiral London,' Emerald said.

After a moment Shelia reported: 'His office doesn't answer.'

'Then put out a planetary bulletin: Admiral London

has one minute to report to me via this network, or he will be disciplined.'

'In process, sir.' She made her connections, and in a moment Emerald's face on the screen was replaced by that of a staff officer.

'By order of Hope Hubris, Admiral London to report within sixty seconds or be disciplined. All units advise.'

Coral emerged, clean and fresh. She was in her mid-thirties but possessed the figure and features of a woman a decade younger. 'I begin to get nervous,' she murmured.

'It's being handled,' Ebony said.

The minute finished without response by the admiral. 'Admiral London is as of this moment relieved of command,' I said. 'Admiral Emerald Mondy is elevated to that command. Notify all units immediately.'

Shelia got busy again, sending out the word. Emerald's face reappeared on the screen. 'Further orders, sir?'

'Consolidate your position,' I said. 'You know what to do.'

'Aye-aye, sir,' she said, saluting smartly.

I returned the salute. For an instant it was like old times, when I had commanded my own task force. But now we were playing for larger stakes.

'Sir,' Shelia said. 'Broadcast from Admiral London.'

'Put it on.'

The Admiral's face appeared on the screen. '. . . usurper,' he was saying. 'Repeat: There is rebellion in the Navy. All loyal units to declare for President Tocsin and against the usurper. Report immediately.'

But Emerald was on the job. 'The Constitutional Convention is the ultimate authority of North Jupiter. It has appointed Hope Hubris to govern the planet. Hope Hubris has appointed me commanding admiral of the Jupiter Navy. Neither Tocsin nor London retains power. Verify this for yourselves and do as you deem proper.'

She smiled. She was the same age as I, fifty, but still a compelling woman.

The units, for the moment perplexed, did just that. Then, one by one, they declared for the new order. My authority, however precedent-breaking, *was* legitimate; Tocsin's was illegitimate, and it did not require any great amount of research to verify that. The ongoing news of my elevation to power had been dominating the media; very few citizens, whether civilian or military, could be in ignorance of it. When it became apparent that the majority supported me, the conversion of those in doubt was prompt. Only a few units held out, and these were promptly isolated and nullified without violence.

I relaxed. 'So the Navy supports me,' I said. 'I know that the majority of the people support me too.'

Later there would be stories published about the supposedly horrendous campaign I waged to tame the rebellious elements of the Navy, making it seem as if Planet Jupiter was the centre of a blazing battle, with several ships holed and several more plummeting into the deadly depth of the atmosphere. The truth was otherwise; it was really only a minor question, settled peacefully in a few minutes. No blood was shed at my accession. If this makes my own narration seem trivial, so be it; I have seen more than enough genuine bloodshed and do not care to enhance my notoriety by fiction. Admiral London was guilty of a misjudgement, no more, and was permitted to take early retirement with an unblemished record.

The irony is that though many of the dramatic stories about me are false, there are true episodes that would have been equally dramatic in print but that were never published. In some cases the reasons for nonpublication are as interesting as the items themselves, for I never practised censorship. My enemies could have blasted me with the truth, but their attention was so firmly fixed on what was false that they overlooked the reality. In this manuscript I mean to present as much of the truth as is warranted. About the only ugly action was in connection with ex-President Tocsin. He was holed up in New Wash, in the White Bubble itself, and refused to acknowledge the change of government. I realized that I had to deal with him directly.

Tocsin was a completely unscrupulous man He had shown his nature during his campaign against Megan for a seat as a senator, twenty-two years before. It had become a textbook example of scurrilous politics. He had proceeded from height to height – more properly, depth to depth – until I defeated him for the highest office. Then he had used several nefarious devices to block my ascension, until the Constitutional Convention had swept the entire prior government aside and appointed me. Now he fought a stubborn rear-guard action, perhaps believing that the people would in the end support him as the defender of the status quo, rather than me, as a completely new order. I was not concerned about the people, but there were records in the White Bubble that I wanted to recover intact, and I did not want to give him the opportunity to destroy them. He had to be dealt with swiftly.

But the White Bubble was a very special place. It was associated with New Wash, where the major portion of the North Jupiter governmental apparatus was, and I knew that had to be preserved. Even if I had not had a care for the population there, I would not have threatened the administrative structures of the nation. How could we get the worm out of the apple without harming the apple?

I discussed it with my limited staff, there in the flagship, and we concluded that there was only one feasible way. I had to make a deal. The only way Tocsin would ever let those records fall into my hands was if he was assured that nothing in them could be used against him.

I really had no choice. 'Call him,' I told Shelia.

Tocsin had evidently anticipated the call, because in a moment his homely face was on the screen. 'You know what I want, Governor,' he said when he saw me. Since the last public office I had held was that of governor of the State of Sunshine, it was a legitimate address. This was a public call, open to the media; there would be no secrets here, and because it was to our mutual interest to make a good impression, he was polite.

'I want an orderly transition of administration,' I said. 'I presume your interest is similar.'

'The Supreme Court denied you, but the Navy supports you,' he said. 'You have taken over by force, not by the political process. But might makes right, eh? You've got the power.'

I did not care to debate with him the ethics of my ascension. I had taken power legitimately if unconstitutionally; the force had been required only because of his intransigence. 'I have the power,' I agreed.

'But I have the White Bubble,' he said. 'And you want it. What do you offer for it?'

This galled me, as I had known it would. He was trying to make me pose the offer when I would have preferred to have him ask for it. 'A safe conduct out of it,' I said shortly.

He shook his head. 'You can do better than that, Governor.'

I ground my teeth, almost literally. 'A pardon,' I said. My reputation as governor had suffered grievously when I pardoned four unfairly condemned men. Tocsin was certainly guilty – and I had to let him off. My mouth tasted of gall.

He nodded. 'Your word on that, Governor.'

'I give it,' I said grimly. I felt unclean. I had long dreamed of bringing this man to trial, of making him pay for everything – and now he would not.

That was all there was to it. Tocsin knew that my word was good, though his was not. But to the best of my knowledge he never again conspired against me, because he could be held accountable for anything he did following the pardon. If he gave me a legitimate pretext to go after him . . .

In this manner I consolidated my power. Oh, there were pockets of resistance scattered around the planet, but I was now in control, and the population seemed satisfied to have the matter settled.

I thought the worst was over. I thought, in that early day, that I really could do it. Such was my hubris, my namesake: the arrogance of pride and passion. Hope Hubris, the foolish dream of glory.

3

The Tyrancy

Emerald took us to New Wash. The Navy landed the troops to safeguard my arrival, but Emerald did not trust this. She made sure that no segment of the public had access to me during the transition. 'There are always the crazies, the kamikaze assassins,' she said. 'We need to get you installed alive, sir.'

The White Bubble, so recently vacated by Tocsin, was a short distance from the massive New Wash city-bubble, like a satellite, though, of course, it did not orbit the city. It was now flanked by three cruisers and a number of smaller ships; nothing short of a direct military invasion could penetrate that defence.

We were funnelled in on another destroyer. Emerald kissed me at the lock. 'Take care of yourself, sir,' she cautioned me.

'My staff will see to that,' I said.

'For the moment,' she agreed obliquely. 'Remember, the Navy is always at your service.'

She meant more than militarily. I wished I could take her up on it; the Navy had been a competent home for me, in the past. At the moment I wished someone could take me by the hand and guide me to some quiet, safe place where I could just relax for a time. But there was too much to be done; I did not know when I could afford to rest. 'I'll remember,' I agreed wanly.

Then we were moved to the White Bubble. There, at the entrance lock, was my sister Spirit. She was three years my junior but, I think, looked younger. Somehow I still remembered her as a child of twelve. As a woman of twelve.

I moved into her arms. Suddenly I felt much better. Spirit had always been my strength; how glad I was that she had got here as fast as I had.

Spirit got right to work. 'You have done a good job of consolidating power, Hope. Now you need to establish a government, at least a temporary one.'

'I will declare the present mechanisms of government to continue until further notice,' I said. 'Then I will revise them as convenient, piecemeal.'

She nodded appreciatively. 'You are better organized than I thought you might be.'

'It's not my notion,' I confessed.

'Oh?'

'Beautiful Dreamer.'

'Oh.' She understood the reference, of course, but took a moment to digest the implication. 'Then let's make notes on your speech.' She turned to Shelia. 'Set up a planetary address at the earliest auspicious moment.'

'Twenty-one minutes hence,' Shelia said evenly.

'We'll make it,' Spirit said.

We huddled over it, working out suitable phrasing. The essence was: I am the new government of North Jupiter, by the authority of the Constitutional Convention to Balance the Budget. I declare all the current institutions to remain in force until further notice, on an advisory basis. Life will proceed unchanged until further notice. The leaders of Congress and the governors of all the States of the Union will have twelve hours to acknowledge their acceptance of this state to my office. The members of the Supreme Court will acknowledge similarly. Any failing to so acknowledge will be summarily removed from office thereafter. Announcements of new posts and appointees will follow in due course, and the first major effort will be made to balance the budget as of the present.

Of course, the actual wording was more sophisticated and polite, with due compliments to the good sense of the population. But the message was plain: Accept the new order or else. I didn't like putting it that way, but I had already been convinced by the problems I had encountered that absolute firmness was required, if there was not to be anarchy in short order. Once the new administration was established, I could relax.

The broadcast was planetary, and the monitors indicated that a goodly portion of the remainder of the System was picking it up too. Of course, the interplanetary scale is such that it would be hours before all the other planets received it, but their local news representatives were relaying it from Jupiter. It seemed everyone was interested in what was happening on Jupiter.

When it was done, we turned to the matter of appointments. As candidate for president I had been aware of the need to set up a Cabinet and prepare a programme of legislation; I had expected to finalize that after the election, if I won. Severe complications had interrupted that, and now I did not have any proper programme. The fact that I had assumed power outside the normal framework added a dimension of complication. I was now pretty much flying by the seat of my pants.

Fortunately Spirit was better organized than I was. 'We have a guideline of sorts,' she said. 'That campaign speech you gave on the eve of the election.'

'But that was scripted for me by the opposition!' I protested. 'It was made up of impossible dreams.'

'But you presented it,' she reminded me. 'And you won the election. The individual points were not necessarily bad; it was merely not feasible to implement *all* the

40

programmes simultaneously. Now, with a completely new government, that may have become feasible.'

I nodded, appreciating the scope of the opportunity. Part of the complications I had encountered were a two-month abduction and a memory-wash that cleaned out much of my recent life. I had recovered most of that, but some gaps remained. I wasn't necessarily aware of a particular gap until I came across it by chance, so my own ignorance torpedoed me at odd moments.

'You'll have to do a lot of interviewing,' she continued. 'It might save trouble at the beginning if you drew on people you already know, for the key posts, and then interview at greater leisure to fill the lesser ones.'

I spread my hands. 'You know what to do,' I said.

'I'd *better*! We've got a planet to organize.' She brought out a notepad. 'Now what people do you want closest to you, who are competent to act in your name?'

I sighed. 'She won't come.'

She patted my hand. 'Aside from Megan.'

'I contacted Senator Stonebridge about the budget – '

'Yes, he should be put in charge of economics. But you'll need a mandate for him. It's not enough simply to say "Balance the budget", You have to have your priorities aligned before he gets into harness.'

'So I discovered,' I agreed ruefully. 'My last four months haven't been very good for economic priorities.'

She laughed. 'Sometimes I think of you as the fifteen-year-old boy I knew when our situation changed,' she said. Then she leaned across and kissed me, as I sat startled.

But, of course, if I could remember her as twelve, she could remember me as fifteen. Certainly that had been the period of our reckoning, of our coming of age. We had shared more joy and tragedy then than ever since. Whatever else might happen, that common experience bound us together in a way that no other person was equipped to understand.

'Crime,' she said. 'We have taken steps to deal with it in the past, but it's like a hydra, always sprouting new heads. We want a competent, dedicated person to tackle the problems of violence in the streets, illicit drugs, gambling – '

Gambling. That summoned a picture of Roulette, my last Navy wife, as she had been then: eighteen, fiery, and with a body crafted by the devil himself for man's corruption. I had been required to rape her –

'Why not?' Spirit asked.

I jogged out of my reverie. 'I – '

'Only one body compels a trance like that. But she always was competent, and at thirty-eight she's had a good deal of experience. She could tackle the problem of crime as well as anyone could.'

'But – '

'Of course, we need her husband even more. He is under our power, while she isn't, so we'd better assign him first.'

'Admiral Phist?' I said, not quite keeping up.

'The same. When it comes to efficiency, he has no peer.'

She had been married to him for several years in the Navy. 'You ought to know,' I murmured. But, of course, it was true; Gerald Phist had been held back in the Navy because he was a whistle-blower, until he joined my unit. He had done marvels for our procurement. Certainly I wanted him on my team now – and if Spirit asked him, he would serve. He was now in his mid-sixties, but I knew his mind remained sharp. 'What position?'

'Well, I would have thought defence, because that's his area of expertise, but he has already taken care of that.'

I knew what she meant. After Spirit and I had left the

Navy our unit had continued, and its personnel had extended their influence, thanks to Admiral Mondy's – the male, Emerald's husband – sinister expertise. Emerald's own position had been proof of that; my recent promotion of her had only completed a twenty-year process. My people had in their quiet way assumed the reins and reorganized the Navy, making it a far more effective fighting force than it had been. Gone were the days of paying hundreds of dollars for nickel and dime parts and of spending billions for exotic equipment that didn't work. The Navy had become the canniest of buyers. President Tocsin would have squelched that but had realized that it was better simply to take credit for the improved efficiency, and since my people did not seek credit, that had worked out well enough. But when it had come to the crunch, the Navy had supported me, not Tocsin. *That* had been the payoff.

Spirit was right. The Navy no longer needed Admiral Phist. *We* needed him – to do the same job in the civilian sector. 'But if not defence, then what?'

'The Navy learned to deal effectively with the industrial part of the military-industrial complex,' she said. 'Thanks to Gerald. But the political power of industry has only been blunted, not broken. Waste and fraud are rampant, and both the government and the consumers suffer. We need to bring down the prices of food and goods for the average citizen, bringing inflation to a complete halt. He's the one to do that.'

'He surely is,' I agreed. It was evident that Spirit had done more thinking on these matters than I had.

'And we'll need someone for interplanetary relations – '

'Sir,' Shelia said from across the room.

I got up and went over to her.

43

'The opposition members are walking out of Congress,' she explained.

'Walking out?' I repeated blankly.

'To prevent a quorum,' Spirit said, rejoining me. 'So that no official business can be done. It's an old ploy.'

'Maybe I can appoint replacements,' I said.

'Easier said than done,' Spirit said darkly. 'Those Congressmen are supposedly the representatives of their various districts. Your appointees would represent you, not their districts. That wouldn't go over well.'

I nodded sombrely, seeing her point. 'And we're having enough trouble figuring out who to appoint to the major offices; filling congressional seats would be impossibly cumbersome.'

'Agreed,' she said. 'As I see it, we have two convenient routes.'

'Sir,' Shelia said again.

I sighed. 'Another problem? I haven't grasped the last one yet!'

'Not exactly. A delivery from Ganymede is here. They need your clearance.'

'A delivery from Ganymede?' I repeated blankly.

'A baby,' she said succinctly.

A baby! Abruptly I remembered. I had made a deal with a woman from Ganymede I called Dorian Gray: to return her baby to her, in exchange for her help. Her help had enabled me to survive my situation, but she had died. I had nevertheless contacted the premier of Ganymede, who had agreed to locate the baby. Now, two or three months later, he had evidently done so.

'Perhaps I should contact the nursery – ' Shelia murmured.

'No,' I said. 'This is my responsibility. Bring it in.'

She spoke into her mike, giving the clearance.

'One is to nationalize Congress,' Spirit resumed unconcerned about the interruption. I regrouped my attention; we had been discussing ways to deal with the opposition walkout. 'That would put the members under the authority of the government – '

'But they *are* the government,' I protested.

'No, *you* are the government,' she reminded me.

'But still, what use is their advice and consent if they are compelled to be there by a government they oppose?'

She shrugged. 'Not much, I suspect. The other alternative is abolition.'

'What?'

But again we were interrupted. A Hispanic nurse entered, carrying a little boy. She approached me. '*¿Senōr Hubris?*' she inquired.

'*Si,*' I responded; evidently she did not speak English.

'Robertico,' she said, holding out the baby boy.

'Robertico,' I agreed somewhat numbly, taking him.

She turned smartly and exited, leaving me holding the baby. I was the cynosure of all present. I felt like a fool.

Robertico contemplated me. He was in doubt and considered crying, but I anticipated him and distracted him with a remark. 'I promised to fetch you for your mother, Robertico,' I said. 'This will be your new home. Meet your new friends: Spirit, Coral, and Shelia.' Naturally he did not understand the words, for he was too young to talk, and in any event, I was speaking in English, but my tone and the manner in which I held him reassured him. He decided that this place was all right.

'May I?' Shelia inquired, holding out her hands. With relief I gave Robertico to her. She sat him in her lap, facing him forward. His gaze fixed on the little transceiver screen and his expression became rapt. Evidently the moving picture was new and fascinating to him.

'Abolition,' Spirit repeated, picking up where she had

left off. 'Simply abolish Congress, since it is no longer representative.'

'But that would be – '

'Dictatorial,' she finished. 'You have the power and would be foolish not to use it. You gave them a chance and they refused to cooperate. Why not make an example?'

'But without them who will represent the people?'

'Do you suppose that very many of those folk represent the people?' she asked dryly.

Robertico started to cry. Evidently he had seen something on the screen that upset him. 'We've got to make better provision for him,' I said.

'I have seen to it,' Shelia said. 'But we are strangers to him. I suspect he has not been in as stimulating an environment as this before.'

'He needs some sleep,' Spirit said.

'It will be another half hour before the child-bed arrives,' Shelia said.

'Give him here,' I said, taking the little boy back.

'He needs changing,' Shelia said. 'But the diapers – '

'Aren't here yet,' I concluded. So I simply held him and he quieted down.

I returned to the matter at hand. 'To deprive the people of all representation – that was never my intent.'

'You can appoint people to represent them,' Spirit said.

'I don't know. I – ' I broke off, for my arm was wet. Robertico was dripping. When would those diapers arrive?

'Sir,' Shelia said. 'Call from RedSpot.'

RedSpot was our neighbour-nation to the south, whose city-bubbles occupied the great Red Spot of Jupiter. They would want to know my policy towards Latin Jupiter, since for the first time a Hispanic had ultimate power in

North Jupiter. I could not avoid that call, lest I precipitate a diplomatic incident before I get properly established. 'Put it on,' I said wearily.

The face of the president of RedSpot appeared on the main screen. His eyes widened as he saw me standing with my shirt stained by leaking urine. '*¡Señor Presidente!*' he exclaimed.

'We're waiting for diapers,' I muttered in Spanish.

'Diapers!' he repeated, evidently suppressing a smile. 'Surely these are available locally?'

'*Si*,' I agreed tightly.

The smile struggled to get out, causing his lips to twitch. 'If not, perhaps we might arrange a shipment from RedSpot.'

'Unnecessary, thank you, *señor*,' I demurred.

'Lend-Lease, perhaps.' Oh, he was enjoying this! 'We prefer to be generous to our less fortunate neighbours.'

'What is your business, sir?' I inquired through teeth that threatened to clench.

'Just to wish you well in your endeavours,' he said, stepping on another smile as he glanced at the spreading stain on my shirt. 'And to express my government's support for your new policy.'

'*What* policy?' I demanded, lapsing into English. 'I haven't been able to organize my own wets, uh, wits yet!'

'Well, naturally you, as a Hispanic leader, are sympathetic to our concerns. I am sure relations between North Jupiter and RedSpot will be very close.'

He was getting ready to put the touch on me! Naturally RedSpot wanted more favourable terms on things like the debt owed to our big banks. I didn't want to alienate him, for I did appreciate his expression of support, but I simply wasn't ready to talk finance.

I was saved by the arrival of the diapers. 'Señor, I am sure they will,' I said quickly. 'We must talk again soon!

47

But at the moment I wouldn't want to burden you with the sight of a diaper being changed – '

He laughed. 'In RedSpot we teach our women to do such things, but then, we are not as liberated as you of the North.' He faded out, shaking his head.

I looked around. 'Where's a table?' I asked. 'It's been about fourteen years since I changed a diaper, but I remember the principle.'

Spirit showed me to a suitable table. She did not offer to do the job for me; she had had less experience at this than I, and Coral and Shelia were no better off. We stripped Robertico of his clothes and the sodden diaper. It turned out that he had done more than one number; the result was a real mess. Naturally we lacked the equipment to deal with this problem properly. Coral fetched towels and tissues from the bathroom, and we used a damp washcloth for the cleaning. But the cloth was cold, and Robertico reacted with a howl of distress.

'Sir,' Shelia said.

'You know a better way to do it?' I snapped.

'Call from Senator Stonebridge.'

Oh. He would be concerned about the opposition walkout. What could I tell him?

I sighed. 'Put him on,' I said.

Stonebridge's face appeared on the main screen. He glanced at what was going on, seeming perplexed. 'Minor crisis,' I explained as I dried Robertico's bottom and set him down for the new diaper.

'I think you need a baby-sitter, Mr President,' he said gravely.

'I can't trust this boy to a stranger,' I said. 'He doesn't speak English.'

'Few do, at that age,' he pointed out.

All three women smiled. It was true: babies of this age did not speak at all. 'But he has a Spanish heritage,' I explained. 'All he has heard spoken is Spanish. I would rather break him in to English gradually.'

'There are bilingual baby-sitters,' Stonebridge pointed out.

'None I know well enough to trust at the moment.'

'With all due respect, Mr President, I suggest that this is surely untrue. You have a fully competent bilingual baby-sitter available that you can trust.'

'Evidently you know something I don't!' I gritted as I stuck my thumb on a pin. The diaper had some kind of self-stick fastener, but I had been unable, in my distracted state, to decipher it, so was using the old-fashioned pin that had been on the old diaper. Diapering an active baby, I was rediscovering, is no simple task.

'Your daughter.'

I paused, my mouth dropping open. My daughter Hopie – of course. She was fifteen years old now and eager for just such jobs as this. But she was with Megan.

I looked helplessly at Spirit. 'I can't take Hopie away from Megan!'

'She would be safer here,' Spirit said. 'She has to attend school, and she will now be more of a target. Here she could be tutored and provided the same protection we are.'

'But Megan – '

'I will talk to her,' my sister said firmly.

I sought to spread my hands but could not, because I had to hold Robertico. I picked him up, not bothering with the soiled pants; the diaper would have to do for now. My eye was caught by Senator Stonebridge's eye in the screen.

'If I may now bring up a somewhat less important concern,' he said with a straight face.

'The walkout,' I said.

'Exactly. The present government of North Jupiter is

disintegrating. Prompt and decisive action is required if we are to retain a viable framework.'

'I am not sure the *prior* framework remains viable,' I said. 'I have assumed power outside the normal framework, and I suspect there is no way the opposition representatives will accept that.'

'Probably correct,' he agreed. 'Columnist Thorley has already dubbed your administration "the Tyrancy".'

'The Tyrancy!' I exclaimed. That was the first time I had heard that appellation applied to me, familiar as it was later to become. 'Well, I suppose I am, technically, a tyrant. The original term refers to one who assumes power illegally. I am legal but not by the standard of the system that has hitherto governed Jupiter. Some of the ancient Greek tyrants were enlightened rulers.'

'And some were despots,' Stonebridge pointed out.

'Still, upon reflection, I think the shoe fits. I will try to be an enlightened tyrant. So Thorley can call my administration the Tyrancy if he wants.'

Stonebridge frowned. 'You are not going to have him arrested?'

'Of course not! I have always respected freedom of the press, and of speech in general. Thorley will always be free to express himself in public.'

'Then I think you are not a tyrant by my definition.'

'No, let me be called the Tyrant,' I said, liking the sound of it better as I considered it. 'That solves the problem of my title.'

'Surely you jest!'

'No jest. I am the Tyrant, and my administration is the Tyrancy. I am making no pretence of honouring the old order.'

'As you prefer, Mr Tyrant,' he said awkwardly.

'Just Tyrant,' I said. 'I will make that my title of honour. It will set me apart, appropriately.'

'As you prefer,' he repeated disapprovingly. 'Now as to the walkout by the opposition – '

'That becomes immaterial. I am abolishing Congress.'

'Sir?' he asked, startled.

'Let's face it, Senator,' I said briskly, while Robertico played with the buttons on my shirt. 'The average member of Congress is a tool of the special interests, regardless of his party. He is beholden to the political action committees that provide the bulk of the money he needs for his election campaigns, and a fair number are corrupt apart from that. Few actually, honestly, represent their constituents. The present – *prior* – system of government is monstrously nonrepresentative in everything except name, and excruciatingly inefficient. The average man would be better off without it.'

'But this is treason!' he protested.

'Not any more,' I said. 'I *am* the new government; I merely have to find new avenues to implement my power. I'm sure I will find it much easier to balance the budget if I eliminate fraud and waste in the government – and Congress is a nest of both.'

'Sir, this – this is unfeasible,' he said, shocked. 'All our institutions . . . there would be anarchy – '

'Not if I appoint competent and honest people to run things,' I said. 'As soon as I get my priorities organized, I will be asking you to serve. In fact, I am asking you now: will you serve as my adviser on budgetary matters?'

His mouth thinned. 'What is the force of that request, sir?'

'You mean, will you be arrested if you refuse? No, this is voluntary. I need good people to serve as my lieutenants, and I will heed the advice of those who do serve. I am committed to the balancing of the budget, and I feel that no individual is better qualified to advise me on that than you. Will you serve?'

51

Stonebridge was obviously upset and uncertain. 'Let me take time to consider, sir. There are implications that – '

'Of course,' I agreed. 'But bear in mind that the sooner I get competent advice, the better it will be for Jupiter.'

He faded out. I saw that Robertico was getting sleepy, so I cast about for a way to put him down.

'Hope, we have Hopie on the line,' Spirit said.

'Put her on!'

Hopie's face appeared. 'Oh, isn't he cute!' she exclaimed.

'Uh, I need – ' I began somewhat lamely.

'Yes, Daddy, Aunt Spirit explained. You're all upheavaled! You need a bottle, and a formula, and a crib, and some toys and a whole lot of time.'

'I don't have any of those!'

'I know. I'd better get up there and take over.'

'But your mother – '

'Daddy, she understands.'

'I'm not sure she does.'

Spirit touched my hand. 'She understands.'

Evidently Spirit had talked directly to Megan. 'Oh. Then – '

'I'll catch a priority flight,' Hopie said happily.

'The Navy will take you, dear,' Spirit put in. 'Can you be ready in . . .' She glanced at Shelia.

Emerald's face flicked on the screen. 'Fifteen minutes,' she said, and flicked off.

'Yes,' Hopie agreed.

'You'll be here in two hours,' Spirit told the girl.

'He'll wake before then, hungry,' Hopie said. 'Give him something to chew on.'

'We'll try,' I said.

'And change your shirt,' Hopie instructed me.

I glanced down at myself. Yes, I needed a change. I started to work my way out of the shirt.

The screen blanked. 'Now we'd better make the announcement about the abolition of Congress and assure the citizens that their interests will be represented,' Spirit said briskly.

'But Robertico – '

'We'll put some pillows on the floor; he'll be safe there.'

They fetched pillows from the nearest beds elsewhere in the mansion and piled them on the floor. I set the baby down, but the moment I let go of him, he woke and screamed, and I had to pick him up again.

In addition, I discovered that I had no replacement shirt. In our rush to get here and get started, that detail had been neglected. 'I will order more,' Shelia said. She knew my sizes, of course; she knew everything about me that a secretary should know – and more.

So I sat in a plush easy chair, shirtless, holding Robertico, with pillows braced about me. He settled back to sleep, and Spirit and I made notes for my next announcement.

'Sir,' Shelia said.

I was coming to dread that word! 'Not another crisis?'

'The Saturn Embassy,' she said.

I sighed. 'Put it on.'

The face of the ambassador from Saturn came on the main screen. He took in my situation and scowled. 'Perhaps I should return when you are less domestic, Mr President,' he said.

'Just call me Tyrant,' I said. 'What is your business?'

'My government wishes to clarify the status of interplanetary relations between Jupiter and Saturn, considering your recent change in government.'

'Unchanged,' I said.

'We would prefer an improvement.'

'I'm amenable.'

He seemed disconcerted. 'Specifically – '

'No specifics yet,' I cut in. 'If you come to us with positive proposals for the diminution of interplanetary tension, we shall reciprocate. It's up to you.'

Still, he seemed unpleased. He was trying to measure me, and I wasn't giving him much substance. 'Surely – '

'So good to have this dialogue,' I said, signalling to Shelia, who cut him off.

'We'll have trouble with Saturn,' Spirit said darkly. 'They always work over a new administration.'

'Precisely,' I agreed. 'I mean to be ready for the vultures as they descend.'

We returned to work on the announcement, punctuated by calls from every type of party. I dealt with them as well as I could, making no commitments. We formulated a list of prospects for service in the new administration; Spirit had largely prepared that beforehand and needed only my concurrence. It was complicated because there were so many necessary offices and so many people; matching the two together was a headache. We knew we had to get at least a patchwork government organized promptly, so that anarchy would not erupt.

Suddenly Hopie was there, lifting the sleeping baby from my shoulder; I had hardly been aware of the passage of that time. My daughter did know her business; she set up shop in a corner of the room (because Robertico felt comfortable with me but not apart from me) and saw to a feeding and another change of diaper. Coral brought in another shirt for me; evidently Shelia's order had arrived.

We continued, calling the people on our list, asking their participation, accepting their excuses, stressing that there was no coercion here: we wanted only those who would be committed to the welfare of Jupiter without

54

reservation. Some were belligerent and some were afraid, but when they learned that it truly was voluntary, a number of these softened and did accept the positions. Some who turned down the offer later called back with a change of heart, and we accepted them. Slowly but satisfyingly the new framework was being erected.

I don't pretend that this was any genius of mine. Spirit had done the groundwork and now prompted me on the execution. I was like a duffer who assembles a complex device by following the simplistic step-by-step instructions provided. I was the figurehead to Spirit's strategy. That was nothing new; my genius is reading (and making an impression on) other people, while Spirit's is organizational. We have always been a team, and there is no shame in that. While it is true that I would be a sorry figure of a politician without Spirit, it is also true that she would be unable to perform without me.

Then Coral approached me. 'Sir, it is time for you to rest,' she said firmly.

'But there is so much to do!' I protested.

'You have been working without pause for ten hours,' she informed me. 'The others are dead on their feet, but they will not stop until you do.'

I glanced around and saw that it was true. Spirit was drawn, and Shelia's eyes were red-rimmed. Hopie was asleep on the pillows with Robertico. Still, I demurred. 'Just a little more work, and the list will be complete – '

'That list will never be complete,' she asserted. 'I am charged with the preservation of your body, and that charge I shall honour, preserving it from all threats – including that of your will. You must rest now, at least for a while.' She took my arm and drew me firmly along.

The others did not protest, and I suffered myself to be conducted to the master bedroom. 'Strip, wash, change,' Coral ordered, and I obeyed. It did not bother me that

55

she watched; she had seen me in dishabille many times before, for she was always close. Once there had been a trap set for me in a urinal, so now she accompanied me to the bathroom too. One might suppose that a man would be nervous about having an attractive woman with him on such an occasion, but Coral was really part of my nuclear family.

In pyjamas, I lay down on the huge empty bed, now feeling my own fatigue. Then another thought occurred. I sat up. 'I just remembered another appointment to –'

'Down, sir,' Coral said.

'But it will only take a moment to –'

She moved to me, her arms about me, and bore me down on the bed. She had changed herself, to some kind of feminine robe that I knew concealed some unfeminine hardware; Coral was never without armament, ready for any emergency. She put what is called the Scarf-hold on me, her right arm circling my neck, and, gripping my right shoulder, her left hand hauling on my right sleeve, her legs spread and braced against the surface of the bed. I think I could have broken that hold, had I wished to make sufficient effort, for my strength was greater than hers, but I wasn't sure, and in any event, it wasn't *worth* the effort. So I lay there, conscious of her right breast nudging my cheek as she breathed and of the sight of her left breast, through the parted robe, and I relaxed.

When she saw that I was willing to rest, she released her hold and kissed me. Then she stretched out beside me on the bed and slept herself, lightly and instantly, like a cat. It is intended as no affront to Coral that I wished she was Megan; the separation from my wife remained fresh and painful but final; when Megan had consented to unite with me, that had been final, and when she sundered that union, for reasons that were certainly sufficient, that, too, was final. It was I who had changed, not her; I had

56

passed from the stage of Politician to the stage of Tyrant, and she had never consented to be married to the latter. I understood, respected her decision fully, and did not question it, but still there was a void without her.

My tension alerted Coral, who woke. 'Damn it, sir, *sleep*!' she whispered. She changed position, took hold of my head, and drew it in to her bosom. It was a fine and fragrant bosom, but I think it was more the feeling of her arms around me, holding me close, that brought my submission. Helse had held me that way, so long ago, and Roulette, too, less long ago, and Shelia, recently. I relaxed, comforted, and suddenly slept.

4

Between CT and BH

I woke many hours later, somewhat refreshed. Coral was up, of course; she had always had a fast recharge time.

We assembled for breakfast – I'm not sure what the hour was, but we treated it as morning – at the White Bubble dining room, served by the WB staff. Spirit, Coral, Shelia, Ebony, Hopie, and Robertico. I don't remember what we ate; my attention has been increasingly absorbed by concerns other than food as I grow older, so I tend not to notice meals, anyway, unless they are for some reason remarkable in their own right.

I deliberately kept the conversation on trivial matters. I would soon enough be overwhelmed by the consequential ones. 'Hopie, we'll have to arrange for your education,' I said.

She made a wry face. 'Daddy, I'm fifteen years old. Most of what they teach in school is useless, anyway. I'd be better off without it.'

The others ate, remaining carefully neutral. They knew I supported education.

'I had in mind bringing in a competent tutor,' I said. 'Surely she would teach you useful material.'

'But the required courses are jokes!' she protested. 'Even the best teachers can't make a pointless course worthwhile.'

I frowned. 'What course is pointless?'

She hesitated, realizing that she could walk into a mire of her own making. Teenagers can be imperious, but they are not, despite some appearances, total fools. 'What courses did *you* take, Daddy, once you were my age?'

58

That set me back, for my formal schooling had abruptly stopped at that age. That had been by no choice of mine, however. 'I had some lessons from life,' I said. 'I would have preferred those of school.'

'So you had no more school – and where are you now?' she demanded triumphantly.

'But I did have further education,' I pointed out. 'I took many courses in the Navy – more than I would have in normal school. I learned a great deal.'

'But those were military classes. At least they had some application to life.'

'Many were,' I agreed. 'But many were necessary to fill out the education I had not gained from school.'

She changed her tack. 'Well, did they teach you geometry?'

'Certainly. In space, manoeuvres are three-dimensional, and a proper understanding is essential to – '

'*Plane* geometry,' she said with disdain. 'How to solve triangles by erecting perpendiculars with a compass and straightedge. You did that?'

'Well, no, not exactly. We used the computer simulations to do the underlying calculations and projections, but – '

'*We* must do it by hand,' she said witheringly. 'Two years of it. We've had computers for ten centuries, but they won't let us use them!'

'Six centuries,' I said. 'But it is necessary to know the fundamentals, in order to appreciate what the computers do.'

'Seven. Does it take two years of ever-more-obscure two-dimensional examples to appreciate what the computers do in three-dimensional space?'

Spirit turned away, masking half a smile. I was in trouble! 'I suppose the basics could be abridged,' I

59

said. 'Perhaps one semester, and then the computer applications for the more advanced work.'

'Exactly!' she said triumphantly. 'I've already had three semesters of it, and none of it about computer applications. Why should I continue?'

'Name another useless subject,' I said.

'English.'

'Now I realize you are bilingual, as are a number of Hispanics,' I said, 'but English *is* the primary language of Jupiter, and it behooves those of us who have adopted this planet to – '

'Verbs and nouns,' she said. 'The same things, every year, over and over.'

'Well, again it is necessary to know the basics before – '

'No, it isn't,' she said. 'I learned to speak English *and* Spanish before I ever heard of the parts of speech. Everyone else did too. It is no more necessary to know the names of the parts of speech in order to use the language correctly than it is to know the names of the muscles and ligaments of the body in order to live and breathe.'

I sat back, considering that. She had a point! 'But surely those who were brought up in less literate homes than your own require this form of education, so that – '

'No, they don't!' she said hotly. 'They need to be instructed in the correct forms directly. The parts of speech are merely a means to an end, and the educational system has let the means *become* the end! They're trying to turn out illiterate students who can name the parts of speech!'

'Surely you exaggerate!' I said, daunted. Where had I been warned before about means becoming ends? 'The basics remain useful as underlying knowledge, much as the knowledge of the basic principles of mathematics remains useful in the computer age. Speaking correctly is not necessarily a simple – '

'Define a gerund,' she said.

I concentrated. I remembered the term but had forgotten to what it applied. 'An animal like a hamster?'

'Gerbil,' she said, correcting me in the manner I had corrected her about the period of computers but refusing to be distracted by the humour. Now Shelia turned away, smiling. 'It's strange that you cannot define a gerund, Daddy, since you just used one.'

'I did? Where?'

'A gerund is a verb used as a noun, ending in "ing". You said "speaking", and that's a gerund.'

Now I remembered. 'I guess I did, daughter.'

She closed in for the kill. 'You knew how to use it before you learned the name of that part of speech in school, and you knew how to use it after you had forgotten its name. *Of what use is the name of it to you?*'

I spread my hands. 'No use that I can fathom at the moment, Hopie.'

'Would *two more years* of instruction in gerunds and participles and indirect objects and dependent clauses and parallel structure improve your ability to speak?'

I laughed, as much at her vehemence as at her point. 'I suspect not.'

'Then why foist off this useless drill on me? It won't improve my speech, either.'

Indeed, it would not, for she had been speaking to me most effectively. I was privately proud of her ability to make her point. She was a bright girl who reminded me a lot of Spirit, and I was always pleased to be reminded of that.

'What would you have me do, Hopie?' I asked. 'Abolish school?'

She considered. 'No. School could be useful – *should*

be useful, if correctly instituted. What you need is to make the schools relevant.'

'And you know what reforms contemporary education requires to make it relevant?'

'I know where to start,' she said.

'Well, start there.'

Her eyes widened. 'What?'

'I think that's an incomplete sentence.'

'What are you telling me, Daddy? That I don't have to take those stupid courses any more?'

I glanced at Spirit. 'The Department of Education remains unassigned?'

'Unassigned,' she agreed. 'We got tired last night.'

I returned to Hopie. 'You are now in charge of the Department of Education. Do your job.'

'My job?' she asked, dumbfounded.

'Reform education.'

'But I'm only fifteen!'

'So?'

'That's too young to – '

'By whose definition?'

'But the minimum age – '

'The old order changeth. This is the Tyrant speaking. You are old enough.'

'But – but – I really wouldn't know how to – I mean, who would even *listen* to me?'

'The school system,' I said. 'Of course, you will want a staff to advise you and implement policy. I suggest that you select it carefully. Perhaps some of the really good teachers you know.'

'You mean – honest? Me?'

'Honest, honey. I think the experience will be as good an education for you as the conventional system would have provided. Just keep in mind that many other people will be profoundly affected by your decisions.'

'Um,' she agreed, daunted.

Breakfast broke up, and we got to work. Hopie saw to Robertico's needs – she was certainly good in that capacity – while she assimilated the magnitude of the responsibility I had laid on her. Spirit and Shelia and I adjourned to the conference room.

'First you will want to look at these,' Spirit told me, showing a sheaf of papers.

'What are they?'

'Your daily news summary. It's a normal presidential service. The top man has to be kept informed.'

'You have gone over these, of course?'

'Of course,' she agreed.

'Just acquaint me with what I need to know to function.'

'Saturn is making a move,' she said.

I sighed. 'That's to be expected, isn't it? They always work over a new president.'

'Always,' she agreed. 'But this is not a normal presidential transition, and so this may not be a normal Saturnist move.'

'Exactly what is it?'

'They are shipping troops to Ganymede.'

I frowned. 'That's their prerogative, isn't it? It *is* a Saturnian puppet-state.'

'Less so than it was, thanks to your tenure as ambassador there. I think you should talk to the ambassador from Ganymede.'

'I can call the premier himself, if – '

'No. That call would be tapped and entirely too official. This has to be private.'

'Shelia, get me the ambassador,' I said. My secretary had evidently profited by the night's rest; she looked perky again.

'He is on his way, sir,' she said.

'I see.' A personal meeting signalled something sensitive indeed.

We got down to the remaining appointments. All of the top ones were to people I knew personally and trusted; trust was more important than competence here. Senator Stonebridge was in charge of economics, Admiral Phist would handle industry, Spirit herself had the interplanetary arena, Hopie had education, Roulette Phist had crime, my other sister Faith had poverty, and our gofer Ebony had population. I confess that this was something of a hodge-podge; there would be plenty of redefinition later. But it was a start. Meanwhile the existing institutions of the state level, from governor on down, remained in force, and, for now, the Supreme Court. So we had a haphazardly functioning government. I planned to do substantial interviewing, approving all the top personnel of these departments, so that they would be both loyal and competent. That was, of course, my special skill; there would be no bad apples in our top echelons.

Next we would turn to policy. But before we could get into it, the Ganymede ambassador arrived. He was a somewhat harried man in his fifties, a political nonentity, basically a mouthpiece. I had never met him before but hadn't needed to. At this point I don't even recollect his name, but that doesn't matter.

We exchanged normal amenities, then got down to business. 'What is this about Saturn troops?' I asked.

'Señor, I am instructed to be absolutely candid with you,' he said nervously. 'The premier begs complete privacy.'

'Granted,' I said.

'The Saturn troops – they are not coming to bolster the present government of Ganymede. They are coming to assume it.'

This was electrifying news. Now I understood the need for secrecy. 'The premier – to be deposed? Ganymede to become a complete puppet-state?'

He nodded gravely. 'Señor, this is not at the behest of the premier. He cannot ask your help, but – ' He shrugged.

I pondered. Naturally the premier could not formally enlist my aid; he governed a Communist planet that owed substantial credit to the Union of Saturnine Republics. If they pulled the rug out, his administration would collapse in days, unless bolstered by some other power. But if he permitted them to depose him and assume total power, he would be finished.

I did not agree with all of the premier's objectives or methods, but I had come to know him well enough during my own term as ambassador, and we had what would pass for a private friendship. In addition, I was sure that his administration posed a great deal less of a problem for me than a straight Saturnist puppet regime would. I remembered how Saturn had tried to implant interplanetary missiles on Ganymede not that many years ago and triggered the Ganymedan Missile Crisis, which had brought Jupiter and Saturn to the verge of war. It was entirely possible that Saturn would be trying this again, under the cover of the confusion of my assumption of government. Such missiles, once in place and activated, would represent an almost literal dagger poised at Jupiter; our interplanetary policy would be severely circumscribed, and the balance of interplanetary power would shift decisively to Saturn.

This was a crisis worthy of my immediate attention, certainly! 'You know that Jupiter cannot tolerate such a change in our sphere,' I told the ambassador.

He nodded gravely. 'The premier believes you will know what to do.'

'I will figure *out* what to do,' I agreed. 'Meanwhile tell the premier to arrange a leak of information, so that Jupiter can be apprised of this development without implicating him. You understand, Señor.'

'The premier understands.'

'There must be no further private communication between us. We must play our parts perfectly.'

'You will support . . . the present regime?'

'In my fashion,' I agreed. 'But my words will not necessarily indicate that. The premier understands.'

'*Gracias*,' he said with perfect sincerity.

That was it; the ambassador departed, and we considered. 'I think we shall have to have a confrontation,' I said.

Spirit nodded soberly. 'We shall have to be prepared to go to war. If our resolve falters, even momentarily . . .'

'Get in touch with Emerald. She'll have to get the Navy ready, without making any obvious moves yet.'

Shelia placed the call. Emerald's dusky face appeared on the main screen. 'You have a small crisis or two, sir?'

I hesitated. I knew that the Saturn monitors could intercept supposedly private communications; to tell her the real problem now would be a giveaway. 'Um, Admiral, I'm considering reorganizing the Navy. Naturally I want to consider the input of those most concerned. The details may become tedious – um, suppose you stop by here, so we can discuss them at leisure?'

Her eyes narrowed slightly. She read me well, as all my women do; she knew that something important was up. 'A personal visit? I'm not sure my husband would approve, sir.'

I smiled. 'I won't lay a hand on you, woman!'

'He isn't worried about *your* hands, sir. It's *mine* that concern him.'

I laughed. Emerald certainly had facile hands; how

well I remembered! She and I were both fifty, but it was mutual fun to imagine that we were twenty-two again. 'Then bring him along!'

'One hour,' she said. Her ship was not far from New Wash, as she was guarding me personally, in her fashion, but she needed time to fetch her husband, Admiral Mondy (retired). Of course, I needed to talk with him, too, for he was the expert on intelligence. He would be an excellent consultant for this crisis, which was, of course, why Emerald had suggested his presence. It was possible she already had an inkling of the Saturn threat.

The press of contacts resumed. Shelia shielded me from all but the most important calls, but even those were constant. Already we were instituting a subsidiary network of secretaries, to screen out the barrage of junk calls. It seemed that every member of Congress, including the opposition contingent that had walked out as a bloc, was outraged by my decision to abolish that institution, and every one of them felt it incumbent upon himself to advise me of his distress personally. But wherever possible we were appointing the same people, whether of my own party or the opposition party, as representatives of their districts: true representatives with no other function than to advise me of the needs and concerns of their constituencies. Those who accepted such appointment – which entailed a concomitant acceptance of my authority as Tyrant – were granted access to me or simply provided with what they requested by someone in my developing chain of command. I may make it seem, in this narration, as if nothing much was happening apart from my dialogues with particular individuals, but that was not the case. Spirit had a number of aides who understood her purposes, and they were doing much of the job of organization while Spirit and I focused on the high spots. I repeat: I was in many respects a figurehead, while my sister actually ran the show. Our campaign organization was converting rapidly to our administrative organization. This was not intended to be an application of the notorious spoils system, but the most convenient way to post responsible people in responsible positions rapidly. So we did have a mechanism for handling specific problems but needed to broaden it enormously, and the former members of Congress represented prime candidates for the new offices. They would not be given power until we were satisfied that they would use it properly, but they were given token recognition – and when one called, I had to answer, even if I did no more than congratulate him on his patriotism in facilitating the new order. You see, in politics, appearance is generally more important than reality, and the reassignment of existing representatives facilitated the appearance of a smooth transition.

Thus the hour passed, hectically, until Emerald and Mondy arrived. Then Spirit and I took them into another room, leaving Shelia to fend for herself, which she was competent to do. She would let me know what decisions she had made in my name when I returned. There are those who think that a cripple is necessarily a nonentity; this is never the case, and Shelia was as intelligent, competent, and experienced a person as I had on my staff. Ninety-five per cent of the time she knew my answers before I did, and she could make a pretty good guess on the other five per cent. I suspect, in retrospect, that my act of love with her was neither as spontaneous nor as strange as it seemed at the time; it was my recognition of her importance to me. It was not the type of recognition I could give while my marriage to Megan was sound, but the moment my marriage ended (in fact, if not in name), the overt expression of that relationship was possible and perhaps necessary. It was not that I loved her, though she loved me; I have had only two true loves in my life, Helse and Megan. All of my women love me, but all recognize the limitations of my nature. I do for each what I can, when I can, inadequate as this may be.

My romance with Emerald, of course, was long dead. We retained the dream of the past, but today our respect for each other had other forms of expression, as her husband understood. We got right down to business.

'Saturn is sending troops to take over Ganymede,' I said. 'What do we do?'

Mondy had been middle-aged when I met him; now he was old. For some men seventy is not old, but for him it was. He looked terrible: bald and fat and pallid. But his mind remained murkily penetrating. 'You underestimate the problems, sir,' he said. 'Those are not mere troops; they are technicians.'

'Technicians? I don't see how – '

'Bearing sophisticated new equipment to recode the locks at Tanamo,' he concluded.

Spirit whistled. 'That puts a different complexion on it!' she exclaimed.

'We thought it might,' Emerald said, a trifle smugly.

Tanamo was the big naval base on Ganymede, whose transfer I had arranged during my ambassadorship. It had moved from the control of Jupiter to the control of Ganymede. In exchange Ganymede had agreed to cease all covert fomentation of revolution and shipment of arms to dissident elements of Latin Jupiter. This had eliminated a prime source of irritation and saved Jupiter much mischief. Former President Tocsin, of course, had done his best to undermine this accord, preferring open hostility, as hostility facilitated his endorsement of the monstrous military-industrial complex of Jupiter. There were great profits to be made in the fever of threatening war. It was my intent to dismantle that complex, and Admiral

Phist was just the man to do it. But this move by Saturn – that could torpedo everything.

I shook my head. 'Why?' I asked. 'I was ready to get along with Saturn!'

'Did you suppose Tocsin was the only tool of the special interests?' Mondy inquired. 'The ruling council of Saturn is engaged in a continual and savage struggle for power, both internal and external. They perceive an opportunity to achieve a significant advantage during your period of indecision, which will not only put Jupiter on the defensive but will thoroughly refute dissent in their own population. That dissent has been growing in strength in recent years, spearheaded by people like Khukov.'

'Khukov!' I exclaimed. 'I have no quarrel with him.' For Admiral Khukov had been the other party to the compromise of Ganymede; together we had helped both Ganymede and ourselves. I had taught him Spanish, privately, and he had taught me Russian; these secret abilities were most useful on occasion.

'It is the Politboro that has the quarrel with him,' Mondy said. 'He has criticized their inefficiency, such as their repeated failure to become self-sufficient in food grains, but his power base is such that they cannot liquidate him. But a coup like this would enable them to eliminate threats both external and internal.'

It was becoming clear. 'The Ganymedan ambassador said they planned to depose the premier.'

'That would be the premier's first concern, naturally,' Mondy agreed. 'But that is only the initial step. It is necessary because the premier insists on honouring the covenant he made with you. He will not pervert Tanamo or resume clandestine arms shipments. Once they have changed the government of Ganymede, there is no practical limit to their mischief.'

'We'll have planet-buster missile bases there again!' Emerald put in.

'Obviously this must be stopped before it starts,' I said. 'Emerald, you can call an alert – '

'No, sir,' Mondy said. 'That would not be expedient.'

'But we can't let it happen!' I protested.

'There are ways and ways,' he said. 'Jupiter has mismanaged interplanetary relations for so long that it has come to be expected. You have a chance to change that.'

'But if we don't intercept that ship before it reaches Ganymede, there will be hell to pay!'

'And if we do, Saturn will know who told,' he countered. 'The premier of Ganymede will be finished – by assassination, if not by political means.'

'But *you* knew!' I said. 'So I didn't have to find out through the premier.'

'I found out, once given the hint,' Mondy said. 'My source was coerced, and connected to the premier. I must not betray it.'

I sighed. 'No, you must not, and I must not. But we can't sit idly by while that ship lands. How do we proceed?'

'We assess our resources and our desires. Then we formulate a programme to best utilize the former to achieve the latter. We stand to gain considerably if we manage this correctly.'

'*Gain?*' I demanded. 'If we even come out even, I'll be surprised!'

'Ganymede could shift orbits, from Saturn to Jupiter,' he said. 'That would be the minor gain.'

'It would be a phenomenal gain! It would signal the failure of Communism to establish any lasting foothold in the Jupiter sphere. And I can see how, if we save the premier's hide, that shift could occur. But if that's minor, what would be the major gain?'

71

'We could in effect shift Saturn itself to Jupiter orbit,' he said seriously.

I whistled. 'You had better spell out the details!'

'If an issue is made and Saturn loses, the present government there will fall. The man who manages to resolve the crisis will probably step into power there.'

'And that man would be – ' I said, seeing it.

'Admiral Khukov.'

'Admiral Khukov,' I echoed.

'Who remembers his benefactors, by whatever device.'

'Who remembers,' I agreed. 'With him in power, there – '

Mondy nodded. 'You could end the cold war.'

'And make the Solar System safe for mankind,' I said. 'What a dream!'

'But at a price. The confrontation could destroy the System.'

'Is it worth the risk?' I asked musingly.

'That doesn't matter. The situation is already upon us.'

I sighed. 'It is indeed!'

We hashed it out, and Mondy and Emerald departed. We had devised a strategy, but we all knew it was risky. We could indeed precipitate a devastating System war if we miscalculated at any stage or even if luck went against us. I would not have entered into such a programme had I been able to avoid it, but as Mondy said, we were already committed. If Ganymede became a Saturnian military base, Jupiter would be in dire peril. And Ganymede *would* become that, if we did not act.

First we had to develop a legitimate source of information, so that Saturn would not know that the premier had told us. Until we had that we could not afford to make our first move.

Meanwhile, the job of setting up our new departments proceeded irregularly. Senator Stonebridge advised me that he was assembling a package of programmes that should halt inflation and balance the budget but that there would be formidable resistance to it.

'Resistance – to accomplishing what I have been installed to accomplish?' I asked. 'Why?'

'Because the standard of living of the average citizen will have to be materially lowered,' he said. 'This entails a universal income tax of fifty per cent, and – '

'Fifty per cent!' I exclaimed. 'Impossible!'

'I told you there would be resistance,' he said.

'Suppose we make it a flat tax of twenty-five per cent? That seems more equitable.'

'Suppose you find me an additional source of revenue that will produce six hundred billion dollars per year?' he returned.

'I'll look for it,' I agreed. But I knew I was in trouble. There were no easy answers economically, but somehow I had to find a way to balance that budget without triggering a revolution on Jupiter.

We watched the Saturn ship as it moved steadily through space towards our sphere. Theoretically it was one of a regular supply convoy, relatively innocent; we had no reason to intercept it, other than the one we could not reveal. It was scheduled to arrive in seven days if we did not find a pretext to stop it.

We tapped its communications with the home base and with Ganymede, hoping to intercept a revealing message. The transmissions were coded, of course, but our technicians decoded them as rapidly as they were sent. Saturn was aware of that; Saturn did the same to ours. Saturn was too canny to put anything truly private into any such transmissions. So we got nothing, as expected – and the ship moved on. Six days till arrival now.

My sister Faith came to see me. I had appointed her to the Department of Poverty: it was her job to eliminate it.

She was having a problem getting started. 'We need full employment, at fair wages, with fair working conditions,' she said. 'My consultants tell me that there simply aren't enough jobs and that legislation will be required to define the wages and conditions. The only possible answer . . .' She hesitated.

'Out with it,' I said.

'Is for the government to become the Employer of Last Resort, for all those who cannot otherwise find work.'

I called Stonebridge. 'What's the price tag for the government to become the Employer of Last Resort for all the unemployed?'

'Three hundred billion dollars minimum,' he replied without hesitation. 'That assumes a thirty-three per cent cost of administration, which I fear is conservative.'

'But if they were working, paying their way – '

'At what jobs? Believe me, Tyrant, it would be far cheaper to put them all on welfare – and cheaper yet to simply hand them each the money.'

'But that would lead to complete indifference to working for a living!'

'Exactly. Therefore, that is no solution to your problem. Don't try to eliminate unemployment that way.' He faded off.

I sighed as I returned to Faith. 'Let's see whether Gerald Phist is making progress at providing new jobs.' I called him.

'Good news, Tyrant,' Phist said as he came on screen. 'I am developing a programme that will virtually eliminate waste and fraud, and reduce the cost of industry by enabling us to produce the same products and services with only seventy per cent of the personnel!'

'Seventy per cent,' I said, not reacting with quite the joy he expected. 'That means – '

'About thirty million jobs saved,' he finished. 'No more inefficient duplication of effort.'

'And thirty million more unemployed,' I concluded.

'Well, perhaps new industries can be developed to take up the slack – '

'Work on it,' I advised him, signing off.

I looked at Faith, and she looked at me. 'Believe me,' I told her, 'when I find an answer, you'll be the first to know. Meanwhile, work things out as well as you can.'

'I think you're in over your head, Tyrant,' she replied.

'In more than one respect,' I agreed wanly. Certainly the Tyrancy was not getting off to a polished start.

Meanwhile, that dread ship moved closer to Ganymede. It might as well have been a planet-buster headed inexorably for the heart of the Planet of Jupiter!

We tried to arrange for a 'coincidental' encounter with the ship: a playboy yacht that lost its bearings and strayed into the Saturn vessel's path. But the ship was the soul of courtesy, putting on the screen an English-speaking officer, who provided meticulous and accurate bearings for the stray. Now there were only five days till arrival.

Roulette called. She was in charge of crime – the elimination thereof. 'Crime is costing the planet hundreds of billions of dollars per year,' she informed me. 'Much of it relates to drugs and gambling. But to eliminate those we have to eliminate the hard-core criminal element. We can spot most of the bad types, but can you keep them out of circulation?'

More unemployed! 'I'll work on it,' I told her without conviction.

'She's on to an ugly truth,' Spirit said. 'Ninety per cent of the crime is done by ten per cent of the criminals. That is, most people may stray once or twice but aren't hard-core, while a few are solidly into it. We have to deal with them.'

'How?' I asked. 'I seem to remember a debate with Thorley that bore on this, and he was tearing me up. If we imprison all the hard-corists, we are in effect supporting them at the expense of the state, and that will, as Stonebridge will surely advise me, add to the deficit. But I really don't like capital punishment.'

She half smiled. 'Maybe you should put Thorley in charge of crime.'

'Thorley is a good man,' I said seriously. 'We differ on principle, but I respect his competence and integrity. If I thought there was the ghost of a chance that he would work for the Tyrancy – '

She shook her head. 'Not even the suggestion of the ghost of a chance. Have you seen his recent columns?'

'I've been too busy.'

'You have been most eloquently castigated. He makes you seem a complete ass, and dangerous as well.'

'All true,' I said, smiling.

'Most of the other critics are silent. They are waiting to see what happens to Thorley.'

'*Nothing* will happen to Thorley!' I snapped. 'I honour freedom of the press; you know that.'

'*All* dictators promise freedom and reform,' she reminded me. 'Few follow through.'

'Asoka did,' I said.

She shrugged. 'As I recall, Asoka had some consolidation to do at the outset.'

'And so do I. What next, on that Saturn doom ship?'

'How about a Naval exercise that happens to cut off its approach to Ganymede?'

We explored that. Emerald had sent a representative, a lower officer who was conversant with the current situation of the Jupiter Navy. That enabled me to get the information without going on the beam to her ship and also protected my privacy.

'Sir,' the officer said, 'that isn't feasible. Such exercises have to be scheduled well in advance and planned meticulously. The Saturnines know all of our schedules, as we know theirs. Such a deviation would be well-nigh impossible, and even the attempt would alert them to our real problem. They are not fools, sir.'

Which was exactly what I had suspected. Naval fleets are not turned on a dime; I had learned that well during my own Naval command. If we tried to arrange something on the spur of the moment, it would be a virtual advertisement that we had some pressing ulterior motive. We might as well challenge the ship outright.

But that I was not ready to do. Mondy's advice was sound: Do not let Saturn know that the premier of Ganymede had tipped us off. Learn about the ship some other way.

Hopie came to me in her official capacity, distraught. 'I went to my teachers,' she said, 'and they gave me all sorts of fancy reasons why all the present subjects are necessary. I don't believe them, but I can't convince them. I can't find anyone who agrees with me to advise me.'

I smiled. 'All Tyrants should have such a problem! Most men of power are surrounded by yes-men who only echo what the leader wants to hear. That's no good.'

'Daddy, you aren't helping,' she said severely.

Something clicked in my mind. 'I can give you an excellent source of advice whose notions will agree with those of no one you know but who can really critique contemporary education. Listen to him and argue with him, and you will surely emerge with some positive ideas.'

She viewed me somewhat distrustfully. 'Daddy, you're up to something.'

'Of course I am,' I agreed. 'But what I tell you is true.'

'All right, I'll bite. Who?'

'Thorley.'

'Thorley!' she exclaimed, shocked.

'Go to him. Tell him your problem. Ask his advice. If he fails you, I'll suggest another name.'

'He wouldn't help you in anything!' she said.

'But *you* he just might help. You're not the Tyrant; you're just an underling trying to do a job. That, he might understand.'

She shook her head doubtfully. 'All right, Daddy, I'll call your bluff. But you'd better be ready with another name.' She flounced off.

Spirit nodded. 'Tyrant, you play an interesting game.'

'You know he won't turn her down.'

'I know. Still – '

'She's fifteen. Old enough to wrestle with reality. And it's the only way we'll ever get Thorley's input for the Tyrancy.'

Spirit shrugged, not debating it. We returned to the problem of the ship.

'QYV has sources,' I said.

'But do we want to risk exposure of that connection?'

'If that ship lands, that and the status of Jupiter may become academic.'

'There is that,' she agreed.

'I have something for Reba, anyway.'

So I put in a call to Q. A diagram flashed momentarily on the screen. 'Got it, sir,' Shelia said, and put it on again as a still picture. She had captured it on her recording so that now I could study it at leisure without holding open the connection. QYV (pronounced 'kife') was a very private party.

The diagram was a stylized map of a section of New Wash. One chamber was marked. 'I'm not ready to go there yet myself,' I said. 'I'll send Ebony with the package.' The package was my private narrative of my twenty years as a politician, leading to the moment I assumed the office of Tyrant; I had taken a few minutes to scribble the last sentences, so that it ended at the very point at which the present manuscript begins. QYV had become the repository for these manuscripts; I knew they were safe there.

I gave the package and the address to Ebony to deliver. She could no longer run errands as she had when she was only our gofer, for now she was head of the Department of Population, and a Secret Service man tagged along with her, but I doubted that anyone would pay much attention. Ebony was very good at being anonymous.

'And tell her this,' I said. '"I need a pretext." She will understand.'

'Got it, sir,' she said, and departed.

I brooded over the blip on the screen, now four days distant. 'Maybe a rogue ship, a pirate,' I said. 'Something out of control, seeking plunder.'

'Can't,' Spirit said. 'We cleaned the pirates out of space, remember?'

'For the first time I wish there were a pirate left!'

'Even if there were, it wouldn't have either the nerve or the power to take on a Saturnian ship. That's a cruiser, theoretically converted to merchant duty, but you can bet she can blast anything less than a Jupiter cruiser out of space – and will, if provoked. The Saturnians aren't lily-livered the way we are.'

'I'll gild that lily-liver before I let that ship dock!' I swore. But she was right, as she always was. We could take out that ship, but we would have to do it directly, using the Navy – and that would be an act of war. That was to be done only as a last resort. For one thing, if we challenged the Saturn ship and it did not turn back, we would have to blast it – and that would destroy any proof we might have had of its designs.

It seemed that we were caught between being in the wrong, which would be a very bad beginning for the Tyrancy on the interplanetary scale, and allowing Saturn to achieve a significant, perhaps critical, tactical advantage. Scylla and Charybdis – or in the contemporary parlance, CT and BH. To be caught between contraterrene matter, whose very touch would render a person into something like a miniature nova, and a black hole, that would suck him in and crush him to the size of the nucleus of an atom. I rather liked the imagery but not the situation.

'See Tee and BeeAitch,' Spirit murmured, echoing my unspoken thought.

We continued to handle routinely hectic matters, trying to get the new government formed enough to function while reassuring parties of both the planetary and interplanetary scenes that everything was under control. Many functions had continued for a while on inertia, but the existing structure was deteriorating, and we had constantly to shore it up on a patchwork basis.

Ebony returned. 'She took your package and sent you this one,' she reported, handing me a small box. 'She said it's a fair exchange but that there need be no messenger for the next.'

'Thank you, Ebony,' I said. I would certainly have to deal with Reba directly – but not until this crisis had been negotiated. 'How is your own project going?'

'There are too many people,' she said simply. 'I went to the library and did some reading. We'd be better off with half our present number, but more keep coming in from RedSpot, and more keep being born. But the resources are running out.'

'Have you a programme to deal with this threat?'

She spread her hands. 'Sir, short of a planet-buster war, I don't think anything would work.'

'Keep working on it,' I told her. 'Root out some experts – Shelia can find their names for you – and see what they say. You're one of the common folk; I want to know what you think is best, once you know the full story.'

'I'd rather just be your gofer,' she said.

'Think larger,' I advised.

We opened the QYV package. It was a miniature holo projector that projected the image of a sheet of paper on which was scribbled the military designation of a ship. As a former Navy man, I knew the system, but I didn't recognize the type.

We summoned the Navy officer and showed him the designation. He squinted at it, puzzled. 'That's not one of ours, sir.'

'It has to be,' I said. 'That's a JupeNav designation.'

He frowned. 'I realize that, sir, but I also know our listings. There's no ship by that designation.'

I got a glimmer of a notion. 'How about a sub?'

'Sir, I wouldn't know about that. All subs are classified.'

'Precisely. Because their location must be secret at all times, so the enemy cannot take them out by blind fire at the specific coordinates. But this could be one such.'

'It could, sir,' he agreed, discomfited. Regular Navy personnel did not feel easy about subs, because a sub was a ship-destroyer. In my term in the Navy I had never dealt with a sub. I had, however, had some rather recent experiences with them and fully respected their devious potential.

'Put out a call, Navy protocol, for that ship to contact the Tyrant,' I said.

'But sir, without knowledge of its location, a sealed beam communication is impossible!'

'An open call,' I clarified.

'But a general call – anybody could read it!' he protested, appalled.

'Saturn reads our sealed transmissions, too, and deciphers them as fast as we do,' I pointed out. 'But how much attention do they pay to unclassified, uncoded calls?'

'Very little,' he conceded. 'It would hardly be feasible to track every open call. There are thousands of routine transmissions every minute. Still – '

'So an open call may be the most private kind we can make, in practice.'

'Well, sir, if you look at it that way . . .' He was obviously distressed.

'That is the way I look at it,' I agreed.

He stiffened and saluted, and he turned stiffly and departed.

'Sir,' Shelia said.

'Woman, one of these days I'm going to gag you!' I exclaimed. 'You don't even let me have five seconds to relax between crises!'

'You told me to cut you off at ten o'clock, local time,' she reminded me. 'It is that time.'

Coral came forward. 'Day is over, Tyrant. To bed with you.'

'But that sub – '

'Won't answer you directly. Those vessels don't keep their locations secret by sending any kind of transmission. It will reach you in its own time and fashion. You can relax.'

'But there's still so much to – '

She reached up and caught me by the ear. 'Move, Tyrant!'

Spirit smiled and sent Shelia an end-of-shift signal. I knew that the enforced break was for them as much as for me; we could not afford to run ourselves down to the point of irrationality. I went.

But the notion of that sub still held me. A sub could

take out a ship readily enough, but that would still be an overt act of war. Reba must have had something more sophisticated in mind. How could – ?

Coral did not nag me. She simply led me to the bathroom, undressed me, and shoved me into the sonic shower. I continued to mull over the sub. Could it make the attack seem like an accident? Yet the Saturnians were fully as canny about such things as we.

'Enough,' Coral announced. 'You're clean.'

Damn it, there was no way to make a torpedo from a sub seem like an accident! And what of the innocent personnel aboard that Saturn ship? I was sure that they had not been told of its mission; only the technicians would know. I had destroyed whole ships in space during my Navy career but had never enjoyed it, and my taste for carnage was no greater now. What was needed was not destruction but to make that ship turn back.

'Sir, you aren't moving,' Coral said. 'Come out and retire; I don't want to have to remind you again.'

Suppose there were some way to preempt that ship's controls, forcing it to deviate from its course? If it drifted out of its assigned spacelane, we could legitimately challenge it. But, of course, there was no way to take over a ship from the outside; we would have to sneak an agent aboard, and I doubted that that could be done. Saturn was no slouch at counter-measures.

'I warned you, Tyrant,' Coral said severely. 'Now you shall pay the consequence.' She stepped into the shower.

Startled, I looked at her. She was naked and lovely. There are those who believe a woman to be beyond her prime after her twenties, but Coral had kept herself in top physical form from her martial arts, and from my vantage of fifty, the mid-thirties seemed young enough. She was of Saturn stock, with typically golden skin and Mongoloid facial features, which can be most appealing to males of any race. Certainly I found her attractive, though, of course, I had never made any move on her. I had been loyal to Megan – while I had her. Now . . .

The atmosphere changed. I mean, the physical one. Warm air blasted up from the floor grille. 'What?'

'A froth massage,' she explained. 'The consequence.'

'Oh. I was thinking about – '

'You mentioned Asoka. I happen to have an interest in that part of the System. The roots of my culture are there.'

'But you're from Saturn!' I protested.

'And Saturn was colonized from the old Asian continent of Earth,' she said. 'Six centuries ago I would have been called Chinese. But aspects of our culture were spawned in the southernmost region of that continent, called India, and so I have an interest in that, too, even though India did not go to space.'

'India – ' I repeated, working on the connection. It had been a long time since I had studied ancient history! 'It took over Earth!'

'My point is, Asoka was an Indian conqueror. At first he was called a tyrant, but later he became perhaps the finest of all great rulers. He is certainly a worthy model to follow.'

I would have paid more attention to her comment, but there were distractions. Not only was she nudging against me so that her marvellous body forced a masculine reaction in me, but also the warm air around us was thickening. Now the froth was manifesting, coursing upward around our bodies, tickling intimate places.

'Is your mind off business yet?' she inquired.

I laughed. 'Yes. However, if one of us doesn't get out of this shower soon – '

'I have wanted to do this for a long time,' she said. She

pressed her warm, slippery body against mine and drew my head down for a kiss.

The froth thickened further. It creamed up against and around our bodies, pushing, kneading, almost lifting us off our feet. I had never experienced anything quite like this before, but it was a thing worth learning about. The fact that I was next to a well-formed woman added to the effect.

'Now let me introduce you to the Tree,' Coral murmured.

'The what?'

'You Westerners tend to be unimaginative about sexual expression,' she said. 'Sit there.'

'But this is the shower! There's no – '

'There is now.' And indeed there was; a seat had emerged from the wall.

I sat, and she got on to my lap, facing me, her legs spread to circle me, as the froth coursed by ever more thickly. I felt as if I were being borne up on a cloud, high in some planetary heaven, with an angel embracing me.

She lifted her body, bringing it into position, then settled firmly on me in the amorous connection. 'Now,' she said, 'as you arrive, stand.'

'Stand!' I exclaimed. 'But you would fall!'

'No way, Tyrant,' she breathed. Then she tightened certain internal muscles, and suddenly I felt the eruption developing. I lunged to my feet, assisted by her weight leaning back, and sure enough: she was supported and could not fall. The mass of her body pressed down most solidly, however, heightening the sensation as I pressured all that I had through that connection.

We stood there amid the moving froth, my feet planted on the floor, our two bodies branching outward at the mid-point, our heads apart. We were the Tree, without doubt! The sensation was almost painfully intense.

Then she drew her upper body into mine and reached for my lips with a frothy kiss. I felt her quiver, inside and out, and knew that she had reached her own climax.

But soon she had to put her feet down, for her support was waning. She got off me, and the froth swirled between us and cleansed us anew.

At last she turned off the froth, and we stood there, spent. 'Next time, another consequence,' she said. 'When I tell you to rest, remember.'

But I strongly suspected that I would balk again the next time, requiring her to introduce me to the next consequence.

I stepped out of the shower, feeling cleansed outside and inside, and made my way to the bed, forgetting my pyjamas. It didn't matter; Coral joined me in the same state.

I suppose it seems frivolous of me to make love to another woman so soon after my separation from Megan. I still loved Megan and would always love her, but the physical portion of our relationship was over. My girls were now doing what they deemed necessary to tide me through the transition, and I have no reason in retrospect to challenge their judgement. It was, as it were, all in the family.

Certainly I slept well – when Coral put me to bed.

5

For the Love of God

The Saturn ship cruised on inexorably. I fidgeted, unable to concentrate properly on the details of organization. Shelia handled most of them, and I spoke directly to others only when she prompted me to. When would that sub make contact with me?

'Sir,' Shelia said.

'Sir,' I mimicked her, teasingly, and she smiled. She was in this period my closest and most valued associate, Coral's nocturnal ministrations notwithstanding, because she was dealing with my intellectual needs in the crisis. I had hired her for merit, not body, and that merit remained solid.

'A Navy man to see you.'

'I'm not seeing any other – ' I began, then broke off, looking at her.

She nodded. '*The* Navy man,' she amended.

'I expected a message.'

She spoke into her unit. 'The Tyrant will see him now,' she said.

'But he could be an imposter!'

'No, sir,' she said. Obviously my lower personnel had verified the man's identity.

The man entered. He wore the outfit of a mechanic, and it was dirty. He had the stripes of a corporal. He was middle-aged. Taken aback, I stared at him.

He stepped up to me and saluted. 'Commander Jenkins reporting as directed, sir.'

I returned the salute, bemused. 'You seem to be out of uniform, Commander.'

'No officer leaves the ship, sir,' he said.

So he was anonymous, beyond his ship or this office. I spoke briefly with him, quickly ascertaining that he was familiar with the Navy and had known of my unit when I was there. He did seem to be legitimate. Of course, I trusted the verdict of my lower staff; I just liked to verify things in my own fashion.

'Commander,' I said, getting down to business. 'There is a Saturn cruiser on course for Ganymede. It carries contraband that must not be permitted to reach port. But because we have not been officially notified of this, we need to balk this ship off-the-record, so as to provide Saturn no pretext for protest. Are you able to handle this?'

Now the man's nature came through clearly, as he tackled the problem. 'Coordinates of target vessel, sir?'

I glanced at Spirit. She gave them.

He did a quick mental computation. 'We can reach them in two days, sir. That will be a margin of two days. It would be better to let the target enter the mine field, however.'

'Mine field?'

'Perhaps your predecessor didn't advise you, sir. Ganymede is protected from intrusion by a mine field laid down fifteen years ago.'

I thought back. 'When Tocsin was vice-president. Didn't the administration protest?'

'Why should it? Tocsin was in charge of the project.'

I was stunned. 'You mean, *we* laid those mines?'

'Surreptitiously. To inhibit the Saturn connection.'

'But there has been no news of detonations!' I protested.

'Not in our press,' he agreed.

I digested this. 'What of the Ganymede press?'

'Not there, either. They have preferred to scout paths

through the field and to move some of the mines. Now they do serve as a kind of protection from invasion, because only Ganymede knows the precise route through.'

Spirit laughed. 'So the mining backfired! It helps Gany, rather than hurting it!'

'I am not responsible for the blunders of our leaders,' Commander Jenkins said somewhat stiffly.

'But I went there as ambassador! My ship encountered no mines!'

'Not while you followed the route charted for you by Ganymede,' he agreed.

'The premier never mentioned –'

'The premier keeps his own counsel.'

So it seemed. 'But if the Saturn ship uses a Gany-cleared approach –'

'Errors occur,' he said. 'Sometimes individual mines drift.'

Now, at last, I caught on. 'If one should drift into the entry channel –'

'An unfortunate accident,' he concluded.

'But can you move one to the right place in time? Do you know their specific channel?'

'No.'

'Then –'

'It can be very difficult to tell the difference between a mine contact and a torpedo contact.'

I nodded. 'So, in that region you could take out that ship without making it obvious.' I frowned. 'I wish there were some way simply to turn it back. I don't like unnecessary bloodshed.'

'Saturn cannot be cowed the way pirates can, sir. You cannot bluff it. The ship must be taken out.'

'Besides which,' Spirit added, 'we cannot afford to advertise our part in this. It must seem like an accident.'

The logic was inescapable. We had to destroy that ship. Already I was being forced into exactly the kind of dirty secret dealings I had condemned in Tocsin.

But I couldn't allow Ganymede to be transformed into a true Saturn base. 'Do it,' I said, feeling unclean.

Commander Jenkins saluted, turned and departed. As he left the room his military bearing dissolved, and he slouched into unkempt mechanic status. My respect for this aspect of the Navy increased.

Now I could relax, to a degree. The problem of the Saturn ship was being handled. Perhaps Saturn would suspect what we had done, but it would not be sure and would not know why. That doubt should protect the premier, until we found some other way to 'discover' the Saturn plot. In fact, debris from the ship could reveal that plot.

The rush of setting up continued. Spirit brought prospects in for me to interview; I talked with each, using my talent to read his or her basic nature, and made my judgements. My talent is not a solution to all personnel problems, because it does not tell me how much a person knows or how competent he is, only what his basic reactions are as I talk to him. Yet, if I ask probing questions or stir some emotion in him, his true reaction is clear to me, and that counts for a lot. A person who seeks to deceive me, or who has some guilty secret, rings like a false coin to my perception. I have never been betrayed by one I have analysed in my way, even if I have taken only a few minutes.

The problems continued too. Now that the initial shock of the changeover had passed, the population was asking questions. What were the basic policies of my administration to be? Would the average man be better off than before? Would my supporters be directly rewarded? Would Hispanics be appointed to all the best jobs, at the expense of Saxons? These things were important to them. It was necessary to formulate reassuring messages, to keep the populace quiet until the actual policies were formulated and implemented. I had hardly any greater notion of what the final configuration of my administration was to be than they did.

Hopie called Thorley, explained her mission, and was astonished when he invited her to his residence for consultation. 'But he's your enemy!' she exclaimed. 'He condemns everything you do! Why should he help me?'

'Thorley is not my enemy,' I reminded her. 'Remember how courteous he was when he accompanied us to Saturn several years ago? He is merely an honest man with a differing philosophy.'

'But he still writes the most horrible things about you! About how you have preempted the established Jupiter system of government and become the first true Tyrant we have had – '

'All true,' I said. 'Thorley never lies.'

'And I'm your daughter. I'm trying to do a job you assigned me. Why should he help?'

'The complete rationale of a man as complex as Thorley can never be properly understood by others,' I said. 'But I suspect that in this particular case he realizes that if he is to have any positive effect on the new order, this is the most likely avenue. If he can influence you to make truly effective reforms in education, that is worth his while.'

'But education isn't even important!'

I smiled. 'Try telling him that.'

'I will!' she said defiantly, and flounced off in the manner her kind has. How I loved that child!

Within an hour she was gone, taking little Robertico with her. Spirit had arranged for a small Navy vessel to transport her to Ebor in Sunshine, where she would stay with Megan. Thorley maintained a residence in the vicinity, as he had emerged professionally from roots in that region, much as I had. Hopie would ferry across to interview him as convenient.

I made a formal public address, explaining about the departments I was in the process of setting up and reassuring everyone that I intended to be fair to all parties. 'But my first priority is to balance the budget,' I concluded. 'I suspect that this will require some sacrifices, so I want to do it very carefully. Senator Stonebridge is working on that now.'

Then I turned to questions. Representatives of the leading news services were in the network, and Shelia selected individuals randomly to pose their questions.

The first one, as luck would have it, was from the *Gotham Times*. 'Tyrant, when will the next elections be held?'

There was a murmur of humour at the manner in which he addressed me, but I knew that my preference for exactly that title would soon be accepted. His question set me back. I hadn't thought about elections, but, of course, I had abolished Congress, and I myself had taken power through no elective process. Would I step aside in four years to allow a new president to be elected? I didn't have to. Yet elections had always been vital to our system. There would be broad and deep popular outrage if I did not commit myself to the restoration of elections.

'There will surely be elections,' I said somewhat lamely, 'but I'm not sure when.'

Then they were on me, figuratively, like a pack of wolves. If I was serious about future elections, why couldn't I name the date? Was I in fact planning to remain a dictator for life? Did I think the people of Jupiter would stand for that? How could there be congressional elections if there was no Congress?

I answered as well as I could, which wasn't really

adequate. I felt like a less-than-bright student before a university panel. I had to promise to try to come up with better answers, after researching the matter.

Then a respected member of the Holo Guild had his turn. 'Tyrant, suppose I were to call you a gnat-brained, pigheaded, philandering son of a spic?'

Suddenly there was silence in the chamber and on the air, and probably all around Jupiter, for this was being broadcast live. I knew what he was doing: he was testing my commitment to the freedom of the press, which encompassed all the present media. Actually Spirit had arranged to plant the question without telling me; that was her little bit of teasing.

It took me only a moment to recover. I hauled my open mouth closed. 'I really don't think of myself as gnat-brained,' I responded.

There was a pause as the audience assimilated the significance of that. Then the laughter began, timorously at first, swelling to heroic proportion. It was, I think, comprised mostly of relief. I had answered the true question: there would be no censorship. If the Tyrant himself could be openly insulted, without consequence, then anyone could.

In all my tenure as Tyrant I never suppressed the press. I remained true to my commitment to Thorley, made some fifteen or sixteen years before I assumed the power. In retrospect, that is one of the things I view with greatest pride. I believe Asoka would have approved.

The time proceeded in the usual manner, seeming at once phenomenally extended and laser-swift. My next sharp memory is of the handling of the Saturn ship. It cruised to within a day's range of Ganymede, slowed, and maneuvered through the mine field. Our watching instruments perceived a fleeting little nova; a ship had

93

been blown up. But my regretful relief converted abruptly to dismay.

It was not the Saturn ship. That vessel proceeded on towards the planet, untouched.

What, then, had it been? Our survey of the debris made it all too clear: a sub had blown. Our sub.

What had happened? We consulted with our Navy man and came to a conclusion: either the sub had encountered one of the mines, which would have been colossal bad fortune, or –

Or there was another sub. One that had lurked in ambush for ours and torpedoed it as the opportunity arose.

If there was another sub, the implications were chilling. It suggested that Saturn knew that we knew of their Gany ploy and had anticipated our reaction. That they had planned further ahead than we had guessed and secured their plot from our interference. Or that the premier had acted to lure us into the trap.

I rejected the latter notion. I knew the premier of Ganymede. He was a hard man, but he would not have done that to me. It was not honour so much as the particular brand of acquaintance we had: not precisely friendship but mutual respect.

Yet I was not sure I could accept the other hypothesis, either. Saturn could not have hidden a sub in Gany space without Ganymede's knowledge and acceptance. Had it done so, the premier would have warned me.

'She brought her own sub,' Spirit said.

That had to be it. A Saturn sub could have travelled under the cover of the Saturn ship, perhaps even attached to it. Then, as the ship approached the dangerous region of the mine field, where an ambush would be most likely if any were to occur, the sub could have been launched. It was no easier for one sub to spot another than for a normal ship to spot a sub, but the advantage lay with surprise. Our sub had been intent on the ship it was stalking; it could readily have missed the other sub. But the enemy sub had no such distraction; it was questing only for another sub, and if it nudged ahead of the Saturn ship, it could have spotted the other. Not easily – but as Commander Jenkins (rest his soul) had reminded me, Saturn was no slouch in space. In fact, Saturn was the most sub-oriented of all the planets. If anyone had the technology to spot a sub, Saturn did.

If this was the correct scenario, then Saturn did not necessarily know that we knew of its Gany plot. It was simply exercising normal caution. Or special caution, because of the importance of this particular mission. There need be no suspicion of the premier.

But our sub *had* been there. Why should we have been there, if not to take out the Saturn ship? That had to suggest that we did know.

Spirit sighed. 'Brother, we are in trouble.'

'Double trouble,' I agreed morosely. 'Not only does Saturn now know or strongly suspect that we know, it is about to dock that ship on Ganymede – the one thing we can't afford.'

'Maybe we can still put it out,' she said. 'We can take the offence. We can accuse Ganymede of blowing up one of our strayed vessels and demand reparation.'

'That might shield the premier from suspicion,' I agreed, 'but it won't stop the Saturn ship from docking.'

'It will if we get so outraged by the unprovoked attack that we invoke the Navy. We could pick that ship out of space long-distance if we used a saturation launch of homing missiles.'

'But that would be an overt act of war!' I cried. 'That's theoretically a Saturn freighter!'

'If that ship docks, we'll soon be at war regardless,' she pointed out.

I pondered, ill at ease. 'It would also be a lie,' I said. 'Covert activity is one thing; a lie is another. I want my administration to be based on the truth.'

'The truth is that the Premier of Ganymede tipped us off,' Spirit reminded me. 'Do you want to put that out as news?'

'No. To preserve a confidence is not to lie. We must find a way to act without violating either the confidence or the truth.'

She shook her head as if in frustration. Then she took hold of me and kissed me. 'My brother, you are my conscience. Without you I would be lost.'

I was halfway dazed by the compliment. My sister does not speak often in that manner. But even in my distraction of the moment I noticed Coral exchanging a glance with Shelia and nodding. Apparently the guideline that was obvious to me was not as clear to the others until enunciated.

Spirit regrouped. 'Well, Saturn now knows that we had a sub in there. Would it be fair to say that we had a suspicion about their ship, that we now feel is confirmed?'

'Yes,' I agreed. 'But we can't say what our suspicion is.'

'Suppose we accuse them of renewed arms smuggling? That's not exactly what they're doing, but it is something Jupiter has always been sensitive about. After that business with the impounded ship . . .'

She meant the ploy Tocsin had used to discredit Ganymede and void our exchange of ambassadors. That had been aimed primarily at my candidacy, because I had been the first ambassador to Ganymede after President Kenson reestablished diplomatic relations. I had acted to expose that ruse, but certainly it had heightened Jupiter awareness of that particular issue. It could account for our increased surveillance of Ganymede.

Where was the line between diplomacy and duplicity? What means were justified for what ends? I remained disquieted, finding this philosophical territory murky, but saw no better alternative. 'Do it,' I said.

So it went out to the media: our accusation that Ganymede was violating the covenant and shipping arms again. An alert went out to the Jupiter Navy, and our ships changed course and made for Ganymede. Of course, it would be days before the majority of them were in position, but the order was dramatic enough.

'Sir,' Shelia said.

'Have I mentioned that I plan to have you keel-hauled without a helmet, just to keep you quiet, girl?'

'After the crisis,' she agreed. 'A Saturn defector wishes to see you personally. He seems to have information.'

'He has been checked by our personnel?'

'Now in progress. They are impressed.'

'Information relevant to the present situation?'

'They think so, sir.'

'Then move him on through and bring him in.'

She returned to her equipment, relaying the order.

Within the hour the premier of Ganymede was on the screen. 'Señor Tyrant, we are not guilty of this thing! We are shipping no arms!'

I scowled impressively. 'We sent a sub in to intercept your freighter from Saturn. It did not even wait for our challenge. It torpedoed our sub! What greater evidence of guilt can there be than that?'

'That ship contained no arms!' he protested. It took about three and a half seconds for the signal to travel at light speed, each way, so there was a necessary pause that we accepted as a matter of course. 'It acted only to protect itself!'

'Then what was the cargo?' I demanded. We both knew what it was, but it was necessary to put the mystery on the record.

'Why did you send a sub into Ganymede space?' he countered. 'We offered no provocation! You tried to attack a routine supply ship!'

'That was no supply ship!' I exclaimed angrily.

He gazed at me cannily. 'How can you say that, Señor? Do you accuse me of falsification?'

Of course, he was guilty of just that, but his code was not mine, and this declaration was necessary to clear him of the particular suspicion that counted.

I formed a smile with obvious difficulty. 'Of course not, Premier. If you are giving me your word that that ship carried no arms, I must accept that.' I hoped I did not look as if I accepted it. The agents of Saturn would be analysing my every nuance of expression, trying to determine exactly how much I knew or suspected.

'Thank you, Señor Tyrant. Now about that sub in our space – '

'Sir,' Shelia said.

'I'm on screen at the moment,' I reminded her, nettled. She knew this was not the time for an interruption.

'This may be relevant, sir.'

I caught her tone. I heeded it. 'Premier, if you will pardon me one moment . . .' I said quickly in Spanish.

Seven seconds later the premier made a gesture of unconcern. But I was already inspecting the intruder. He was a man of about thirty, wearing ill-fitting Navy fatigues that had evidently been borrowed recently. Probably his own clothing had been taken by my security crew, to be quite sure he had nothing that could harm me.

'Admiral, I am from North Saturn,' he said in Russian.

I looked suitably baffled, though as it happens, I do speak the language. It was not at that time a talent I

98

wanted to advertise. 'English,' I said. 'Can you speak English? ¿Español?'

'I – from Saturn,' he said haltingly in English. 'Infor – information. Interest you.'

'Perhaps,' I agreed guardedly. 'But right now I'm in the middle of a call.'

'About cargo – ship.' I could tell that he believed that what he had to tell me was vitally important, and I knew that my personnel, including Shelia, had shunted him on up to me as rapidly as possible.

'*The* ship?' I asked, my pulse quickening. 'The one now approaching Ganymede?'

'Think – so,' he agreed. 'I – technician on special equipment. Control brain – distance. Very new.'

'Mind control – without drugs?' I asked, beginning to see the relevance. 'Take over people without touching them?'

He nodded vigorously. 'Experimental – but effective. Sent to Ganymede.'

With new surmise I returned my gaze to the screen. 'Premier, if not arms, what about experimental equipment?' I demanded. 'To subvert our agents without leaving any telltale drug traces or brain-wave distortions?'

'Absolutely not, Señor!' he exclaimed indignantly. 'How can you believe a defector? He would say anything to gain a rich reward from Jupiter!'

'Or the locks at Tanamo,' I said, as if just tuning in on something new. 'Presently coded to our personnel, though under Ganymedan suzerainty. If those personnel could be subverted by such a device without our knowledge – ' My expression abruptly hardened. 'Premier, *what the hell are you pulling?*'

'All a mistake!' the premier exclaimed. 'A lie, to sully Ganymede!'

'Then you won't object to allowing our personnel to

board and inspect that Saturn ship before it docks,' I said. 'To verify that what you say is true, Señor Premier.'

'It is a Saturn ship!' he protested. 'Only the Saturn authorities can permit that! But I'm sure that if you apply to them, they will be happy to assuage your doubt.'

'Señor, I mean to inspect that ship before it docks!' I said. 'Will you deny docking clearance until this is accomplished?'

'I cannot do that!' he countered desperately. 'Saturn is the ally of Ganymede! But I assure you, Señor – '

I cut him off with a Spanish expletive that related to the manner in which he pained my genital member. I returned to the defector. 'What details can you provide?'

He provided what he could. Soon I was satisfied that Saturn was doing research of the nature described and did plan to use it to corrupt the agents of other planets. Whether this was the equipment actually on the present ship was uncertain, but it did provide us with what we vitally needed: the alternate source of information right at the critical moment. Now we could act without implicating the premier of Ganymede. Indeed, on the record, the premier had done his best to conceal the information from us.

Later I learned that QYV had been responsible for producing the defector at the critical moment. I was glad I had put Reba in charge; she had really helped me that time.

We spirited the defector away to a safe and comfortable place and contacted Saturn. Naturally their bureaucracy stalled. They didn't deny our demand, they merely ran it through their labyrinthine channels. It was obvious that nothing would be accomplished within the day's time required for the ship to arrive and dock.

I cut that short by putting through a hotline call directly to the Chairman of the Council of Ministers of Saturn,

Comrade Karzhinov. Any call to Saturn, under optimum conditions, requires a minimum of half an hour, because the orbit of that planet is more than four astronomical units from the orbit of Jupiter, and, of course, one astronomical unit is the archaic measure of Earth's distance from the sun, or about eight and a third light minutes. Normally Saturn is farther from Jupiter than that, depending on the planets' positions within these orbits; at its worst, the separation can be about fifteen astronomical units, or over two hours' one-way signal time. It has been claimed that this slowness of communication is responsible for the deteriorating relations between the two, but I regard that as nonsense. After all, Uranus is never *closer* than fourteen astronomical units to Jupiter, yet our relations with that planet generally have been good. No, it is political, not spatial, relations that generate the problem.

But while we were expending the hours required to contact Karzhinov directly, that Saturn ship was still proceeding to Ganymede. I'm not sure what the Saturn day-night cycle was at that time relative to ours or how long it took the North Saturn leader to read my message and formulate his reply. Probably he took time to consult his advisers. Thus it was about ten hours before I heard from him. I did not stand on one foot waiting; I retired and slept and handled the onrushing routine.

Then, when the ship was within twelve hours of Ganymede, I received Karzhinov's response. It was terse and to the point: the ship was a Saturn freighter, not subject to our interference, and we would respect its integrity or pay the price.

Spirit and I exchanged a glance. 'He's toughing it out,' she said. 'He knows that by the time we exchange many more messages, the ship will have docked.'

'He thinks I am made of putty,' I said. Putty is a

concept derived from the nature of a substance once used to caulk windows; it deforms readily under pressure.

'Saturn does not respect putty,' she said.

'Then let's up the ante. We have time for one more exchange, at this rate, before that ship docks. What can we do to dispel the putty image?'

'We can put the Navy on Full Alert.'

I pursed my lips. There have been various procedures over the centuries for the preparation for action, with various names and codes. At present Alert meant that the Navy would be marshalling for possible battle. It did not signal war, but it was not a thing that was done without reason. We had invoked a partial Alert when we oriented on Ganymede; a Full Alert would involve all our ships disposed around the Solar System, including those in Saturn Space. That could be construed as menacing. Certainly it would signal the seriousness with which we viewed the present situation.

'Do it,' I said.

Shelia made the call. Within a minute Emerald's dark face was on the main screen. 'You sure, Tyrant?' she demanded.

'Full Alert,' I repeated.

'Done. It will take a while for it to be effective in the farther reaches. To what extent do we grant local autonomy?'

Because when it required four hours to send a signal to a ship in the Neptune region, the admiral in charge there could not necessarily afford to wait eight hours for the answer to any query.

'Limited,' I said. 'I don't want some fool starting SWIII on his own itch.'

'Just see that he doesn't start it right here,' she replied, smiling grimly as she faded out.

I smiled in return, though the screen was now blank.

Emerald had called on a private beam, but we both knew that the transmission would be intercepted, recorded, and decoded by Saturn agents. She knew I was making a gesture for Saturn to interpret, in the game of hints and signals that interplanetary relations was. Her informality suggested that we did not know we would be tapped, and her remark about the possibility of accidental launching Solar System War Three suggested that I had that potential. It would not be a comfortable interpretation for the Saturn experts – and that was good. I wanted them to become uncertain. How well Emerald still understood me!

'So much for the indirect message to Saturn,' Spirit said. 'Now for the direct one. What tone do we assume?'

'A reasonable one,' I decided. 'We have information that the ship is transporting equipment that threatens the security of Jupiter, and we cannot allow it to dock. They must turn it back to Saturn or suffer the consequences.'

'And our closest ships will simultaneously orient for firing on that ship,' she agreed. 'We remain out of range, but we can make quite a show.'

'Do it,' I agreed.

This time the Saturn response came within four hours. To fire on that ship would be an act of war, and Saturn would not be responsible for the consequence.

'They're still toughing it out,' Spirit said. 'They are sure you'll back down.'

'Do you think they'll go to war over one ship?' I asked.

'I doubt it. They don't want war, they want the critical advantage that a converted Tanamo base would provide.'

'Then let's fire on that ship.'

She frowned. 'Um, let's keep within protocol. We have time for one more exchange of messages before it docks. We can send an ultimatum, and if they don't respond by the deadline, then we shall be justified in taking action.

In that time our ships will get that much closer, and their fire correspondingly more accurate. We might be able to take the ship out.'

We did it. Knowing that a difficult period was coming up, I took a nap. This might seem strange, but I had been in combat and knew the importance of being properly rested. I had learned decades ago to sleep when I needed to. I would have done so that first night after I assumed power, had Coral not forced the issue. But it had been more comfortable letting her handle it, as I am sure any man would agree.

The response from Karzhinov came just two hours before the docking, and it was blunt indeed. It translated: 'Do not interfere with ship. Saturn will retaliate.'

Spirit sighed. 'They simply *won't* take us seriously! We have no alternative but to do it.'

'Remember when we delivered ultimatums to pirates?' I asked her. For though I regarded pirates as the scum of the System and hated the entire breed ever since they had slain our father, I had tried to be fair. This was not so much for their benefit, as for my own: I needed to believe in the justness of my cause and the rightness of my action. Just as I did now.

'We did have to kill a number of them,' she reminded me.

It was my turn to sigh. I have never liked killing, but I have done it when necessary. I was prepared to do it again.

We contacted Emerald and gave the order. The Navy ships opened fire.

The attack failed; the range was still too great. But there was a virtual explosion nevertheless.

First there was a call from the premier of Ganymede. 'Tyrant Hubris, you are attacking Ganymede territory!' he protested.

'Correction,' I said. 'We are firing on a Saturn ship that our intelligence informs us is a threat to Jupiter. Its location at the moment is coincidental.'

'You are violating Ganymede space! I demand that you desist instantly!'

'Turn over that Saturn ship and we'll desist,' I replied.

'But I have no authority over a Saturn vessel!'

'Then deny it clearance to dock. It will have to return to Saturn.'

He looked truly pained, though, of course, this was what he most wanted to do. That ship represented disaster for him as well as for Jupiter. But he could not express his true sentiment. 'Saturn is Ganymede's ally and bene-factor! I cannot insult Saturn in this manner!'

My expression hardened. 'I had thought that relations between Jupiter and Ganymede were improving. We maintain embassies. We buy your sugar. Now I learn that you have deceived me, Premier. You have tried to bring in technicians to make Tanamo an enemy military base. This is a dagger at Jupiter's heart and a betrayal of my personal trust.'

His protest was already coming in, crossing with my harangue. I overrode it, lapsing into Spanish in my supposed rage. '*I* arranged the transfer of that base!' I roared. 'I trusted your sincerity! And how do you repay my trust, you dog's penis? You try to convert it to a Saturn missile base! You try to destroy me, just as I come into power in Jupiter!'

'. . . only supplies, I swear!' he was saying in English. 'No arms, no special equipment, only food and tools for our agriculture!'

Then, as I paused, my Spanish outburst caught up to him. He changed to Spanish himself. 'You eater of sweet rolls!' he cried, reddening in the face. I should clarify that in the Gany dialect of Spanish, a certain type of food

105

becomes the vernacular for the female genital and is not spoken as a compliment. 'You fire into my space, violating interplanetary protocol, and dare to accuse *me* of bad faith? You look for a pretext to invade our planet and make it a Jupiter colony! But do you know what will happen if you do that, Señor animal fornicator? *Twenty thousand gringos will die!*'

I cut off the contact, then settled back, laughing. 'He understands, all right,' I said.

'He had better,' Spirit said. 'We're going to have to invade Ganymede, you know.'

'With about twenty thousand troops,' I agreed. 'But with lasers set at stun only.'

'The Saturn forces there won't set theirs at stun,' she said.

'He'll keep them clear. Ganymede is not our worry. Saturn is.'

'Saturn is,' she agreed. 'If Karzhinov doesn't bluff, we really will be in Ess-Doubleyou-Three.'

That sobered me. 'We have to risk it, though.'

'Sir,' Shelia said.

'Put him on,' I said.

It was, as I had anticipated, the ambassador from Saturn. There was no delay in transmission here, because he was in New Wash. 'I must sternly inquire as to the meaning of this outrage,' he said.

'The meaning is that Saturn is trying to change the locks on Tanamo Base on Ganymede, and the premier of Ganymede is playing along,' I said severely. 'This cannot and shall not be permitted. Your ship must turn back before docking or we shall take more specific action.'

'It is only a supply ship!' he protested.

'Guarded by a killer sub,' I said. 'Why are you so protective of this particular ship? A true supply ship has no fear of inspections.'

'This is preposterous!'

'I agree. Turn back the ship.'

'But I have no authority to – '

'Then don't waste my time.' I cut him off.

The ship did not stop. We remained unable to knock it out at long distance; we would have had to launch a CT missile at Ganymede itself to take it out, and I was not prepared to do that.

'Ganymede is organizing to repel invasion,' Spirit said.

'Invade,' I agreed. 'But watch Saturn.'

'Emerald's on it.'

We tracked Saturn's ships in the Jupiter sphere. They were now on alert. Ours moved into position to oppose them, even as Saturn ships defending Saturn moved to counter our formation there. Indeed the invasion of Ganymede might be a joke, but the seige of Saturn was not. If any missile was fired at a Jupiter city –

Now the White Bubble was deluged with calls from our own population. We had not censored the news; the people were catching on that real trouble was brewing.

'Sir, you may want to watch this,' Shelia said, and put on a local interview.

It was Thorley, my most eloquent critic, speaking editorially. The startling thing was who was in the background: my daughter Hopie. Evidently she had been consulting him about the prospects for education when both were caught by the Saturn crisis, and the pickup caught them both.

'*That* will make tongues wag!' Spirit murmured.

'. . .'seems to be madness,' Thorley was saying. 'There is no reputable evidence I know of that the Saturn ship carries contraband, and to launch an attack on the mere suspicion – '

'My father's not mad!' Hopie exclaimed. 'He always has good reason for what he does!'

Thorley gave a wry smile. 'Such as appointing a child to be in charge of education?'

'He told me I could do the job if I got the best advice!'

He shook his head. 'Mayhap he is but mad north-north west; when the wind is southerly, he knows a hawk from a handsaw.' He returned to the camera, smiling in the eloquently rueful way he had. 'It seems the Tyrant sent his daughter to me for advice.'

I heard someone laugh; it was Shelia, losing her composure for the moment. Thorley was, as I mentioned, my most effective critic, but it was impossible not to like him.

'. . . yet it remains difficult to see the logic in such brinkmanship,' Thorley was continuing. 'In a matter of hours the Tyrant has brought us closer to the brink of a holocaust than has been the case in twenty years. I am, candidly, appalled.'

Then we had to return to the business at hand. Another message had arrived from Chairman Karzhinov.

'Madness!' he exclaimed, as if echoing Thorley. Actually the word was that of the translator, for Karzhinov did not speak English and did not know that I spoke Russian. 'You are committing an act of war! Desist or we must react!'

'Send a bread-and-butter note,' I told Shelia. She looked pale, but she got on it: a routine repetition of our demand that the ship not dock. Of course, it would be too late by the time that message reached Saturn, but it maintained contact. I wanted it clear that we had reason for our action and that only a Saturnian backdown would avert catastrophe.

But the ship did dock. Our invasion force moved into position, Tanamo the obvious target. We wanted no confusion on the part of the premier of Ganymede; he had to know precisely where and when we would land.

I looked about me during a lull in the activity, if not the tension. Ebony was there, having reverted to gofer status for the crisis. She looked as pale as a Black woman could. I raised an eyebrow at her.

'Sir, how do they know not to shoot?' she asked. 'You sent no message. After the way you yelled at the premier – '

'The premier and I understand each other,' I said.

'But – '

'Any message of that nature would be intercepted,' I explained. 'Therefore there has to be *no* message. But the premier knows what he has to do, as do I.'

'But the Saturn fleet – '

'Do you happen to know who commands the Jupiter-sphere division of the Saturn fleet?'

Wordlessly she shook her head.

'Admiral Khukov.'

'Oh! We know him – '

'As well as we know the premier.'

'But he's a ruthless man, sir.'

'He knows his priorities – as do I.'

'I sure *hope* you do!' she said.

'It *is* a bit chancy,' I agreed. 'but, I think, necessary.'

The Saturn fleet became more menacing. Their dread-noughts were impressive, but it was their formidable subs that concerned me most. Our destroyers were trying desperately to track them, and we had most located but could not be sure of some. In any event, unless we launched a preemptive strike at them, our cities would be vulnerable to their strike. Yet, at the same time, our subs were closing on Saturn and giving their defences similar fits. One CT warhead could do a horrendous amount of damage. In fact, there was a growing question whether the disruption of planetary atmosphere would not generate a greater long-term mischief than the destruction of a city.

But at the moment it was the immediate situation that concerned us. Saturn had to be made to believe that I really would push the final button – if driven too far.

'Sir,' Shelia said.

Wearily I glanced at her.

'Ganymede is carrying it live.'

'So far so good!' I exclaimed, relieved. 'Put it on.'

The screen showed the Gany militia moving into place, ready to repel the invader. They were armed with laser rifles and pistols.

They were evidently outside the Tanamo base, their entry balked by the resistance of our gatekeepers. That was the peculiarity of the compromise I had arranged, about seven years before: Tanamo had passed to Gany control, but the locks had remained keyed to Jupiter personnel. Thus it had been impossible for the base to be abused by Saturn, because the very specialized equipment necessary to recode the locks could be docked only at Tanamo itself, and our personnel would not permit that. Now, of course, that situation had changed; the more sophisticated equipment being landed at the other port could do that job. Once the premier was out of the way, the treaty could be voided by Saturn.

The ships of the Jupiter Navy, naturally, had no difficulty docking at Tanamo; our personnel facilitated their clearance. In short order we had twenty thousand laser-armed troops there. They stormed out, covered by our own cameras, and rushed to shore up the defences of the planet-bound accesses.

There was a blazing battle at the perimeter as the Gany forces charged. They had to expose themselves in the straight access tunnels, and our troops mowed them down.

It was beautiful. The Gany troops clutched themselves

and collapsed. Had I not known they were not hurt, I would have winced. They had been well coached.

Would it fool the Saturnians? I knew it would not deceive Admiral Khukov for an instant, but I also was pretty sure that he would not expose the ruse. He would read it correctly, censor the Saturn records of anything that would undermine the effect, and send the tapes on to his superiors: the clear violation of Gany territory I had initiated. Then he would wait for his orders.

After our troops had cleared the corridor they moved out to secure a broader foothold. Now they were to some extent exposed, and snipers caught them. They died as convincingly as had the Ganys. The *gringos* were starting to get it.

The reaction in our media was immediate: NAVY INVADES GANY! the *Gotham Times* headline read. Others put it more succinctly: WAR! The calls to the White Bubble multiplied but were blocked off; we were now too busy to bother with them. Only communications through channels were accepted – and there were more than enough of those to swamp us.

Very soon the second reaction came: 'This is madness!' a commentator cried. 'For no reason we invade Ganymede? What kind of a fool do we have at the helm?'

That reaction quickly spread across Jupiter. The ousted opposition Congressmen were quick to cry warning: the planet could not afford to tolerate a crazy man in the White Bubble!

But the great ships of the Jupiter Navy remained in place above our cities, orienting on Ganymede, and tracking the Saturn ships and subs. They represented the ultimate power in this region of space, and they answered only to Admiral Emerald Mondy, who served the Tyrant with absolute loyalty. The power was mine.

Actually the sequence took more time than it seems in

111

my memory, and the details were more complex than I can render here, because of the distance to Saturn and the enormity of planetary proceedings. But I must render it as I perceived it, trusting to the official records to correct my confusions. One thing is certain: the System came extraordinarily close to war and possible annihilation in that period. Yet I am not certain that there was any better way to accomplish what had to be accomplished. Some risk is always entailed in surgery, and the dangers of leaving the situation uncorrected were, in the long term, greater. I did what I had to do.

Our invasion of Ganymede proceeded while Saturn expostulated. Because it took four hours for Karzhinov's reactions to reach me, much happened between calls. Now *we* stalled *them*, reversing their prior ploy, and they were as helpless as we. They lacked the resources to defend Ganymede directly; this was, after all, the Jupiter sphere. Certainly they did not desire to initiate System War Three over Ganymede; the planet was a loss to them even under favourable circumstances and hardly worth the horrendous cost of full war. Yet Saturn pride could not let us take over without opposition.

Kharzhinov temporized: he issued an ultimatum. 'With-draw your troops from Ganymede by 1200 hours, January 28, 2650, or the Union of Saturnian Republics will be forced to consider your action an act of war.'

I laughed when Shelia read me the translation. 'Send this reply,' I told her. 'Saturn, keep your nose clear of Jupiter business, lest it get cut off. Signed, the Tyrant of Space.'

'You're sure Karzhinov can be bluffed?' Spirit inquired.

'Who's bluffing?'

She smiled, but I could see that she was worried. She understood me well, but she got nervous when I got like this.

Actually I was pretty sure about Karzhinov. He was typical of the Saturn hierarchy: an unscrupulous, atheistic bureaucrat who had risen to the apex by conspiring against his enemies, betraying his friends, and being lucky. Like most bullies, he was essentially a coward. I had never met him personally, but I had read him through his public pronouncements and interviews and updated my information during the current exchange. I knew I could bluff him out.

The danger was that when he stepped down or was replaced, there would be a new and tougher Saturn leader who lacked the judgement to back off. I could handle a man I had studied; there might not be the time to study the next.

But if the right man seized the occasion –

The Navy spread out and conquered new territory on Ganymede with surprising alacrity. Horror stories of death and destruction were broadcast by the hour, sometimes by the minute, from both sides, and the toll in lives and property mounted. Censorship was clamped down by both sides, but selected tales leaked out. It was, by all appearances, an awful situation. Our body count differed from theirs by the usual ratio: we claimed two and a half times as many casualties inflicted as they acknowledged. The Navy threw in more men as other ships arrived, and the toll of dead *gringos* mounted steadily towards the predicted total.

The Saturn ships manoeuvred, orienting on all of our major targets. Their subs played tag with ours – those that either party could identify. We knew that the greatest threat was from the unlocated Saturn subs, which would torpedo our defensive ships from hiding. Ours would take out their ships similarly, but that would be too late to save our cities from the initial bombardment by those ships. Our real response would not be defensive but offensive: as our subs took out the major Saturn cities. *That* was the true balance of terror: the civilian populations of each planet were hostage to the Navy of the other. Karzhinov was not secure from that, and neither was I; we would both be dead men once the war began.

But Karzhinov was a coward and I was not.

The hours passed. The Saturn deadline drew nigh. I knew Karzhinov would back down, but others did not know that, nor could I tell them. The Gany invasion was fake, a construct of tacit collaboration between the premier and me, but the confrontation with Saturn was not. I had to trust that the Saturn structure had the same discipline as ours, so that no nervous admiral pushed his button and triggered the ultimate holocaust. I was conscious of the potential for error and of the enormous consequence thereof.

I told the others to sleep – Coral, Ebony, Spirit, and Shelia – but they would not or could not. Certainly I would not. Thus as the Saturnian deadline approached, we had been awake for more than thirty hours. I don't think any of us felt it or were aware of our natural functions. We ate and drank and eliminated on a different level of awareness, as though our bodies were disconnected from our heads.

In retrospect I realize that I drifted into one of my visions. I was not then aware of its coming, and I still am not certain to what extent the others were aware of it or participated in it. Helse did not come to me this time; that was one reason I did not realize. Perhaps the others were afraid to bring me out of it, lest in my confusion or reaction I do something rash – such as giving the Order – so I played along. I never cared to inquire afterwards, and they never cared to volunteer. Thus we went through a special experience together, whose complete nature remains opaque.

In my private awareness it seemed that the barriers of space and time dissolved, and I faced Karzhinov via a screen that had no delay of transmission. 'Why do you do this, Tyrant of Space?' he demanded, beads of cold sweat showing on his jowls. 'Why do you force us into this folly of war?'

'You were the one who started it,' I replied. 'You sought to corrupt the pact we fashioned years ago, when Tanamo returned to Ganymede.'

'A lie!' he cried. 'You only sought a pretext to invade Ganymede!'

He had been speaking in Russian, I in English, neither being surprised that we understood each other. Now I addressed him directly in Russian. 'You running dog! You tried to sneak that ship by me, and now you deny it! You make me so angry!' And my finger hovered above the big red button that would ignite the holocaust.

'Don't touch that!' he cried. Then, in a verbal double take: 'You speak my language!'

'That is why you cannot deceive me, you Bolshevik bureaucrat!'

He brought out his own red button, mounted on a little box. His face turned red with embarrassment. 'You knew! You understood my language! You have made a fool of me! I will show you! I will have revenge!' And his fat finger moved to the button.

But I read him better than he read me. I knew he was bluffing. He feared death too much to launch the holocaust. 'Go ahead, imperialist Communist!' I baited him. 'Push the button! Strike it with your shoe! Show the System what you are made of!'

Now, challenged to the point, he realized that he was lost. Slowly he crumbled. He sagged to the floor.

The box with the button fell from his hand and bounced

on the floor. It flipped over and came down on its button. There was a crackle as the connection was made.

'Uh-oh,' I murmured in English.

Responding to that signal, the Saturn fleet opened fire on Jupiter. Our fleet responded, firing on Saturn.

There was a pause. Then the CT missiles, impossible to intercept at short range, scored. Almost simultaneously Jupiter and Saturn flared, their city-bubbles exploding. The shock of the explosions rocked the atmospheres and caused the remaining cities to crack and implode, so that no significant life remained at the planetary level. Meanwhile, other missiles scored on the various moons, taking them out also.

Jupiter and Saturn were sparkling with the pin-point destructions of their cities. But the other planets were not immune. The moment the hostilities commenced, commands went out to the ships of the Belligerents, and missiles were fired at their allies. Uranus erupted, and Mars, Venus, Mercury, and the more extreme planets, and the major settlements of the Belt. Humanity was destroying itself.

I was dead, too, of course, and all who were with me. Together we had brought to a halt man's ascension towards space. Whatever our species might have been or become was ended. Was it worth it?

'Hope, for the love of God!'

The words transfixed me. That was Megan!

I emerged from my vision to discover myself standing before the main screen. Megan's image was on it. She had spoken, and not from the dead. The Saturn deadline was upon us, the moment of decision.

I glanced around me. My sister Spirit stood at my side, her face drawn. Coral and Ebony stood near the door, frozen: of two different races and types but almost alike

116

in this moment. Shelia was as always in her wheelchair, her right hand resting by the computerized communications controls, her eyes fixed on me. None of them would gainsay me; my word was law, here, though it could bring destruction on us all.

But Megan was, and had always been, her own woman. I had kept company with her for almost twenty years, and I would always love her, and she reciprocated. It was in part love that separated us, for she had been unable to join me in the Tyrancy but unwilling to deny me my destiny. Now she was addressing me directly, and it shook me more deeply than the very vision of the end of humanity. Megan was not only the woman I loved; she was a truly great and good person whose instincts were almost unfailingly correct. For her I would give up anything – if she let me.

I gazed at her, and I could not answer her. I knew that she did not know what I knew: that the ongoing conquest of Ganymede was a sham, the tolls of the dead a carefully nurtured fiction crafted by both sides. That the real target was not Ganymede or Saturn but the present leadership of Saturn. This was our best and perhaps only chance to achieve the breakthrough that would enable future changes of enormous significance. My present course could accomplish more of what Megan desired for mankind than any other course could. All she saw at the moment was the concurrent risk. I could not blame her for that, for I had fostered the illusion of madness to which she was responding. Yet I could not at this point disillusion her, for that would damage or destroy the whole of my thrust.

For the sake of all that Megan and I both believed in, I had to deceive her in this. I felt the terrible dread of alienation I was making, for there was no one I wished to hurt less than this woman. But it was necessary.

117

I turned away from her. I signalled Shelia and saw her fingers move, cutting off the connection. It was done.

'I remember when you raped Rue,' Spirit murmured.

That was it, exactly. Rape was an abomination, but I had been forced by circumstance to do it, and my sister had witnessed it. What I had done to Megan was more subtle and more cruel but as necessary. I almost would have preferred the denouement of the vision.

Now we waited. The Saturn deadline was past, and there had been no change in my policy. The action on Ganymede continued. We had secured Tanamo but were broadening our base in an evident campaign of complete conquest. The casualties, as represented by both sides, were high, but the outcome was inevitable: Ganymede would be restored as a satellite of Jupiter, if Saturn did not act. And Saturn could not act – short of System War Three.

The four hours required for the news of my refusal to honour the Saturn deadline passed. Now was the second seige of tension: awaiting the reaction of Saturn. If I had miscalculated, if I had misjudged Karzhinov, then all was over. I was sure I had not done so, yet the stakes were so high that I remained quite tense, anyway.

The time for the response came – and nothing happened. We did not relax; it could mean that there was simply a bureaucratic delay in implementation of the attack command. Yet the longer the delay, the better.

The hours passed without reaction. Saturn neither attacked nor retreated. Was Karzhinov trying to wear me down? I simply waited. All of us were tired, but none of us could sleep.

It seemed that not many others were sleeping, either. Shelia glanced at me inquiringly, having something of

118

interest coming in, and I nodded, and it came on: Thorley, commenting.

'It seems that Jupiter and Saturn are engaged in a contest to see who will be the first to blink. Saturn set a deadline; the Tyrant ignored it; now it is Saturn's move. This would be an intriguing study, if the fate of mankind did not hang upon the outcome.'

'He always was good with a summation,' I said.

'Which demonstrates in more direct fashion than I would have preferred the folly of bypassing our established and time-honoured conventions,' Thorley continued. 'Had the democratic process been honoured, we should not now have a madman inviting destruction for us all. Let this be a lesson, should we survive it.'

'Yes indeed,' Spirit agreed, smiling wanly.

We waited, and the System waited with us. The planet of Jupiter, and probably Saturn also, had paused with bated heartbeat, waiting for the axe to fall – or turn aside.

'Sir.'

I jumped at Shelia's word; I had not been aware I was dozing. 'Um.'

'Admiral Khukov.'

'On.'

Khukov's familiar face appeared. 'Will you meet with me, Tyrant Hubris?' he inquired formally in English.

I knew by his bearing that victory was at hand. Khukov had a talent similar to mine, the ability to read people, and he and I could read each other. That was why we trusted each other, though our motives and loyalties were in many respects quite opposed. 'I will, Admiral.'

'I will send a boat for you and your sister.'

'Agreed.'

The screen went blank. 'Sleep,' I said. 'The crisis has passed.'

'Should we make an announcement, sir?' Shelia asked.

I walked over, leaned down, and kissed her on the forehead. 'That a meeting has been arranged. No more. Then rest until the ship comes.'

She activated her console. 'For release from the office of the Tyrant,' she said. 'A meeting has been arranged between Admiral Khukov of the Saturn fleet and the Tyrant.' She touched a button. 'JupNav, arrange escort for the Saturn ship to the White Bubble.' Then another button. 'No further calls to the Tyrant's office until the Saturn ship arrives.' Then she let her head fall back against the headrest and closed her eyes.

Spirit and Ebony were already gone. Coral took my arm and brought me to my bed, where I flopped prone and slept in my clothes. She must have done likewise.

6
Amber

The next two years saw significant developments in both the planetary and personal schemes. I don't want to dwell unduly on matters that are already a matter of public record, so I will skim somewhat, touching mostly on what is *not* in that record. I want the story of the Tyrancy to be complete, and I have no certainty that those who survive me will care to make it so.

I think it was about ten hours later when Ebony woke us. 'The Saturn ship's pulling in,' she said, touching my shoulder.

'Go away,' I mumbled, turning my face away.

She had been with me for over fifteen years. She knew what to do. 'Get up, Tyrant, or I'll haul you off that bed.'

When I did not respond, she took hold of my chest and turned me over, rolling me towards the edge of the bed. I grabbed her and hauled her down into me. 'You sleep too.'

Captive, she moved one hand to my rib cage and tickled me. 'No fair!' I cried, and wrestled her into place for a kiss.

Ebony was no beautiful woman, but she knew how to kiss. I realized immediately that I was getting into more than was feasible. She, like Shelia and Coral, was ready to take me as far as I cared to go. But I could not afford to go there at the moment; I had business coming up. So I broke without comment, but I squeezed her shoulder briefly by way of saying 'Another time.' I don't know

121

whether those who don't know me personally will understand about this. Helse introduced me to the joys of sex, and the Navy had introduced me to the advantage of doing it with any woman handy. I had been a long time away from both Helse and the Navy, but the old reflexes were returning readily enough. My staff understood me; not one of the girls had touched me while I remained with Megan, but they regarded it as open season now. I am sure that none of them ever spoke to any outside party of what passed privately between us; it was, as it were, all in the family. In this context it was Ebony's turn. When convenient.

I got up. Coral had got up during the scuffle, not interfering. The girls never interfered with each other; they meshed perfectly. It was comfortable being with them, and this helped me considerably in those early days of my separation from Megan.

In due course Spirit and I, both cleaned and changed, boarded the Saturn shuttle ship. I wore a voluminous, flowing cape that someone had deemed to be the fitting attire for a Tyrant making a call of State. It might seem strange to have the leader of Jupiter so blithely step into the power of Saturn, without even his bodyguard, but, of course, I knew Khukov personally, and the whole of the Solar System was hostage to our understanding. I was as safe as I could possibly be, here.

We relaxed and had an excellent meal served by a comely hostess who spoke English. The personnel were uniformly courteous, though they did not speak English. We were permitted free run of the ship.

'Where would you put it?' I asked Spirit in Spanish.

'Officer's dayroom,' she replied.

I nodded. We rose from our completed meal, went to the region reserved for the ship's captain, and knocked on the bulkhead. In a moment it slid open, and we entered.

Inside stood a pool table, and beyond the table stood Admiral Khukov, cue in hand. Without a word I took another cue, oriented on the table, and took the first shot. Spirit took a seat in a comfortable chair and watched. No one seemed surprised; this was the only way a truly private meeting could be arranged.

We played, and he beat me handily. 'Ah, Hope, you are out of shape!' he said in Spanish.

'Tyrants don't get much practice in the important things, Mikhail,' I agreed in Russian. We smiled at each other; obviously our conversation was private, for he would never have betrayed his knowledge of my language to others. My response showed that I understood, for no one aside from my sister knew that I spoke Russian. We had taught each other when we both served on Ganymede. It was one of the private understandings we had.

We continued playing. Now we spoke in English, so Spirit could understand. 'There will be the usual apparatus, every word and gesture recorded and analysed from the moment you board the flagship. Speak no secrets there.'

'My brain is not out of shape, Admiral!'

'When your wife cried "For the love of God!" and you turned away, Karzhinov knew that nothing would turn the madman aside. He faced the gulf of the holocaust, and his mind broke. We of Saturn know the nature of war on our soil; we fear it deeply. He will retire; his successor is not yet known.'

So my ploy had been successful! I prayed that never again would I have to hurt Megan that way. 'We, too, know the meaning of losses,' I said, remembering the destruction of my family in space.

'Yet our two planets proceed to ever greater military

123

effort,' he said. 'We can destroy Jupiter nine times over, and you can destroy Saturn ten times over, but there is no end to the race of new weapons.'

'Madness,' I agreed.

'Madness,' he echoed.

We gazed at each other, each perceiving the pain of the past and fear for the future in the other. No, we did not want this!

'Two scorpions in a bottle,' I said.

He smiled briefly. 'Would that they were male and female!'

'Yet perhaps . . .'

'Is it possible?'

There was a period of silence. Then I changed the subject. 'Shouldn't you be there, not here?' I asked.

'First I must negotiate a significant agreement, to show that I alone can defuse the crisis.'

'What do you need?'

'Your dance with the premier of Ganymede is very pretty.'

'This would be more difficult at light-hours range.'

'Yet the game can be played with caution. I cannot say precisely what moves I will need to make, but if the madman responds only to me . . .'

I nodded. 'And thereafter?'

'What would you have, Hope?'

I glanced at Spirit. 'Disarmament,' she said.

He grimaced. 'Of course. But there is the People's Republic of South Saturn.'

'Which has no significant navy,' I countered. 'It is the interplanetary threat that concerns us.'

'And us!' he agreed. 'We do not desire destruction, but we have had no trust.'

'Until now, Mikhail.'

124

'Until now,' he agreed. 'Yet it must be gradual. First a hold, then failure to replace ageing craft.'

'Agreed.'

We reached across the table and shook hands.

'I have a gift for you,' he said after a moment.

'We did not come prepared for the exchange of gifts,' I protested.

'You give me the power, that is enough. Accept my token with the assurance that there is no harm in it and certain hidden values.'

I shrugged. 'Of course.'

'And for the formal meeting: only a truce and token withdrawal. My present authority is more limited than yours, Tyrant.'

'Understood.'

We played several more games, and I began to give him more of a challenge. Then we had to leave, so that there would be no suspicion. As I had suspected, not even the crew of the shuttle knew that the admiral was aboard.

In due course the shuttle docked at the flagship, and we were ceremonially ushered aboard. We met under the cameras with Khukov, using translators, he addressing us in Russian, I responding in Spanish. We both talked tough but agreed to a temporary truce while Chairman Karzhinov considered his retirement. My words were reasonable, but there was a certain glimmer of madness in my expression, and Spirit cautioned me more than once, quietly as if fearing that I was about to be set off. The Saturn officers present affected unconcern, but they noticed. Yet I responded fairly well to Admiral Khukov's direct attention; it was evident that he had a superior touch. This was hardly surprising; it was that touch that had brought him to his present level of power – and would take him that one step beyond. Saturn was safer when his hand was at the helm, especially when dealing with the lunatic Tyrant.

Thus the official meeting was perfunctory but satisfactory. It was obvious that the admiral and the Tyrant distrusted each other but were ready to deal. What would count would be the success of those dealings.

Khukov formally introduced me to his aide, another admiral, who would be in charge of the Saturn Jupiter-sphere fleet during Khukov's absence. 'Speak to him as you would to me,' he said, flashing a caution signal by his body language that only he and I could read. 'He converses in both our languages, Russian and English, and he is empowered to act without delay.'

So the other admiral could push the button if attacked but did not speak Spanish. He was surely competent, for Khukov knew his personnel as I knew mine. Indeed, as I shook his hand, I felt his power as a person. This was one good, tough, honest man who would not act carelessly.

As we prepared to depart the flagship Khukov held me one more moment. 'Tyrant, allow me to present you with a token of my esteem for you,' he said in English.

A young girl, really a child of ten or eleven, approached. She held her left hand up. On the middle finger was a platinum ring, and mounted on the ring was a large amber gem. In fact, it was not merely the colour of amber; it was amber itself.

I took the child's hand and peered at the amber. It was clear and finely formed, and deep inside it was embedded an insect – a termite. I smiled, taking this as a kind of little joke, for a termite is not a pretty bug. But I was aware of something else: the one whose hand I held was no ordinary child. There was a curious vacuity about her, a lack of human emotion and expression. Had she been lobotomized? No, to my perception her reflexes were normal, merely uninvoked. Mind-wash? Possibly.

'This is an interesting gift,' I said, glancing up at Khukov. 'But it becomes the girl, and I would hesitate to take it from her.'

He smiled. 'No need, Tyrant.'

Spirit caught on. 'The girl is the gift,' she murmured.

'The girl!' I said startled.

'As you say, it would not be kind to take her treasure from her,' Khukov said. 'I know you treat children well, Tyrant, and she is of your culture. You will find her interesting.'

'But – '

'Thank you, Admiral Khukov,' Spirit said firmly. 'We shall see that she is properly treated. What is her name?'

'Amber,' he replied, and at that, the girl's eyes widened and her head lifted in recognition.

'Come with us, Amber,' Spirit said gently. The girl did not change expression, but she stepped towards Spirit. Evidently she understood.

So we returned to the shuttle and to Jupiter, bringing Amber with us. And strange was the avenue that acquiescence opened for me.

The first thing we noted was that Amber was mute. She understood what we said and responded to it, but she did not speak. We had our medical staff examine her and ascertained that she had no congenital or other inhibition; she *could* speak but simply did not.

The next thing we learned was that she was older than she seemed. Without her birth record we could not be sure, but physically she was about thirteen, not eleven. She seemed younger because she had not yet developed. This did not seem to be any artificial retardation, just natural variation. There had been a time, historically, when few girls developed before that age, but modern nutrition and care had reduced the age. Hopie had assumed the physical attributes of maturity by the age of

127

twelve, for example. The intellectual and social attributes took longer to complete, but, of course, this could be a lifelong process, anyway. Amber was healthy, just a little slow. It was difficult to verify her intelligence nonverbally because she did not volunteer things. If, for example, a person told her to assemble the pieces of a simple plastic puzzle, she would do so but without any particular initiative. It was evident that she could do it faster, but she lacked the drive. Our conclusion was that she fell within the low-normal range. Certainly she was no genius.

Why had Khukov given her to me? I was sure he had not done so frivolously. He had to have had excellent reason. Members of my staff worried that it could be some kind of trap, that she carried poison or a weapon, but I did not accept that. First, there was no evidence of anything like that about her person; our personnel were sharp enough to catch anything potentially dangerous. Second, Khukov would not have done that. He didn't operate that way, and he had no motive. His own success depended on my cooperation, and he wanted me to remain in power. So whatever there was about Amber – and there definitely was something – it was no threat to me. He had said I would find her interesting; in that he was correct, merely because of the mystery of her. But there was more than mystery. He had had compelling reason to put her in my hands.

We set her up with Hopie, who had a room with Robertico. Hopie was entitled to a room of her own, but she was generous in this respect; she shared. Robertico was devoted to her and slept quietly when she was near. Amber, though only two years younger than Hopie – possibly only one year younger – was so obviously better off with company that it seemed best to move her in. The two of them became like sisters, and Robertico a baby brother.

Hopie found the riddle of Amber as intriguing as Spirit and I did. She talked with the girl, or rather to her, for Amber never responded in words. Hopie soon became a kind of translator for Amber, ascertaining her preferences and informing us of them. Amber liked Hispanic food and didn't care for sonic showers; she preferred to wash up with a damp cloth. She always wore the amber ring; the only time she became truly distressed was when the medics tried to remove it for examination. They had finally compromised by examining it on her hand, the radiation showing up her finger bones as well as the interior of the ring, and she had no objection. Hopie wanted to teach her to read, for she seemed not to know how, but Amber just stared blankly at the printed words. She was unable to relate to anything more technical than pictures.

Meanwhile, the crisis of Saturn abated. In accordance with the truce we pulled back our ships, which were oriented on Saturn, and they pulled back theirs, which were oriented on Jupiter. The fighting on Ganymede halted in place. Admiral Khukov returned to Saturn and worked his magic there, and in a fortnight he was formally announced as the new Chairman of the Council of Ministers, along with assorted other titles appropriate to the power base. Our Navy cooperated by showing evident respect for his prowess as a leader, retreating somewhat when he challenged and failing to do so when others did. Gradually the citizens of both planets resumed their breathing.

The formal arrangements were to spread out over some months, but the informal ones proceeded immediately. We dismantled our mock invasion of Ganymede, quietly returning our troops to their bases. The official death toll remained at just about twenty thousand *gringos*, but no list was published, 'for reasons of security'. The families of the men were satisfied to know that their particular loved ones were not on the list and did not inquire about the others. That was just as well, for, of course, there were no dead on either side.

Saturn abandoned its effort to corrupt Tanamo Base, and the premier of Ganymede retained his power. Trade, originally limited to sugar, gradually broadened; it again became possible and even acceptable to smoke Gany cigars. Of course, that market was small; the ancient habit of inhaling from burning tubes of tobacco had been banished for health reasons centuries before, and with the addictive compulsion gone, few bothered to draw on cigars merely for the taste. But symbolically it was important to Gany, and it was true that they had always made the best taste-only cigars.

The ongoing business of government socked back in the moment the crisis abated. First to reach me was Senator Stonebridge. He came armed with statistics and graphs, a bewildering array, but the essence was this: 'Tyrant, the budget cannot possibly be balanced without substantial reduction in spending,' he informed me forcefully.

'What does the government of Jupiter spend most on?' I inquired with assumed naïveté.

'Well, that depends on your orientation. The social services – '

'I'll have to consult with my sister Faith before I approve any reduction there.'

'Sir, your sister has grandiose aspirations for the eradication of poverty at the government's expense!'

'So I gather. What other categories?'

'The military. But, of course, no chances can be taken with planetary defence – '

'Suppose we were to put a freeze on all military spending?'

'You mean to hold the level at the current – '

'No. To stop spending for arms entirely.'

He tried to laugh, but it didn't work. 'Sir, in the face of the present System situation – '

'How much would it assist in the balancing of the budget?'

'But it is pointless to – under no circumstances could – '

'I have never seen you at a loss for figures before, Senator.'

He coughed. 'Assuming that other income and outlays remain constant, such a step would, on paper, achieve the objective. But – '

'Assume that Saturn is no further threat to Jupiter,' I said. 'What would interfere with a zero military budget?'

He came to grips with this problem. 'Sir, there are existing contractual commitments that – '

'What commitments?'

'Orders for new weapons systems, research and development costs, maintenance – '

'Who made those commitments?'

'The government, of course! It – '

'The *former* government,' I said firmly. 'Today there is the Tyrancy. I have made no commitments for new weapons.'

'But, sir, you cannot renege on it. It would devastate the credibility of – '

'I expect to make my own credibility. What would be the immediate consequence of a cancellation of all military commitments?'

He got canny. 'Well, sir, a substantial portion relates to pensions and care for those disabled in action.'

Ouch! I couldn't cut off payments to the wounded and retired! 'Keep that portion,' I said.

'And if the contracts with private enterprise are cancelled, quite a substantial portion of Jupiter industry

131

would be bankrupted. Those companies have made heavy investments – '

And the last thing I wanted was wholesale bankruptcy in our major industries. That would throw millions of people out of work and make twice the problem for Faith, as well as being a poor reflection on the Tyrant's ability to manage the economy. 'Point made,' I said. 'It is not feasible at this moment to balance the budget by cutting off all military expense. But I do plan to cancel all new military expense, and that should result in a substantial and increasing savings over the years.'

'But Saturn – '

'Let Admiral Khukov worry about his own planet. Meanwhile I will see what I can do to cut expenses elsewhere. My job is not done until I balance that budget.'

He shook his head. 'Even with the best of intentions and the most favourable developments, sir, it remains a Herculean task.'

'Name another major expense.'

'Well, there is the interest on the planetary debt, which itself is now contributing significantly to the deficit. If present trends continue – '

'Suppose we simply abolish the planetary debt?'

'Sir, you can't be serious!'

'Insane, perhaps, but serious. If thy debt offends thee, why not cut it off?'

'Because that debt is owed, ultimately, to our own citizens! The life savings of retirees are invested in planetary bonds – '

And to wipe out those savings would make instant paupers of a major class of citizens and have Faith on my neck immediately. Also, there was the matter of keeping faith – no pun; Jupiter could not become known as a defaulter. So scratch one simplistic solution. 'What are your suggestions?'

'Well, first there should be currency and tax reform. I believe that to abate inflation it would be wise to consider what is termed the gold standard.'

'Which is?'

'To back all Jupiter currency with metal of value. Of course, that does not mean literal gold; there is not enough of that, and too much of it is in the possession of marginal or even hostile powers. But a so-called basket of metals, including especially iron – '

'But we need iron for fuel!' I protested.

'That, sir, is why its value is assured. Any currency pegged to iron will endure. It would become difficult or impossible to inflate the currency without backing, if all of it could be redeemed for specified metals of verified value. Historically the most stable periods have been when – '

'The gold standard,' I agreed. 'Set about it, Senator.'

He was gratified; he was a hard money man, as the truest conservatives tended to be. 'Now, about tax reform – '

'The flat tax,' I said.

'Well, that would be too extreme. I was thinking of a modified – '

'Why?'

'The flat tax? Sir, the first consequence would be to reduce revenues at a time when – '

'But the level can be set anywhere, can't it? One rate for all, no exceptions, exclusions, or loopholes. Set at the point that would bring in the same revenue as now.'

He took a breath. 'Sir, I am not at all certain you would endorse some of the complications. For example, the people at the lowest end of the earnings spectrum would pay a proportionally greater portion of their income than they do today, while those at the top would save substantially. Since you tend to sympathize with the lower range – '

'What about a minimum wage that prevents them from suffering? So they actually receive the same amount, after tax, as now?'

'That would be effective in that instance, sir. But it would drastically increase the labour cost of industry, which would in effect be paying the added burden. Prices would have to rise, sometimes considerably.'

I sighed. 'There are no easy solutions, are there, Senator?'

'No easy solutions, sir,' he agreed, smiling. I might be the Tyrant, but he was establishing his authority in his bailiwick. We would be balancing the budget his way. Actually, much of my experience as Tyrant was the process of discovering my formidable limitations; I could not simply say 'Do this! Do that!' and have things happen magically. Every action had a consequence, and these consequences hemmed me in, so that my absolute power was far more apparent than real.

I went to Nyork to address an audience personally, as I am, of course, a politician and can't make as much of an impact when distanced from those I talk to. I knew that there was substantial concern about the nature of the newly installed Tyrancy and the recent Saturn crisis, and I simply wanted to reassure them with my human presence. Coral opposed it as a safety hazard, and so did the Secret Service guards, but I had always been a man of the people and needed this contact. After all, every member of that audience would be checked for weapons, and no known troublemakers would be admitted. I should be safe enough.

I was mistaken. From one of the floodlights a laser beam speared down. It scorched into the lectern where I was supposed to be standing. It had evidently been set long in advance and timed for the moment I took the floor. But I had been delayed a few seconds by a trifle – a child had begged for the touch of my hand, and like the vain creature I was, I had obliged – so I had approached the lectern late. The very precision of the trap's timing defeated it. Had it functioned late, it would have caught me. As it was, I felt the heat as the lectern scintillated in the beam and began to melt.

Then Coral's own laser caught the floodlight. It exploded, and the laser stopped.

I proceeded to my address as though nothing had happened, but I was shaken. Not so much by the attempt or its near success; I had faced death many times before and was somewhat fatalistic about it. But the seeming ease with which the assassin had bypassed all the efforts of my safety squad – that showed me how vulnerable I was. It was indeed dangerous for me to appear in public, even a friendly public.

My talk was a rousing success. Perhaps Spirit had arranged to pack the hall with my supporters; I didn't think to ask. But certainly they were with me and were reassured by my explanation of the Saturn crisis, now over, and my plans to balance the budget and improve the lot of every citizen of Jupiter.

But I realized that even if this audience were representative of the majority of citizens, I could not often risk such appearances. The majority would not assassinate me: the deadly minority would. This was the point at which it really came home to me that my old open ways were over; I would have to accept the increasing isolation that my bodyguards urged on me. They could not protect me from every devious threat that some fanatic with endless time and cunning devised. That floodlight, as it turned out, had been in place for a year; its original bulb had at some point been replaced by one containing the

135

laser mechanism and timer. In the future the experts would check all bulbs, but there would be some other mechanism. I simply was not safe in public.

I had condemned President Tocsin, in part, because of his isolation from the public. I still condemned him, but now I had a trace more understanding. Isolation was not necessarily self-chosen.

Yet I hated to give up my public contact. My strength was in relating to people, and I felt deprived when I could not exercise it. I understood the pitfall of allowing myself to be surrounded by those I knew well; that was the true isolation. I had to be freshened by my constant input from the real planet.

I mentioned this to Spirit. 'I am being channelled into the trap of inadequate feedback from the people,' I said. 'Yet, if I don't isolate myself, sooner or later an assassin will catch me. What can I do?'

'I face the same problem myself,' she said. 'I am now too public a figure to employ my male disguise. There have been more attempts on our lives than I have bothered you with; we are all hostages to our position.'

So she – and my staff – had been shielding me from this ugly reality. Spirit had always been my strength in adversity. 'There has to be an answer,' I said.

She quirked a smile. 'Go to Q.'

To Q. She meant QYV, the secret organization that had first bedevilled, then assisted me. To Reba, the woman who was my sole contact with it. She had accepted my manuscript, sent the information about the sub, and let me know that my next contact should be personal.

I sighed. Like most women, Reba was smitten with me. Now that my marriage had fractured, they considered it to be open season on me. Most women did not have access to me, but Reba was one I needed. It was time to make that call.

'We shall hold the fort for a couple of hours,' Spirit said, smiling knowingly.

'Here is the address, sir,' Shelia said, handing me a slip of paper. The same smile tugged at her lips.

'I'd rather be with you,' I murmured to her. The smile disappeared, replaced by a flush. Suddenly I felt guilty; that was not the kind of teasing to do.

Spirit summoned a Secret Service man who was about my size and complexion. 'Take his suit,' she told me. 'Our makeup man will render you into his likeness. That will do for this.'

The makeup man was good. He applied firming paste to my cheeks and colour to my brows and did this and that to the rest of me, and when I stood beside the SS man before the mirror, we looked like twins. I practised walking the way he did, and left, alone, to seek the address on the paper. Neither Coral nor the SS complement were happy about my exposure, but they had to allow it; I was, after all, the Tyrant.

I left the White Bubble in the SS shuttle. Theoretically I was either going off duty or was on some errand for the Tyrant, so no one paid attention. I debarked at a private access in New Wash Bubble and went my way. Of course, I was being tracked by other Secret Service men, so that I could be rescued if anything threatened, but I *seemed* to be alone. It was a good feeling; the tension of my office drained out of me, and I felt like an ordinary working man. It was wonderful.

I took a taxi to the address, for off-duty Secret Service men did not rate limo service. The cabbie zoomed expertly along the vehicle route, seeming at every moment to be about to collide with a wall or some other vehicle. I had almost forgotten the experience! Probably this was one of the lesser things that I was only now recalling, that had been deleted from my memory by my recent mem-wash. I loved it. Cabbies were like Navy drone pilots, in their fashion, careening around the system with hazardous expertise. I tipped him well, but not so well that he would remember me long, and approached the indicated door. It slid open at my approach, revealing a gloomy interior served by a moving belt. I stepped on, and the panel slid closed behind me.

The light went out, putting me in total darkness. The belt carried me into a chamber – I could tell by the sound and the feel of the air that it was of fair size – and deposited me in the centre. Then I was seized by a field I remembered from thirty-five years before: pacifier. It did not hurt me, but it slowed me and robbed me of volition.

Hands came, catching my suit, drawing me forward. I moved as urged, as I had to when under pacifier influence. I wasn't pleased to be subjected to this, as I had come voluntarily to do this woman's limited bidding, but could not protest. It reminded me of the time when I was fifteen and pirates had used a pacifier on our refugee group and slain my father while I watched helplessly. But this was not that, I reminded myself. I knew by the touch that this was Reba, the woman I had come to see. She brought me to the end of a couch or bed and stopped me there. Still I could not see; the darkness was impenetrable.

Then she worked on my clothing. I did not resist. She drew off my jacket and shirt, and I moved my arms to assist, following the implied directives. She took down my trousers, and I lifted one foot and then the other, cooperating. In due course she had me naked, still standing. What did she have in mind? Evidently not ordinary sex.

Now her hands slid lightly across the skin of my body, my arms and chest and back. There are ways and *ways* to touch; this was expertly caressing. The fingers were slippery smooth, perhaps gloved in plastic, and slightly cool.

They moved on down my torso, brushing my belly and spine, down to cup my buttocks, down the backs of my legs to my feet, then up inside. They climbed to my private region and explored it, becoming ticklish. My body reacted, melding from flaccid to rigid, but I remained otherwise unmoving.

The hands returned to my upper structure, and their force increased. Now the fingers kneaded my flesh, squeezing the muscle of the arms, moving up to massage my shoulders. At this, too, they were expert; it felt very good. They worked over my neck, causing unsuspected tensions to ease. They travelled down my backbone, bearing relief of tightness. They kneaded my buttocks and my thigh muscles and my calves. They returned to work on my member, causing it, ironically to harden further rather than soften.

Then the hands went to my shoulders, turned me around, and pushed abruptly. I fell backward, my legs catching on the edge of the bed, so that I landed bouncingly on my back, my feet remaining on the floor.

She took hold of one foot, moving it outward. Then the other, out, so that my knees were widely spread. Then the hands hauled on both legs, so that I had to slide down until my posterior almost overhung the edge. What *did* she have in mind? So far she had not spoken, and I had been able to see nothing; touch was the only communication.

Now she got on me, her naked body straddling mine, facing towards my spread knees. Her thighs dropped down outside mine, her feet remaining on the floor, so that she was able to stand in her fashion. She took my member and guided it, slowly settling down on it, until all her weight was on me and the connection was complete. Still I did not move, obeying her unstated directive. She required my body to play with in her fashion; she had it.

Those hands reached down, caressed that portion of my anatomy that remained exposed, then moved on. One finger slid to the aperture below and nudged and pushed, and, lubricated by something, entered. I felt very much as if I were a woman, being entered by a man, especially considering the intimate contact above that site. That member of hers drove to its full depth, then stroked an interior organ of mine and put pressure against it.

I had been accepting what was happening as if I were indifferent, also in the manner of a woman. I cannot say that I found the situation comfortable emotionally. But now, as that finger squeezed that organ, my system became urgent. I started to thrust, as well as I could in that awkward position.

She moved with me, rocking back and forth, her own anatomy clenching. That finger thrust harder, becoming uncomfortable, almost painful, compressing what it found. I tensed urgently, then fountained, that finger seeming to guide and enhance each spasm. I had thought I had experienced the ultimate intensity with Coral's tree; this was far beyond that, though not actually as pleasurable overall.

It subsided at last. Her finger came out, and her torso lifted, freeing me. In a moment a cloth washed off my anatomy. Then the hands tugged on me again, causing me to sit up, then stand, and they dressed me. When that process was complete, the hands pushed me forward. I stepped on to the moving belt, which now moved in the opposite direction, and was carried to the door panel. It opened, and I stepped out, blinking in the light, abruptly free of the pacifier field.

I had never even spoken to her, yet somehow I knew that she would take care of my need. She had, in a very direct manner, had her will of me; now she would serve my interest effectively.

She had also given me a considerable experience, and food for thought. I was somewhat sore in the crotch, as a woman might be, after a too-violent effort by a man. But I had been forced to respond, and the discomfort had become part of the pleasure. I had never had any comprehension of sadomasochism or of reverse roles, but now I had an inkling. In absolute darkness Reba had shown me much.

Back at the White Bubble, the girls treated me in a manner reminiscent of my female associates in the Navy: knowing, curious, superior, competitive. Perhaps they had reason. 'Did she teach you anything, Tyrant?' Coral inquired.

'Um,' I mumbled, preferring to avoid the subject.

'Are you limping, sir?' Shelia asked.

I straightened up. 'Num.'

'I hear those older women can have a lot of experience,' Ebony put in.

'Um.'

'Did she answer your question?' Spirit asked.

I spread my hands. 'She never spoke!' I said, realizing that I had been so bemused by Reba's touch that my mission had been neglected.

They all laughed. Then Shelia tapped her armrest. 'She sent a message, sir: there will be an alternate identity created for you.'

So QYV was addressing my problem! Reba simply had had to make her impression on me, her way. That she had certainly done. I might be the Tyrant, but she had reminded me how it felt to be subject to the will of

141

another person. To be helpless while one's most private parts were manipulated, leaving no physical refuge. The way most of the citizens of North Jupiter were with relation to the Tyrant. A lesson in humility – and the Golden Rule. That was worth remembering.

My daughter Hopie had been wrestling diligently with the problem of education. I could see the impact of Thorley in her attitude now.

'Daddy, the problem starts with the low respect teachers have,' she said earnestly. 'Very few educated people want to go into that profession; those who can get more challenging or better paying positions elsewhere do so, leaving the bottom quarter of those qualified to go into teaching as their last alternative. No wonder the curricula they fashion lack relevance!'

'No wonder,' I agreed, suspecting what was coming.

'First we have to elevate the profession, to attract the top graduates,' she continued. 'Then we have to give them free rein to revamp the system, stressing excellence. It will take time, but – '

'How do we attract top graduates?' I asked warily.

'Why, we upgrade their pay scales to be competitive with those of industry,' she said.

That's what I had feared. 'More money.' I groaned.

'Well, you don't get something for nothing, Daddy.'

'And where do we get the extra money?'

She shrugged. 'That's someone else's department.'

I sighed. My balanced budget retreated as I approached it, assuming the attributes of a mirage. 'I'll try to raise more money,' I said. 'Meanwhile, see if you can come up with some temporary expedient to improve education using the present personnel.'

She surprised me. 'Thorley said you'd say that. I'm working on it.' And she hurried away, fresh with the vigour of her generation.

I took a break of sorts, going to see Robertico and Amber. The two got along adequately, for neither spoke. Amber was spelling Hopie as baby-sitter, for that did not require words. At the moment they had an entertainment holo on: cowboys and Indians of the ancient Earth that never was. Amber was viewing it with curiosity rather than interest, while Robertico crawled around, trying to grab the three dimensional images.

Hopie had done a good job with both of them, I realized. I had assigned her these tasks in addition to her education post, and these matters had largely vacated my awareness. Hopie had taken hold on all fronts, and that pleased me greatly. I resolved to tell her so, the next time I encountered her. But, of course, her proficiency was to be expected, considering her parentage and upbringing. There were aspects of her appearance and intellect that stamped HUBRIS clearly on her, as well as others that established her independence.

'Come here, Tico,' I said, picking up the boy. He was now in watertight pants, no problem to handle. 'Soon you will be learning to walk – and to talk. You may be a little slow, because of the time you spent in the nursery without proper attention or stimulation, but now you have plenty. What do you say to that?'

Robertico smiled, then scrambled back towards the holo, his fascination unabated. I let him go, smiling.

I turned to the girl, who had watched the interchange without expression. 'And you, Amber – what is your background? I want you to be happy, too, and to learn to be a complete person. Why don't you talk?'

She only shook her head, evidently understanding me but unable to respond verbally.

The mystery of her intrigued me, as it had before. Khukov had given her to me and surely not for any idle reason. Now, still fresh from my experience with Reba, I was highly attuned to the problem of helplessness. This girl should talk and smile and have initiative, instead of being like a person caught by a pacifier field. Teaching her did not work, but that suggested only that she was balked from responding.

My eye fixed on the orange gem mounted on her ring: amber, her namesake, surely somehow linked to her secret. I took her hand, feeling again that strangeness in her, and stared into the ring. There was the embedded termite.

What was a termite? An ugly insect by human definition, and a destructive one. On occasion some got loose in a bubble and methodically devoured whatever organic fibre they could find, silently tunnelling through and through until the structure collapsed. They had to be exterminated. In the old days on Earth they had been a constant threat to buildings. Yet termites were actually a kind of civilization, like the ants and bees, being organized into an efficient society. They were in a sense a parallel to the human species, adapting nature to their need, uncaring about the resulting erosion of prior structures. Why should Amber carry a termite? What did that symbolize?

Then another aspect of the termite existence occurred to me.

They were supposed to have a number of phases, or stages of development. They didn't just hatch from grub to adult; they moved through several aspects, some land-bound, some winged. I really did not know much about it and doubted that I needed to; all that was needed was to grasp the key.

Did Amber have stages? If so, what would they be? How would they occur?

I pondered. The girl seemed to have the potential to speak but did not. That could be like a silent phase.

Perhaps the correct signal could switch her to a talking phase. But what would that signal be?

'Amber,' I said, and her gaze came up to meet mine. Her eyes were pretty, in that large, childlike way, and seemed almost the colour of her name.

'Talk,' I commanded.

She merely stared at me, remaining mute.

I pondered again. If a verbal command did not do it, what kind would?

I looked down at the gem. That was the one thing she would not part with. There had to be a reason, and not any fascination with termites. Was the gem the key? How?

I became aware of a change in her as her gaze followed mine down to seek the gem. Her body relaxed, as if coming home after some difficult activity. Yes, surely this related!

'Amber,' I told her. 'Look at the amber gem. Stare into it. Lose yourself in it.'

She obeyed. Her body relaxed further. I still held her hand, and I felt her going into a light trance.

Hypnotic suggestion – triggered by the gem! Certainly that made sense. Now she would be receptive to my directive.

'Talk,' I repeated.

She remained as she was, unresponsive. That was not the correct directive.

I pondered yet again, sure that I was making progress but baffled by the necessary detail. If only I knew the correct command!

This girl was Hispanic; her aspect conformed, and Khukov had said she was of my culture. Many of us were bilingual; could she understand Spanish?

I tried. '¿Español?'

'¡Sí!' she agreed.

145

I jumped, startled by this unexpected success. 'You do speak Spanish!' I exclaimed in that language, thrilled.

Gravely she nodded.

'But you did not speak it before!'

She nodded again.

'But why not?'

'I – was in the wrong mode,' she explained.

'But you seemed to understand English.'

Once more she nodded. When I did not ask a direct question, she did not answer in words. She was still unusually passive. It remained my task to find the way to full communication.

'You are in the Spanish mode now,' I said. 'In this you can speak and understand, for you are Hispanic. You have learned English, but you do not speak it.'

She nodded affirmatively.

'*Why* don't you speak English?'

'It is a passive mode.'

Not much help. 'What can I do to help you speak English?'

She shrugged. She didn't know.

Apparently Khukov, or some other party, had in some way programmed her to speak only in her native language and barred her from the other she had learned. Why?

I tried another tack. 'Where are you from, Amber?'

'Halfcal,' she said.

I knew it was true; I should have recognized the accent immediately. She was from my home state! That offered a clue to part of Khukov's rationale; he had known I would appreciate helping another of my kind.

'Are you a refugee?'

Her gaze was blank. She didn't know.

'What is your family? Your home city?'

She didn't know. Perhaps she had been mem-washed, so that only her knowledge of her planet and nation of

146

origin remained, stripped of detail. Possibly that information would return, as the effect of the wash diminished with time. It was hard to be sure with children; sometimes they threw off the effect rapidly, and sometimes their loss of memory was permanent. I feared the latter was the case here.

'The gem,' I asked. 'The amber in the ring – that enables you to change modes? From English to Spanish and back again?'

She nodded.

'So you were locked into English, a language you understand but do not speak, until I told you to change to Spanish?' I wanted to be sure I had this aspect right; I did not want to lock her in any wrong mode.

Again she agreed.

'But you remember what happened when you were in English?' She nodded, and I continued: 'You remember about me and Hopie and Robertico and how you came to Jupiter?'

As usual, the nod. She could speak now but lacked the habit.

'Do you know why Admiral Khukov gave you to me?'

Negative nod.

'Would you prefer to return to Saturn?'

Now she showed some emotion, shaking her head vigorously no.

'You are satisfied to be here?'

She smiled, and in that expression I found a familiarity I could not define. Déjà vu – but I could not place its origin.

'Then we shall keep you here,' I reassured her. 'We want you to be happy. You may have a room of your own if you wish – '

No, she did not want that. She liked it as it was.

'We shall have to see to your education. Can you read in Spanish?'

She spread her hands; she did not know.

I went to the blackboard Hopie had set up for Robertico. The old mechanisms are often the best, for teaching. I wrote AMBER. 'Can you read that?'

She concentrated. Then she smiled again. 'It is my name!'

I soon verified that she could read but not well. 'We shall work with you, and soon you will read well enough, in Spanish,' I said. 'Hopie will teach you. She has an interest in education.'

'Hopie . . . is unhappy,' she volunteered.

That got my attention. 'My daughter, unhappy? Why?'

'She said, in English – I cannot translate well, but I remember – she talks to me when she is tired.'

'We all get tired,' I said carefully. 'It is natural to talk to a friend.'

'She said her parents separated, and it hurts her because she cannot put them back together. She worries that it is her fault.'

'It's not her fault!' I exclaimed, disturbed. I had not realized that my daughter felt this way, yet it was immediately obvious. She had said nothing to me, of course.

'She says you sleep with other women and they are good women, but – '

I shook my head. 'Men may be of an inferior species to women. I am guilty of all she says.' *How could I not have realized?*

'I do not understand.'

Of course, she didn't, just as my daughter didn't. Children are relatively innocent creatures, until corrupted by adults. But I could not leave it at that. 'What is it that confuses you, Amber?'

'What is wrong with sleeping?'

148

Oh. 'To sleep as you do, a period of unconsciousness – that is a good necessary thing. All people do it. But to sleep with a person of the opposite sex – that has a different connotation. It means that they are engaging in sexual relations.'

She gazed at me, uncomprehending. I realized that another major aspect of her education had been neglected or washed away. I was tempted to let it go at that but realized that she would have to know about this sort of thing, too, and that now was the time for her to learn, and that it was best that I tell her.

'A man and a woman can develop a close acquaintance,' I said. 'Sometimes this becomes love. Sometimes they give their bodies to each other, experiencing a deep intimacy and pleasure. Sometimes they are intimate without love. Normally this is restricted to married couples, but in some institutions, such as the military, they are unmarried. Whatever the situation, such a union should not be made without careful consideration. Hopie feels that although I have separated from her mother, I should not be intimate with any other woman. She may be correct. But men have different perceptions about these things, and so I act in a manner my daughter does not approve. I am deeply sorry to have hurt her in this way.'

She just gazed at me, unspeaking, and I was uncertain of how much she understood. Well, I had tried to make a fair presentation; that was all I could do.

'I must return to my business now, Amber,' I said. 'But I will talk with you again. I am very glad to know that you are able to talk and to read. There is nothing wrong with Spanish; it is an interplanetary language, as is English.'

Still she did not react. Discomfited, I left her.

I continued with the hectic business of setting up a government, consulting with experts, interviewing prospects, checking my facts.

I talked with Gerald Phist, who was in charge of industry, and his wife, Roulette. We had been close in the Navy, with Phist my second in command (after Spirit), and Roulette my wife. As I had explained to Amber, the Navy was a special situation. When I left the Navy, Rue had married Phist at my behest, but she still loved me, and he still loved my sister, who had been his wife. I think he was disappointed that Spirit was not present; she had had to go to another bubble to organize a chain of command. Spirit, as I have said, was always the true strength of the Tyrancy; she constantly welded the necessary connections, keeping the structure tight. It had been that way in the Navy, too, when she was my executive officer.

Phist was ageing gracefully, being about fifteen years my senior, and Rue remained stunning, being about ten years my junior. My eyes tended to stray to aspects of her form, and when they did, she would wiggle that aspect, and Phist would laugh. Both of them understood perfectly my situation with women, which was one of the things that made them comfortable to be with. My amorous relationship with Rue was long over, but it had not been ended by my choice or by hers, and we all knew it.

'Hope, I propose two major solutions to the problem of crime,' she said briskly. 'Legalization and elimination. Legalize everything possible and eliminate the rest.'

'Um, yes,' I said, apprehensive about what she contemplated. 'But you know I have a problem with costs.' My gaze drifted to her décolletage.

'No cost,' she said, giving her cleavage a little quiver, so that my eyes snapped away. 'Expenses should be the same or less than they are at present, and the programmes may become self-supporting.'

'That sounds too good to be true!' I said.

'She tends to seem that way,' Phist remarked.

'The problem with drugs is the market,' she said. 'Jupiter has been going to phenomenal effort and expense to stop them from being imported, but the suppliers override that effort because of the enormous profit to be made. The same is true of gambling. The solution is to expand on the programme you had in Sunshine: legalize everything. Then there will be no premium for illicit things; the marketplace will determine their value.'

I remembered the programme I had instituted, with her help, when I was governor of the State of Sunshine. We had provided drugs to addicts at nominal cost, undercutting the criminal suppliers. Since a sizable proportion of the crime in the state had been related to such drugs, crime had plummeted. We had obtained our own supply of drugs by confiscation from illegal sources and refined them so that they were as safe as such things could be. A number of other states had emulated our programme, but the majority had not, and the old types of crime remained. As for gambling – Roulette had been named for an aspect of her father's business – she saw no harm in it. With certain reservations I agreed. Compulsive gamblers were a problem to themselves and society, but most people were not compulsive. Prostitution was merely another business, the consequence of the civilian restrictions on sex.

'Legalize those vices that do not harm other citizens,' I agreed. 'But what of lasers, projectile weapons, theft, violence, embezzlement, child abuse, and so on? We can't afford to legalize *everything*.'

'Elimination,' she said. 'Lasers and other weapons hurt other people and often their owners. A laser-pistol in

151

amateur hands is six times as likely to injure or kill a friend or family member as a criminal. Ban them all, unless the person is with the police or military or has a special permit.'

'But there must be twice as many weapons in the hands of private citizens as there are citizens!' I protested somewhat rhetorically, for I knew her rebuttal. During my years as a politician I had more than once locked horns with the nefarious PLA, the Planetary Laser Association, whose guiding principle was that every citizen should have completely free access to laser weapons. 'LASERS DON'T KILL PEOPLE, PEOPLE DO,' they proclaimed. 'We can't even *find* them all, let alone take them away from citizens who believe they need them for protection. The best we could achieve would be the disarming of the law-abiding; only the criminals would still have weapons.'

'Not if you eliminate the criminals,' she said. 'Then the law-abiding citizens will have no need of weapons for private defence. Outlaw the weapons. Anyone possessing one will be a lawbreaker by definition. No criminal will give himself away by carrying a weapon that clearly identifies his nature.'

'And how do we eliminate the criminals? I don't like the death penalty.'

'I have discussed that with Gerald,' she said, glancing at her husband. 'He advises me that there are a number of inclement positions in space – jobs that few people volunteer to perform despite increasingly high pay scales. One-man isolated planetoid stations, missions on Io, outposts on Charon, ice-scavenging in deep space – that sort of thing. Those jobs could be done by criminals.'

'But some of those jobs are important!' I said. 'We don't want some criminal messing them up.'

'Any criminal that messes up in space dies,' she said.

'This is not execution; it is the law of space. Space does not forgive a little error in judgement. One tiny hole in a suit, unpatched – poof!' She spread her hands expressively, and her bosom bounced, my eyeballs with it. 'That's why people don't like space. But if a criminal were sentenced to three years of that, his term to be extended if he did not perform adequately, he would make very sure he would perform. It's not a judgement call; in space either you survive and accomplish the job or you don't.'

I turned the notion over in my mind, liking the configuration of it. How well I remembered the rigors of space! As for the station on Charon – that was the satellite of Pluto, farthest conventional planet from the sun – at that distance the sun seemed to be no more than a bright star, and the cold of space seemed to infuse the domes. Physically it was reasonably comfortable; emotionally it was devastating. There was a high attrition due to personality breakdown. And Io – that was the true hell of the System, on the face towards Jupiter. My mother had died there, as well as most of the women of our refugee party, destroyed by the savage volcanic activity. It was true: that was a fitting punishment for even the worst of criminals – and the study missions there were scientifically productive.

'I like it,' I said. 'Set it up and consult with me when ready to implement.'

She smiled and approached me for a kiss. I accepted, feeling awkward not because of the presence of her husband but because of my recent discussion with Amber. My daughter Hopie did not like my intimate associations with women other than Megan; she understood intellectually but not emotionally.

'You can do better than that, Captain!' Rue snapped, shaking me by the shoulders.

'I – my daughter is disturbed by – ' I faltered.

'The one they think is *my* daughter,' she said. 'You had *better* show me some respect!'

I had to laugh. I took her and kissed her again with greater vigour, and she was still man's desire. I loved Megan, my true wife, but that did not subtract from what Rue had been.

Even so, her mouth quirked when we broke. 'Someone's been at you,' she said. 'Someone with real experience.'

I felt myself blushing, remembering the devastating experience with Reba in the dark. How had Rue known? Somehow my women always knew my secrets!

Now it was Phist's turn. I had put him in charge of industry, knowing that his experience as a military equipment procurer and whistle-blower made him supremely qualified. I suspected that he had the most difficult task of all those that the Tyrancy would be coming to grips with, for the relation of the Jupiter military-industrial complex to the government most resembled that of a multi-headed hydra to its prey. Our task was to tame that monster without killing it, for its disciplined survival was crucial to the welfare of the planet.

But as he opened his mouth we were interrupted. Hopie hurried in. She had free access to me always; Shelia never stopped her. 'Daddy, something's wrong with Amber!' she exclaimed. Then she paused, noting my company. 'Oh!'

'You know Admiral Phist and his wife Roulette,' I said. I turned to them. 'My daughter, Hopie.'

Roulette smiled. 'Well, I ought to!' she exclaimed.

Hopie flushed. 'Are you really my – '

Roulette sighed. 'I wish I could answer you, Hopie.'

'Talk to Amber in Spanish,' I said quickly.

154

'I don't care what other people think!' Hopie said, flustered. 'I just want to know who – '

'Amber talks in Spanish,' I said. 'Not in English. I discovered that today.'

Roulette shook her head sadly. 'It isn't right to mislead you, Hopie. I am not your mother. I would like to have been, but that privilege was not destined to be mine.'

'Then who – '

'If you will just say something to her in – ' I started.

'Butt out, Daddy,' Hopie snapped. 'If not you, Roulette, then who is it? I believe I have a right to know.'

'It is not my place to answer that, dear,' Roulette said. 'But does it really matter? You have a life that others would envy, and a family – '

'*Half* a family!' the girl retorted. 'And a philanderer for a father.'

Phist looked at me, but I gave him a take-cover signal. It was better to have this out, and better in company than alone. Hopie could be an imperious girl, and there was some justice in her complaint.

Roulette patted the couch beside her. 'Come sit by me, Hopie, and we'll talk. There are things I *can* tell you.'

The girl joined her, perching uncomfortably. 'If you know who knows – '

'Things that Hope Hubris believes but that are not necessarily true,' Roulette continued. 'To understand him you have to understand the Navy. In the Jupiter Navy, men and women are not encouraged to love, but they are required to make love. That is, enlisted personnel are not permitted to marry, but they must perform sexually every week or be rebuked. Officers have greater privileges, but still, it is difficult to have children or a normal family in the civilian manner. To survive in the Navy they must conform, in this as in other things. A person can leave

155

the Navy, but his way of life is likely to be set – his underlying values.'

'What has this to do with my – '

'Now, Hope is separated from his wife, just as he was separated from me when he left the Navy. This has nothing to do with love and everything to do with circumstance. When he left me, he had relations with other women, and I with another man. He would have stayed with me if he could, and I with him. It could not be. We each had to make our separate lives. Now he is apart from the wife that followed me, and that is not his choice, but he must make his separate life again. Of course, this means other women. That is the Navy way. That is what those in the Service know is right, however the civilian sector may perceive it. You must not condemn him for being what he has been conditioned to be. I am sure Megan understands.'

'She does,' Hopie said. 'But *I* don't!'

'She loves him, as I do. As many women do. We love him for what he is, not what we would choose him to be. We know that he believes he has loved only two women in his life but that, in fact, he loves only one.'

Now Hopie was startled. 'One?'

'It was no easier for me to accept than it is for you. I wanted him to love me, but he was only smitten with me because of my shape and my youth. His first romance was with one not much younger than I was then – '

'Helse. She was sixteen.'

'And his second romance with one older – '

'Megan. She's fifty-six.'

'So there really wasn't room for Juana or Emerald or me. We were passing fancies, relatively. Just as his present women are. Just as, to a lesser extent, his two major romances have been. You have to keep that perspective on him. For your sake, not his.'

Hopie was obviously shaken. 'How can you say such things about him, with him right here listening?'

'Because they are true. Because you need to know. Because he will not tell you. You must not let your misconception damage your relationship with him. He is a man destined for women, and a worthy one despite or because of that.'

'My misconception!' Hopie snorted. 'That's a neat way to put it!'

'Because you are of illegitimate birth,' Roulette agreed smiling. 'But your origin is no fault in you, just as Hope Hubris's nature is no fault in him. You are a good girl, and he is a good man.'

Hopie cocked her head. 'Did he really rape you?'

'He really did, dear.'

'And you call him a good man?'

'Yes. He is a good man *because* he raped me. A bad man would not have had the courage or the ability.'

'I don't understand that at all!'

'He was the third to try it. I killed the first two. Hope Hubris was the first and the last to master me.'

Hopie glanced at Phist. 'But – '

'She tolerates me,' he said. 'For the sake of the situation. It is the Navy way – and the pirate way. I never mastered her.'

'You never even tried!' Roulette said, reproving him.

'But – ' Hopie repeated. 'To – to have sex with – '

'As I said, we do not always get to have sex with the one we love,' Roulette reminded her. 'If I had my true choice, I would be in bed with Hope Hubris right now. But – '

'Why not?' Hopie said stoutly. 'Everyone *else* is – '

'No. *He* has lost his wife. I have not lost my husband. Hope is free; I am not.'

'But from what you say, your husband would let you – '

'Of course, he would,' Roulette agreed. 'But we honour the code that we live by. As does Hope. I am sure he has not touched any married woman or any unwilling one. You must not condemn him; your standards are civilian and do not apply.'

Hopie shook her head, neither positively nor negatively. 'I'll try, Roulette. But you must tell me one thing.'

'One thing,' Roulette agreed.

'You said he only truly loves one woman. Who is that?'

'Your natural mother.'

'But I don't know who she is!'

'One day you shall know, dear. Until then you must keep an open mind.'

Now Hopie was close to tears. 'But if I don't know who she is, how do I know she loves me?'

'She loves you,' I said.

'But she never cared enough to keep me!'

'She couldn't keep you,' I said. 'She was single, and your father was married. That sort of thing is not understood in the better families.'

'But she doesn't have to be anonymous!'

'I think I understand,' Phist said. 'If she were to reveal her part in this, it would destroy the reputation of your natural father. She must love him – '

'She does,' I said before I thought.

He turned away. I understood why but could not speak of it. He was the best of men.

Roulette glanced up at him. 'Oh, Gerald, I'm sorry!'

Hopie looked from one to the other, perplexed. 'What – '

'We deal on levels, and *levels*,' Roulette said. 'Let me share my song with you, Hopie.'

'Your – '

'After Hope mastered me I became part of his culture. I had to take a folk song, in the manner of all the personnel in his unit. That is how I became Rue, instead of Roulette. I want you to share my song, because I fear you will one day need it. It will do until you are given your own song.'

'But we don't have songs here!' Hopie protested.

'Then it is time to start. Hope is called Worry, after his song, "Worried Man Blues", Gerald is Old King Cole. Your Aunt Spirit is the Dear, after her song.'

'The Deer? An animal?'

'Dear, as in "I know who I love, but the dear knows who I'll marry". Make her sing it for you sometime.'

'I will,' Hopie said, brightening.

Then Roulette sang her song:

Come all ye fair and tender maids
Who flourish in your prime, prime;
Beware, beware, make your garden fair
Let no man steal your thyme, thyme . . .

'That's beautiful,' Hopie said when she finished. 'But so sad.'

'Life can be sad – and beautiful,' Roulette said.

Hopie looked around. 'But I'm interrupting,' she said, her realization coming somewhat belatedly. She stood, glancing at me. 'Spanish.' She departed.

'Who is Amber?' Phist inquired.

I summarized the history of Amber.

Roulette pursed her lips. 'You had better brush up on your song, Hope. That girl is mischief.'

'You haven't seen her!' I protested.

'I don't need to. I can tell a missile by its description.' And she smiled in that private, sometimes annoying, way women have.

Phist resumed his presentation. 'My preliminary study shows phenomenal waste, fraud, and inefficiency through-out the planet. I had supposed that this was largely a function of military purchases, but I see now that it is endemic. The entire framework requires overhauling.'

'I dread to ask the cost,' I said.

'Ideally there should be no net cost. The object is to make the apparatus function more efficiently, so that it serves the planet better than before and leads to further improvement. But initially – '

'We don't have initial cash,' I said.

'Then it will have to be done indirectly. I think the best approach is to nationalize key companies in key industries.'

'But they did that on Saturn,' I protested. 'Everything is run by the state, and every season they have record crop failures and industrial inadequacies.'

'Because the fundamental Communist philosophy is flawed,' Phist said. 'It provides inadequate motive for individual effort. When a man is not rewarded for his accomplishment, he loses incentive. When that extends to an entire planet, that planet is in serious trouble.'

'But if we nationalize, we'll be in the same trouble.'

'Not necessarily. We need to do it right. We have to take incentive into account and make our selected companies models for the others. To produce the products more efficiently at cheaper prices and higher quality and better reliability than the competition. Then the other companies will have to match our level or suffer erosion of their markets.'

'I hope you're right,' I said doubtfully.

'We'll start with the most troublesome companies in the key industrial sectors,' he said briskly. 'One in metals, one in construction, one in transport, one in agriculture – '

'Agriculture?'

'That's an industry too,' he said. 'And a vital one. Without food we'll starve.'

160

'Um, yes,' I agreed. 'Now, I mean to reduce military hardware production, so – '

'You're sure that's wise?'

'I have a tacit deal with Admiral Khukov. There's an enormous amount of resources to be saved in defence, and for the first time we have a trustworthy opportunity to reduce Jupiter–Saturn tensions.'

He nodded. 'Khukov's like you in certain respects. He's trustworthy and he handles people well. Very well. I'll dismantle the military industry, But I'll need cover.'

'Cover?'

'The powers-that-be aren't going to like this.'

'*I* am the powers-that-be!' I said.

'You are the nominal power. You'll need Mondy to make that power actual. Meanwhile stand by me, and I'll do the job.'

'I'll tell Spirit,' I said.

He sighed. 'I do miss the old days.'

'Don't we all, dear,' Roulette said, taking his arm. I was surprised by her manner; she had softened considerably in twenty years and was no longer the fiery pirate lass I had known. It was obvious that whatever she might say about her passion for me (which was perhaps more complimentary than actual), she had developed a genuine fondness for her husband. She had not been soft during our association. She had been able to appreciate only violent passion; I had had to hit her to make her respond. Now I knew that she could respond also to gentleness – and Phist was a gentle man. He still loved Spirit, but surely Roulette gave him much to appreciate. To have a woman like that again –

'Don't we all,' I echoed.

'You're jealous of Gerald!' Roulette exclaimed, pleased.

'You never called *me* "dear",' I grumbled.

161

'Oh, that makes it all worthwhile!' she chortled. Even Phist had to smile. 'You broke her in well, sir.'

'*Too* well,' I agreed.

Smiling, they departed.

Several days later I had another opportunity to visit Amber. Her face brightened when she saw me, and again I experienced that déjà vu. It was as though I had seen her before, but I could not place where.

This time Hopie was there. 'You know, Daddy, about what Roulette said . . .' she began somewhat diffidently.

'All true,' I murmured, embarrassed.

'It helps me to understand. I shouldn't have judged you.'

'You are my daughter,' I said. 'Judge me as you will.'

'Just hug me, Daddy,' she said.

So I hugged her. I knew that her adjustment was not complete, but perhaps, in her deepest emotion, she was coming to terms with the new reality. I could not blame her for not liking a sundered family; at her age I had lost mine, except for my sister Spirit, and I knew the horror of that. I would have protected her from this experience if I could have.

Amber was watching, her face blank. Hopie glanced at her. 'Oops, I didn't think,' she murmured. 'You'd better hug her, too, Daddy.'

Because the girl did not understand affection shown to one and not to another? Perhaps Hopie was right.

'Amber, I will hug you too,' I said in Spanish.

She came to me somewhat timidly, and I took her in my arms and squeezed her. She was somewhat stiff, unfamiliar with this, but I could tell by her bodily reaction that she liked it. She had probably been denied such simple, direct expressions of familiarity or affection.

'I'll have to give her hugging lessons,' Hopie said

judiciously in English. Then, in Spanish: 'Amber is improving in writing.'

'Good enough,' I said, turning the girl loose. 'Did I explain to you, Hopie, how she changes languages?'

'No. She's been locked here in Spanish ever since you changed her. She doesn't understand English any more.'

Which was odd, now that I considered it. She had been able to tell me what she had heard in English, yet could no longer understand it directly. 'Amber, may we experiment with you?' I asked.

She shrugged, not objecting.

'Look at the gem,' I said. 'Look deep at the termite; go into your trance.'

She obeyed. Hopie watched, fascinated.

'English,' I said.

Amber did not react. 'Do you understand me now?' I asked in Spanish.

She gazed at me, uncomprehending.

'Do you understand me now?' I repeated in English.

She nodded affirmatively.

'But you cannot speak in English?'

She spread her hands, acquiescing.

'She's back the way she was before!' Hopie exclaimed, also in English.

'It is the gem that does it,' I said. 'It puts her in a trance, and then the spoken name of the language puts her into that mode. But she only actually speaks Spanish.'

'Does it end there?' Hopie asked.

'Why, I hadn't thought – ' I said, surprised.

'Amber, look at the gem again,' Hopie said.

The girl did. '*Le français*,' Hopie said. She had been studying French in school. This was not a language I knew, other than the merest smattering of words.

There was no reaction from Amber. 'Remember, she

163

doesn't speak,' I said in English. 'But we can verify it.' I faced the girl. 'Do you understand me now?'

She did not react.

'*Ce chemin, où méne-t-il?*' Hopie inquired. I may have misrendered that; I can't be sure.

Amber looked at her, smiling as if she had spoken foolishly.

'*C'est tordant, c'est rigolo,*' Hopie said.

Amber smiled, agreeing.

'*Voilà ce qu'il me faut!*' Hopie said, pleased.

'Now will you enlighten me?' I inquired with a bit of an edge, though I was pleased that my daughter shared my facility with language. I can learn any language I choose to, but, of course, it requires time and effort, so I don't do it without reason. I had mastered Spanish, English, and Russian but never had occasion to learn French.

Hopie smiled, enjoying my discomfort. 'First I named the language,' she said in English. 'Then I asked "Where does this road lead?" I thought – you know, it's a kind of road we are following here, and maybe – '

'Understood,' I said. 'Good question.'

She smiled, pleased. 'Then I said, "It's terribly funny!" and she agreed, and I knew she did understand, because she doesn't smile unless she has reason. So I exclaimed, "That's exactly what I want!" Daddy, it worked! Now she understands French.'

'And nothing else,' I agreed.

'She's like an old-fashioned computer. You tell it the code, and it is instantly set in that mode and doesn't react to anything in any other mode, even though it has all modes in its circuitry.'

'Like a primitive computer,' I agreed, nodding. 'But she is a human being.'

'People do funny things to people,' she said, frowning. 'They mem-washed you, Daddy.'

'I recovered,' I said. 'But Amber – I don't know how far we should meddle until we understand exactly what has been done to her. We don't want to hurt her.'

'Of course, we don't!' she agreed. 'But checking languages shouldn't hurt her.'

'It shouldn't,' I agreed. I felt a certain unease, fearing that we were doing something risky or wrong, but I couldn't define it. 'If we proceed cautiously.'

7

Helmet Love

The next two years were filled with activity of every sort. Again I don't want to slight the very serious business of government, but the truth is that Spirit handled most of the scutwork, so I merely had to make my appearances and statements as directed, make basic decisions of policy, and sign documents where indicated. As I have made clear, Spirit really ran the Tyrancy. Had others realized this, she would have had less freedom, and I more. I realize that seems backward. I had more time to myself than she did, but I was also the subject of increasingly determined attempts at assassination, so I had to restrict my life for the sake of safety. Spirit was always busy, and I would not even see her for weeks at a time, but because she was not known as the Mistress of the Empire, she was not such a target. She could go fairly freely around the globe, negotiating in my name, and others believed that if anything happened to her, it would only evoke the fury of the Tyrant (true) and bring a similar replacement for her office (false).

I gave Ebony her turn with me. I find myself being slightly defensive here but can only repeat that my way with women is the way that seems correct to me. Ebony was part of my staff-family, and she deserved her share. That does not mean that I loved her or necessarily found her physically attractive. But I had known her many years and respected her as a person. She had never made any pretence at being beautiful or brilliant; she was good at running errands and absolutely conscientious in that. When any of us gave her a thing to do, we had no further concern; it would be done properly and on schedule. She had been especially useful to Shelia, who could not get around freely in her wheelchair. Of course, I paid all my staff members a decent wage – well, Spirit did; I don't even know what the figure was but knew it was fair. They served me with a devotion that deserved a greater recompense, and now was the time of payment.

Thus it was that I found myself in bed with Ebony, though I confess I would have preferred Coral. I admit that this period following the Navy and my marriage left me somewhat out of sorts sexually. Some prefer to believe that folk in their fifties have little remaining interest in sexual expression. This is not the case in my experience. My interest remained as strong as ever, though my performance had slowed somewhat. Thus an act that might have been completed in two minutes when I was twenty was more comfortable in half an hour at fifty, not because my body had slowed to that degree but because my urgency had. The young tend not to understand about timing and savouring.

Ebony introduced me to an oral technique she called 'Around the Planet'. She began at my navel and proceeded in a kind of tightening spiral, her tongue covering every part of me. I had not imagined how stimulating this could be when properly performed. She moved me around as suited her, closing in on my centre of gravity, and the effect became so strong that I felt compelled to warn her: 'Pilot, that ship is about to take off without you!'

'Ships don't make single flights,' she said, and proceeded unabated.

Maybe not, but this one fired its drive thereafter, unattended. She proceeded as if it hadn't happened, and in an amazingly brief interval, the drive was ready to fire again. She continued to use her tongue and her mouth, and presently the urgency overcame me a second time, this time attended by her lips.

I thought it was over, but I was mistaken. Still she continued, the detumescence that should have occurred was halted, and the ship was fuelled for a third takeoff. When she deemed the occasion appropriate, she mounted me in the normal manner and moved in such a way that I did indeed come to a final culmination. She had not had pleasure in her own body before, but now she joined me in a pulsing climax.

'Did Q match that?' she inquired as we subsided.

'Once,' I said. Indeed, I was not sure I had ever before had a triple conclusion. I had not known that men were capable of multiple performances, especially at this age, but it seems they are, when suitably managed.

She relaxed, satisfied. She had evidently proved her point.

Thereafter I felt no disappointment when it was Ebony's turn; she had her own expertise. And for a year or so I had, if it is fair to phrase it that way, three mistresses, who scheduled me somewhat in the manner that the multiple wives of ancient sultans had, seeing that I had no sexual frustrations. Perhaps one would look askance that I include Shelia in this number, but though she could not move her legs, she was worthy in other respects, and I always felt comfortable with her. I should clarify that our time together at night was not always physically sexual; the companionship of these three women was just as important to me.

Yet, gradually, a dissatisfaction came upon me. That may seem ungracious in the extreme, and certainly I did not voice it to the three, but in retrospect I must say it was so. I think it was the fact that these were working personnel. They had been chosen for reasons other than sexual, and while I deeply respected them all, I did not love them. They were too close; I knew them too well. They were *not* my mistresses; they were the members of my personal staff, who served me to the best of their ability in all things. Their sexual accommodation had to be a secondary thing, temporary, until I found a woman who was not a respected associate. I did not view it that way at the time; I view it that way now, in my effort to understand the subsequent events. I believe that I desired some new romance, with some less knowledgeable woman, so that I could take the initiative and feel more like a man than a pampered creature.

I called my first formal cabinet meeting, on Spirit's advice. It was in the hallowed Oval Office, and the media were excluded, with one exception.

'As Tyrant, I have no need of conventional organization,' I informed the group. 'This may be the only cabinet meeting held. But I felt I should introduce you formally to each other, so that there is no confusion about the offices you hold or the rationale for them. All of you will report directly to me, or, in my absence or unavailability, to my sister Spirit, or to Shelia, who will see that I am kept current.' I put my hand on Shelia's shoulder, for her wheelchair was beside me. 'She has my complete confidence, and she will respect yours; if she tells you something, you may rely on it. If it sometimes seems that she is running the planet, that is probably the case.' I smiled, and the others smiled with me, but we all knew there was a fair amount of truth in the statement. If Shelia made a commitment in my name, and it turned out to be in error, I would do my best to honour it, anyway, to avoid mutual embarrassment.

I turned to the man on my right. 'Senator Stonebridge is in charge of economics,' I said. 'He will take what measures are necessary to balance the planetary budget and thereafter to reduce or eliminate the planetary debt. This has not been accomplished in centuries, but it is my mandate and I mean to honour it. The United States of North Jupiter at this point is on the verge of becoming a net debtor nation; we shall restore it to creditor status.'

I turned next to Gerald Phist, seated next right. 'Admiral Phist is in charge of industry. This includes farming, food procurement, and the preservation of the environment, which has, at times in the past, been degraded by the excesses of industry. He will restore Jupiter to a position of leadership in technology and production and efficiency, and will eliminate such waste and fraud as has existed in the past.' I spoke as though this would be easy to do, but we all knew that Phist's job would be as difficult as Stonebridge's.

Roulette, Phist's wife, was next. 'Rue Phist is not a citizen of Jupiter,' I said. 'As Tyrant, I have abolished that requirement for service. She is in charge of crime, and she will eliminate it as a factor in Jupiter's economy. This includes all types, violent and monetary and sexual.' Roulette nodded and smiled and leaned forward, and Stonebridge's eyes nearly popped as her deep cleavage flexed. I knew he would be meeting with her individually, as economics and crime interacted; he would discover that she had a competent head above that competent bosom. I had selected mostly from my own closest circle, because I understood these people best, but I had not ignored competence.

Spirit was next. 'My younger sister, Spirit Hubris,' I said, 'is in charge of interplanetary relations and implementation of policy. She is my second in command and will govern in my absence. This has been so throughout our relationship.' And I suffered a flash of memory of Spirit as a child, with her finger whip, using it in my defence. She no longer had the whip, but nothing had

170

changed between us. At forty-seven she remained a fine figure of a woman too.

Ebony was next, looking somewhat out of sorts in this company. 'Ebony did not ask for the post of population,' I said. 'I thrust it on her. She will find means to bring our burgeoning population under control, so that it will not devastate us. She will consult with the others to see that such measures as she implements will not interfere with their projects.'

'Tyrant, if I may . . .' Stonebridge said cautiously. I nodded and he continued: 'A significant portion of our population problem originates beyond the territorial boundaries of North Jupiter. I doubt that the domestic problem can be solved without reference to the external problem. Immigration – '

'Illegal aliens cost us twenty-five billion dollars a year,' Ebony said. 'But if we try to wall them out – '

'Jupiter industry would suffer,' Phist said.

'So we must solve the international and interplanetary problem first,' Roulette said. 'Illegal aliens are my concern too. We shall have to have an early meeting, Senator – those of us whose concerns overlap, as in this case.' She flexed her cleavage at him again.

'By all means,' Stonebridge agreed immediately, as any man would.

I was privately pleased. Ebony was no intellectual giant and made no such pretension, but she did do her homework. She had, by this interchange, achieved a measure of acceptance in this group, in Stonebridge's eyes and in her own. They would get the job done.

Next was Faith. 'My older sister, Faith Hubris,' I said. 'She is in charge of poverty. She will abolish it – again, consulting with others of you to be sure that her programmes do not conflict with your own.' I glanced around the group. 'I expect there to be constant interaction among you. When you come to me with a programme, be sure you have already cleared it with whoever overlaps. If you cannot agree on policy, then I will arbitrate. Shelia will coordinate any required meetings.'

I came to Hopie. 'My daughter is in charge of education. She will arrange for it to become competent and relevant. Whether this includes job training or retraining you will work out among those who overlap. I suspect that means most of you.'

Then Mondy: 'Admiral Mondy is in charge of intelligence. He will probably not be interacting often with the rest of you, but Shelia will show him all of your reports, and he will inform you of what he deems relevant to your interests.'

I completed the circle with Thorley. 'As you know, I agreed never to infringe on freedom of the press,' I said. 'Though Thorley's political philosophy differs from mine, and he opposes the Tyrancy on principle, he is enough of a realist to accept the situation, and I do not keep secrets from him.' I paused, remembering how the man had stepped into a laser beam intended for Megan and won my lasting gratitude – and hers. I mught differ from Thorley on every other matter, but I respected his courage, integrity, intelligence, and dedication to principle, as he respected mine. I was about to surprise him.

'Sir, I know you want no part of this administration,' I told him directly. 'You came here in your capacity as a commentator, and you are free to publish what you will. This is to be an open administration in every matter other than immediate planetary security or private scandal, and of those you will also be advised. I believe you now know the actual nature of the Jupiter invasion of Ganymede.' He nodded, with that wry quirk of a smile. 'I am now asking you to participate in this administration, in a capacity I doubt you can refuse.'

'I *do* refuse!' Thorley said, startled. 'I do not care to lend any portion of my reputation to the Tyrancy.'

'The position of censor,' I said.

Thorley actually spluttered, and there was a ripple of laughter around the circle. 'The only censorship I would approve is *no* censorship!' he exclaimed. 'I would consider any such institution a clear and present breach of – '

He paused, for I was nodding affirmatively. He smiled ruefully. 'You wish me to enforce the *absence* of censorship.'

'I can think of no one better qualified for that post,' I agreed. 'It is necessary that the person in charge have the discretion to distinguish between legitimate privacy of individual interests and the right of the public to be informed about the nature of its government. The integrity to abuse neither.'

'And if I should decline, I would be by implication condoning what I abhor.'

'You know that even the best intentions can be corrupted by time and circumstance,' I said. 'Today I support total freedom of the media, but how will it be after I have wrestled with error and inadequacy? It is better to have a censor who is not otherwise committed to the policies of the Tyrancy.'

Thorley raised his hands. 'Sir, you have mousetrapped me. I am left with no choice.'

'That is the nature of tyranny,' Spirit said, smiling. But she knew, as I did, and as Thorley did, that this appointment signalled more emphatically than any other my intent to honour the commitments that had brought me to the Tyrancy. I did not intend to be corrupted by power.

I was dangerously naïve, of course.

* * *

We brought in linguistic experts, folk who practised many languages, and explored Amber's potential. She was indeed not limited to Spanish, English, and French. She knew Russian, Arabic, German, more than one dialect of Chinese, and sundry others, though she spoke in none but Spanish.

The specialists explained it to me in terms I could understand. Amber had not been mem-washed or otherwise abused. She was a member of the class sometimes called *idiot savants*. Her brain was in effect miswired. The material was there but could not be properly applied to the ordinary concerns of normal folk. Her intelligence, in Spanish, was low-normal; in other languages, she was technically a moron. But she could remember a certain amount of what she heard.

Khukov's specialists had evidently found a way to utilize her severely compartmentalized brain. They had programmed each segment to a different language. Had they all been programmed in Spanish, Amber would have understood Spanish in any mode but have spoken it only in one. In short, she would have had no advantage, because her brain operated only, as it were, in parallel, not in series. But this way, she had an enormous array of languages to draw on, without sacrificing the one complete one. She was indeed like a computer – one with a number of memory banks, each bank set up in a specific language, which could be hooked in at will. But only Spanish could print.

One might wonder of what use such a child might be to a political tyrant. But it did not take me long to fathom that. I did not know all the languages of the System, but it seemed that Amber did. My secret knowledge of Russian had on occasion served me well, when Saturnians spoke among themselves in my presence, supposing their consultation to be private. With Amber I could spy similarly on any other language. All that I needed to do was bring her with me, letting it be known that she had been given into my care, was of substandard intellect, and would not cause any mischief. Indeed it was so – up to a point.

When the iron magnates of Mars dickered with me on prices and policies, Amber was there. She sat in her chair, staring at her hands, her fingers twitching erratically. What the magnates did not realize was that the solitary child, tuned in to Arabic, had been instructed to make certain simple gestures if certain things were said. Amber did not understand the significance of those things, but she dutifully made the gestures with her fingers, and I noted these. It was a simplistic task, but, coupled with my own talent in judging people, it gave me invaluable information. I became aware of the limits to which the magnates were prepared to go, muttered among themselves, and that greatly facilitated my bargaining.

The same was true when I dealt with executives from the various nations of Uranus, who spoke French, German, Italian, or other tongues. I became a far more prescient negotiator than those others took me for. After the sessions I would return Amber to Spanish and question her in detail, gathering yet more information. She was normal, in memory; I had to catch her early, or she would forget most of the detail in a few days. That was all right; in a few days the information became passé.

Somewhere along about here – I regret I can no longer keep the chronology straight, but it really doesn't matter – I received an interesting message. It was in the form of a feelie chip. Shelia gave it to me with a wry expression. 'I think you had better read this one yourself, sir.'

'You can't give me a digest?' I asked, mildly perplexed.

'The effect would be diminished.'

'I don't need effects!' I said, mildly exasperated. 'I need efficient information. That's why I keep you.'

'It's from an admirer,' she clarified. 'Female.'

Oh. My position did lead to some communications of this kind. Men are mostly attracted to physical beauty, women to power. As Tyrant I attracted more than my share of offers. In the earliest days some voluptuous women would strip part or all their clothing as I passed, showing their wares much as shopkeepers might. And you know, I did find it appealing, not merely for the elegance of the flesh but also for the fact that it was being offered to me, a physical nonentity. Vanity may be as much a male trait as a female one, and flattery has power even over those who know better. Sometimes I dreamed about those proffered bodies that I had to pass up.

Shelia filtered most of them out, not through any jealousy but because a power-seeking woman really has little to offer me but mischief. Also, she knew my bias for known elements; I prefer to know a woman well before I get intimate with her, and it was difficult to know any ordinary woman when I could not go out without my security guards. Finally there was my marriage: it existed in name, no longer in substance, but for Megan's sake I did not want to sully that name openly. As far as the public knew, I had become celibate. (I use that term in its popular sense, rather than its dictionary sense. In centuries dictionaries have not caught up to the fact that celibacy refers to a person's state of sexual inactivity, rather than to his state of unmarriage.) All my women protected me in that respect. There were surely suspicions and insinuations about our night life; in fact, some uncomfortably accurate conjectures were published (and some I rather wish *had* occurred), but Coral, Shelia, and Ebony invariably turned blank stares on questioners, as if soiled by the very notion. Women tend to be better at such deception than are men.

Shelia had to have good reason to give this one to me. I accepted it, and on the next occasion when I had private time, I relaxed in an easy chair and donned a holo helmet. This came down to about the level of my eyes and ears. When I set in the chip and turned it on, the helmet sent its field through my brain, stimulating my visual, auditory, and tactile centres. This, in effect, put me right into the picture.

I found myself in a nondescript chamber, not ordinary so much as never properly visualized for the projection. This was evidently an amateur effort. Feelies come in two kinds: the professional, which are carefully staged and formed, and the amateur, which tend to be fuzzy. In order to make a feelie sequence, it is necessary to don a recording helmet such as this one and formulate the desired images. The helmet's magnetic fluxes pick up the patterns of impulses and preserve them, much the way a holo recorder does with direct physical things. When these impulses are played back, the imagined scene is recreated in whatever detail was originally provided. Some minds have better conceptualization (by that I mean the full gamut of sight, hearing, and touch) than others, which is what makes those with such minds professionals. They also enhance imagination by contemplating relevant physical objects. Thus a pro would not necessarily imagine a chair; he would fix his gaze directly on it, and the helmet would record the precise impressions, including the unconscious ones. That makes for a relatively sharp and realistic picture. An amateur is more apt to imagine the chair from whole cloth, as it were, and that chair could be lopsided and malproportioned.

Yet there can be a certain appeal to amateur efforts.

177

The fuzziness of detail lends a dreamlike quality, which is often the desired effect. Some psychologists employ feelies as therapy; they encourage the patients to make any rendering that satisfies them and then analyse the distortions that appear in the images. Apparently there are definite neurotic and psychotic patterns, and these become more normal when the designated condition is treated. The doctors can verify the effect of treatment through the subsequent recordings. Some employers require feelalysis of prospective employees. However, a competent mind can distort the results by emulating either the normal or an abnormal pattern, and there have been some real embarrassments there. So, mainly, the feelies remain a popular entertainment device, with millions of people tuning in on published chipisodes. There is, of course, a sizable business in pornographic chips; I had encountered these in the Navy.

Now I let myself experience the scene. It was of a figure, a man in some sort of cape, a deified man, for he glowed, literally, as if imbued with some inherent phosphorescence. He walked, he turned, flinging his cape about.

Then I saw his face – and recognized it as a version of my own. Well, of course, Shelia had said this was from a female admirer. I had anticipated some sort of stripping scene, a woman tempting me with her body, but this was nothing of that kind. It seemed to be the way my admirer perceived me, glow and all. Flattering in its fashion but hardly realistic.

The me-figure strode on – and came into the neighbourhood of a veiled woman. This was evidently the admirer. In imagination, a person can, of course, be anything; the dumpiest of women may become the loveliest of damsels. Yet this one was neither beautiful nor seductive; she was concealed from head to toe by an all-encompassing shawl or poncho. She was merely there, standing silently.

The me-figure paused, orienting on this woman. Her chin lifted, the motion evident under the veil. And there it ended.

I turned off the projection and sat pondering. This was a love missive? Where was the incitement, the come-on?

And why had Shelia given it directly to me? There had to be more to this than was immediately apparent.

I played the scene again but perceived no further clues. This was simply a vision of admiration from afar, with no solicitation. Merely the me-figure becoming aware of the veiled woman. No erotic import at all.

I found myself intrigued by the very simplicity and brevity of it. It was like a fragment of a dream. I have a certain penchant for dreams or visions.

At last, privately cursing myself for my foolishness, I decided to answer it. There was plenty of room remaining on the chip; those things are good for up to an hour's recording. Some professional entertainments run to two or three or more chips. I simply invoked the recording feature of my helmet and picked up where the original scene left off.

The me-figure's glow reduced, for I did not see myself as supernatural. He contemplated the veiled woman for another moment, then stepped towards her. He extended his arms and embraced her.

I stopped it there. There was no point in pushing this too far; it was only a gesture. Even so, I realized that I probably shouldn't be doing it. The chip had simply intrigued me, so I hoped to intrigue it back; that was all.

I removed the updated chip and took it to Shelia. 'Return to sender,' I told her.

'You are rejecting it?'

'No, I am responding to it. Play it if you wish.'

'With your permission, sir.' She brought out a helmet, set it on her head, and inserted the chip.

I watched her face as she experienced the feelie but might as well not have bothered. The top half of her face was concealed, and her mouth was set in Standard Neutral. Shelia had been my secretary for a long time, and knew me well, both as employer and lover; she gave away nothing unless she chose to. There are those who suppose that a cripple is inadequate in more than the physical way, as I may have remarked before; Shelia was deceptive, because she acted with quiet caution, but, in fact, her mind was brilliant and her will was immovable. At first I had thought she could make a good executive secretary despite her handicap; very soon I knew that she was just about the best I could have chosen, on an absolute basis. Her physical handicap had prevented biased employers from considering her, so she had been available for me. That was my great fortune.

She removed the chip and the helmet. 'It will do, sir,' she said.

I smiled, dismissing the matter. The rush of other concerns caught us up again.

'I have worked out a basic programme,' Senator Stone-bridge advised me. 'I have cleared it with the other cabinet officers, including your daughter, who requires a great deal more funding for education. But the measures I propose will have such an impact on the planet – ' He shrugged.

'If the others have cleared it, I should have no objection,' I said. 'But perhaps you should summarize it for me, so that I'm not caught ignorant when the public reaction strikes.'

'By all means. The programme, in broadest outline, is to balance the budget by economizing on existing programmes and by bringing in new revenues – about half of each. The cuts come largely from the projected military allocations, in reductions of the generous military and civil servant retirement programmes, and virtual elimination of the government bureaucracy. There are presently more than two million government employees, with five major layers of authority, and the inefficiency and waste – ' He shook his head. 'Appalling. But there will be repercussions.'

'Against cutting waste?' I asked.

'The typical Navy careerist retires at age forty, with sextuple the benefits accruing to a civilian with commensurate service. He feels this is his right. The typical civil servant retires with triple the private sector benefits. Retired presidents have extremely generous settlements and perks.'

'They'll all be screaming,' I agreed. 'But my own Navy retirement benefits will be cut too.'

'They are not your primary source of sustenance,' he pointed out.

'True. But Faith will see that no one is reduced to poverty.'

'Sir, I'm not sure you grasp the potential reaction against such reductions. When the average person is hit in the pocketbook, he becomes – '

'I'll handle it,' I said, unconcerned. 'It is the job of the Tyrant to take the heat. You just do what you have to do.'

'Now, the revenue enhancement aspect is similarly difficult,' he said.

'Tax increase, you mean.'

'Not precisely. The present system is patently inequitable and is to be reformed and simplified. Naturally we shall be closing the loopholes, and this will cause a certain backlash – '

'To hell with the backlash!' I exclaimed. 'It's high time we had fair taxation!'

'Every person's definition of "fair" differs,' he said, 'and tends to be somewhat self-serving. For example, the elimination of the mortgage interest deduction – '

'Which means that the poor will pay more taxes,' I said, seeing it. 'What does Faith have to say about that?'

'We, ah, bargained,' he said. 'Your sister is an attractive and dedicated woman.' I realized with a start that Faith's initial considerable appeal for men had not entirely abated; Stonebridge had felt the impact. There was nothing serious in this, of course; this man was not about to dally with any Hispanic woman of any age. But evidently he had been satisfied to work things out with her, economically. 'She realizes that some sacrifices have to be made, in the interest of the greater good. Since one of the objectives we share is that of full employment at fair recompense – '

'Gotcha,' I said. 'She has to worry first about the people who have no homes to mortgage because they have no jobs. They will be glad to pay taxes on the interest they pay on mortgages, as long as their overall lot is improved.'

'Precisely. Now the actual mechanism for broadening the tax base includes a flat twenty-per cent rate on earned income, interest income excluded – '

'But didn't you just say that interest *would* be taxed?'

'If it is taxed when paid, it would be unfair to tax it again when received,' he explained. 'We propose to encourage savings and investment by eliminating all tax on interest earned. This will, of course, reduce one source of income for the government, but the resulting incentive to business – '

'Aren't you taking it from the poor and giving it to the rich?' I demanded.

He smiled with a trace of misgiving. 'Your sister also broached that question. In that sense, in that particular case, it might be possible to interpret it that way, as it is true that the rich do have more money to invest than do the poor. However, the importance of encouraging investment, in the interest of expanding business and generating jobs for everyone – '

'Faith doesn't mind if the rich get richer, so long as the poor get richer too,' I agreed.

'Actually the rich are not benefitting that much. We are implementing a currency change to eliminate the underground economy, and that will bring an enormous new segment of the economy into the tax base. Since many of the sheltered income and tax havens relate, this will result in considerably increased costs to the wealthy. I suspect the earliest protests we have will be from that quarter.'

'But how does changing the currency eliminate tax havens?'

He smiled. 'The new currency will be coded, so that its origin and location can be traced. When large amounts collect in one place and the tax for the transaction is not paid, our agents will, ah, pounce. I worked this out at Ms Phist's suggestion – '

'Roulette,' I said. 'Rue to her friends. She's a remarkable woman.'

'A remarkable woman,' he agreed. I was not certain whether he was thinking of her physical or her intellectual endowments. 'Her interest is in tracking the illicit sums involved in drugs and gambling, but we realized that this would also track other types of activity. I suspect that, for perhaps the first time in the history of Jupiter as a nation, the appropriate tax will be paid on virtually all earned income. On that basis the flat twenty per cent rate should bring in substantially more revenue than the prior graduated tax system did, though that went up to a fifty per cent rate. This, coupled with the five per cent VAT – '

'The five per cent what?'

'VAT. Value Added Tax. It has been used successfully for centuries on Uranus but not here on Jupiter. It is essentially a planetary sales tax, collected at every stage in segments, so that – '

'So, between the two, it will be a twenty-five per cent tax rate,' I said.

'Not precisely, because income and sales are not identical. The dynamics – '

'And this will eliminate the deficit and balance the budget?'

'Well, not as first. As with any venture, there are initial costs and qualifications. But once the system is in place, this is the objective.'

I wasn't satisfied. 'I told you I wanted the budget balanced! What's this about initial costs and qualifications?'

'Full employment is not achieved in a day. Not via the private sector. Admiral Phist estimates that it will take at least two years before the industrial base expands enough to accommodate the entire labour force. Until that time the government must be the Employer of Last Resort, and that means – '

'One hell of an expense for the unemployed,' I finished. 'Faith is really making you pay for that mortgage deduction!'

'Initially, yes. But the long-term trend is definitely healthy.'

I nodded. He knew what he was doing; my passion for the instant fix was misplaced. 'How does the gold standard relate?'

'Nothing permanent can be accomplished without a

stable currency. We expect to eliminate automatic raises, because we expect to eliminate inflation. The only sure way to do that is to back all of our currency with value, and that means metals and goods. A value-backed currency does not erode. With that certainty we can perhaps work marvels.'

I smiled. 'You're enjoying this, Senator!'

'I'm afraid I am, Tyrant,' he confessed. 'I have always wanted to see what could be accomplished with a genuinely competent administration.'

'Me too.' So far, it looked good.

'Sir.' Shelia had a call for me. 'Tocsin.'

Now it started. 'On,' I said shortly.

Tocsin's homely face appeared on the main screen. 'Tyrant, what the hell is this nonsense about cutting the allotments? Those were set up by Congress; they can't be touched!'

'I abolished Congress,' I reminded him. 'I am a dictator; I am bound by no prior governmental commitments.'

'Listen, we made a deal. You pardoned me. You can't start going after me now!'

'I'm not. These reductions apply to all civil service and military retirees at all levels. No one is exempted; there is now a single standard of retirement. Your predecessor has the same limit.'

'Kenson? He's getting no more than I do?' he asked, brightening.

'Slightly more, because he was in office longer. But no more than a retiree of similar level in the civilian sector.'

He became crafty. 'What happens when *you* retire, Hubris?'

'There is no provision for my retirement. I don't expect to collect any benefits.'

'You mean you plan to stay in power forever?' he demanded.

'No. I expect to be assassinated in due course.'

He started to laugh, then cut it off, staring at me, realizing that I was serious. He faded out.

Shelia caught my eye. She held a chip.

'What?' I asked, perplexed.

'Remember your anonymous girl friend? The veiled woman?'

'Oh,' I said, feeling inane. It had been a month or more – again, my memory is imprecise, for at that time I did not realize the significance of this correspondence, and the matter had faded from my awareness. Now memory brought another concern. 'This – something like this could be used to embarrass me. Maybe I shouldn't – '

She shook her head. 'This one can be trusted, sir.'

If Shelia said so, it was so. I put aside my concern.

I took the chip, and later, when I had a suitable break, I donned the helmet and turned on the scene.

I was back in the blurry chamber, watching the glowing me-figure. Though feelies like this are generated in the mind, they generally do show scenes from an anonymous third-party view, as if a camera were there. I think this derives from conventional holo technique, which portrays a person as being alone, though obviously someone is tracking him with a camera; we learn to suspend our logic for the sake of the story, and we imitate that technique in our fancy. It isn't necessary, just convenient.

The me-man spied the her-woman, strode across and took her in his arms. That was where I had left it; this reply refreshed my memory completely. What was her response?

The me-man bent his head to kiss her, and she tilted up her head to receive it, but the heavy veil was in the way. She drew back a little, raised her hand, and drew aside the veil so as to bare her face.

The me-man looked – and now the picture jumped, holo-style, to a close-up of her head.

Her face was blank. It was nothing more than a pink-white curvature of flesh without eyes, nose, or mouth. It resembled a dressmaker's dummy, the head a mere shape, because one did not, after all, measure a dress on a person's face.

There the scene ended. Jolted, I considered. Was this person trying to tease me? Somehow I doubted it; nothing in the sequence suggested humour. This is one thing about amateur scenes: they lack the cleverness of professional efforts so are more believable. Also, I was able to use my talent to read the woman a little. This may seem odd, but it is true. I read the minute physical reactions of people, normally unnoticed and uncontrolled, a constant signal-ling of their state of mind. Because they originate in the mind, these signals are transmitted to imaginary figures, and the body of this woman had them. Not lucidly but still suggestive of a most serious intent. She had, it seemed, a genuine passion for me. She was amateur, but she was not jesting.

Why, then, was her face blank? Not as a joke. It was more like an appeal. A blank to be filled in.

There it was. In life she might be a homely woman; certainly passion is not limited to the beautiful. She was afraid that her true face would turn me off, but she had no other. But in a feelie a person can be anything, and they generally do prefer to take advantage of that. Making a scene, as it is termed, is a dream-fulfilling business, where people can portray themselves as they would like to be, to the extent their imagination permits.

She wanted to be beautiful, obviously – but not in just

any way. She wanted to be the way I wanted her to be. Her dream was to be the realization of my dream.

This was a game I could play, except for one thing. There were only two faces I really desired. One was Megan's which I would not tolerate on any other woman; the other was Helse's.

Well, Helse had assumed the bodies of other women on occasion, to please me, as she could no longer do so with her own body. She could certainly assume *this* body.

Would it be right to do this? This was no purely personal vision of mine when my reality changed; this was an interactive vision, shared with an anonymous admirer. Well, if I were willing, and Helse were willing, and the woman wanted it, why not? It was, after all, limited to the helmet. It was only a kind of game.

Or was it?

I nudged that caution aside, intrigued by the possibilities. To have a living woman playing my lost love in the privacy of the helmet. What might come of that?

I gazed at the blank face and let my longing manifest. The face blurred and changed, and there was Helse's face. Helse, as she was at sixteen, when I had known her in life and loved her. As I still loved her.

Then I moved to kiss those precious lips. But I stopped just before the contact, for I wanted *her* to do it, to kiss me actively. Kissing a construct of imagination is like masturbation; it is better if there is truly another person, even if her appearance has been changed.

Roulette, for a change, was in an outfit that showed no cleavage. She wore a light green sweater and plaid skirt, like a college girl, and even had a green ribbon in her red hair. I discovered to my chagrin that she was every bit as sexy that way as she had been with the cleavage.

'The place to start,' she said briskly, 'is to legalize

everything possible. There is no point in wasting effort suppressing victimless crimes.'

'Like what?' I asked, trying not to look as she crossed her legs so that her skirt slid across her thighs.

'Gambling, drugs, sex, pornography.'

Indeed, such concepts came readily to my mind as I fought to bring my errant gaze under control. Those thighs! 'Porno is Thorley's problem; he's in charge of censorship.'

She laughed. That sweater! 'He's a rock-ribbed conservative! He hates porno almost as bad as he hates censorship. I'd like to watch him reviewing sex.'

'He'll simply ignore it,' I said. Would that I could do the same! 'But about the others – I know you have no case against gambling, but what of the casinos run by organized crime, which fleeces the clients and pays off the authorities?'

'Organized crime I mean to abolish. When it takes over gambling, then there's trouble, but the evil is in the crime, not the gambling. Keep it honest, it'll be all right.'

'But the compulsive gamblers who can't stop, who run themselves into monstrous debts – '

'Strictly cash,' she said. 'No credit, no IOUs. That keeps them to what they can afford. The truly sick ones can put up segments of their lives for rehabilitative treatment; they lose, they go in. Truly compulsive gambling is a disease; it can be treated, but the client has to be willing.'

She seemed to have her answers! But, of course, she was the daughter of a professional (and honest) gambler; this was her home turf. 'Drugs, then,' I said. 'Some of them devastate the human system. If we legalize them – '

'Make the drugs legal, the abuse illegal,' she said firmly. 'Most drugs are good and necessary for human health. A lot of the harm in drugs is *because* they are illegal. Drug addiction is the single greatest cause of chronic crime against property: addicts have to steal to get the money for their habit. With government clinics like those you had in Sunshine when you were governor, the money motive is gone and the crime stops. The rest is education: teach the people the truth about drugs, all drugs, what they do and what their abuse costs in health and independence. Most people will stay clear or at least stick to the relatively harmless ones. But any dangerous or addictive drug has to be given at the clinic; nobody doses himself or anyone else. There'll be some new addictions, sure, but there'll also be some who learn better at the clinic and never get addicted, when they would otherwise. Because they'll *see* the true addicts, coming in for theirs, and that will open eyes.'

'I don't know,' I said. 'Everyone knows the perils of alcohol addiction, but it progresses anyway.'

'Because they have unlimited access. They get soused, drive their bubble-cars, crack up, kill people – ' Her face hardened. 'We're going to get those drunk drivers out of the channels! Man kills another man, I don't care if he's drunk or crazy, I want him gone. Get all killers out of circulation, same as the hardened criminals.'

'We'd have to spend billions on new prisons!' I protested.

She frowned. 'Somehow I just knew you weren't going to want to put 'em out the space lock suitless,' she said. 'All right, you don't have to. Just guarantee that no killer will ever be free in the society again and I'll be satisfied; I don't care how you do it.'

'But – '

'Ask Gerald; he can work anything out. Just so long as we eliminate the repeat criminals of any type.'

I sighed, partly for the situation and partly for those

supremely fleshed legs. 'I expected you to solve my problems, not complicate them!'

'After more than twenty years you retain that delusion?' she inquired sweetly, spreading her legs. Damn her! She *knew* what she was doing to me!

'Which reminds me,' I said doggedly. 'Sex. It may be natural, but not when it's forced. You don't propose to legalize rape, do you?'

She laughed enthusiastically, causing her sweater to ripple. 'He remembers that day! And I thought he'd forgotten! Who says romance is dead?'

I had walked into that one. I had for the moment lost awareness of the fact that I had raped her according to the pirate ritual. I found myself blushing.

She shook her head. 'You're hopeless, Hope. God, I'd like to reenact that occasion!' She made as if to remove the sweater, and suddenly I knew that she wore no undergarment. No wonder it rippled! 'But I do know what you mean. Your typical humdrum civilized Jupiter woman doesn't care to get raped. For her I'd say voluntary sex is fine, but involuntary is a violation of her civil rights, and those who violate the civil rights of others should be taken promptly out of circulation.'

'More prisons!' I moaned. 'But you sound as though you think any voluntary sex is all right. What about children?'

She considered. 'Yes, there had better be an age of consent. But you know, some children like it. They –'

'No!' I snapped.

She sighed. 'You conservatives! Well, let's establish a realistic age of consent, say twelve or thirteen, that can be modified by a magistrate when warranted. When a girl grows woman's equipment, she's at the age of consent; that's easy enough to verify. Below that, there has to be legal approval.'

191

'And I thought I was a liberal,' I muttered.

'You're a bleeding heart,' she said. 'There's a difference.'

'Live and learn.'

'But you miss the point on rape,' she continued. 'You debate whether it is a crime of sex or a crime of violence, when, in fact, it is a crime of opportunity. If you jailed every man who would rape if he had a safe opportunity and ability, seventy per cent of the men and thirty per cent of the women would wind up behind bars. The only way to eliminate it is to restrict opportunity.'

'But we can't segregate all the men from all the women!' I protested.

'You assume that rape is strictly heterosexual. No, you can't eliminate it entirely, but you can liberalize society's attitude. After all, what is rape but a difference of opinion? The same act, consenting, is victimless; non-consenting, it is rape. If we make more women consenting, we'll have less rape.'

'That's preposterous!'

'That's practical,' she corrected me. 'Do you really want to solve the problems of Jupiter society or merely impose your moralism on it?' She drew up her sweater, showing her bare right breast. What a wonder! She was correct: if I were not constrained by social awareness, I would fling myself at her and rape her, as I had more than two decades before, knowing that she would welcome it. She was deliberately taunting me with her body, and it would be her victory if I succumbed.

I shook my head, bemused, my gaze locked exactly where she wanted it. 'Work out your programme, but consult with me before you implement it.'

She rose, inhaling. 'Anytime, Tyrant.'

* * *

There was another swell of outrage as the crime reforms were announced. Newsfaxes editorialized, condemning me roundly for encouraging promiscuity, child abuse, and drug addiction. One planetarily syndicated cartoon showed me naked, with erection and a hypodermic, pursuing a child. That stung, but I had to smile; the Tyrancy had legalized pornography, so such pictures were now quite legal.

The last laugh, though, was mine, for the statistics on crime showed a sharp drop. Part of this was, as my critics claimed, because many acts had been decriminalized, so no longer counted as crimes. But more of it was because we were systematically getting the habitual criminals out of society, and the drug addicts had no further incentive to commit crimes. We were, indeed, making the halls safe for the common folk.

It was only two weeks before the chip came back, and this time I remembered it immediately. Shelia held it up with a wry expression; naturally she had played it through, as it was her job to do, insuring that nothing directly harmful to me was in it. It was, of course, quite clear to her where the progression was leading, but she was understanding and tolerant, knowing that she herself had gone farther with me than this anonymous woman was ever likely to.

This time the initial scene had been modified slightly. The me-figure glow had been diminished, in accordance with my prior tailoring of it, and my appearance was closer to the reality. The veiled woman was also more sharply drawn, as if she had more confidence now that she had a face. When she parted the veil, Helse's face was clear and animated.

My face came down, and our lips touched. But hers were not properly responsive. They were there but quite inexperienced. It was as though she had never kissed before.

No, it was something else. Her lips were there only as my expectation; they had no substance apart from that. Well, substance, but not reaction. It was like kissing a woman who had no knowledge I was there, as if I were a ghost.

I broke the kiss and considered. Well, I had expected expertise and was mistaken. This woman had a passion for me but not experience in seducing men. She was *not* Helse, regardless of the image.

Again I considered. Feelie helmets were sophisticated devices with properties that unsophisticated users could readily overlook. Obviously this woman did not realize that there were potential multiple tracks and had confined herself to one. That meant that she could craft a scene as perceived by a camera or as viewed by one participant or the other, but could not merge the two. For true interaction such merging was essential. So her kiss was what she thought I should feel but inadequate because she didn't *know* what I should feel.

I could correct that. All that was required was some simple instruction – in the use of the helmet.

I drew back. 'Woman,' I said in English, 'I must show you something.' Then I pictured myself with a feelie helmet on. 'This setting is for one viewpoint,' I explained, touching the appropriate place on the helmet. 'Normally it should be for the third-party impressions. This is the one you have been using. This setting is for a second viewpoint.' I touched the next. 'Normally you should use it for your own impressions – the way you personally see and feel. You have not been using this. Set it this way' – I had the third-party camera pan in close, so the detail was clear – 'and it will continuously record your impressions without your conscious effort. And this setting' – I showed

194

the third – 'this is for a third viewpoint. You should leave this one alone. *I* will use it for my impressions.'

I removed the helmet in the scene, and it disappeared. 'Now what do we have?' I inquired rhetorically. 'We have channel three, recorded by me, for me. We have channel two, recorded by you, for you. And we have channel one, recorded and modified by both of us, so it is a composite camera-eye picture.'

I paused, then spoke again. She had never spoken in the scene, which probably meant that she hadn't realized that it was possible. If a person recorded the mental pattern consistent with the effort of formulating certain words, that recording would reproduce as the formulated words. 'Now, those three channels are not the whole scene,' I continued. 'They do not provide proper interaction. For that we need a special modification. When I kiss you, I need to feel not what I expect to feel but what you arrange for me to feel physically. Otherwise I am kissing a ghost. I must feel your reaction to my action or it becomes nothing.'

I caused the helmet to reappear. 'It works like this. After you have recorded your impressions on your channel, you do some recording on my channel, using this special setting that augments mine without erasing it. You place there the impressions you want me to experience. So when I kiss you, your lips must kiss back. That's there on my channel, so that when I do kiss you, I feel what you have prepared for me to feel. Similarly I will set it up for you on your channel. With the two together' – I spread my hands – 'a great deal can be experienced, when a scene is properly crafted. But it requires careful attention and work by both parties.'

I caused the helmet to fade out again. It had been a long time since I had really played with one of these devices, and I enjoyed showing off my expertise. 'Now, obviously there is a problem here,' I said, in a kind of lecture. 'How can I provide my reaction to something you haven't yet put in the scene? Well, there are two ways. First, I can react to what you have already put in the scene, and you can replay that section and get a more accurate notion of the total effect. But that can be tedious. Second, I can anticipate what you might do and prepare for that. Of course, that can lead to peculiar effects. Let's say I anticipate that if I kiss you, you will kiss back. But, in fact, you slap my face. Then, when I kiss you, I will instead feel the slap. That would be a funny kiss! Or you might slap me, and I would feel your lips kissing. The viewpoints have to integrate. So here we go into a slightly computerized function built into the helmets. This insures that a given action meets with an appropriate response. So if I kiss you, you either kiss back or slap me but not both – or if both, at least one at a time. If I do something you have not anticipated, so that you have prepared no response, then it becomes dead stick – like your present kiss. That means you have to go back and prepare an appropriate set of responses, so we can go on from there. It is, in its fashion, like a chess game, wherein each player must consider the various possible responses to the move he makes and prepare for them. Of course, he can't go too far; normally he sets up only a single, negative response to an action by the other party that he doesn't want and a number of more positive responses to actions he does want. When two people have a similar course in mind, the scene can go quite far before being returned for more input.'

I paused again. I didn't worry that this was too much information for a helmet novice; she could play the scene over and over until she understood. 'Now I will prepare several alternatives, which the helmet will automatically key in according to their types; this is a function of this special interactive mode. You may explore them and then prepare your own sets of responses. I suspect that our next exchange of chips will be more interesting.'

Then I set up my scenelets. In one, I kissed her, her lips were closed, and it was a long, quiet contact. I planted in her channel the pressure of my hands at her back and my arms encircling her. In another, her lips parted, and I planted the feel of my tongue passing through my own lips to touch hers. In another, she turned a bit, and my left hand slid down to cup her right buttock through the material of her voluminous cloak. In yet another, she resisted, drawing back her head as I approached, and I paused, then let her go and turned away without kissing her. Nothing was forced here; she had to select the alternative in order to experience it, and she could cut it off at any time simply by turning off the helmet. In each of the cases I also prepared the appropriate camera-view sequence. The kissing ones were similar and really didn't need modification, but the turning away one did.

Satisfied, I returned the chip to Shelia for shipment. I discovered that I had expended two hours; the time had flown!

8

Helmet Sex

'Yes, I have answers,' Phist said. Evidently his wife had already advised him of my misgivings about the elimination of criminals. 'Where feasible, there must be restitution; where not, elimination.'

'How can there be restitution for murder?' I demanded.

'An eye for an eye, a tooth for a tooth, a life for a life; it can be done literally. We can continue to execute murderers.'

'How can killing ever be justified?' I asked, troubled. 'To execute a murderer – that doesn't bring the victim back, it just makes two people dead. That's no good!'

'There was a time when you seemed to feel otherwise,' he reminded me gently.

'I killed,' I said. 'I never liked it.'

'A decade or two with a gentle woman has nevertheless had its effect on you.'

'And has two decades with a violent woman affected you?' I returned.

He smiled. 'Perhaps. But to address the present problem: there is use, within industry, even for murderers. Inclement assignments. I suspect we can absorb all the murderers you can provide, and a number of lesser criminals.'

I knew he wasn't bluffing. 'Tell me how.'

'In deep space there are posts that few accept voluntarily. Guard duty on remote planetoids of the Belt, the Charon tour, close Solar duty, that sort of thing. Men don't like being sterilized by the radiation of their working environment, or being exposed to a fifty per cent risk of death, or being left alone for months at a time. A criminal would not like it, either, but would not be in a position to protest this as punishment. He either performs appropriately or he spends the rest of his life in deep space, isolated from all other human contact.'

Now I remembered: Roulette had mentioned this alternative, and I approved it. In the rush and stress of events, it had entirely slipped my mind.

I pondered. I thought of being confined alone in space myself, and I knew I would shortly go mad. Only the promise of restoration of human company would sustain me. Even the least social criminals would feel that lack to some extent. Yes, the criminal would perform!

'Maybe so,' I agreed. 'It does avoid the brutal alternatives of killing or letting criminals back into society, and it does seem to be a way to get personnel for inclement assignments. I'm glad these intra-cabinet consultations are working out so well.'

'They are working,' Phist agreed. 'But these are the halcyon days of creation; implementation may be another matter. There is apt to be a massive reckoning when the tide touches the public.'

'I assumed this post to do a job, and I mean to do it,' I said. 'The people should understand, when the new order emerges. It is for their own good.'

He smiled warily. 'Do you remember my fortune in the Navy?'

I realized he was not referring to his recent rise to the heights. 'As – a whistleblower?'

'The same. It was my job to procure equipment for the Navy as economically as possible, for a given standard of performance and quality. I discovered that we had been paying a hundred thousand dollars for a hundred and ten dollars worth of spare parts. We were being charged $9,606 for wrenches that could be had for twelve cents on the civilian market. Antenna motor pins worth about two and a half cents were going for over two thousand dollars. Thirteen-cent bolts for one thousand – '

'Now wait,' I protested. 'How can a thirteen-cent nut go for twice as much as a sixty-seven-cent bolt? I mean – '

'I refer you to the ancient saying: The Navy moves in mysterious ways, its blunders to perform.'

I smiled. 'I remember.'

'Naturally I put a stop to such purchases and instituted an investigation. And – '

'You were fired,' I finished. 'Or put on Navy hold. Same thing. That was why I, as an upstart young officer, was able to leapfrog you on promotion and eventually add you to my command.'

'Where you gave my talent for effective procurement free rein and protected me from the backlash and did my career more good than ever would have been the case otherwise,' he said warmly. 'All this in addition to your sister.'

'You were worthy of Spirit,' I said honestly. 'She would gladly have stayed with you, if that had been possible. Just as I would have stayed with Rue.'

We were silent for a moment, remembering our past loves.

'My point,' Phist resumed in due course, 'is that virtue is not always rewarded. You may install the best of all possible governments, but you will not necessarily be hailed for your achievement.'

'I am already in the process of discovering that,' I said, emulating one of Thorley's rueful smiles. 'Still, it will be worth doing. I swore when I was fifteen to extirpate piracy from the face of the System. I found as I proceeded that there was always a higher source of the corruption. Now I am in a position to complete my vow – and to fulfil the other one I took: to put Jupiter's financial base in order. Success will be its own reward.'

'If success comes,' he agreed with the caution of experience, 'I have a rather challenging programme.'

'Implement it,' I told him.

'Don't authorize it until you know its nature,' he warned. 'I feel it may well be an exercise in futility to attempt to regulate anything as massive and fragmented as Jupiter industry. Over the centuries the government has not been able to get an accurate accounting from any of the large iron companies, let alone effectively police their operations, and I see only one way to achieve any of that now.'

I knew about the iron companies. They had grown rich and powerful in fair times and foul, because they controlled the single most vital substance in the System: the magnetic-power metal, iron. Without it our mechanized civilization would grind to a halt. The metal was intrinsically inexpensive, but somehow its value magnified by the time it reached the black-hole labs for conversion to contra-terrene iron. The same magnets could handle CT iron, moving it without physical contact with any terrene matter, until the time came for its merging with normal iron and total conversion to energy. There was our literal power base: iron. Of course, the key was in its conversion to CT, which was accomplished by the enormous concentration of gravitrons by very special gee-shields. Those artificial black holes could convert any matter to antimatter -- this was a fairly straightforward operation, so long as the change was to the same type of substance, which is to say tin to tin or iron to iron – but not just any matter could be handled magnetically. So far, all things considered, nothing better had been found than iron. 'So how do you propose to make the iron companies behave?'

'Nationalization,' he said seriously.

I sighed. 'Saturn nationalized everything, and look

what they have: the System's most monstrously inefficient industry! With the most massive farm bubbles extant, they still can't feed their own population and have to purchase grain from us. Apart from their military machine, they are a second-rate industrial power. I can't see any particular promise in that route.'

'It is not nationalization that is at fault but deprivation of individual incentive,' he reminded me. 'I mean to keep incentive. What I propose to do is nationalize at least one major company in each key aspect of industry and revitalize that company so that it can become truly competitive. This will accomplish two things: first, it will give the government, for the first time, an avenue to ascertaining the true nature of the business, from which we can extrapolate an honest tax base for Senator Stonebridge to implement; second, it will enable us to enter the market competitively, forcing restraint in pricing by example.'

'How can we control prices by example?' I asked. 'We can control the prices of the companies we operate but not those of the ones we don't.'

'If the others raise their prices in an unjustified manner, ours will gain a larger share of the market,' he explained. 'For centuries the Big Iron has colluded to increase the price of crude ore, overcharging clients and cheating the government unmercifully; but *our* iron company would not cooperate. It will represent a gap in the dyke. No consumer company is going to pay more than it needs to for iron, and we shall offer a fair price – and the lowest price, if need be. This is the essence of free enterprise; we shall bring it to iron at last – without any direct government coercion. Prices will drop across the board, I am certain.' He actually rubbed his hands together.

I liked the notion. 'Which companies do you have in mind for nationalization?'

'The Planetary Iron Company,' he said.

'Planico? I thought that was the one large iron company in trouble!'

'True. With annual revenues in the billions, they managed their affairs so disastrously that they were the subject of an attempted takeover by a competitor. Their reserves are as good as any, but their present management is so wrong headed as to be laughable.'

'Surely it would be better to take over a sound company!'

'No. Two reasons. First, we can acquire Planico relatively cheaply, merely by buying up a bare majority of their stock at the present devalued rate; no one will even realize we're doing it, until it is done, if we handle it correctly. It really will be best not to disturb the economy by drastic overt takeovers; the senator satisfied me on that score. Second, we can make our point better by turning an ailing company into a healthy one than by keeping a healthy one healthy. If our management is good, we'll wind up with the best-run company on the planet, regardless.'

The notion appealed as it came clear to me. 'Selective nationalization,' I repeated. 'Of ailing companies in various sectors of the economy. I wonder if this will help provide jobs for the unemployed.'

'No. We'll be firing inefficient employees. There will have to be a planetary work programme for Employment of Last Resort. That will be expensive.'

'But if the work programme trained people to fill the jobs in the nationalized companies?'

'Then we could hire them. Of course, if they're really qualified, they could be hired by the private companies too.'

'Maybe there could be training branches of the nationalized companies, so that we could slowly convert the unemployed to employable – '

'That could do,' he agreed.

If the poor had protested the seeming raising of taxes, while the rich had been silent, the nationalization of key companies reversed that reaction. The billionaire scions of industry were virtually unanimous in their outrage, while the unemployed folk flocked eagerly to apply for jobs in the nationalized companies. Evidently they regarded this as much preferable to the make-work employment the government would otherwise provide. A lot of hiring was done, but this saved the government no money. It merely changed the pocket from which the money leaked.

The hiring of the poor was counterbalanced by the flight of the highly trained technical personnel. The majority of them seemed to regard working for a government-owned company as anathema. Perhaps the standardized wage scales had something to do with it. Our scales were not actually inferior to those of private enterprise, but there were no perks – no unofficial benefits that avoided the tax rolls. Also, though private industry was by law equal opportunity for all races and ages and both sexes, somehow that did not manifest perfectly in practice, while the government companies truly did operate by merit alone. That seemed to upset many qualified workers.

The next time Shelia handed me the chip, she pursed her lips in a silent whistle. Evidently she was enjoying this in a certain voyeuristic way. Well, she had a right to.

My instruction had had dramatic efffect. Now all three major channels were in use, and the detail was much improved. The action was unchanged up to the point of the kiss.

I took her in my arms, as before, and brought my lips to hers. This time she did kiss back, passionately, her lips parting for my tongue. Her body pressed close to mine, and I felt her breasts nudging me. When my hand slipped down to her buttock, her buttock twitched in acknowledgement.

Well, now. Obviously she had understood my words and taken pains to master the helmet. The seduction that had been lacking before was now present; she evidently wanted my hands on her body.

I experimented. After the kiss I looked at her Helse-face – and that face still stirred me deeply, though I knew it wasn't her – and asked in English, 'Will you remove your cloak?'

She had anticipated this. She shimmered, and the cloak was gone. Evidently she liked the magical effect I had demonstrated with the appearing and disappearing helmet. Feelies are fantasy worlds; anything can happen in them. That is much of their appeal.

Underneath she wore only a red bra and panties. Her hair descended to her shoulders in the manner that Helse's had at the end. Her body was voluptuous; it had evidently been crafted from the contemplation of holos of lush starlets. There were nuances about it that satisfied me that it was not her own; the natural body signals were absent. Still, my curiosity led me to experiment further.

I reached out and touched her full bra. She did not shrink away. Instead the bra dissolved, leaving her bosom bare. But her breasts did not sag, as masses of that magnitude should; they remained supported. I had suspected as much.

I touched her panties. They too, dissolved, showing her genital region – quite innocent of pubic hair, in the manner of holo stories but not of real women.

I paused again. It was evident that this woman was willing to go as far as I might wish, in the holo. Indeed, I understand that in some circles this is the preferred mode of lovemaking, as the protagonists remain technically uninvolved, true to their spouses or whatever. A spouse who might be quite jealous of his partner's physical affair with another individual might accept the holo version with equanimity and even participate in it. Physical purity was evidently more important than emotional purity. Perhaps it was ever thus; what man was ever really certain of what passed through the mind of his woman? The feelies merely made it more evident.

However, this was not the real woman. Her face was that of Helse, her body that of some holo representation. Even in imagination I preferred more reality than this.

So I stood back. 'We must talk,' I said.

'Talk,' she said hesitantly.

So she had anticipated this too. Good enough. 'What we do here in the helmets, on this chip, has no legal force in the real world. It is only a shared fantasy. But even so, I prefer greater realism than we have here. I'll let you keep that face, for I understand your desire for anonymity, even though I myself am not anonymous. But the body – that isn't natural. Is there anything wrong with your own body?'

'My body . . . is not . . . this good,' she said hesitantly. Her voice had a peculiar quality, as if she were having trouble registering it for the recording. All she needed to do was to speak aloud and the helmet would pick up the essential impulses; evidently she was trying to do it entirely by imagination, and that's tricky.

'Well, enhance it a little,' I said. 'But start with your own, as it is, so that your flesh responds naturally when you move it.'

She did not respond; she had not anticipated this answer, so had not programmed for it. Still, we had made considerable progress.

* * *

'Hitherto,' Mondy said, 'certain insiders have had their hands on the levers of economic power. We must now assume control of those levers.'

'Isn't that paranoid?' I asked. 'Blaming the problem of society on mysterious, anonymous culprits?'

'It is paranoid,' he agreed. 'But also true. These few people have always played the economy like a game, constantly milking it for their own benefit. The only barriers to their complete success are the unpredictable vagaries of chance and their inability to unite for their common advantage.'

'Just what do you propose to do with these people? If they aren't criminals – '

'Recruit them,' he said. 'They will in the future work for us instead of for themselves. This will have an enormous impact on the economy.'

'But surely they won't simply cooperate!' I protested.

'They will if they understand that the alternative is extinction.'

'But – '

'Tyrant, what kind of a game do you think we're in? These are not marbles we're playing with, and these people are not school children. We need them, and we won't get them unless we talk their language. They are sensible; when they see that we have the will and the power to eliminate them, they will elect to cooperate. We simply have to do what is necessary, at the outset. Otherwise the Tyrancy will be a joke.'

He had spoken magic words. Reluctantly I gave him the go-ahead.

'The key is Machiavelli,' he concluded. 'The infamous Italian schemer. It is safer to be feared than loved.'

'I'd rather be loved,' I said, and it was not really a joke.

'Be loved by the common, ignorant people. Appearance is more important to them than substance. You must seem to possess the classic virtues of mercy, faith, integrity, humanity, and religion. Then they will be satisfied.'

'I *do* have these things!' I exclaimed.

'Of course, Tyrant. Just don't take them too seriously.'

I left him, disquieted. I trusted his judgement but not his cynicism.

Ebony shook her head. 'It's not just Jupiter,' she said. 'Overpopulation is threatening to overwhelm the whole System. Earth itself has more people now than it did before the diaspora to the System. We don't have to worry about System War Three; our own numbers will do us in in another generation regardless.'

'But we can't do anything about the population of other planets,' I said.

'Tyrant, we *have* to! Every day thousands more cross over from RedSpot and from Callisto – '

'I'm an immigrant from Callisto,' I reminded her.

'And if they had proper government there, you wouldn't have had to do it,' she retorted, unfazed. 'Your folks would have been okay and you'd have been happy. It all starts with population control, so nobody gets squeezed out.'

'Could be,' I agreed, impressed. It was not exactly the way I saw it, but she did have a case that could be argued.

'But how do you propose to solve the population problems of other planets?'

'Same way as here. Start with contraception – put your Navy medicine in the civilian water, or the food, or the air, so no more children for a couple of years. Then ease

208

up selectively; give the neutralizer to only those families who are good prospects for good, healthy children.'

'But no one would agree to that,' I cried, half appalled, half intrigued.

'Who said they had to? Just do it. You're the Tyrant.'

'There'd be a revolution!'

'Not while you control the Navy. They'd settle down soon enough.'

'I never realized you were so cynical, Ebony.'

'I wasn't – till I studied the problem. Then I saw what had to be done. We've got to control our population or it will destroy us; it's that simple.'

'But other planets – '

'The countries of Latin Jupiter will do it if you make them a bargain. Carrot and stick – give them money, give them food – tell 'em why. They'll do it, and it won't take much pushing. They're hurting a lot worse than we are.'

'I don't know,' I said. 'It's such an ugly policy.'

'Would you rather line 'em up and laser 'em down? We can pass out euthanasia pills – effective, painless, work in a few hours if no antidote taken – but we really need to get it at the other end, the birthrate. We can impose the death penalty for every little crime, but it's better if the criminal is never born.'

'But it's a fundamental right to reproduce!'

'Is it? Does every individual have the unlimited right to make babies, whether or not he can care for them? If he can't take care of them, does the government have to do it for him? Or should they just be allowed to starve? In some places they have forcible abortion, sterilization, and they kill girl babies. They also murder the old folk and the ill folk. You want that?'

'No!' I said. 'But we need to take time to consider – '

'Tyrant, we're out of time. The problem is now. We can't wait for the people to get around to doing something about it; they never will. If we don't act now, population will wipe us out all too soon.' She stared into my face. 'Tyrant, we've got to act now, while it can still be halfway gentle. You know that.'

'I *don't* know that!' I protested. But inside, I did.

There was a longer interval before the next chip returned. I wondered whether my anonymous woman had had second thoughts, being too shy to present her own body to me, even if enhanced. Well, it had been a nice diversion. Certainly I did not need to expend time on foolishness of this nature.

When it showed up, I knew by my own reaction that my interest was greater than I had let myself believe. There was something about this woman, perhaps her quality of naïveté, that intrigued me. Also, I realized that I did, after all, need this type of diversion. My tenure as Tyrant was becoming increasingly restrictive, both physically and intellectually; I could neither go freely out in public, lest I get assassinated, nor readily solve the problems of the society. Everywhere I turned, the barriers were formidable and complex, not admitting any simplistic answers. So I needed simplistic relief and distraction, much as a child needs candy or fairy tales as a counterpoint to grim reality. This exploration of love and sex with the anonymous woman, an enjoyable challenge that had no substance, risk-free – this was helping me to cope with the rest of my situation. Pleasure without responsibility – what a treasure that can be!

I played the scene. It went through the kiss. Then she removed her cloak and stood before me much less fully endowed but also far more natural. When I touched her undergarments, they dissolved, as before, but now her breasts had human nipples and human heft, and her cleft had down.

I paused. This was only a feelie, not real, yet on a certain level it was real enough. Did I really want to do this? Did she? I had possessed many women in my day, but she had evidently possessed no men.

I asked her. 'You have offered your body to me. Are you sure you want to do this?'

'Yes,' she said. I realized that this simple answer could have been keyed to any number of potential suggestions. Still, it did seem to be what she wanted: to make love to the Tyrant. After that act was completed on the chip, I might never hear from her again; if so, that was the way it had to be.

'Then I will show you my body,' I said. I disrobed, carefully, so that she could protest if she wished to. She merely stood there and watched.

When I was naked, my member expanded and became erect, ready for the act. Then, yet again, I paused. There had not been sufficient reaction on her part; this could be beyond what she had programmed for. 'Do you know what this is?' I asked.

'I have not seen . . .' she said hesitantly.

Never seen a man naked? An erect organ? This was too risky. I decided to postpone the act. 'Consider and prepare,' I told her. 'If you still wish to do it, we shall do it next time.'

Then I prepared some alternatives for her to explore at her leisure: the feel of a firm member pushing into her orifice, of a male body pressing her down, of a mouth at her breast. Increasingly I suspected that she had not engaged in any kind of sexual act before, not even hugging and kissing, and I did not want to overwhelm her. I did make an attempt to complete the act with her and found that while she lay down on her back at my command, she did not otherwise cooperate; she really

211

didn't know what came next. So I erased that sequence; it was indeed too soon for it.

The population control measure stirred up literal riots. The Navy had to move in to restore order in a dozen cities, and quite a number of people were shipped out to space. When we announced that anyone caught committing vandalism against property in the name of reproduction would be permanently barred from restoration of such rights, the violence abated, but it was evident that much bad feeling remained. It seemed that the people wanted me to solve the problems of society but did not want to be personally touched by the necessary measures. My sympathy for the common man was diminishing in the face of this hypocrisy. Had they really expected to breed without limit, while the government covered all costs of child care and good employment for all the offspring?

Actually they could enjoy children via the helmet too. There were chips available that covered all the details of child rearing, so the population could be controlled without depriving families of the experience of having children – just the reality. But, of course, that wasn't enough.

The next tape showed how correctly I had judged her. She knew almost nothing of actual sexual expression, not even what was available on the more graphic holos. She had led a sheltered life. She was willing and eager but ignorant. I would have to take her through it step by step.

First I did what I should have done earlier: I explained it to her verbally. I described how a man and a woman came together, how she spread her legs and he set his organ carefully in her. Then I set out to demonstrate.

I had her lie on the bed that appeared in the scene,

naked, while I approached with my erect member and ran my hands over her body. She had improved that body greatly; now the flesh felt as it should. But when I mounted her from above, she did not respond properly; her legs remained closed. I realized that she still did not realize the extent to which her cooperation was necessary. I ran my hands along her thighs and tried to separate them, but there was no response.

Again I paused to consider. I had grown accustomed to experienced women and took certain things for granted. This woman had no sexual experience. Perhaps that was why she had come to me, via the helmet: she wanted to learn at the hands of a public figure she respected, one who was reputed to be very good with women. Then she could apply that knowledge to real life and suffer few, if any, of the false starts and errors that inexperience brought. It did make sense.

I remembered Juana, my first roommate in the Navy, some thirty-five years before. A lovely girl who was terrified of sex because she had been raped, yet who had to get through it because of inflexible Navy policy. How had I handled that?

'Let me show you a different way,' I told my helmet woman. 'One that requires less of you. I will describe it to you now, and the next time we can do it.'

I told her to lie on her right side and draw up her legs. 'I will embrace you from behind and enter you in the normal manner. You will feel my legs against the backs of yours, and my left arm will circle your body so that my hand can caress your breasts. I will go into you slowly; there will be no discomfort. Do not be concerned about being a virgin; here in the helmet there need be no complications.'

I continued to describe the expectations, so that she

213

would have no surprise, and would be able to accommodate me in anything I might do that she chose to accept.
This is easier to do when limited to a single position. I
tried to describe what her feeling of me inside her should
be, but, of course, this was difficult. I couldn't act it out,
because I lacked the feminine anatomy. Finally I drew on
my long-ago memory of one of the reverse-role chips, in
which a male could experience the sensations of the
female during the act and projected the memory as clearly
as I could.

I returned the chip to Shelia. What she would think of
the content I could not say. But she did know me well
enough to accept it.

My memory suggests that only a few days later the
chip returned, but either it was longer or there were
intermediate missives that my recollection has compressed
into a single episode. Again it hardly matters; the essence
is accurate. I was eager to don the helmet; my secret
romance with this anonymous woman had quite taken my
fancy. Perhaps it was the novelty of introducing her to
sex, which is a special type of pleasure for a man. The
nervous excitement of her learning process fed back to
me, making the familiar become new.

I played through the routine opening sequence, then
got her on the bed. She assumed the position I had
described, and I got on the bed beside her and brought
my member into play. Her flesh was ready, responsive,
and wet where I positioned myself for entry. I advanced
slowly, and she had keyed in the crossover tactiles so that
the distinction between this and reality was not great. I
moved into her all the way, and my hand took hold of
her left breast and squeezed it gently. Oh, yes, this was
good!

Then her vaginal muscles clenched. Surprised, I thrust,

and suddenly we were in the culmination, moving almost together, thrust and clench and squeeze. Very soon I jetted into her . . . and then the scene ended, and I realized I had soiled my trousers. This is a consequence of careless use of the helmet; I should have taken a precaution.

I removed the helmet, took a shower, and changed my clothing. Then I returned to the helmet and played through the alternatives. She had indeed learned well; we completed the act in several slight variances.

But though she had reacted well, she had not actually climaxed; careful study satisfied me on that. So I explained what I contemplated for the next occasion and told her how to accommodate it, so that she, too, could experience the thrill of culmination. I complimented her on what she had done so far and invited her to play through my personal channel to verify the joy she had brought me. There are ways in which feelie sex is better than the reality, and this is one of them: the partners can actually feel each other's pleasure. I had recorded a formidable dose of it this time, and it only excited me further to realize that her first experience of orgasm might be mine. Later I would have the special pleasure of feeling hers.

Faith was now fifty-three, but her recent years of service to the community had revitalized her, and she was indeed a beautiful woman again.

'Full employment is easier said than done,' she said earnestly. 'Many who are called unemployed are actually migrant labourers – '

'We want to take proper care of them,' I said firmly. 'I spent a year as one myself; I know their lot.'

'Fair wages and fair working conditions will do them

the most good. Another group of the poor is the home-
less; people who used to exist comfortably enough until
rising rents forced them into the halls to become drifters,
shopping-bag ladies, and such. Give them decent housing
and they can become productive again.'

'Housing for all,' I agreed.

'And the women with children,' she continued. 'They
can't work because they have to stay home with the
children, but they *want* to work, and *would* work, if they
had proper day care for those children.'

'Day care, definitely,' I agreed.

'And the ill – physically and mentally. If the handicapped are hired for suitable positions, they can be self-
supporting, and the mental cases can be got out of the
passages – '

I thought of Shelia. Certainly the handicapped could
be effective workers! 'Why aren't the mentally ill in
institutions?' I asked.

'They were, but it was too expensive to maintain them,
so as an act of generosity, they were returned to society.
That means they wander the halls, panhandling, and they
sleep in the crannies of storage chambers. Most are
harmless, but shopkeepers don't like them because of the
thefts – '

'But they can work productively?'

'If the right jobs are provided. Many are of low
intelligence, but for them, routine jobs that would bore
normal people to distraction could be fine. Some would
need to work in confinement, but they could still operate
computers. Some of them have minds that resemble
computers, actually.'

'Like Amber,' I murmured.

'The child who translates for you? Yes. If we make a
diligent effort, we can put many of these people to useful

work, and they will be better off for it.' She glanced at her notes. 'We'll have to do something about racism.'

'Racism causes poverty?'

'Indirectly. It tends to isolate minorities and reduce their employment opportunities. Blacks and Hispanics can become ghettoized, and their rates of unemployment – '

'Deal with racism,' I agreed. 'But I'm not quite sure how.'

'Education,' she said firmly.

'Hopie's department,' I said. 'I hope that doesn't overwhelm her.'

'She's a bright girl; she'll think of something. Now another class of poverty is the prostitutes – '

'The what?'

'Most of them are only in for economic reasons; if they had any better way to earn a living, they'd take it.' She smiled. 'I happen to know the route. Roulette agrees. She means to decriminalize sex. Provide decent jobs for those women, so they don't *have* to look for money that way. The minority who really do like that sort of work can get jobs at what she calls the civilian Tail. No more hallwalking.'

'That should do it,' I agreed. 'But I don't know how we can stop some from hallwalking if they decide to pick up some extra income.'

'No need. They can do what they want. But they won't be forced to for economic reasons, and the men will know that they can get it at a set price in the Tail, so there won't be much demand. No hundred-dollars-a-night stuff, unless the girl is something special. Now we come to the problem – '

'The problem,' I repeated, dreading what it might be.

'The major problem of poverty is health. Either health care is so expensive that it impoverishes ordinary people, or the poor are dying because they can't afford it. Now, we could provide free health care for all . . .'

'The Senator has already braced me on that,' I said. 'Health care now costs ten per cent of the gross planetary product, and is rising towards fifteen per cent.'

'And it's not really helping,' she agreed. 'Free care is not making folks healthier; they continue with their unhealthy habits and let the state pick up the tab for the consequence. Stonebridge tells me that half of all the medical costs of the average person's life occur in the final year. Now, if we could just cut off that year – '

'How can we know when a person's final year is starting?'

'I hashed this out with Stonebridge,' she said. 'We agreed that some people are better risks than others. If we consider age, general health, and life-style, we can get a pretty good notion when expenses are going to mount. Or we could simply set a cap: when any person uses up the allowance for free care, that's it, and he's on his own. That seems fair.'

'That seems callous,' I said. 'I expected you to argue the other side.'

'I *did* argue the other side, but Stonebridge showed me that we could do a lot more good for many more poor people if we put a cap on calamitous medical expense and used the money to help those who could benefit most by small amounts. If we use Ebony's euthanasia pills for the terminal cases . . .' She shrugged. 'I must confess, things do look different when you're trying to solve the whole problem instead of pushing one particular view. The greatest good for the greatest number – it does make sense.'

'If we have a set limit,' I pointed out, 'some bright young man might have an accident and go over, and have to die, when just a little more money would have paid to make him fit for forty more years of productive service, while an idle old man who has been lucky might be saved.'

'A limit to state care,' she said. 'If an employer wanted to pay for extra care for a good employee, that would be satisfactory.'

'Could be,' I agreed, not entirely satisified. We were coming to difficult decisions.

The helmet affair continued thereafter with increasing sophistication. Every few days the chip would arrive, and it always meant a new position or a new variation, wonderfully detailed. My anonymous woman had become a very fine lover, always eager to please me and herself. She learned to use her hands to excellent advantage, and her mouth, and to accommodate my hands and mouth in phenomenal ways.

We mastered all the positions I could think of, and many variations. Sometimes we did it fast, sometimes slow; we filled up a second chip, and a third, saving all the versions. That's another thing about a feelie: long after the initial episode, you can play it again and again. After a while the familiarity dulls it, but still, it is much better than nothing. I understand that some men – and women – have saved their early feelie recordings for decades and played them back in sequence when old and unable to perform similarly. Via the feelie, a luscious young wife can remain that way forever. Naturally all this was available on the porno market, but there is a special quality to the scene of your own loved one, and of one you have actually experienced.

I tried to talk with her on occasion. 'You have never given me a name,' I complained. She only smiled, preferring to retain anonymity. She would not talk politics or anything of substance; she merely expressed her love of, and joy in, me. She thought I was a wonderful person and a wonderful lover. I found this easy enough to take; I was now in my fifties and knew she was young, perhaps twenty, and her continuing interest was very flattering.

'But you must go to your real life,' I cautioned her. 'You have now mastered sex and are ready for marriage or whatever relationship you choose.'

'I am satisfied with you,' she responded. 'I want only you.' Actually this did not occur all in one sequence; it developed over the course of several episodes, just as our sexual events did. But it would be tedious to render it in fragmented form.

'You know I am married,' I said. 'I am separated, so I can and do indulge privately with other women, but I cannot marry any of them. Even if I were not the Tyrant, I could not take up another formal relationship.'

'There is only one thing that would bring me greater joy than the helmet has with you,' she said.

'And what is that?' I asked, for she seldom volunteered information; she had to be asked. By that token I knew she was not any of the women I knew. Even had Coral or Ebony or one of my old Navy mistresses chosen to communicate with me in this manner, they would not have had the diffident mannerisms of this anonymous woman. I rather liked this quality in her. She was not pushy; apart from her devotion to me, she made no demands.

'To be with you physically,' she said.

I smiled. 'That would ruin your anonymity,' I pointed out. 'I think that I would be interested in being with you physically, though I know you would not look the way you do here, for you have accommodated my tastes as well as any woman has. But it would be both awkward and dangerous for you, for I am a target for assassins. I would not care to expose you to that.'

'I would gladly die for you,' she said.

'But I would not gladly have you die for me!' I responded. 'If there were some way we could be together, without generating danger for you, I would do it. But there is not.'

'There is,' she said.

'Oh? How?'

But that she would not answer. When I pressed her, she would only say that I would have to fathom it for myself.

'But I don't even know who you are!' I protested. 'How can I find a way to be with you physically when I have no knowledge of you physically?'

'If you knew me physically, you might not like me,' she said. 'I would rather keep you with the helmet.'

'Are you physically ugly?' I asked. 'Are you afraid I would be revolted by your appearance?'

'I am very much as you see me here,' she said, spreading her hands. At this moment she was standing naked before me, and her proportions were modest; she had gradually diminished them as she discovered that I did not mind. In fact, she was now virtually nascent in development; her breasts were developed but not full, and her hips were almost boyishly slender. No, it truly didn't matter; I had loved slender women as well as voluptuous ones, and this one had mastered the techniques that made actual flesh superfluous. When a man is *in* a woman, the flesh on her outside matters less. Flesh is mostly an attractant, bearing much the same relation to her performance as smell does to taste. Not to be ignored, but not the full story, either.

'I can accept that,' I said, going to her and taking her in my arms and kissing her.

'But if you knew me physically, you might not,' she demurred.

'How can I convince you that you are wrong?' I asked.

'When you find me, you will know,' she said. 'Then – ' She shrugged, and I saw that she was genuinely afraid.

Hopie was getting her programme shaped up. '*No required courses, no exams*,' she said. 'No mandatory attendance, but anyone who isn't in school beyond a certain age must enter the work force. If he doesn't know what he needs, he'll get fired soon enough. The kids'll get serious quick enough. Absolutely no hazing – anyone practising it to be summarily dismissed. Freedom from fear – most kids miss at least one day a month, just because they're afraid they'll get beaten up in school. That S-blank-blank-T will come to a screeching halt. No more robberies or attacks.'

'But how do you propose to prevent them?' I asked.

'Hall monitors, replays of tapes, undercover agents – we'll catch the perpetrators and get rid of them. Pretty soon it'll be safe enough. Any student who sees anything had better report it, or he's in trouble.'

I shook my head. 'Hopie, these are police-state methods!'

'So?'

I sighed. 'You've been talking to Roulette.'

'Well, she's right. What we've got now is a school system largely run by thugs. Better a police-state than that! At least until we get the thugs out. You know that most of the crime is committed by kids aged fourteen to twenty-one. Catch 'em then, a lot of your crime problem is solved.'

'Perhaps so,' I agreed, again with reluctance. How readily people accepted tyrannical methods! 'What of the quality of education itself?'

'Oh, sure. Thorley's right. The school system's problems are like those of the Navy: low pay, low standards, irrelevant requirements. Double the pay, so as to attract better people. Train them so they really know how to teach. Revamp the organization, so that things are run efficiently instead of having teachers spend all their time taking attendance and collecting slips of paper. With voluntary attendance that stuff won't be necessary. Make the courses relevant to real life. Give the teachers a real sense of mission, so they know what they're accomplishing and feel good about it. TROMP.'

'What?'

'TROMP,' she repeated. 'Training–Relevance–Organization–Mission–Pay. The formula for fixing education.'

'So education has been reduced to a formula?'

She bridled. 'Daddy, you're making fun of me!'

'I wouldn't dare,' I said hastily. 'Do it your way. But how do you expect to handle racism?'

She glanced at me cannily. 'Think you got me, don't you! But that's one of the relevant classes. To cover exactly what racism is, and why it's wrong. They'll learn.'

'But if you don't require tests, or even attendance, the racists won't take that course,' I pointed out. 'And without school records the kids can sign up for school, then go out into the halls for mischief, since they won't be in the labour force.'

She frowned. 'Um. I'll think about that.' She moved away.

My helmet love was not wasted on Shelia, who monitored every episode, each way. She did not conceal it from me. 'Sir . . .' she would say, and not continue.

I knew it was unfair to subject her to this without recompense. She loved me, as all my women did, and deserved better. 'Get us private,' I would mutter.

She would, and we would make love. There were ways in which Shelia was similar to the helmet woman, in that

223

she could not initiate the act. After that first occasion her legs had never moved, if indeed they had then. She was Shelia, not Helse, and that left her paralysed. But apart from that they were good legs, and I gave them proper attention and brought her to her joy.

'I was never jealous of any woman before,' she confessed. 'I never thought I would be jealous of this one. But those scenes – '

I snapped my fingers with realization. 'Shelia, we can do it with the helmet! You can have the same and not be – '

She shook her head. 'No, Hope. That is *her* territory. I must not intrude.'

This might seem a strange ethic, but I understood it. All that my helmet woman had was the feelie sequences, while Shelia had my physical body. They were indeed separate territories, and Shelia honoured that the way she honoured and protected my personal privacy and my liaisons with Coral and Ebony. The truth was, these had largely abated by this time, but the principle remained.

'You know who she is,' I said.

'Of course.'

'You know whether she is correct about my not wanting her if I learn her identity.'

'She is wrong about that.'

'But you won't tell me her identity.'

'I promised not to.'

That was that; Shelia would not break her given word, and I would not ask her to. 'But will you talk to her?'

'Sir, this is a thing you must do for yourself.'

'I remember when my Navy women used to manage my affairs, for my own good,' I grumbled.

'Yes,' she agreed.

But it was not to be long thereafter before my ignorance was abated, with serious consequence.

9

Hell to Pay

There was a problem at the zoo. There was a white elephant at the New Wash facility, and it cost a fantastic amount to maintain it, for elephants are not native to space. A lively public debate had developed: keep the elephant or abolish it? Spirit had decided to let the issue be settled by a referendum, for this was exactly the type of nonpolitical matter that could arouse and divert public attention from the problems of the Tyrancy. We tried to keep the population as contented as possible, giving it small bonuses to distract it from the more serious issues. That may seem cynical, and surely it is, but it helps keep the peace. The ordinary citizen is equipped by neither education nor temperament to decide affairs of state, but he *thinks* he is, so it is best to divert him. That is one reason why politicians, historically, have had very little substance in their campaigns.

However, I wanted to make sure of the situation, because the vote promised to be divisively close, and that would force me to make the final decision. I wanted to get out of the White Dome for a while, anyway. So I arranged to take the girls to the zoo. Of course, my security force would be along, but this would be anonymous. I had to put on common-man clothes and a little holo-camera, and Hopie and Amber donned girlish jumpers so as to look like innocent teenagers. We would go see the elephant.

The excursion was fun. We followed a circuitous route, changing bubbles several times, making sure no one realized our origin. There was no sign of the security men; of course, they had infiltrated the crowd before I arrived. Coral acted as a cabbie, taking us through the city in a cab rented for the purpose. The girls chattered merrily in Spanish; there was no point in setting Amber to English and having her mute. Certainly we could all three pass for Hispanic tourists, and there were a fair number of those here too.

The zoo was impressive. It was set up in a cluster of small bubbles in the New Wash vicinity. We didn't bother with the others; we headed straight for the elephantarium. We had agreed that after we saw the elephant, and if our anonymity remained intact, I would go home, but the girls could stay and enjoy the rest of the zoo.

We entered at the null-gee lock at the bubble's admission pole and proceeded to the central orientation chamber. The animal, of course, had the favoured equatorial rim of the whirling bubble; the spectators could make do with low-gee for their temporary visits.

We were, of course, accustomed to the city-bubbles. This one was different. The naturalistic environment extended in a full sphere around us, like a giant map: plain, jungle, desert, and lake, all there in living colour. The sun-beacon projected the concentrated light to half the sphere, leaving the other half in deep shadow, simulating day and night. It rotated slowly so that a complete circle was made in twenty-four hours. This was mostly for the benefit of the living plants; the elephant could choose its place and time, obtaining the light or the darkness whenever it desired.

We became part of a party of about twenty-five sightseers, mostly children. The canned tour announcement came on: 'This is the Elephant Dome. It was constructed in 2586 and has been in continuous service since. Its ecology is completely self-contained except for the elephant and its diet; the insects, field mice, snakes, and

226

assorted birds reproduce themselves and maintain their populations in equilibrium without interference by man. We do monitor the air, but this is minimal; it regenerates naturally. If mankind were to disappear tomorrow, this community would continue indefinitely.'

'Not likely,' I muttered. 'The necessary concentration of the sunlight, twenty-seven-fold, has to be done by geelens, and that technology has to be maintained by man.'

'Oh, Daddy, don't talk back to the recording,' Hopie said impatiently. She nudged Amber. 'Isn't he funny? He argues with canned announcements!' Amber grinned dutifully. She was a great deal more expressive than she had been when she arrived; two years of our influence had been good for her.

'Elephants are the largest of all contemporary land animals,' the voice continued. 'More than six hundred varieties have existed in the past, but only two survive naturally. The one in this bubble is a genetically crafted *Mammut americanum*, or American mastodon. We call her Mammy, of course.' The announcer paused to allow suitable chuckles of appreciation. Naturally *Mammut* became Mammy! 'She stands seven feet tall at the shoulder and would weigh six thousand pounds if subjected to normal-gee. However, she is fifty-two years old and in indifferent health, so we have scaled down the gee to eighty per cent.'

'That's not very big,' Hopie said. 'I read where African males weigh twelve thousand pounds and are over ten feet tall.'

'Don't talk back to the recording,' I admonished her.

'I'm *not*!' she protested. 'I'm just making a clarification.'

'So good to know the distinction.'

'Fifty-two,' Amber said. 'Your age.'

227

'Thank you so much for reminding me,' I said, frowning, and I knew she was smiling. 'But I'm not quite as fat as the elephant.'

The recording continued with information about elephants in general and Mammy in particular: how large her brain was; how padded her feet; how versatile her trunk. 'There are forty thousand muscles and tendons in her trunk; it is an extremely precise appendage. Her ears are large and have many blood vessels; she flaps them to make a breeze and cool her blood.'

'I want to get in close and get some pictures,' Hopie said.

'Let's hear the spiel through first,' I said. 'Then there'll be the tour through the habitat.'

'Mammy consumes fifty thousand pounds of hay every year,' the spiel continued, 'in addition to thousands of gallons of mixed grains, about six thousand pounds of dried alfalfa, and thousands of potatoes, cabbages, apples, and loaves of bread. She drinks about eight thousand gallons of water.'

I considered those figures. The cost was phenomenal! We could feed a lot of people with fifty thousand pounds of grain! The water use wasn't so bad because it was recycled, but the food – well, surely they recycled that indirectly, via the manure, but still I had to consider whether it was worth it.

'. . . relatively inefficient,' the voice continued. 'Mammy actually eats twice the food that would be required by an animal of her mass with superior digestion.'

It looked bad for Mammy.

Then we proceeded to the tour of the grounds. Our party descended to the rim. The canned lecture followed us, explaining that the elephant was very careful where she went and would not cross a ditch more than five feet

228

across and five feet deep. Thus we could walk in perfect safety along the marked path that was protected by naturalistic ditches and barriers. The elephant could swim well enough, with all of her body submerged except the tip of her trunk, but concealed vertical mesh under the lake region prevented her access to the marked trail in that direction.

We filed along it. 'Oh, there she is!' Hopie exclaimed, pointing. 'Coming towards us.'

'You don't want to wait here,' a more experienced visitor said. 'Watering time in five minutes.'

'Oh.'

We moved on, not wanting to get wetted down in the simulated rainstorm coming up. We skirted the shore of a pleasant little lake.

I heard a little hiss. I looked – and there was a smoking spot on the turf at my foot.

My military experience gave instant recognition. That was a laser score!

'Girls, get out of here!' I said, and dived into the lake. Lasers are deadly but not through water. I was under attack, but my guards would manifest almost immediately to cover the situation. All I had to do was stay out of range long enough to let them function.

There was a splash beside me, and a thrashing. Someone else had jumped or fallen in. In a moment I saw it was Amber. Did she know how to swim?

It was evident that she did not. I stroked to her and caught hold. 'Relax!' I shouted at her head. 'I've got you!'

She heard me and stopped thrashing. I hauled her to the most convenient shore, which happened to be in the elephant's domain. We staggered out, my arm around her waist. I had to trust that my would-be assassin had been routed by my bodyguards and would not fire again.

Still, I hauled Amber under a thick bush, to get us both out of sight.

It could only have been a minute, perhaps less, that we were there before the guards found us. But it seemed like a small eternity. Because I had made a remarkable discovery.

Amber, completely soaked, had her hair and dress plastered to her body. But she was not a mess; she was beautiful. Suddenly I saw the features of Helse on her. Not precisely but approximately. Amber was about fifteen years old, just a little younger than Helse had been. She was Hispanic, as Helse had been. She was very much like a younger version of Helse.

I gazed at her silently. I saw now that she had developed in two years. Of course, it had been happening all along, but I had not been noticing.

Not only that.

Her development paralleled that of my anonymous helmet lover. So did her appearance, now. And her manner, as she gasped and clung to me, frightened.

I focused my talent on her, reading her, and in a moment I had no doubt. *This girl was that woman*.

The guards appeared and brought us back to the marked path and out of the zoo. I hardly noticed. My mind was in a whirl.

Amber had not realized that I had caught on. That was the way I wanted it, because I had some complex thinking to do.

Things were falling into place: these mysteriously appearing chips; Shelia's attitude; the anonymous woman's inexperience – they all fit now. Amber, lonely, liking me, unable to express it directly because she couldn't talk in English and knowing she shouldn't talk about this in Spanish . . .

But the helmet woman had talked in English! How could that be?

It could indeed be, I concluded. Amber could not speak English, but she did know the language. In a feelie a person's imagination governed. If she imagined she could speak there, then she could – and so she had. And she had got what she wanted.

What *she* wanted? I pondered the past year of helmet love, and knew that I had wanted it too. Had I realized the identity of the woman, I would never have done it; but now I did realize, and though I was shocked, I knew I still wanted that woman.

Fifteen years old. Fourteen when it started. Below the age of consent. Yet the age of consent had been all but abolished by the Tyrancy; any two people could do what they wanted together, provided both understood and acceded.

But the fact remained that she was younger than my daughter. That bothered me.

What was I to do? I wrestled with it, then went to Shelia. 'I have caught on,' I informed her grimly.

She made no pretence at ignorance. 'Then you know why she wouldn't tell you.'

'Yes. I would have cut it off at the outset, before – '

'Before you loved her,' she agreed.

I nodded. 'But you – why did you collude in this?'

'She needed you – and you needed her.'

'But she's a child!' I protested.

'Not any more.'

I thought again of our year's affair. No, not any more! 'What do I do now?'

'Why, you love her, Hope.'

'But she's younger than Hopie!'

'So?'

'Don't you see – she – how can I – ?'

231

'Helse was sixteen,' she reminded me.

'Helse was a woman!'

She nodded agreement.

And, of course, my definitions were skewed. I had been fifteen when I knew Helse. She had seemed adult then. Now I looked back on that age, and it seemed to be that of a child. It was not so.

'Don't you see the complications?' I argued. 'She came as my . . . my ward. Like another daughter. How can I – '

'We shall keep your secret, Hope.'

'Coral, Ebony – they know?'

'They know. It was Coral who first recognized Helse. That was why Chairman Khukov gave her to you.'

Obvious – in retrospect. Khukov shared my talent and perhaps my tastes. He had recognized the physical potential in the girl and seen what she would become. The fact that she was a variant idiot savant was incidental. 'You demon!' I muttered.

'You would have done the same for him,' Shelia said. 'In fact, you gave him his position.'

'Let me think,' I said. 'She doesn't know I know, and I don't know how to tell her or what to do after I do.'

Shelia handed me the chip. 'Tell her here.'

Maybe so. I didn't feel free to talk to the child Amber, but I could do so with the anonymous woman. I took the chip.

I donned the helmet and played through our latest scene. It happened to be of violent sex. I had hit her, and she had hit me, and then we had clutched each other and done it standing up. In the scene our blows had been painless; we were playing at violence, just for the variety of it, knowing that we would never have done it in real life.

Playing at violence. Playing – as children did.

No wonder! She was a child! And I in my second childhood.

After the act we stood together, just holding each other. Children?

'Amber,' I said, not sure how the helmet woman would react to this.

'You found out,' she said.

'I found out,' I said, half appalled that she should have had this programmed, anticipating my realization.

I moved back to a prior congress and repeated the word.

She responded similarly. I went back to our very first act together – and she responded to the name.

From the outset she had been ready, just waiting for me.

For a year she had waited.

A child?

I returned to the most recent scene. 'I finally realized,' I said. 'But what are we to do now?'

'Whatever you will,' she said simply.

'No!' I protested. 'You are the one at risk here. You must decide. You must come and tell me what you want – in life.'

'Hope, I cannot speak this language in life.'

'And I cannot touch you like this in life,' I retorted. 'But now that I know, I cannot continue this way, through the helmet. Come to me, tell me in Spanish if you must, but tell me. To love you – or to leave you alone.'

She was silent. We had progressed beyond her preparation. I removed the helmet and took the chip and gave it to Shelia.

'I think I shall not monitor these any more,' Shelia said.

'As you wish,' I said curtly, and proceeded to my other business.

* * *

Megan was now speaking out in public, not exactly criticizing the new policies of the Tyrancy but making constructive suggestions. She wanted attention paid to slum clearance, conservation, women's rights, and planetary aid. She had travelled to Latin Jupiter and bought a bright and beautiful scarf there, which she wore proudly. 'The people are talented and good,' she said. 'But many are oppressed by their governments. We of wealthy North Jupiter cannot be satisfied while hunger and misery remain elsewhere. We must help in whatever way we can but especially through education. The poor people cannot wait for gradual reform; in their frustration they will turn violently against their governments. The Tyrant should go for himself to see the situation to the south; then perhaps he would better appreciate the need.'

Megan refused to participate directly in my government, but I valued her input in whatever manner it came. 'Set up a Latin tour,' I told Shelia.

The ship lifted above the great rushing band of clouds that was the base for the United States of North Jupiter and slid south around the planet. I watched with my usual goggle-eyed tourist's fascination. I had been over twenty years on Jupiter, but still its atmospheric dynamics awed me. You can, as the old saying goes, take the man out of space, but you can't take the space out of man. I had been raised on a surface that was solid, with no atmosphere beyond the dome; later I had spent fifteen years in space, mostly aboard ships. Atmosphere remained a strange thing to me, in my unconscious mind. The way it thickened and swirled as if possessed of its own volition, its cloud patterns never quite repeating themselves in detail despite their consistency on the planetary scale . . .

We crossed into the mighty maelstrom that was Red-Spot. I saw the endless swirls and eddies that rimmed it, stormlets paying homage to the Lord of Storms, and for a while I flirted with the trance state. To my eye the vortex seemed to accelerate, to make its grand counterclockwise rotation in seconds, so that I could appreciate the whole of it. It became a monstrous mouth that consumed the smaller swirls, one after the other, or at least sucked away much of their power. That was, of course, how it nourished itself: it was the System's hungriest vampire.

I felt a hand on mine and emerged from my reverie. It was Amber, beside me, for, of course, I had her along as I normally did when contacting the officials of other nations. It had become accepted as one of the idiosyncrasies of the Tyrant, this constant presence of his ward, the mute girl; in fact, it was now expected. It seemed to lend an air of validity to the encounters, in the minds of the officials.

So she was with me physically. And emotionally, via the helmet. But the two were not yet merged, for she had not come to me in the manner I required, to tell me that she wanted me to love her in life as I had in the helmet – or not. I had to have that independent statement from her before I could act. My memory of Reba's lesson remained clear, and I did not want to impose a relationship of this nature on a virtual child who was in most other respects subject to my will. This much would be Amber's choice – and if she did not tell me yes, then I would leave her alone, and all would be as it had been, overtly. I had to have this much assurance of the fairness of my position. This much.

Now we descended into the vortex of RedSpot, and the great swirl of it took us in, perhaps an analogue of our emotional situation. The clarity of it was lost with proximity, and soon it was as if we were in a normal

235

atmospheric current. That was the way of human objectivity, I realized: from up close, the daily routine seemed ordinary even if from afar it clearly was not. We could appreciate reality on the physical plane, on occasion, by rising above it, but how could we ever do so on the emotional plane?

We docked at RedSpot City, the capital of this nation. Externally it was a cluster of giant bubbles, much like any other complex. Internally, I knew, it had its own identity. But I was not properly prepared for the reality.

The halls of the upper class were spacious and elegant. Parks, gardens, and fountains abounded, and there were many statues. We toured the Plaza of the Constitution and saw the majestic cathedral there, whose spires reached up towards the centre of the bubble. Amber was plainly awestruck, and I was mightily impressed myself. Then we were received at the National Palace, and the phenomenal Castle, traditional home of the president of RedSpot. We admired the University Library, its enormous facade reflecting ancient Aztec and Toltec art.

'But what about the residential areas?' I inquired.

There was a certain confusion while they tried to persuade me that such regions were not really of interest to me. Ah, but they were, I insisted innocently. I reminded them that I was Hispanic myself and had come from a Hispanic planet; they were my people and I wanted to see them personally. What I did not remind them of was that it was evident that much of the aid rendered in prior years to this and other Latin Jupiter nations had been wasted. So I needed a closer look at their real nature, to justify the intransigence I had in mind – and they preferred to deny that justification without stating why.

They could not deny me, though misgiving was manifest on every RedSpot face. Soon Amber and I were treated

236

to an impromptu ride through one of the neighbouring sections. They tried to confine it to the favoured gee-norm level, but I asked to see the upper reaches, where the poor folk resided. Because courtesy required that I be humoured, and because my lone say-so could cause another massive North Jupiter loan to be approved for RedSpot, they obeyed again. We went directly to the top.

Gee was noticably diminished here, for this was nearer to the centre of the mighty city-bubble, with correspondingly smaller centrifugal force. That was why it was not a favoured level; prolonged residence here would weaken the body, making activity on the full-gee levels difficult. It had been to avoid a similar fate that my family had emigrated from Callisto, the better part of forty years before. We had been threatened with residence in the half-gee coffee bean plantation, and we could never have won free of that, once committed. This level of RedSpot was not that extreme, but still it was not healthy.

The travel-hall was a complete contrast to the broad lanes of the display region. It was low and narrow, the lighting was bad, the air was polluted. The fact was that RedSpot City was so congested, so overpopulated, that its recycling mechanisms were unable to keep up with the demand. The diameter of the main bubble was no greater than that of Nyork or Cago in North Jupiter, but its population was swelling so grotesquely that it was now the largest city of the planet, and soon it would be the largest of the entire System.

Amber coughed, unused to such foul air, and I was not enjoying it myself. In addition to the pollution there was a certain stench, suggesting that the sanitary mechanisms were also over-capacitated. But I held firm; I wanted to see the people of this nation as they really were.

We came to a park area, but it was no longer a park.

Instead it was a grotesque conglomeration of junk. Old containers, crates, segments of packing material and things I could not quite identify were piled around haphazardly, filling the chamber.

'The park . . . is now a rubbish dump?' I inquired, appalled.

'We shall send a crew to clean it up!' my guide promised hastily.

I knew this was more complicated than that. Remember, it is my talent to read people, and this man was excruciatingly eager to get me away from here. Therefore I resisted. 'Let's take a look at it now,' I said.

I helped Amber to get out of the vehicle, remembering as I took her hand the secret that lay between us. She was now in the Spanish mode, so could talk, but she had remained silent. Perhaps my insistence on extending this tour to the seamier side of the city was also a sublimation of my need to gain some sort of commitment from Amber, whatever its nature might be. As long as we were here, we were together without suspicion. Or perhaps it was more sinister: if she disliked this oppressive region, she would have to initiate some sort of gesture to inform me, and once she had done that, she might find it easier to inform me of the more important decision.

I studied her covertly as she stepped to the floor. She was slender but attractive enough in her public dress. For this occasion her outfit was in the style of RedSpot, a full skirt with a frilly border, and she had a flower in her hair. She looked completely Hispanic and completely innocent, a little girl just merging into maidenhood. I found her wholly desirable and condemned myself for that. I had always had contempt for those older men who took very young mistresses; now I understood their position better than I liked.

As we approached the piled junk a small boy emerged. He spied us and retreated.

'Wait!' I called in Spanish. 'Let me talk to you!'

But the boy did not reappear. 'Please, Señor Tyrant,' our guide said. 'We must get clear of this region.'

'In a moment,' I agreed. I stepped to the crevice where the boy had vanished. Sure enough, there was a passage there.

This was no dump. It was a region of makeshift housing. The poverty-stricken masses of RedSpot had had to fashion their own residences, squatting in the park.

The odour was worse here, suggesting that these folk did not have proper access to sanitary facilities. I was appalled that such conditions should exist in the middle of a giant city-bubble of Jupiter, but not really surprised. I had verified what I had suspected. RedSpot really did need economic improvement loans!

Amber stood beside me, not reacting, so I pushed farther. I hunched over and entered the aperture, drawing her in after me. In retrospect I realize how foolish an act this was; I had been too long away from poverty.

'Señor! Señor!' the guide protested, horrified, and the guards strode forward.

But I moved on into the labyrinth – for so it turned out to be – of the slum village, Amber behind me. I found myself in a kind of twisting alley that wound through the jammed hut-chambers. There was literal garbage on the floor, and the passage was fraught with projecting ridges of plastic, for the chambers were not neatly fashioned.

I heard something behind and glanced back. A man had materialized, and he held a knife.

Now, belatedly, I realized my foolhardiness. I had left our guards behind and entered a largely lawless region. I could get myself killed before the guards could break through to rescue me.

But the man's attention was on Amber, not on me. 'Girl, come here,' he said gruffly.

Amber shrank away from him and towards me. 'She is with me, *señor*,' I said.

Another man appeared on my other side. He, too, bore a blade. 'What is your price for her?' he demanded. I was armed, of course. I had a laser, and I put my hand on it in my jacket. '*Señors*, I wish you no mischief,' I said. 'But the *señorita* will not go with you. Now, if you will stand aside, we shall depart; I regret intruding on your territory.'

Both men closed on us, knives extended. I fired at one through my jacket, scorching him on the right ear, then spun to cover the other. He hesitated, so I seared him on the same ear. I knew better than to bluff with this type.

There was a stirring in the chambers of this region, and I knew we would soon have more company. I hustled Amber back, watching all around us. In a moment we were out, standing before the alarmed guards. I knew why they had not pursued us into the slum passage; they had feared this would only get us immediately knifed, and themselves as well. Their relief at seeing us unharmed was manifest.

We returned to the vehicle and moved on through the level. I saw the two guards and the guide were tight with apprehension, despite our safe return, and in a moment I realized why. 'I did a foolish thing,' I said to them. 'You warned me but, of course, could not prevent me without causing affront. If you three will be so kind as to forget this embarrassing incident completely, it will be a great favour to me. I would not like to have to explain it to either my kind hosts or my own people; it would damage my image.'

The three exchanged glances, then smiled with relief. 'It is forgotten!' they agreed emphatically. Of course, they would keep the secret; their own heads were on the line, for their neglect in protecting me.

'And the people of the slum – I wounded two in the ear,' I continued as an afterthought. 'If they should appear with some complaint – '

'There will be no complaint,' the guards reassured me grimly.

Yes, I was sure of that. We had a minor conspiracy of silence, to mutual advantage. In the process I had been reminded of something I should never have forgotten: that is not smart to attempt too boldly to mix with the disadvantaged. They may have been wronged by their society, but they are not necessarily nice or polite people.

Amber sat very close to me now. She, too, had been shaken, realizing how precarious existence can be for all of us. Perhaps that was a worthwhile side effect.

We docked at Callisto, winding up my Latin Jupiter tour. My people were nervous about this, because I had departed this planet as a refugee, not as a legitimate emigrant. But politics and power change things, and I suspected I would be safer here today than I was back on the colossus. I felt nostalgia for the home planet; my roots, however brutally severed, were here, and I wanted to walk on the soil of Halfcal again. Also, I had a specific mission here, an ironic one, that was best handled personally and privately.

I took Amber to the city-dome of Maraud, my home turf. It was good to see the barren, airless terrain of Callisto again, with the great old ice mine and the hemisphere that sealed in the city, with the gee-lens above it that concentrated the sunlight twenty-seven fold.

How the old, once-familiar things tugged at my soul today!

But the neighbourhood where my family had lived was gone, or at least changed. Increasing population had forced more crowded quarters, and the look of it differed. The streets where my lovely sister Faith had been braced by the scion, setting off our ruin – I could not tell to which one it was now. Our old domicile – impossible to tell exactly where it had been. Too much time had passed, too much recent history had intervened. It might have been easier to locate Amber's root-location, elsewhere in Halfcal, but she had no desire to do that, and I didn't push it.

What of that scion, the young punk whose misshapen vengeance had so threatened us? I didn't even inquire, knowing that today, if he lived, he would be nearing sixty years old, a completely different person. I was not here for this sort of retribution.

We were received at the domicile of the current leader, Junior Doc. The name had become a kind of title in an ongoing repression that had endured for centuries. Junior was actually about my age, which meant he hadn't been in power when I departed Callisto; that helped. It made it possible for him to assure me that things had changed and that families like mine would not be forced to flee today.

'I am most gratified to hear you say that, *señor*,' I replied. 'Because Jupiter is being overrun by illegal immigrants, and this is causing us considerable expense. I have talked to the authorities of RedSpot about this, and they have graciously agreed to take positive steps to restrict the flow of people from their border.' Because I had made it plain that no loans or financial guarantees would be extended otherwise and that the all-important rate of interest on the loans extant could be raised or

242

lowered at my whim. Every point those rates increased was like a sledge hammer blow to the economy of RedSpot.

'But you are of Halfcal stock!' Junior protested. 'Surely you cannot turn your back on your own kind!'

'Surely not,' I agreed. 'But there are ways and ways.'

'As you know, Señor Tyrant, we are very poor,' he said cunningly. 'A good loan would enable us to take better care of our poor.'

'Odd thing about good loans,' I remarked. 'In the past the money has somehow found its way to the coffers of the richest class, while the poor have been benefitted very little, and, of course, those loans are seldom, if ever, repaid.'

'Much of our budget goes necessarily to defence,' he continued almost without pause. 'If we were to receive sufficient military aid, then more of the basic resources would be available for our basic needs.'

'Odd thing about military aid,' I remarked in the same tone as before. 'Somehow it seems to have made the military commands of Latin nations so strong that they have then taken over the governments of their countries, replacing republics with military oligarchies or outright dictatorships.'

'There may be something to be said for an enlightened dictatorship,' he observed, glancing at me sidelong. 'Certainly when conscientious reforms are undertaken. If Halfcal were to receive, for example, a preferred price for its coffee exports, I'm sure certain reforms – '

'Odd thing about reforms, *señor*. Either they fail to proceed far beyond the stage of rhetoric or they become too effective. An oppressive government that ceases to torture its citizens can be overthrown by those who are less concerned about human rights, so the effort is wasted.'

243

'Small danger of that here,' he murmured, but for some reason did not push the point. 'However, direct economic aid should be effective – '

'Odd thing: the donations of food and machinery and materials we have made in the past have somehow turned up for sale on the interplanetary black market.'

Junior sighed. 'You are a hard man to bargain with, *señor*! But surely we could find some accommodation?'

'If the bubble-folk were to stop arriving in our atmosphere, so that we were not constantly distracted by these unfortunates, we might be inclined to contribute somewhat to their betterment at home. Food, perhaps – the same we use on Jupiter.'

'Yours is dosed to make people sterile!' he protested.

'Temporarily infecund,' I agreed. 'The antidote is in the hands of the government. Your birthrate would decline, of course. Is that too great a sacrifice?'

He considered. 'Antidote available to the élite – assuming any of them used that food? No, I think we can accommodate that sacrifice.'

'We do expect most of that food to go the the poor.' That was the same pitch I had made to RedSpot: food that would not only help feed their impoverished but would drastically curtail the birthrate of that class – the class that was encroaching on the territory of the US of J. If that food found its way to the black market, it would be easy for us to withhold the antidote; that enforced proper distribution. RedSpot had been similarly hospitable to the notion. Thorley and other commentators were to castigate me roundly for this device, but it seemed at the time to be the expedient course. I was, after all, the Tyrant; the hard decisions were mine to make.

His eyes almost glinted. 'Certainly they would be more inclined to remain at home if their situation were bettered. I think it very likely that few, if any, would seek your skies.'

I nodded. Underlings would work out the details: aid for Halfcal, a cutoff of the flow of refugees for Jupiter. We parted with understanding smiles.

But on the ship, on the way home, Amber spoke up. She addressed me in Spanish, of course. 'I do not know about these things, but I think Hopie would ask – '

'How can I torpedo my own kind?' I finished with a sigh. 'I would just have to explain to my daughter that no matter how bad things may seem to the poverty-stricken natives of Halfcal, they would be worse in space. We cleaned out the pirates, to be sure, but space remains dangerous for those inadequately prepared, and the chances of any given refugee making it safely to Jupiter are only one in three or four. And what will he find there? Only unemployment, if he can't speak English – and most of them can't. He will hardly be better off than he was before.'

'She would say. "But you were a refugee!" '

'I would reply: "I am no longer a refugee. I am the government of Jupiter. My loyalties have changed." '

'She would say, "You have been corrupted by power." '

'I am the Tyrant,' I agreed.

And it came home to me with special force now: I was, indeed, the Tyrant. Power had not corrupted me, it had merely changed my perspective. But how was any Halfcal refugee to perceive the distinction? I was now acting exactly the way any dictator did, with seeming callousness for the common man. Yet what else could I do? The rationale, as stated indirectly to my daughter, was valid. No single man could repeal the basic laws of economics.

'Who is Megan?' she asked abruptly.

I was not entirely comfortable with this question from this source at this time, but I answered. 'She is my wife.'

'Why isn't she with you now?'

'She cannot bring herself to participate in the Tyrancy.'

'But she loves you?'

'Yes.'

'How can that be?'

'She would say that it is possible to hate the sin but to love the sinner.'

She was silent. I was braced for questions about my relations with other women and with Amber herself, while I remained married to this great and good woman, but they did not come. Apparently Amber now understood as much as she needed to.

Amber came to me when I was alone in my room. I knew Shelia and Coral had arranged to provide us this privacy. My skin experienced a cold wash; I was abruptly afraid.

She stood before me silently. I forced open my mouth and whispered: 'You are in English?'

She nodded. I would have to change her over to Spanish to have her talk. I was tempted to avoid the issue by declining to do that. I compromised.

'Amber, it is you in the helmet,' I said.

She nodded again.

'But there you can speak.'

Once more the nod.

'But not in life.' I sighed. 'Amber, I am afraid of you now. I don't know whether I should change you over to Spanish and let you talk.'

She remained mute and unmoving. I looked into her face and saw a shine in her eye. Tears were forming.

They melted me. 'Oh, Amber!' I exclaimed, and stepped into her and embraced her. She hugged me back, and our tears flowed. No, I could not deny her!

But neither could I accept her – yet. 'Amber,' I said gently to her hair as I held her. 'I do not truly love anyone, in the sense that love is normally understood. But you – what I feel for you is close.' I kissed her, and she returned the kiss, exactly as she had always done in the helmet. 'But this – this is not yet right. There are things I – we – must clear first.'

She merely gazed at me. I thought again of putting her into Spanish mode but delayed it again. I knew that she would go along with anything I decided; I was the one who was hesitant. So I tried to explain, to myself as much as to her.

'Amber, I am fifty-two years old. You are fifteen. You have been placed in my charge. It is not right for me to do this with you.'

Again the tears formed in her eyes. She thought I was rejecting her.

I embraced her again. She was not Helse, and I knew that; she differed markedly in personality and abilities. But the way she looked – it was as if she were just coming into Helse's range, physically. Perhaps all girls, all Hispanic girls, have a similar aspect at that age. Megan, who was Saxon, had also resembled Helse, and in that resemblance my fascination had been caught, though Megan was a totally different person. I knew better, but I knew I had to have this girl. Maybe it was a retreat to an impossible past, but it was necessary.

'Amber, I'll do it,' I told her. 'But you will have to help. We shall have to tell my daughter Hopie, and that will be the most difficult part. Then I must notify my leading critic, for reasons that you would not understand. But for you: Hopie will come to you, and then you must tell her how you feel. She may then become your enemy. Are you prepared to face that?'

Slowly Amber nodded.

I felt, almost, regret. This was going to complicate my life significantly. But my nature gave me no choice.

I talked to Hopie. It was every bit as bad as I had feared. I tried to come at it obliquely, but I suspect that there was no approach I could have made that would have avoided her reaction. 'Hopie, I have to ask you to do something that I fear you will not like,' I said.

'What else is new, Daddy?' she inquired brightly.

'This does not relate to education. You have been doing well enough on that, and I'm pleased.'

Her eyes narrowed. 'You're up to something.'

'I will need your cooperation, and this may not be easy for you,' I continued grimly. 'And I must ask you to go to Thorley and inform him of the situation.'

'Thorley's not so bad,' she said. 'He really helped me on education; you know that. I could almost like him, if he weren't so conservative.'

'You will not like telling him this.'

'I can tell him whatever I need to; he doesn't have to like it,' she said confidently. 'But what is this big mystery?'

'It involves Amber.' My throat tried to tighten.

'She's doing very well, Daddy; she's got taller and she's filling out and she's happy.'

'I am aware of that. But her status is about to change.'

Hopie abruptly sobered. 'Daddy, you can't send her away! She's like a little sister to me! She's very good with Robertico, and she makes no demands at all. And she thinks the world of you.'

'Not to send her away,' I said with difficulty.

She relaxed somewhat. 'What, then?'

'I want you to continue to – to treat her as a sister. To go places with her, to help her deal with those who do not understand her nature. To be her friend.'

'Daddy, that goes without saying!' she chided me. 'I love her!'

'So do I,' I whispered.

'Of course! You understand her best of all. So what's the problem?'

'She will not always be spending the night with you any more. You must accept that without being angry.'

'Not with me? Where would she sleep, then? Daddy, she doesn't like to be alone.'

'She will not be alone.'

'With whom, then? There's really nobody – '

'With me.'

'Oh. You have special languages for her to listen to?'

'In a sense.' I wished I could postpone this indefinitely.

'Daddy, exactly what are you trying to tell me?' she demanded.

'I want . . . to take Amber . . . to be my mistress.'

This was so far from her expectation that she missed the implication entirely. 'Mistress of what, Daddy?'

I took a shuddering breath. 'To be my sexual companion.'

Now it dawned. 'To *what*?'

'I – she and I have had a relationship via the helmet. An affair. Now we want to make it real.'

She stared at me. 'Helmet – the feelies? You and Amber?'

I nodded.

'Sex? As in the Navy?'

'Yes.'

'With *her*?'

'Yes.'

She considered. 'I don't believe this!'

'Believe it,' I said miserably.

'You – she – Daddy, *she's younger than I am!*'

'Yes.'

'And you mean to – to force her to – to satisfy your lusts?'

'No force.'

'No force!' she exclaimed, her face flaming. 'Fifteen years old, absolutely dependent on you for her very life and you want her body, and you say there's *no force?!*'

'She wants it too,' I said.

'She wants not to be thrown out into space if she says no!' she cried. 'She's afraid she'll be tortured if she tries to resist the mighty Tyrant!'

'No. No fear. She came to me, via the helmet. She – '

'And you raped her in the helmet? And now you want to do it for real? And you expect me to go along?'

'Hopie, I wish you would try to understand,' I said. I put my hand on her arm. It was a mistake.

She became violent. She threw my hand off. 'How *could* you!' she cried, and punched me in the right eye.

The pain flared, but I did not move or resist. 'I do love her, in my fashion.'

'*In your fashion!*' she exclaimed derisively. 'The way you loved Roulette in the Navy?'

'Somewhat like that,' I agreed. 'But without violence.'

'And what of Megan?' she screamed.

'Your mother and I are separated. She understands.'

'She's not my mother!' Hopie said. 'I don't know who my mother is! Sometimes I hate her for being secret – and for making me a bastard! Why did you have to do it, Daddy? What was wrong with your *wife*? You just had to – '

'You misunderstand – '

She slammed me in the nose. The pain exploded, and almost immediately the blood flowed from a burst blood vessel.

I let it flow. 'I'm sorry,' I said.

'Sorry!' she mimicked. 'Why weren't you sorry before you started all this?'

'If you would talk to Amber – '

'I'll talk to her!' she cried. 'You bet I will!' She ran out of the room, and I knew that her rage was forty-nine per cent grief.

Coral came in to medicate me and clean me up, for my blood was all over my face and shirt. 'I didn't think you wanted protection this time,' she murmured.

I nodded. 'There is some punishment a man must accept.'

'She'll settle down, in time.'

'I knew she would be angry,' I said. 'But I didn't realize *how* angry.'

'Daughters don't have to be understanding of adult weakness.' Under her skilled hands the flow of blood eased and stopped, and so did the physical pain. 'You'll be bruised, sir.'

'Not only physically,' I agreed.

Hours later, when I was lying sleepless in my bed, my nose bandaged, Hopie came quietly to me. 'Oh, Daddy!' she said.

I sat up and gazed at her, unspeaking. She threw herself into my arms and sobbed. She cried for about fifteen minutes, then disengaged. 'I will tell Thorley,' she whispered, and left. Then I slept.

Next morning Shelia handed me a feelie chip. 'From Amber?' I asked, startled.

'From Hopie,' she said. 'I have not played it.'

I was thankful for that. 'Hopie said she was – '

'She's already gone.' She glanced sidelong up at me. 'That must have been some session you had.'

I touched my bandaged nose. 'You guessed!'

'She shows similar wounds.'

I nodded, knowing it was the emotional carnage she meant. I took the chip and played it at the earliest opportunity, apprehensive about what it would show.

Hopie had evidently forgiven me my transgression, but the whole story was not yet clear. My talent blurs when applied to those I love; I did not know my daughter's mind.

The scene was of Amber, sitting in the room they shared, the helmet on her head. Hopie entered, saw her, and took up a similar helmet.

My muscles tightened. The helmets show the programmed scenes when used separately with the chips, but because they tune in on the user's brain signals, they can interact when used close to each other. This can cause unpredictable effects and is not recommended for amateurs. It is the closest approach to telepathy that we presently possess. Hopie was within the interactive range, deliberately.

The scene dissolved and re-formed: now it was no longer what Hopie had programmed to set the situation; it was the shared dream of the two girls.

Amber's scene was a field of pretty flowers, the horizon far distant, showing that this was not the interior of a bubble or dome. The sun as seen from Earth shone brightly down, warming her. She was in a simple print dress, sitting cross-legged. She held a daisy, and she was picking off the petals in the age-old 'He loves me, he loves me not' ritual. But the query was never completed; no matter how long she picked, there were always more petals. She could have been at this for hours.

Then a man strode towards her, his boots trampling down the living flowers. I winced; the man was me, imperfectly rendered but recognizable. In real life I would never trample flowers; they were too valuable. But this was hardly intended to be the real me; it was something else, and I doubted that I would like it very much.

Amber looked up and saw the me-figure. She smiled welcome.

The me-figure smiled. He reached down and more or less lifted her to her feet. Then he took her by the hair and held her cruelly while his free hand ripped off her dress.

Amber's face showed surprise and shock. Obviously she had never expected such an approach from me. But she did not resist. She even tried to help with the removal of the clothing. Perhaps she did not realize that the me-figure was not being animated by the real Hope Hubris but by his angry daughter, who was attempting to show how badly I was acting.

In moments Amber was naked. The me-figure leered and developed an impossibly monstrous erect phallus, one that would have torn the girl apart if forced into her. He started to do just that – but then was engulfed in flames. He screamed as his hair blazed up.

The scene shifted to show the source of the flame. It was a dragon with a long and sinuous neck, burnished scales, and a switching tail. It inhaled, reorienting on the target, then belched out another fierce jet of fire.

The me-figure tried to flee, but the flame pursued; it was obvious that he could not escape a horrible death by burning. But as the fire arrived naked Amber leapt to intercept it, spreading her arms to take the brunt of it on her breast. She, the ravished, was sacrificing herself to save me.

Abruptly the dragon vanished. The scene reverted to its original state: girl with flower. Evidently Hopie had not intended to have Amber burned, but Amber had power over her own scene-figure and could do what she willed.

Again the me-figure approached, and again he attacked the unresisting girl. This time the act was halted by the arrival of a huge turbanned pirate bearing a sword with a

253

blade four feet long. He swung it violently at the me-figure, lopping off an arm. The sword evidently had a laser-buttressed edge, so that it cut right through flesh and bone.

Again Amber leapt to protect me. She jumped to intercept the next cut, losing one of her own arms. And again the scene abruptly abated; Amber was not supposed to be the target.

The third attack was more subtle. This time the me-figure did not rip off Amber's dress; he merely took hold of her, dragging her away. She scrambled around to get her feet properly under her, so that she could come along willingly.

The scene darkened. A quick pan of the sky showed that a storm was forming, the clouds roiling in great grey masses as they never did in a Jupiter bubble. A wind came up, flattening the flowers and tearing at the me-figure's clothing and Amber's dress.

Then snow pelted down, and its very touch froze the flowers, for they turned instantly grey and stiff. Soon the two figures were ploughing through ankle-deep drifts.

A poncho appeared, settling around Amber's shoulders, but there was none for the me-figure. Instead the wind tore at him so persistently that his clothing tore away, exposing him further to the elements. He would soon freeze to death.

Amber removed her poncho and set it on the me-figure, trying to protect him from the deadly chill. But the poncho dissipated into mist as she did so, and was gone. Another poncho formed around her. She tried to give this also to the me-figure, but again it misted out, re-forming about her. The message was plain enough: only she could be warm.

The snow quickly became knee-deep, and the wind cut through cruelly. The me-figure faltered, his motions slowing; he was literally freezing to death. He tottered and fell face forward into the snow.

Amber got down and tried to lift him up, but her strength was inadequate. She turned him over, brushing the snow from his face. His features were frozen; he did not respond to her ministrations. He was preserved as an icy statue.

Amber bent to kiss his frozen lips, but still there was no response. She tried once more to wrap the poncho around him but, once more, to no avail. He was gone.

Then she gazed up at the snowy sky, and her face was wet with tears, not with snow. 'Why are you doing this?' she cried in English, the language she was locked into.

For an instant the scene froze, not in the cold sense but in the still sense. I knew what was happening: Hopie had never before heard Amber speak in that language and was so astonished that she was forgetting to animate the scene.

Then she recovered. Her own figure appeared in the scene. 'You're talking English!' she exclaimed. 'How can you do that?'

'This isn't the real world,' Amber reminded her. Then, realizing: '*You* are doing this?'

'Yes. I'm in the adjacent helmet. They interact.'

'But – why are you killing your father?'

'Because he means to abuse you,' Hopie said grimly.

'Oh, no, no!' Amber cried. 'He is a great and gentle man, and he would never hurt me!'

'Amber, don't you understand? *He wants to have sex with you.*'

'Yes. And I with him. I love him.'

Hopie was flustered. 'But you – you're a child! It isn't right! He's abusing his position, his power over you!'

'Oh, Hopie, please understand! I have no life without

255

him! I love him utterly! All I want is to be with him completely.'

'To be ... one of his women?' Hopie asked disdainfully.

'Oh, yes!'

'But you know he can't love you! He doesn't love anybody, really! He only uses women! They love him, but it's one-sided. How can you even consider letting yourself be – '

'He loves each one a little,' Amber said. 'None of them as much as Helse or Megan or you. But enough.'

Hopie paused, shaken anew. 'You really mean it, don't you? You want to be one of his mistresses! You don't care what it means!'

'He only touches those he really respects or cares about. I thought there was no chance for me, and when I found there was – oh, Hopie, don't deny me this, my only real pleasure in existence! You know I have no life of my own! You're his daughter; you have everything, but I have nothing!'

'I'm his daughter,' Hopie repeated. 'His illegitimate offspring. You call that everything?'

'He only ever loved one woman enough to have a child by her. What could be more precious to him than that child?'

Hopie considered. Then, slowly, her militancy crumbled. She began to cry.

Amber went over to her. 'Oh, Hopie, don't be sad. You have been so good to me, I don't want to make you unhappy!'

Hopie reached out to embrace her. The two girls clutched each other, both crying, while the snow melted away and the flowers returned.

'Show me how it is with you,' Hopie said at last.

Amber was perplexed. 'How it is?'

'We're connected now. How do you feel about my father? Just let your feeling go, and I will read it.'

Amber let her feeling go. It expanded to fill the scene – not a picture, not a sound, but sheer, incoherent, encompassing emotion, such total longing, need, desire, passion, and love that it swept aside all considerations of age, sex, propriety, legality, status, and doubt. Her body might be marginally adult, but her feeling was the essence of womanly abandon.

I, the object of it all, found myself awed. This emotion – it vaporized anything childish or playful or innocent. This was the very depth of reality. To be loved so utterly – could I possibly be worthy?

A brief eternity later it ebbed, for it had been only a glimpse. A peek into Heaven, Hell, and Purgatory combined, into Nirvana and Nothingness. Amber's entire brain was misorganized, without the normal feedbacks and governors. Her love was absolute.

'I never understood,' Hopie breathed.

Neither had I, I realized.

'You never felt the lack,' Amber responded.

The scene dissolved.

'Missive from Thorley,' Shelia informed me, handing me the letter. Thorley, of course, clung quaintly to the printed page, despite its inefficiency, because he identified literally with the press. It is a bias I appreciate, for when I wish to express myself with unstressed candour, this is the medium I choose. The written word. Its magic supersedes technology.

At my leisure I broke the archaic wax seal on the envelope and read:

My Dear Tyrant:

I feel it incumbent upon me to advise you of a private interview I had most recently with your adopted daughter,

Hopie Hubris. She came to me with what I assumed was to be a concern relating to her post as Minister of Education, but which turned out to be of another nature.

She advised me that you had required her to inform me of a private peccadillo: your passion for a rather young woman in your charge, by name Amber. It seems that Amber was given to you by Chairman Khukov two years past and serves as a kind of translator, being conversant in her fashion with a number of tongues. Now it is your intent to make of this young woman a mistress, she being amenable.

Obviously it is not my prerogative to pass judgement on your private affairs, nor is it my desire to do so. The secret passions of any man, I suspect, would embarrass him were they made public. As this particular one appears to relate in no way to your performance in office, I see no need to expose this girl to the kind of notoriety that would develop if the matter were to become public. In sum, sir, I will keep your secret. I am sure you would do the same for me.

However, there is a related matter that I found necessary to impart to your daughter. After completing her mission, which, it seems, was not entirely to her liking, she unburdened herself to the point of inquiring rhetorically why she has had to be the one to perform this office.

'Because, my dear young woman,' I said to her, assuming that familiarity that our labours on the organization of education facilitated, 'the Tyrant, knowing that news of this nature could not be entirely concealed from those with a keen nose for the nuance of human fallibility, wished to advise me in a fashion which could not be doubted that the object of his amorous intention was not yourself. Had other been the case, it would indeed have been necessary to expose – '

Here I had to abate my explanation, for she was staring at me with such chagrin that I realized that further discussion was pointless. She departed forthwith. May I say, sir, that if I have caused your daughter unwarranted distress, I am deeply disturbed. Certainly I bear her no malice and consider her to be a fine young woman with an attractive penchant for literary expression. It may be that I spoke carelessly in this instance. As it is too late to mitigate such damage as I may have done, I am taking the liberty of informing you of the situation. I leave the remainder in your hands.

> Your Most Humble & Obedient Servant
> Thorley

There are levels, and levels, to Thorley that are seldom properly appreciated. In the guise of his consciously affected style he had informed me of what I most needed to know and had done a portion of my dirty work for me. Now Hopie understood why it had been necessary for Thorley to know from Hopie's own lips the truth about my passion for Amber. Indeed, Hopie's statement, and her reaction, could not be doubted. There are things that even a Tyrant does not do.

There may be those who suppose Thorley to be my enemy. How little they know!

10
Company Man

There had been a number of rallying points of opposition to the Tyrancy, and these intensified as our reforms were implemented. The common man, it seemed, did not really want reform – not when it inconvenienced him. Already editorials were lamenting the good old days of President Tocsin, 'the last legitimate leader' of North Jupiter. There was a climate of rebellion that was coming to permeate every level of society.

I had never realized how unpopular I could get, but I had no doubt of it now. I knew I would be lynched if I walked openly down any hall of any major city-bubble of this section of the planet. Perhaps if I had acted to control the press, it would have been better, but I refused to do that. So the editorials lambasted me continually, and the people followed, convincing themselves that they were worse off than they had been, despite the manifest fairness of the reforms the Tyrancy had made.

But I was riding the tiger. I could not simply step down; to do so would be to throw the society into chaos and to wipe out the groundwork we were laying for the new society. No revolution is painless, and the Tyrancy was a revolution: a revolution of reform. Once the benefits began to manifest themselves, the common attitude would change. We knew that, and it was what kept us going. But now we were in the darkest seige of the long tunnel, seeming to make very little progress.

The day I received Thorley's missive, the bubble shook with the force of a nearby detonation. It rocked us all. In moments we learned the cause: a missile had been launched at the bubble, one with a black-hole shield similar to that of a sub but smaller. That protected it from most observation, but if it had collided with the bubble, it would have caused a deadly implosion. The Navy had intercepted it, but this one had come uncomfortably close. An investigation would be made to ascertain the source and why it hadn't been intercepted long before becoming an actual threat to the bubble; someone's head would roll.

'But we just can't be secure from this type of threat,' Spirit informed me seriously. 'You are too much of a target, Hope, and the threats come too thickly, from too many directions. Some of the ones we have stopped without fanfare have been frightening: poisoned food, flawed oxygen supply, hypnotic devices – anything. It isn't enough to put away the perpetrators; more keep developing. Sooner or later we're apt to be overwhelmed.'

'What's our best course, then?' I asked.

'I think it's time to remove the main target. You are the Tyrant; the people are convinced that if they can just get rid of you, all their problems will abate. It isn't true, of course, but it's hard to argue effectively against that sort of ignorance.'

Remove the main target. 'So it's time for me to go into hiding,' I said, hardly surprised.

'At least until the furore subsides,' she agreed. 'Once the policies start taking proper hold and things improve – '

'I feel as if I'm running out,' I complained. 'The budget is further out of balance than ever, and that's my – '

'You won't be running out. You will just be going to work on a more specific aspect. Our biggest present problem is industry: we nationalized companies in key industries, but when we used them as our Employers of Last Resort, they became not more efficient but less

261

efficient. We are taking enormous losses on those companies, and that isn't going to change until we can make them efficient – *with* the last-resort employees.'

'Get me some really good managers, and we'll get them efficient,' I said.

'The best managers fled to private enterprise,' she reminded me. 'Unless we want to get coercive, we'll have to develop our own from scratch – and that takes time. Which is where you come in now.'

'*I* don't know how to manage a company!' I protested.

'You'll learn. Reba set it up. For over a year a man answering your general description has been shifting from job to job and company to company, showing proficiency but moving on when he was unable to get promotions fast enough to suit him. He blew the whistle on one inefficient practice and was eased out of a bubble company.'

'But we protect whistle-blowers!'

'We *try* to protect whistle-blowers,' she said. 'The company found another pretext to suppress him so nothing could be proved. That is often the way of it. So he has a reputation for erratic brilliance, but he can't get along with management.'

'Put him *in* as management,' I said. 'See what he's made of.'

'Exactly,' she agreed. 'You will enter our Jupiter Bubble Company as a trainee manager, slated to run the company after you master the details of its operation. You should be able to make something of it – and then to make something of the other Jupiter companies. That will turn the tide on the economy and the budget.'

'Just like that!' I exclaimed wryly.

'As you said, get some good managers . . .'

* * *

The front offices of the Jupiter Bubble Company were palatial, but I saw them only briefly. I was introduced as Jose Garcia, an ambitious Hispanic who was smart enough but not patient enough, now granted the position of prospective Manager of Jupiter Bubble, provided I could master the business. It was very like a patronage plum, because the Tyrant was known to favour whistle-blowers and Hispanics, and the prior management of the company was not particularly pleased. However, the Tyrant had spoken, so they had to tolerate me, hoping I would foul up badly enough to be displaced before I assumed the actual power.

Not the most delightful situation, but it was evident that despite my similarity to the form and age of the Tyrant himself, no one even thought of connecting me with him. Minor spot surgery had been done on my face to change its configuration, so that I simply didn't look like the Tyrant despite being fairly close. My throat had also been treated, so that my voice had a different timbre and was not recognizable as that of the Tyrant.

Amber was with me, also subtly modified. Her hair had been changed in colour, length, and styling, and her nose and mouth as well. In fact, she now resembled my lost love Helse remarkably closely. Was that coincidence or Spirit's teasing design or my imagination? Did it matter? She remained Amber to me, and her revised appearance did not bother me, and it did protect her from possible recognition. She was now to be called Amena, close enough to be familiar, far enough to eliminate the possible connection. She was my underage girlfriend: before the Tyrancy, relations with her would have been considered statutory rape, but now they were legitimate because she was nubile and consenting. My prior association with her, in the mock identity, had been the reason given for my disfavour; though the association was legal, it remained socially awkward, and a company was not required to promote those who were in such poor favour with their peers that a managerial position would be unlikely to work.

We were rapidly shunted to the most basic aspect of company business: prospecting. I was supposed to gain experience from the bottom up, and this was taken literally. I found myself with Amber (I have no need to call her Amena here, so am not bothering) in a mini-scoutship. It had facilities for two, for a month at a time: food, water, air, energy, sleep, entertainment. Now, this might sound like fun, but in fact, it was not considered so.

For one thing, the prospect-ship was cramped. There were no passages; there were crawlways. No separate kitchen or bathroom: one tiny chamber served both capacities. It was assumed that since the ship had to be under acceleration for the kitch/head facilities to work properly, one person would be piloting while the other did the job here. Thus the merging of plumbing made sense – to an executive who didn't have to use it. Food prepared here was, in the vernacular, termed fart-fare. Mark one item to be corrected when I had power.

'It facilitates the processing of garbage,' I explained wryly to Amber. 'You can put it in one end and out the other without having to move.'

She smiled, because this was evidently meant to be funny, but she didn't really understand. She was not, and would never be, a 'clever' type of woman. She was just glad to be alone with me at last. I hoped she would not find the next month excruciatingly tiresome.

The operation of the ship was simple enough for any duffer. I would have had no problem regardless, because of my time in the Navy, but this facilitated things for Amber. She was able to use a joystick to guide it in any direction, a lever to control acceleration. The screen showed a panoramic view of what was outside, with an inset and cross hairs for specific detail. Anything more complicated she could safely leave to me.

Our mission was to locate suitable bubbles for exploitation. We were in the bubble-band of Jupiter, the nether region of the atmosphere where a combination of density, temperature, and turbulence caused substances to be dredged from the hellish interior and precipitated out before settling down. I am no chemist, so this may be somewhat garbled, but my understanding is that among those exotic substances are carbon, silicon, aluminium, tungsten, and tantalum, and that some of the precipitates are natural crystals of exceeding hardness. Not as hard as diamond but harder than sapphire. It is said that the bubbles are formed of carborundum, but I believe it is more complicated than that, with an admixture of boron. At any rate, that material is just about the toughest stuff extant in nature. It isn't economical to form it in such quantities in the laboratory, considering the high pressure required and the rarity of the trace elements at our level of the atmosphere. Nature does it best, so we harvest it wild.

Of course, nature doesn't form many perfect hollow spheres of enormous size. The bubbles were seeded centuries ago and allowed to grow. Again I am hazy on the technical detail and can only say that an enormous number of very small moulds were sent out – hardly larger than molecules – crafted in such fashion as to attract deposits of crystallized bubblene (that is, the boron, carborundum, or whatever mix) but with a very special quality. The deposits become unstable beyond a certain size, so that they tend to shed their inner layers even as their outer ones are forming. One might picture a tree, rotting from the centre as it puts on growth outside, only more disciplined. Thus the spheres do become hollow and become proportionately thinner-shelled as they grow larger. The result is the bubbles, ranging from pea-sized to city-sized.

But the Jupiter atmosphere is large. Though there is a tonnage of bubble formations at this level that can only be crudely estimated, the individual bubbles are spread far apart, and there is a murk of inchoate material that clouds whatever view there might be. Thus, searching for the forming bubbles is like the proverbial needle in the haystack. They are there, but it is a challenge to find them.

That was our job, as prospectors. Once freelance individuals had prospected for nuggets of gold on the surface of archaic Earth; now they sought spheres in the wilder reaches of the Jupiter atmosphere. Bubblene was just as precious as gold had been; without the bubbles, civilization as we knew it would not be possible. Oh, certainly the fundamental breakthrough had been the gee-shield; that made System exploration possible. But the bubbles, combined with the shields, made extended settlement feasible. It was the same on Saturn, Uranus, and Neptune: all had their bubble-bands, and all harvested the bubbles and fashioned them into ships and cities. Nothing but a bubble could withstand the rigors of atmosphere and space, for bubblene was virtually impervious to accidental destruction. Gravel-meteorites merely scratched the superhard surface, and neither heat nor cold (within reason) weakened it. A new bubble was a treasure indeed!

So we quested, but the chances of our discovering a good bubble within a month were small. Some prospectors searched for years before making a decent strike, and some never succeeded. Some died in the effort. But those that succeeded could have their fortunes made, depending on the size and quality of the bubble they staked. Thus there were many volunteers, despite the discomfort and danger; man tends to be foolishly optimistic, or perhaps he just likes to gamble.

Our ship's hull was of bubblene, of course, and it was thick. The pressure here was about a thousand bars – a thousand times that of Earth-normal. The natural bubbles were porous, so that atmospheric pressure inside equalized that outside, but the ships had to provide and protect the human environment. Implosion was definitely a threat, and I felt it as a kind of claustrophobia, though I knew that the ship was designed to withstand the pressure. I fought the feeling, knowing that it was merely the legacy of my rearing in the relative vacuum of space, where explosion was the threat. I could not afford to be handicapped by emotion. Amber didn't seem to be aware of the pressure; perhaps she didn't grasp its nature or extent. I was not about to educate her about it; her ignorance was bliss, in this case.

We proceeded through the soup, and I gave her practice in the handling of the ship. The gee-shield prevented it from descending, even when stationary, but mishandling could still generate mischief. The ship manoeuvred by planing with its wings when accelerating, so could lift or descend, and it was theoretically possible to skim too deep and encounter pressure too great for the hull to withstand; it was best to be careful. To turn left or right one merely rotated the ship so that the plane acted sidewise. Simple in theory, sometimes tricky in practice, because of the murk and the turbulence.

Outside all was wind and dust and streamers of gas. Sometimes we spotted larger blobs of substance, but they were generally misshapen, useless for our purpose. Some ships were harvesters of amorphous material, scooping it in and carrying it up to the factories for processing. Such mining was big business. But we were going for bigger game.

After several hours I was satisfied that Amber had the hang of it; henceforth we could take turns piloting. Normally one pilot was on duty at all times, even if not actively searching; it was prudent to keep an eye out for both danger and bubbles. Most discoveries were actually random, though innumerable search systems existed that supposedly enhanced the chances. The longer someone looked, and the more sharply he looked, the more likely he was to score: that was the essence.

But at the conclusion of this first shift we put the ship on auto-pilot, for we had another matter in mind. We had not before had the chance to be completely alone and private, together. We wanted to make love.

One might suppose that this would be a simple matter. It was not. First, there was the social aspect. Remember, at this time Amber was just fifteen years old, and though she had the body of a young woman, there were ways in which she remained childlike. I wanted her, in part, because of that youth, so like that of Helse when I had known her. But I was fifty-two and conscious of the disparity in ages. We had made love many times and in many ways – via the helmet – but this was real and therefore hazardous in its own special way.

Second, there was the physical aspect. This was a ship designed to support two – in different places. Sleeping was definitely conceived as a solitary matter. The bedroom cell was a niche that opened from a rear wall, just about big enough for one large man or, possibly, two small ones. We discovered that we could, by dint of much effort and discomfort, jam in together, but the fit was so tight that sexual activity was really not feasible. I suppose if a man and a woman were experienced, so that each knew exactly what contour fitted what and were not ambitious for mutual satisfaction, it could be done. That was not the case with us. We wanted to do it gently and well. That pretty well eliminated the bed.

That left the kitch/head: not the most conducive locale. If one person sat on the vac-pot, there was just room for the other to stand. I looked at the pot, disgusted, but didn't see a much better way.

'This isn't the way I wanted it to be the first time,' I said. 'But . . .'

She smiled, not concerned. Amber never complained about anything.

She retreated to the entry tunnel, giving me room to strip. When I was naked, I sat on the pot, giving her room. And you know, as her clothing came off, this awkward situation brought a powerful sense of déjà vu. Seeing a young woman's private parts in the chamber for natural functions – that was the way it had been with Helse when I had had to help her urinate in free-fall. You see, Helse had masqueraded for safety's sake as a boy and therefore had to use the male facilities, and they were awkward for a woman to use in free-fall. So I had had to hold her to the funnel while she squatted to relieve herself. It had been a tremendously stimulating experience for me, at age fifteen, the guilt of my reaction adding to the excitement. The facility for elimination differed here, being designed to be used while under gee, but the similarity of situation was close enough to evoke the same effect in me. In an instant I had a rigid erection.

Amber stared. I realized, belatedly, that this was the first time she had seen such a thing in life. In the helmet she had seen it many times and handled it and felt it inside her, but this was a different level of experience. She paused, evidently daunted, and I suffered a siege of embarrassment. Perhaps I should have arranged to do this in darkness this first time.

Then she laughed. 'It's real!' she exclaimed.

I relaxed. At least she wasn't horrified or terrified. I reached for her, and, of course, she was within reach because it was impossible to be out of reach of anything in this chamber.

I brought her down to me, but she hesitated. 'I can't sit on that!' she protested.

'Certainly you can,' I informed her.

'But . . .'

I showed her how. It seemed it had not occurred to her that both it and she could occupy my lap simultaneously. When she discovered how this worked, she was delighted.

And so she sat on my lap, facing away from me, divinely impaled, and I reached around to squeeze her young breasts in my two hands. I had in mind a considerable period of dalliance in that position before the culmination, but I had misjudged my tolerance. No sooner were we fairly set than I erupted.

'Damn!' I swore, for, of course, she had barely started on her own course of pleasure.

But she had a different reaction. 'It worked!' she exclaimed. 'You went inside me and you did it, just like the helmet!' She put her hands on mine, so that now her breasts were double-cupped, and squeezed them, pleased at this success.

I decided not to argue. There would be plenty of time for her to discover the other type of pleasure. For now her verification of her own performance seemed sufficient.

Of course, we didn't stay in the ship all the time. Periodically a sub descended to take us aboard. Amber was given a brief fling at the comforts of civilization, such as a soft and roomy bed, non-canned food, and relief from the stress of prospecting. I had no such reprieve; it was necessary for me to make periodic public appearances so that the populace would not realize that I was in hiding. I might have broadcast interviews, but that would have meant communicative contact with the prospect-ship, and that was too dangerous to risk. So I went physically, which was an odd mechanism for secrecy.

'The former congressmen have announced a government-in-exile,' Spirit informed me. 'And challenged you to meet them in debate.'

'That can have no legal status!' I protested. '*I* am the legitimate government of the US of J.'

'Legitimate but not conventional – or popular,' she reminded me. 'The people are paying a lot of attention to this movement. Because these are all former members of the former government, they possess a certain status in the eyes of the majority. We can hold down the random rebellions, but these people can sow the seeds of endless mischief, leading the majority into resistance.'

'I'd better tackle them, then,' I said. 'If they want to debate, I'll debate. The facts support my programmes.'

'Yes. But they may be up to something else. We have to be careful.'

'Of course. Set up electronic weapon detectors and have a pacifier ready.'

'They have nullifiers,' Coral said. 'But we have null-nullifiers. They will not be proof against pacification.'

'So I can go into their midst personally and brace them and make points for the Tyrancy,' I said. 'It should be fun.'

I went, after my personnel had made their arrangements. I really wasn't worried; this was a group of twenty former senators, of both major parties, all with excellent reputations. Obviously they intended to awe the audience with their credentials and to impress upon the audience – which should include most of Jupiter – the obvious justice of their cause. They stood foursquare for the old ways, the

271

good ways, the ways that should be restored. However, I was prepared to remind that same audience of the phenomenal problems those old ways had engendered – problems that my reforms were now attacking. Soon the results would begin to show, if we just stayed the course. I didn't expect my message to be completely popular, but I was sure it would make the more sensible people pause. The very fact that I, the Tyrant, came in person to debate those who pretended to be a counter-government – that demonstrated the extent of free speech that existed today and the openness of my dialogue. Repressive dictators did not indulge in this sort of thing.

They were seated in a large semicircle on a stage with the media pickups for an audience. Shelia parked her wheelchair at the edge of the stage where she could prompt me, and Coral stood beside her. I tried never to make a big thing of my personal protection; the Navy was never far from me, but Coral looked more like my mistress than my bodyguard. Indeed, on this occasion she wore a fetching red print dress that made her look more like a college girl than a mature woman, and she had a mock rose in her hair. Because of the rigid precautions against weapons, she carried none on this occasion, but, of course, her entire body was a kind of weapon when required.

This chamber was elegant. It was fashioned in the manner of an ancient Roman hall, with decorative columns and sculpture, and the walls, floor, and ceiling were of brightly phosphorescent material, so that external illumination was hardly necessary. This lent an ethereal quality to the proceedings.

In addition, there were mock stone alcoves set up as fountains, where water flowed and formed little falls. These were made up like portals to the outside, and beyond them was a panoramic holo scene that changed visibly to show the seasons, in accelerated manner. It had been fall as I entered; as I watched, intrigued as I often am by the innocent marvels of civilization, winter approached. The falls congealed to ice, and icicles spread across like bars. Delightful!

The programme began. I expected an opening diatribe against my policies but was surprised. A senator from my own party rose from his chair, strode forward, raised his hand, and proclaimed: 'Hail, Caesar!'

The power failed. The artificial lights went out, leaving only the glow of the walls, and the susurration of the air refreshing system ceased. Of all times for a breakdown!

But in a moment I realized that it was more than that. The senators were rising together and stepping to the mock windows. They were reaching for the icicles.

Coral was at my side, almost at a bound. 'Out, sir!' she hissed. 'Exit by Shelia!'

I started towards my secretary, but several senators were already moving to cut me off. Shelia, realizing what was happening, wheeled her chair to clear the exit.

As if in slow motion, while I was striding towards her, I saw it happen. Two men bent to grab her chair. They heaved it up and forward. The chair skidded sideways, then tilted over as the wheel struck the edge of the stage. It overturned, dumping Shelia down into the audience section.

I changed course to reach her, horrified. The drop was not great, but she had been pitched out head first, the chair coming down on top of her. If she was hurt –

'To me!' Coral snapped. I saw that the men had closed off the exit, and now all twenty were advancing on me, holding icicles.

Obviously this had been most carefully rehearsed. The setting, the freezing water, generating weapons where there had been none, the power cutoff that prevented either the pacifier from being used or any message from going out. The holo-cameras were dead; no one could see what was happening here. They had never intended to debate me! Now they had twenty against two, and the two were unarmed, and one a woman. In scant minutes a crack Navy unit would burst in here and take over, but evidently the senators believed they had time enough.

'Straight defence won't do it,' I muttered to Coral as we stood back to back.

'Build a wall,' she replied tersely.

I recognized another Oriental concept of hers. 'Right.'

The first senator came at me like a kamikaze, his icicle held clumsily in an overhand mode, stabbing down. I ducked under, whirled, caught his descending arm, and heaved him the rest of the way over my shoulder. He landed heavily, his arm outstretched and in my grip, and I quickly twisted his wrist and took the slippery icicle from it. Then I kicked him hard in the head, so that he would lie still, and whirled to face the next.

I heard a thunk behind me and knew that Coral had landed her client beside mine. She might look like a delicate young lady, but she was a more efficient and deadly combat specialist than I was. Then I stabbed forward with my icicle, plunging it into the belly of my attacker. The ice shattered, but it didn't matter; as he collapsed in agony I simply took his weapon.

Another body landed behind: Coral's contribution. Four down, sixteen to go. We were building our wall. When it got high enough, we would use it as a barricade.

Now the senators paused. They were obviously ready to give their lives in this cause, this treacherous assassination of Caesar in the Senate chamber, but they realized that they were giving their lives without cause at the moment. It was evident that Coral and I could eliminate them handily, one by one.

'All together!' one cried.

They tried to charge together, but it was impossible. One stumbled, his legs tangled with that of his neighbour, and went down in front. I knocked him in the neck with my booted toe, putting him down to stay. Meanwhile Coral spun around in place, and her dainty-seeming foot flung out to score on the side of the head of another, tumbling him unconscious into the throng. Another lost balance, and I caught his flailing arm and brought his face down to my rising knee.

But I felt the stab of an icicle in my left shoulder. There were too many men, all stabbing clumsily with their weapons; I could not avoid them all! I whirled, catching that arm, hauling the man further off-balance, then using an aikido twist to send him back into the throng.

The Navy arrived. Lasers flashed, catching the remaining senators in rapid order. In a moment, of the original party, only Coral and I were standing. She was bleeding also, but it didn't look serious.

I hurried across to help Shelia. She was bruised but unbroken; she had had the sense to break her fall with her arms and then to stay quiet, knowing she could not help us.

Now a Navy medic was seeing to us, expertly treating our wounds. An officer saluted me. 'Sir, how shall we dispose of the prisoners?' he inquired.

Abrupt rage overcame me. 'Interrogation, trial, execution,' I said. 'Root out the plot.'

'Yes, sir.' He turned to his business.

That was about all there was to it. Coral and Shelia and I had escaped without serious injury, thanks to our immediate and effective action. But I was not pleased. I should never have fallen into that trap!

One might suppose that the public would rise up against

the would-be assassins. It was not so. The news media, in a position to ascertain the facts of the case, elected generally to pretend that I was the one at fault. Three sterling senators were dead, several more injured, and the rest were gone from Jupiter society – all because of the whim of the Tyrant.

No, I did not clamp down on the press. I would not violate my oath. But this marked the turning point in the Tyrancy's handling of assassination and terrorism. After this they were publicly executed.

The job quickly became routine, despite the evident hazard. We quested interminably for bubbles, but though dust and rocks were plentiful, large objects were rare. Once we thought we spied one, but it turned out to be another prospect-ship.

Tedium was the greatest problem. Oh, certainly we made love, but the novelty of physical sex soon passed. At my age it took time to recharge; I found that about once per twenty-four-hour period was all I really cared for, and even though we did our best to make a production of each one, that left about ninety-five per cent of the time available for other things. To some, paradise is isolation with a pretty and willing woman; no one who has actually tried that believes in it any more. For one thing, the challenge is gone. For another, a desire fulfilled is a desire eliminated. When Amber had been anonymous via the helmet, she had been fascinating; each contact was an act of discovery. When she became known but forbidden, she was still fascinating. Now both her mystery and reticence were gone, and there was not a great deal remaining. She was not an intellectual partner; she did not know how to play challenging games. I couldn't even argue with her; she accepted everything I said or did without significant resistance.

Oh, we got along. But the glow was off. I became eager to find a bubble and get out of the ship, and I suspect that Amber, could she have been persuaded to hold an opinion of her own, would have felt the same. The quest became everything.

Naturally, when we finally scored, it was at the wrong moment. We had tried just about every possible variant of sex, struggling to relieve the boredom, and had discovered a promising game: Pin the Tail on the Donkey. No, no pin, no tail; we used our own anatomy, seeking to make the sexual connection. Naked, we took turns freezing in place, in free-fall, while the other closed his or her eyes and sought to make physical contact at only the key site. The closer the first touch to the bull's-eye, the higher the score. Amber was leading, having landed her bottom on my left knee, but I had figured out by elimination and by sound what her position had to be and believed I could home in on the site this time. Doing it blind was much more exciting than doing it sighted, and I was really getting into the spirit of the game. If I scored, I would get to complete the act, while she was bound by the rules to remain in a fixed position, ravished without reprieve. If I missed, she would get another turn, would probably score, and I would have to remain frozen while she had her way with me and won the game. The victory, at this stage, was more important than the sex.

I drifted through the short space, in my blind free-fall, head, hands, and feet held back, only my centre extremity forward – and felt contact with her body. I opened my eyes and saw that I had scored; it was her cleft I was touching. 'Ha, wench!' I exclaimed.

And the alarm sounded.

Amber laughed. It was a rule: the alarm severed any play. I had lost my opportunity and would have to start from scratch next time.

'Damn nuisance!' I muttered, and launched myself to the cockpit, my bare anatomy squeezing past hers in what at any other time would have been an interesting fashion. She made as if to bite at my member, and I made as if to knee her in the head. I squeezed into the pilot's seat, which was clammy to my skin, and she followed to peer over my shoulder.

Ahead was a blip, a monstrous one. 'Oops – we've drifted out of zone,' I said, disgusted. 'That's a city !'

But immediately I realized that it couldn't be; we were well below the inhabited level. Any true city-bubble would implode here. It was a city-sized bubble!

We homed in on it, and the size expanded as we got close. This thing was huge! It was like a planetoid, a perfect sphere. This was our strike!

We circled it, making sure there were no flaws, before planting our strike marker.

And spotted a marker already in place. This bubble had a prior claim.

For an instant I confess that I felt temptation: to remove the other marker and set our own, claiming this phenomenal strike ourselves. But quickly I suppressed the urge. For one thing, it was illegal and unethical. For another, claims were normally booby-trapped against just such an intrusion.

Sadly we moved on.

About a month later we found a bubble we could keep. It was smaller than the first but still well worthwhile. We staked our claim and contacted the company office, and our tour as prospectors was done. But somehow the disappointment of that first, denied strike remained with me. To have been so close to such a fortune in commissions . . .

I was not so foolish as to meet physically with my opposition again. I confined myself to more formal news conferences, and I was confined to my interview chamber: they could attack only my holo image. But that they did.

Some questions were routine, but one man stood and cried, 'I call upon all decent citizens to fight without let up to end the terrible Tyrancy! We are being oppressed by a madman and must free ourselves of this yoke by destroying him!'

He paused, evidently having run out of initial material. He had not expected to get this far before being lasered down or hauled out.

'Continue,' I told him. 'Free speech is one of the guarantees the Tyrant makes'

There was a ripple of laughter. But it wasn't very strong, and I could see that there was considerable support for the man's position. I had indeed progressed from saviour to enemy in the minds and hearts of the average folk. They simply weren't interested in my substantial reforms; they saw only the inconvenience that they themselves suffered at the moment.

Normally the discoverer of a bubble either took his bonus and retired, or if it was a small strike, went on as much of a binge as it would finance, then returned to prospecting. But I was a management trainee, so we stayed with our bubble, following it as it proceeded from the wild state to the civilized state.

First it had to be brought to the processing level. A gee-shield was installed, so that it was no longer dependent on the turbulent currents for support. Tugs nudged it upward, until it floated just below the inhabited level. Then it was cleaned up and rendered airtight, and a lock installed. The atmosphere was pumped out, the pressure reduced to Earth-normal, and breathable air was instituted.

Then they began fashioning the bubble into a residential sphere. They got it spinning, so there was internal gee, and installed prefabricated units and plumbing and electrical lines and all the rest. Amber and I participated, working on one crew and another, getting the overall picture.

I worked under a Saxon foreman named Gray, who evidently had not been given the word about Jose Garcia's manager-trainee status. Gray was no bigot and no genius; he knew his job and wanted it done right. His job was to establish secure foundations for the residential section of this bubble, so that there would never be a collapse after the apartment chambers were installed. Under his direction I had to drill holes into the hard shell of the bubble, to anchor those foundations. This was simple in concept but not in detail; those holes had to be positioned so precisely that they were surveyed in, and the drilling had to be done by heavy-duty laser. Bubblene is the hardest commercially viable substance available and is resistant to breakdown, but the same properties that make it excellent for ships and cities make it hellish to penetrate. Certainly a suitable laser will vaporize anything, but vaporized bubblene is dangerous, as it naturally precipitates the moment the vapour leaves the heat, coating everything it touches with bubblene. That means that the body of the laser drills itself and perhaps the hands of its operator. The first worker to encounter that effect had to have his hands flayed, literally, to get them clean. I used hefty protective gloves, of course; in fact, I was in a light space suit, because though there was now air in the bubble, accidents and leaks were always possible in the early stages of conversion. Still, I had no hankering to play with such vapour. So my unit was set to heat the

280

material to the softening point, so that it could be drilled. My laser was focused in a ring, and a diamond-sonic bit was in the centre of that ring, gouging out the material and sucking the debris into a holding chamber. I had had to take a spot course in the use of this instrument, and I watched its indicators carefully, doing my job right. It was tedious, but each successful hole was an accomplishment; I knew that a century hence, this bubble would probably still be in use, and these same holes would be containing the bolts that anchored all its internal structures. That's a kind of immortality.

As the days passed I came to know Gray. He had a wife from whom he was estranged, and a six-year-old daughter he visited at every opportunity. He shared custody, but now that she was entering school, she couldn't be with him in the bubble. He was evidently irritated about that; he had no objection to education, but he loved his child and didn't like the separation. Thus the school became the focus of his ire.

'You see the kind of books they're using to teach those kids to read?' he demanded rhetorically. 'Dick and Jane?'

I admitted that I hadn't. 'My ward is fifteen,' I said. 'She's beyond Dick and Jane, though she's still perfecting her reading. She's . . .' I shrugged. 'They call it retarded. She doesn't take well to schools, so I had to have her tutored. Now she's carrying on alone; if she passes the test, she'll get her credit, anyway.'

'Ward?' he asked. It seemed he hadn't been informed about this, either.

I shrugged again. 'She – we wanted each other, and it's legal now, but some folk don't understand. I . . . lost my other job because of that, but we're together.'

He nodded. 'Man's business with a woman is his own, if she's consenting.' I knew from the records I had checked that he was tolerant on this score, for his interest in a woman not much older had been responsible for the damage to his marriage.

'You mentioned the early reading books,' I said. 'I was educated on Callisto, and I learned English as a second language. We didn't use Dick and Jane, but I know they've been around for centuries. I guess they're pretty stodgy.'

He laughed. 'You haven't seen 'em? Then you sure don't know! They aren't stodgy any more! I was helping Lisa to read from them, and I nearly got a hard-on! What the hell are they teaching our kids these days?'

I remembered that Hopie had set out to reform the school system in many ways, but this sounded strange. 'Just what is in those books?'

'I'll tell you what's in 'em!' he exclaimed, getting his ire in gear again. Those who are tolerant about man's business can be less so about children's business. 'Here she was reading this book, "See Dick run. Run run run." Then next page it says, "Dick runs to Jane's house. Jane says, 'I'll show you mine if you'll show me yours.' Dick says, 'Great!' Then Jane lifts up her dress. Dick looks. Look, look, look!" I mean, it goes on like that! Playing sneak-peek behind the couch. And that's only the beginning!'

I managed to avoid a smile. Hopie had certainly reformed the first grade reader! My daughter, who had been so shocked at my relationship with Amber! Surely Thorley had not been responsible for this suggestion; she must have got it from Roulette. 'How did Lisa react to it?'

'She thought it was great!' he said indignantly. 'She couldn't wait to turn the page. She couldn't even handle all the words on the one page, but she wanted to get to the part where Dick showed his. "See it grow. Big, big, big!" My six-year-old little girl!'

282

'Well, curiosity is natural in children. If such material encourages them to read – '

'It did that, all right!' he agreed. 'But, my God – if that's what's in the first-grade reader, what the hell's in the second-grade reader? What's in the high school reader?'

'I don't think they've changed those yet,' I said. 'Amena's in that one, and it's copyrighted 2650. They're probably stair-stepping it up, following one grade through, until the whole school system's been updated.'

'Then it's not too late to get rid of this smut!' he said.

'Lots of luck,' I said. 'The Tyrancy's pretty set in its ways.'

'The Tyrancy!' he exclaimed. 'I thought it was great at first, but now with this shit, and the med cutoff – ' He grimaced.

'You're over the limit?' I asked. This was an excellent way to survey the reactions of the common man to the new programmes.

'My mother is. She's seventy-five, and the cutoff's at seventy. First time she gets sick, they'll just let her die. How can they do that? She's a good woman!'

'Well, I heard that medical expenses were getting up so high – '

'Sure, and they need to be cut back. But not out of my mother's hide!'

There, of course, was the rub. People who agreed with the thrust of the new programmes still didn't want to pay the price themselves. But ultimately every programme had to be paid for by the people; there was no other way.

'I wonder . . .' I said. 'Your Lisa . . . my Amena can't speak English, but she understands it. She might listen, and she could signal "no" if the word was wrong. That way you could use books outside the Dick and Jane trainer.'

His face brightened. 'Sure thing! Let's try it.'

We tried it the next time his daughter came to visit. Amber had learned how to read English now, which made it possible for her to study in that language, since it was not necessary to speak what she was reading. We found a fairly simple book, and little Lisa read aloud, and Amber nodded affirmatively for the right words and negatively for the wrong ones. The two girls liked the arrangement, and it seemed to help both.

The work progressed, and by the time I drilled my last bolt hole, the first tier of apartments was anchored on the region where I had started, and the second tier was in progress. So, things were moving along, but I saw that it would have been far more efficient had all the holes been drilled together by a skilled crew that travelled from bubble to bubble, so that in one day the next step could proceed. As it was, my speed of work limited the following work, making it inefficient. I mentioned this to Gray, and he agreed. 'But don't bother suggesting it to the front office,' he advised. 'This is JBC, guaranteed inefficient. If we started doing things the way they should be done, we'd get halfway competitive with the private bubble companies, and the bureaucrats would be out of work.'

'But I thought this company was planetized in order to *make* it competitive!' I protested.

'Fat laugh! No government ever made anything competitive. There's no incentive.'

'Something I've got to tell you – ' I began.

'That you're in training to take over? I found out.'

'It wasn't supposed to be a secret,' I protested.

'The damn inefficient paperwork took so long to come down, I might never have been informed,' he said. 'But you're such a bright one, I couldn't figure what you were doing here in the bottom echelon. So I inquired.'

'You aren't angry that I didn't tell you?'

'I *know* why you didn't tell me! You figured you wouldn't learn much if you walked up and said, "Hey, boss, I'm going to be *your* boss soon, so watch your step!" '

'I really hadn't thought of it that way,' I protested.

'I guess you didn't. You're a decent guy; you really want to learn. So you just kept your mouth shut and learned, and I let you. Comes to the same thing. My recommendation's already in; you got a good one, same as it would have been if you'd been for real. You did good work.'

'I tried to,' I said. 'But, look – when I do get there, I really do want to turn this company around. Certainly I'll change the hole-drilling routine. But that's only one facet of a huge operation; I can't learn it all from direct personal experience. So if you have any notions, I want to hear them.'

'Thought you'd never ask. I have this bright idea for a new kind of bubble, but nobody'd listen. I think it could put one like this on the market at half the price.'

'A fifty per cent saving on a city-bubble? If there's no catch – '

'See, there're a thousand little bubbles down there growing, for every big one. And a lot of fragments. They don't all grow perfect. Those pieces bobble around a while and drop out; when they're not hollow, they get to weigh too much. But there's a lot of good stuff there. Bubblene is valuable no matter what shape it's in. I figure we could fish out all the little bubbles, twenty feet in diameter, that we throw back now, and some chunks of solid bubblene, and take 'em into a big workshop bubble and melt 'em together so we have maybe a hundred little ones making one big one, like a bagful of balloons, tied in together by the spare bubblene. Put a lock in each one, make it an apartment. The whole thing spins for gee. Can leave the centre hollow, even, or use it for storage. Could have a hundred home-bubbles in one big ring, even, spinning for gee. Because they're so much more common than the big, perfect ones, and no complex internal structures are needed, the cost would be much less.' He paused to see how I was taking it.

'Makes so much sense, I don't see why they aren't doing it already,' I remarked. 'Are you sure there's no catch?'

'If there is, I don't know it. Some apartments are set up isolated, anyway; the people seem to like them. This is just bigger-scale.'

I remembered the apartment complex where I had found Megan twenty years before. Spheres on the ends of rods, the whole complex rotating for gee. Larger bubble arrangements like that, or in other shapes, each apartment separate – I saw nothing against it. 'There has to be some reason they wouldn't go for it,' I said. 'It makes too much sense to ignore.'

'Well, when you get there, you look up the files and find out which one my suggestion's filed in. Maybe they put the reason there.'

'I will.'

'You'll be moving on now,' he said.

'To the apartment installation crew,' I agreed. 'I have to learn something about every facet of this operation.'

'They don't seem to be rushing it much,' he said. 'You didn't need to spend a whole month on holes just to learn how it's done.'

'I'm not their choice for top exec,' I confided.

He burst out laughing. 'So *that's* it! They figure if they drag you around in it long enough, you'll get tired and quit.'

'Or foul up, so they can fire me before I get power,' I agreed.

'Why don't they just torpedo you, then? There're lots of ways you can make a person foul up, if you've a mind.'

'I have to wash out legitimately. I think the Tyrancy's getting fed up with bungling, and if they were caught messing up the new boss – '

'Maybe,' he agreed. 'Or maybe they're bungling that job, like everything else.' He pondered a moment, then said, 'You know, the boys've been staying clear of you, because of what you are. But you seem okay to me. Why don't you come into town with us tonight? You can hear a lot of ideas, if you're really interested.'

I had been aware that there was not much socializing, but since many of the times that I went into town alone or with Amber were actually secret returns to my role as Tyrant, I had found it convenient. Still, I did want to know the pulse of the common man, and this seemed like a good opportunity.

Five of us went stag to a bar and had alcoholic drinks. I was afraid they would also go to a civilian tail, but they knew of my situation with Amber and spared me that. Instead they went to an execution.

I am not sure I have discussed this before. It had been my original intention as Tyrant to eliminate the death penalty for crime, but circumstances had overtaken me. We were undertaking a programme to control population, and also to save money. It turned out to be nonsensical to allow old sick folk to die without medication and to prevent new babies from being born, while preserving the lives of murderers. There had turned out to be plenty of lesser criminals to man the inclement space stations: those that had some potential to reform and return eventually to society. So the death penalty had remained, despite my initial misgiving. But with a twist. Roulette had worked this out, and I had lacked the gumption to overrule her.

A large audience had formed for the occasion. Men, women, and even some children. On the stage in front were the prisoner, the judge, and a woman in black: the representative of the victim. The prisoner was bound beside a wall.

'The accused has been found guilty of murdering John Jones, as charged,' the judge said, and his amplified words carried throughout the chamber. 'I hereby sentence him to be lasered until dead.' He turned to the woman. 'You, Mrs Jones, widow of the deceased, may execute him yourself.' He handed her a laser rifle.

The woman shied away from it. 'Oh, I could not do that!' she protested. There was a murmur of mixed emotion from the audience.

'Then it is your privilege to give the order to the execution squad,' the judge said. At his signal a troop of six men entered, each carrying a laser rifle. They lined up and took aim at the prisoner.

The woman tried, but the sound would not come out of her mouth despite the yelled encouragement of members of the audience. Some were eating candy, I noted. I was disgusted, not so much at them as at myself. How could I have let such a scene be legitimized under my government?

'If you do not choose to take vengeance yourself,' the judge said sternly, 'then I shall select at random another person to do it.'

When the woman backed away, demurring, the judge looked across the various interested spectators and halted at the one who had the greatest doubt about the proceeding. 'You,' he said.

I started. He was speaking to me!

'I can't . . .' I protested.

'On pain of being found in contempt of this court,' he said firmly, 'I direct you to perform this office for the representative of the deceased. Only in this manner will justice be fulfilled.'

Still I hesitated. I had never expected to be tapped for this! Yet it *was* my doing, however indirect. Was I to lack the stomach to carry out my own policy?

'Do it! Do it! Do it!' the audience chanted.

'Order!' the judge rapped, and the chant faded.

Now his gaze returned to me. 'Come up here. Address the execution squad.'

Numbly I mounted the stage. I faced the firing squad. I took a breath. 'Fire,' I said.

Six lasers fired. They were heavy-duty; in an instant the body of the prisoner was charred black. It fell to the floor.

A cheer went up. Justice had been served! But somehow I did not find it satisfying.

The judge handed the woman in black a slip of paper. 'Here is your certificate for one birth,' he said. 'In this manner may the life lost be returned to you.'

That was it. The woman now had permission to have a baby; the paper would gain her a spot antidote to the universal contraceptive in the environment. But how would she conceive it with her husband gone?

The answer became apparent. Already men surrounded the widow, proposing marriage. The demand for the right to procreate was enormous. She might come out of this in better condition than before the murder. If that was what counted.

Suddenly I appreciated on a gut level the common man's objection to the Tyrancy. I was beginning to feel it myself.

289

11

Revolutionary

I proceeded on through the other stages of my apprentice-
ship, learning how to install apartment cubes, lay out
major halls, organize waste processors, put in power
and communications lines, and handle the mountainous
paperwork required for every stage. By the time I was
ready to assume the helm, more than a year had passed,
and I was none too certain I was ready. But I knew it had
to be done.

The fundamental problem with Jupiter Bubble Company was that it was huge, impersonal, and inefficient.
There was little dedication to speed, price, or quality,
and those who attempted to improve these things were
either fired or shuffled elsewhere. Paperwork had become
an end in itself, and experimentation was discouraged.
There were no values, no company spirit. The structure
was rotting from the core and didn't seem to care.

On my way up I had taken note of the minority of
genuinely dedicated workers and supervisors. My first act
as company president was to summon these people for a
conference. Gray was among them but only one among
many.

'You, all of you, are about to assume the management
of this company,' I informed them. 'Each of you will be
put in charge of a particular aspect or programme relevant
to your expertise. You will select your own personnel
from those remaining in the company and designate their
duties. They will answer directly to you, and you will
answer directly to me. This will be done personally; if
you find it necessary to write a memo, it shall be confined

290

to one page, preferably less. There will be no paperwork, apart from minimum specifications for complex aspects. I trust your judgement, and I will hold you responsible. If you tell me a programme is good, I will support it; see that you do not let me down.'

They turned to each other, not quite knowing what to make of this, but I was serious. I put Gray in charge of the Micro Bubble task force: to develop a viable programme for producing the type of small bubble complex he had described to me, and then to implement it. I put others in charge of programmes relevant to their interest and competencies. I gave them autonomy and authority. I stressed that our company interest, as of that instant, was first for quality and reliability, then for value, then for service to our customers, then for efficiency, and finally for profit. 'We shall be losing money for a time,' I admitted. 'But we've been losing money for three years; that's nothing new. Once we change, that will change.'

Then I got more personal. 'I have come to know you men as I worked in this company,' I said. 'But you are the minority. We all know that we have quite a number of inadequately trained and motivated workers and deadwood executives. We are not going to fire any of them, but we are going to demote them. If they wish to leave the company, we'll gladly let them go. But those who stay will be well treated here. We are going to treat every worker as a winner, as someone special. We are going to treat every client as someone special. We are going to care about our people. We are going to be like one giant family. We are going to provide medical assistance for any worker who wants it, and day care for the children of any worker who wants it, and honest counselling for any worker who asks for it. Each of you will be like a parent to your group, and I will be a parent to you and a grandparent to them. We are going to have love here –

love of our product and love of our customers and love of each other. We are going to have company-sponsored entertainment. If one employee marries another, we will give them a wedding on the company premises at company expense. If one of our employees dies, the company will cover the memorial service and will offer what support we can to the survivors. Religious services and political meetings will be welcome, provided that no proselytizing or recruiting is done on company premises. And we shall sing together.'

Still they gazed at each other uncertainly, half suspecting that I was not serious. The changes I was proposing were too great, too different. They simply didn't know what to make of it. No paperwork? Weddings on company premises? Singing?

'Now, we are going to make mistakes,' I continued. 'That is inevitable. We shall be tolerant of errors, while avoiding total foolishness. We are going to be highly hospitable to new ideas, to innovation, to alternatives. We . . .'

I paused, for one of the company men had moved quietly to a door and flung it open. A man was revealed there, listening.

'Ah, a spy!' I exclaimed, recognizing the intruder. I had checked out all suspicious characters and knew that this man was in the employ of Saturn, an industrial agent. I had used my facilities as Tyrant privately to get information on him directly from the source: Chairman Khukov had provided it. 'Come forward!'

Apprehensively the man approached me. 'Comrade, we have nothing to fear from Saturn!' I informed him. 'We need have no secrets here. Come to my office in the morning, and I will provide you with any information you desire. I hope that your planet will reciprocate. I appoint you company liaison to Saturn. Now we shall welcome you warmly.' And as the others stared with astonishment, I began to sing: 'Meadowlands, Meadowlands, meadows green and fields in blossom!' I gestured to the others to join me. Most were blank, but some did know the song; hesitantly they joined in. Gray laughed and sang loudly; he was no Saturnist and loved the joke. In due course we were singing it with greater enthusiasm, and indeed, it is a pretty song.

That, I think, was what broke the ice. After we had sung together we felt more like a family. The people I had chosen began to believe in this seemingly crazy dream of mine, to fathom the way in which it could operate. I stepped off the platform, still singing, and took the hands of those nearest, and they took the hands of others, and soon all of us were linked in a big circle, including the Saturn spy, moving our feet in time and swaying our bodies in a kind of dance. One one level it was indeed crazy, but on another it was the essence of what I wanted: company unity.

I was taking a serious risk in this, and I knew it, but I felt that the importance of the move warranted it. You see, what I was doing here was very like what I had done as an officer of the Jupiter Navy, thirty years before, and much more recently as Tyrant. Few people had my talent for understanding and influencing others; it was the principal trait that had brought me to the Tyrancy. I was using it freely here, openly for the first time. If any of these caught on . . .

I think, in retrospect, that it is possible that some did. But if so, they did not betray my identity to others. Perhaps it was curiosity that moved them, waiting to see what I was up to. Or perhaps they liked what I was doing with the company, so supported it despite their knowledge.

It was very much like chaos at first. Our output and our cost-effectiveness plummeted. But I had expected this, and I had had a good deal of experience in this sort of thing. The new lines of command rapidly took form, and as the new formations formed, the work improved. Naturally, great numbers of employees left, in perplexity or horror, but we worked to keep the ones we really wanted. Always we fostered the feeling of family, of total commitment and support, of the importance of every single person associated with Jupiter Bubble. We stressed endlessly the concurrent commitments to quality. Every worker became a quality control expert, passing on no work that was not, in his judgement, up to snuff. We hired personnel to take care of the increasing number of children in the day-care unit. There were none under two years of age, because of the procreation cutoff, but women with children in the three- to five-year-old range flocked to our banner, because here they could work for a fair wage without having to sacrifice their children. A number of them were quite competent, and they were dedicated from the start.

We also attracted creative males: those who had been stifled at their companies, who wanted to be respected, to have their novel notions seriously considered, and to feel important. We soon had capacity employment, and a waiting list developed for potential employees. Indeed, they liked it here – not for superior pay, for our scale was standard, but for the feeling of worth as individuals they experienced here. In return they gave us their best effort, and in an amazingly brief time the benefits accrued.

Of course, I am over simplifying here; there were endless details to cover and continuing minor crises to accommodate, and the process took years. But Spirit ran the Tyrancy while I made spot appearances as Tyrant, and Amber was the appropriate contrast to the stresses of company and Tyrancy management, being a completely malleable young woman who lived only to please me. It may be unkind to say it, but had my other lives been anything other than hectic, I would soon have got bored with Amber. But as it was, she represented a calm haven and constant sop to my ageing masculine ego, and I found I could live with that. Oh, true, at times I dreamed of the glories of my past life, when Helse had initiated me into the magic realms of sex and love, when Emerald had managed my Navy career towards the apex, and when fiery Roulette had dazzled me . . . as perhaps she still did. But I knew I was no longer fifteen, or twenty-two, or thirty; I was passing my mid-fifties, and physically and sexually I was not the man I had been. Emotionally and intellectually I remained viable, I trusted. The proof of my current manhood was in the progress of the company – and that was part of the progress of the Tyrancy.

But at this stage that proof was far from apparent. When I was about a year into my presidency of the company, a significant event occurred, though I was not to appreciate just how significant for another year. My business took me to the great city of Cago, in the State of Prairie, a centre for the food industry. I had a peripheral interest in food production, a matter I shall go into in due course. I was travelling as Jose Garcia, of course; it would hardly have been feasible as Tyrant.

I had just about concluded my business when the trouble started. I was departing the mayor's office, having taken care of some paperwork, and saw that a demonstration was in progress. Curious, I joined the throng in the main hall to watch. The demonstrators were mostly young, and a number of them – perhaps the majority – were female. They held placards proclaiming, GIVE US OUR BABIES and NIX ON NULL-POP!

Now I understood. These were the first people who felt the onus of the population control measure now in force. I knew that it was necessary to halt the exploding population of the System, and that the United States of Jupiter could not dictate population control to the other nations of the planet; we had to set an example ourselves. That was working, but at this stage, the benefits were less apparent than the sacrifice. The festering slum-cities of RedSpot, the result of overpopulation that depleted its resources, seemed far away, while the denial of babies to the families of Cago seemed immediate. Naturally they felt it keenly. I understood this, but, of course, the policy could not be changed until planetary growth had been got under control. So the young would-be mothers marched in protest, and they certainly looked ready to reproduce. As Tyrant I knew why this had to be, but as Garcia, I had sympathy for their cause.

I knew that such demonstrations had been increasing, for as women grew older, their chances of bearing healthy children diminished, and their desperation increased. The ban on babies would be lifted in due course, but for some women, that would be too late. The situation had been especially serious here in Cago; I had been warned of this before I travelled here, but that had not dissuaded me from getting my business done. There had been some unpretty episodes.

There was one today. As I watched, a quite comely young woman strode to the entrance of the mayor's complex, carrying a suitcase. The police guards at the entrance watched, evidently more interested in her appearance than her message.

The woman stood before the entrance, set down her case, and removed her blouse. One guard had taken a step, about to escort her away from the region, but stopped. What man would interfere with a beautiful woman in the process of disrobing before him?

Disrobe she did. In moments she stood gloriously naked. Then she stretched out her arms. 'What use is this body to me if I cannot have my baby?' she cried. Then she bent to touch a stud on the case.

'Watch out!' a guard cried. 'That's a bomb!'

The guards charged, but the case had been activated. It flared, bathing the woman in the intense light.

'No – that's an incendiary laser!' I exclaimed, starting forward myself.

All of us were too late. The woman shrieked as her skin was scorched from her body, a thin veil of smoke rising. Those lasers were used to incinerate garbage, eliminating the problem of collection and disposal; they were normally set at intervals in residential areas, for neighbourhoods to use. This one had evidently been partially dismantled, its protective housing removed, so that it represented a danger to the user.

The woman fell, writhing. Her hair and much of her skin had been burned away, and she was dying in as painful a manner as was possible. The two guards stood over her body, appalled. So was I; I was sure that her medical expense limit had been used up, so that she would not be treated. She would certainly die, which was what she had intended.

'What a waste!' one grunted. 'Body like that – '

'Pigs!' a woman in the crowd cried, and hurled a fruit.

The guard whirled, drawing his sidearm. His laser flashed, and someone in the crowd screamed.

I did not see much more than that, for I was making a hasty retreat. I knew that real trouble was about to flare, and for my own safety I wanted to win clear of it while that was possible.

For a while I wasn't sure of that possibility. The

immolation had electrified the crowd, and the lasering of a demonstrator had galvanized it to action. All manner of objects were flying at the mayor's office now: vegetables, shoes, coins, and even faeces.

More guards rushed out of the office complex, lasers drawn. More beams were fired, and there were more screams amid the crowd. I ducked low, knowing that anything could happen, while the missiles and beams crossed over me. I found myself beside a young woman, a demonstrator, who had similar sense. 'Oh, this is getting out of hand!' she exclaimed. 'There'll be the Tyrant to pay!'

Interesting figure of speech. 'Would the Tyrant really get involved?' I asked. 'This seems to be focusing on the mayor.'

'The Tyrant would do anything,' she said darkly. 'The mayor couldn't stay in power a moment if the Tyrant didn't back him.'

I pondered that as the mayhem increased. It was no longer feasible to retreat; the throng was surging angrily forward, growing as it came. We remained huddled in an alcove. I, in my guise as Tyrant, had not favoured the Mayor of Cago, though he was of my party; I regarded him as a regressionary force and perhaps a racist. But his power was solidly entrenched, and I had had plenty of problems to keep me busy without seeking new ones. Thus Cago had been relatively untouched by the Tyrancy; its local political machine remained intact. Only Tyrancy programmes like population control affected the natives here directly. It was a programme the mayor supported, however, so evidently he had become the symbol of its implementation here. The Tyrant was a more distant figure, therefore less objectionable. An interesting perspective.

But now, as I observed the viciousness with which the

police of Cago pitched in to the fray, it occurred to me that the population measure might be only an incidental symbol of a greater grudge. I had known that the mayor kept a tight rein on his domain, running the city mainly to please himself. Apparently direct force was the principal component of this control. Those lasers were dangerous, even if set at nonlethal intensity.

A beam seared into the wall above my head, gouging a channel. Nonlethal? That was kill-focus!

The incident had become a pitched battle. The broad hall was now jammed with people, most of them ploughing determinedly forward. There were bodies on the floor, but far too many living people for a few police with lasers to stop. The throng surged on, overrunning the police, and I heard the cursing and thudding as fists and feet pounded the downed men. This crowd was now more than angry, it was vicious!

Then they were crowding into the office complex, whence new screams sounded. 'They're raiding the mayor's staff!' I exclaimed.

'We hate the mayor and all he stands for,' the woman said. 'It's a den of thieves.'

Evidently so! Now the throng in the hall was thinning as it drained into the office complex, and we were able to stand. 'This isn't over,' the woman said darkly. 'I never meant to get involved in violence. I'm going home.'

'And I'm going back to the airport,' I agreed. 'Nice meeting you, Miss – '

'Mrs,' she said. 'Culver. My husband didn't want me to get involved in the demonstration; now I know why!' She glanced at my good clothing. 'And you are – ?'

'Jose Garcia,' I said, expecting her to forget the name as soon as she heard it.

I was disappointed. 'Garcia!' she exclaimed. '*The* Garcia?'

299

'Uh, I don't know how many there are – '

'Jup Bub? The good employer?'

'Yes, I am with – '

'Oh, you must come and meet my husband!' she said. 'He's always admired your style.'

'I'm just trying to run the company properly,' I protested. But she was hauling me on, and it seemed easiest to follow. At least it would get us clear of this region of riot.

As we reached her cell the news was being broadcast: a mob had taken over the mayor's office and was holding him and his staff hostage for city reforms, starting with the Pop-Null programme. That was wrongheaded, I knew, but how was one to reason with a mob?

Mr Culver was indeed happy to make my acquaintance. It seemed that I had become something of a hero to the working class in the year I had been running Jupiter Bubble. I had not realized this and was flattered. It had been some time since my days as a rising Hispanic politician, honoured by the masses, and I enjoyed the return of this role. In the persona of Jose Garcia I had returned to the essence of Hope Hubris.

But events proceeded inexorably onward. The mayor had sent out a distress call, and it seemed that the Tyrant was indeed answering. I was sure it was Spirit at the helm, operating in my name as always. But I discovered that firm action did not appear the same from the worm's-eye view I now had, as it did from above.

Because the mob had threatened to murder the mayor and his staff if any attempt were made to rescue him, and because it had the power and evident incentive to do it, the Tyrancy acted indirectly. A valve was opened in the hull of the city-bubble, and the Jupiter atmosphere started leaking in. It would take some time for the pressure to rise significantly, but there was horror the moment this was announced. The pressure of the external atmosphere was a terror, and any break in the integrity of the hull was alarming. The valve was filtered, so that no actual poisons entered, but still, the threat was potent.

'The valve will be closed when the mayor of Cago and his staff are released unharmed and the offices vacated without vandalism,' the Navy officer in charge of this proceeding announced on the city-address system.

'I knew there'd be the Tyrant to pay!' Mrs Culver wailed. 'He stands behind his own.'

This bothered me. Of course, the Tyrancy had to support the mayor, but this was nothing personal. Privately I would have preferred to be rid of the mayor. I disliked being in the position of brutalizing an entire city to save this brutal mayor's hide. But what could I say?

'This has gone too far,' Mr Culver said. 'That mob will never give over – and neither will the Tyrant. We'll all pay for this foolishness – and for what? For opposition to a policy we know in our hearts is necessary.'

I was getting to like this man.

His wife was subdued. 'You're right, of course. There's nothing I want so much as having our baby, but riot and murder isn't the way! We've got to get out of this somehow.'

Easier said than done. Hard on the news of the valve came the news of the city's reaction. Angry workers attempted to storm the valve – and were mowed down by the disciplined lasers of the Navy troops. There was no bluffing here; they were shooting to kill. After fifteen were dead the attack abated, but the city as a whole was twice as fearful and angry. I was wincing at all of it; this was being seriously mishandled. No further deaths had been necessary, and it was doubly unfortunate that they were occurring in the name of the Tyrancy. But what could I do from this vantage?

'Maybe a negotiator,' I suggested. 'Someone that both parties would listen to, who could work for a compromise. If you contact the Arbiters Guild – '

'Those deals are fixed,' Mr Culver said flatly. 'We've been screwed before.'

Oh? That would be something for the Tyrancy to look into! 'Well, some public figure, perhaps, who – '

'Like the president of Jup Bub!' he finished, though that had not been my notion. 'You'll do it, won't you, sir? You understand the needs of the working man, and you rank high enough, so maybe the Tyrant would listen to you!'

'I, uh . . .' I said, for the moment overwhelmed by this development.

The woman took my hand. 'You will, won't you, Mr Garcia?' she beseeched.

What choice was there? I did, in a guise they didn't know of, have a certain responsibility in this matter, and I probably could do something, both because of my talent with people and because my sister Spirit would surely recognize me. 'It is difficult to deny a beautiful woman,' I said.

She flung her arms around me and kissed me. I suppose no matter how many women a man knows, that particular type of thrill never abates.

Thus I found myself approaching the mayor's office, where he was being held hostage. The mob leaders were glad to see me, now that they were aware of my identity and mission. I sensed immediately that they had got themselves into more than they cared for but were riding the tiger and couldn't get off.

'Give me an open public line to the Tyrant,' I said. 'I will try to achieve a compromise settlement.'

The mob leaders acquiesced. Jose Garcia was indeed a man they respected, as the Tyrant was not. Of course, they had little to lose; if I could not strike a fair bargain, I could become their hostage too.

The mayor's screen illuminated, and in a moment the White Bubble was on the line. The mayor's secretary had been released for this duty; the mayor remained bound and looked somewhat the worse for wear.

'I am Jose Garcia, of Jupiter Bubble,' I said. 'May I speak to the Tyrant, please?'

The secretary at the other end kept a straight face. Of course, the average citizen could not call in and be put right through to the Tyrant! 'One moment, sir; I will put his secretary on.'

Shelia appeared. She, too, kept a straight face, but I knew she recognized me. 'I am Jose Garcia,' I repeated. 'I have been selected to negotiate for the City of Cago, and if I could perhaps talk to the Tyrant – '

'The Tyrant is not available at the moment,' Shelia said smoothly. 'But if you will describe your business further, Mr Garcia, I will try to determine whether a direct interview is warranted.'

Of course, the Tyrant was unavailable! But I had a role to play. '*Señora*, this is important. Twenty people have died, the mayor is held hostage, and the city is under seige by order of the Tyrant. I must talk to him directly!'

'Hey, don't push your luck,' one of the mob leaders whispered to me. 'You aggravate the Tyrant, he'll send a ship to blast us all out of the atmosphere!'

What kind of a reputation did I have? But Shelia was responding: 'We are aware of the situation in Cago, Mr Garcia. We did not know that you were there, but if you are in a position to negotiate, I can relay your statement to the Tyrant.'

I became visibly excited. 'People are dying here!' I repeated. 'The mayor and his staff are hostages, and they

303

will be killed if something is not done. If the Tyrant cares at all for the common man, as I do . . .'

Shelia didn't respond immediately, taking stock. 'Let me check,' she said. She spoke inaudibly into her intercom. Then: 'The Tyrant is tied up in a meeting he cannot leave at the moment, but he is cognizant of the situation in Cago and will negotiate privately through me, if it can be kept brief. Will your party accede to that, Mr Garcia?'

I turned to the mob leaders. 'This is the Tyrant's personal secretary,' I said. 'I believe she knows almost everything the Tyrant knows, and she has his ear at the moment. I think we can trust what she says. Is it satisfactory to deal through her?'

The mob leaders exchanged glances. 'We care only about results,' one said, and the others agreed. 'If she can deliver – '

'The trouble started because of the Pop-Null programme,' I said to Shelia. 'The women here want their babies.'

'If they get their babies,' she replied, 'then every other woman on the planet will want hers, and all the ills of overpopulation will return. The Tyrant will not relent on that.'

Indeed he would not! But there were avenues for compromise. 'We know that babies will have to return, or the species will end,' I said. 'Can the schedule for return be established, so that at least our women know with what they are dealing? As I recall, the women supported the Tyrant when he sought power, and some reciprocal gesture now – '

Shelia consulted with her other party, whom I suspected was Spirit. The schedule for the return of babies had already been set but not announced, pending the appropriate time to announce it. This seemed to be that time.

'The Tyrant agrees that in one year, pending good

behaviour, permits matching the death rate will be issued in Cago. In two years that will be extended to the nation as a whole.'

I heard an intake of breath. Suddenly there was news of the schedule of the restoration of births! Surely the women of Cago would eagerly accept that. We had planned to start it in certain major cities, then expand a year later. But I pushed for more. 'There have been deaths here, because of the overreaction of the mayor's police and the murders at the valve. Those police must be put on trial and restoration made.' I saw the mob members tense; I had already got them much of what they wanted, and they were concerned that I was pushing too far.

'The Tyrant will grant permits for births to match the number of deaths resulting from this crisis,' Shelia replied. 'An investigation will be made into the incident and appropriate action taken. That is as far as the Tyrant will go.'

I knew the mob leaders would accept this. 'But how can we be sure the Tyrant will keep his word?' I demanded.

'We accept!' a mob leader cried, shouldering me aside.

'But no action to be taken against the people in this room!' I exclaimed. 'Amnesty – '

Shelia smiled. 'Amnesty,' she agreed. 'But I think if you open your mouth again, Mr Garcia, the Tyrant may reconsider.'

'Agreed!' another mob leader cried, hauling me back. They had had to act to prevent me from throwing away all that I had gained, for the Tyrant was known to be mercurial when challenged. But they were vastly relieved and pleased.

That ended the occupation of the mayor's office. The mob dispersed peacefully, and the valve was closed. The mayor was suspended from office, pending the completion of the investigation; no action was taken against the known mob members, and twenty birth permits were issued to the women of the city. Those at the head of the 'eligible' roster would profit. And Jose Garcia was a hero.

Yet soon after my success as a popular figure came a personal tragedy. It started, for me, with an article by Thorley. In it he set forth the suggestion that a member of the Tyrant's cabinet had been corrupted by a person of the opposite sex and that funds for that department were being abused. 'Does the Tyrant know?' he asked rhetorically. 'If so, why doesn't he act?'

Now, this was fighting language. Shelia showed me the column and awaited my reaction. I read it with anger. All my cabinet members were good people, dedicated to their jobs; I knew I had not misjudged any. Yet Thorley was not a man to manufacture charges from air. 'We'll deal with this openly,' I snapped. 'Issue a news release: my challenge to Thorley to name the cabinet member.'

'Are you sure that's wise, sir?' she asked. 'If the name becomes public, you could be placed in an awkward position.'

I should have paid closer attention to the warning, but I was in the office only briefly, about to return to my role as Garcia. 'I don't believe there *is* anyone,' I said. 'But if there is, I'll deal with it openly. The Tyrancy may not be popular right now, but we cannot afford to have any suggestion of scandal touch it.'

'As you wish, sir,' she agreed.

In due course the challenge was published, and thereafter Thorley named the member. It was my sister Faith.

'*Now* I wished I had listened to Shelia! It had not occurred to me that the suspect would be a family member. Certainly I would have preferred to handle this quietly. But I was stuck with an open situation.

I talked to Spirit, as I also should have done before. 'What's going on here?'

'It seems to be true,' she said. 'A handsome and poised man has been courting her for influence. She meant well, but he was recommending corrupt cronies, and she has authorized their appointments. I don't believe she suspected, but she should have. She's blinded by love.'

Faith – once the most beautiful of young Hispanic women, then the plaything of pirates, finally a respected member of my cabinet. She had enormous support among the masses, for she had truly laboured for the welfare of the poor and had accomplished many excellent reforms. But this was scandal, and now I had to act.

I summoned my sister. When she appeared at the White Bubble, I was struck by her elegance. In her mid-fifties, she was a handsome woman, and her dedication to her position enhanced the aura of class. It was hard to believe that she had got involved in this sordid thing.

'Is the charge true?' I asked, and knew that it was; her reaction betrayed her.

She spread her hands. 'I love him, Hope.'

'He has interfered with the Tyrancy,' I said. 'An example must be set.'

She gazed at me and turned away. That hurt me; I wish she had protested in some more obvious way.

We arrested the man and put him on public trial within days. We suspended Faith from her office. I hated this, but it had to be done.

There was no question of the man's guilt. The facts came out quite clearly. All of the suspect appointments were nulled, and the man was sent to labour in space.

And Faith was found in her Ami apartment, dead. She had taken a euthanasia pill.

Now the storm broke in earnest. For the condemnation of the man there was applause, but for the fate of Faith there was horror. Demonstrators marched and not only in Ami. WHY DID FAITH HUBRIS DIE? the banners demanded.

The answer I remember best is the one made by Jose Garcia. In that guise I was known as an ardent supporter of the common man, so I was one of the ones the media sought for comment. 'I believe she died because the Tyrant lost track of basic human nature,' I said, expressing the recriminations of the Tyrant far more accurately than they knew. 'He has become insensitive to the feelings of others, including his closest family members. He failed to realize how seriously his sister would take the scandal and the destruction of the man she loved. He should have handled this matter privately, allowing her to retire and to join her lover in exile if she chose. Perhaps this is a reflection of his isolation from the passions and needs of the common folk. I'm sure he is extremely sorry now.'

'Now that the damage has been done?' a reporter asked, and I nodded affirmatively.

'Do you believe that the Tyrant is losing control and perhaps should be deposed?' another pressed.

Now, that was a leading question, well worth avoiding. But in my mood of grief and regret I stepped into it. 'Sometimes I think so,' I agreed.

It was not long after that the Resistance contacted Jose Garcia. 'Do you believe that the Tyrancy should be ended?' an anonymous visitor asked.

I controlled my reaction. The Resistance had been bedevilling the Tyrancy increasingly. This was a non-violent movement that spread ideas rather than physical mischief; it seemed to have no organization, which made it almost impossible to uproot. It supported the return of Jupiter to democracy without reversing all the reforms made by the Tyrancy. The problem with that notion was that every out-of-power movement espouses lofty ideals, but few retain those ideals when they achieve power. I was sure that it would not be safe to give over the reins until the reforms were complete. But it didn't necessarily appear that way to the common man. Thus the Resistance was dangerous, and we needed to be rid of it but had no handle on it.

I realized that Jose Garcia might represent that handle. If he joined the Resistance and worked his way into the confidence of its leaders, this could be the key to an important success.

But it disturbed me deeply to think that it had taken the death of my sister to open this particular avenue. Certainly, if I could have travelled back in time and replayed that matter, I would have acted to protect Faith. I had indeed neglected her; I had hardly paid attention to her in the past two years. Now, too late, I thought about her constantly.

I think, in retrospect, that this was the true beginning of my madness. Something had snapped in me, and it could never quite be mended. Perhaps Faith's demise only foreshadowed my own. But this was not apparent at the time, and indeed my grief gradually faded into the background, so that I was not aware of the change that was occurring in me.

So I answered that I did have some questions about the Tyrancy but did support many of its reforms, so was not ready to commit myself to any rash course. After all, I reminded my querant, I owed much to the Tyrancy; it had put me in charge of a major company and allowed me to reorganize it to my satisfaction.

That, it seemed, was the correct answer. The Resistance was not looking for rabid partisans but for thoughtful, concerned citizens who had sensible doubts about the Tyrancy. I certainly fitted that description at the moment.

Thus I became a revolutionary. But this was only the beginning and really did not intrude on my life. Later that was to change, but only gradually, so that most of my life was unchanged.

* * *

My promise to balance the budget had seemed a mockery in the early years, as the deficits became greater than before. But as the company improved, became competitive, and then was the leader in Bubble technology, and other companies emulated our methods in order to become competitive with *us*, what had been a financial liability became a financial asset. Jupiter industry began contributing massively to the health of Jupiter society. Similarly the reduction in medical expenses helped, and the population control programme, spreading to RedSpot and other Latin Jupiter nations so that their population pressure was easing in the same fashion ours was. Already the reduction in illegal immigration was measurable, and the related expenses were dropping proportionately. The Tyrancy might be condemned for the cutoff of procreation, but the job was being accomplished. And you know, as the economic situation improved, so did the attitude of the citizens. When the Tyrancy was two years old, I was being lasered in effigy in every major city; by the time it was five years old, I was being accepted as a necessary evil, and when it was eight years old, I was being hailed as an economic genius. Of course, by that time the antidote to the sterilizing agent in the food was being made available to just about anyone who asked for it, and babies were being born again, to families whose situations were secure. The hardships of the immediate past seemed to be forgotten. Contrary to belief, popular memory is short, and the conditions of the present colour the public impression of both past and future.

I won't say that everything was wonderful, just that we had at last balanced the budget and were now retiring the planetary debt at a significant rate. Jupiter had again become the economic and social leader of the System. Buoyed by this, the people tended to overlook the remaining problems, such as the persistent illicit drug trade and the inability to fit every citizen in the job he most wanted. But we were working on these too.

Let me just give one example, the one that pleases me most, perhaps because it can be indirectly traced to my own management policy at Jupiter Bubble. I had set up task forces to explore new notions and develop them if that proved feasible. Some of these cost the company a good deal of money, because not every bright new notion makes sense, but that is only evident after it has been tried. Some merely wasted time. But some few did pan out, and these made up for all the rest.

One of our executives, Caspar Yonner, had transferred in from the Jupiter Fungus Company – known colloquially as Jupfun – and he had fungus on the brain. He had a notion to develop a strain of fungus that would grow outside a bubble, directly in the atmosphere. Naturally that nonsense had not been tolerated there, but naturally we had considered it more carefully. It did sound scatter-brained, but the potential reward was so great that we decided to take the risk.

You see, much of our food is bacterial in nature. It is relatively inefficient to grow grains and vegetables, and colossally inefficient to grow animals for slaughter. But the right kind of fungoid cultures, yeasts, or bacteria can generate an enormous amount of protein in a very short time, to just about any specification. From the vats emerged imitation animal flesh of many flavours, nutritious and inexpensive, and this was shaped into steaks or bacon or chicken legs to supplement the plant-derived food. Thus the fungus industry was one of the vital ones, which was why the Tyrancy had nationalized one of the inefficient fungus companies. It had floundered under our tutelage in the usual fashion, losing its best personnel. We had hired Yonner because his credits were good.

Culturing bacteria was a tricky business, because the cultures propagated extremely rapidly and mutated often. The solar radiation seemed to be mostly responsible. If a single cell were mutated, remained viable, and bred true to its modification, in a single day we could have a thousand tons of pseudo-vanilla pudding that looked and smelled like rotten eggs, and tasted worse. In such event, about the only thing to be done was to flush out the bubble to kill off the mutated strain, repressure, flood it with saprophytic agents to digest the refuse, and start over. Yonner had been this route several times and had noticed that sometimes the mutated culture returned in the same form in the replacement batch. Either a similar mutation had occurred, which was highly unlikely, or somehow one or more spores had survived the depressurization.

Actually the terminology is deceptive. Originally the farm bubbles were all in space, orbiting beyond the Jupiter atmosphere, so that opening a lock meant depressurization. But in this case the bubble had been in-atmosphere, just below the residential level, where the pressure was about six bars and the temperature slightly higher than Earth-norm. So despite the term, it was actually pressurization that occurred, as the hostile gas of Jupiter squeezed in to stifle the living organisms. Then, when it was pumped back out, it flushed out the dead material with it. Except that it seemed that not all of it was quite dead.

Yonner had reasoned that if some spores could survive depressurization, they might be selected to grow and replicate in it. That could lead to atmospheric farming, dispensing with the need for agricultural bubbles. Perhaps

312

a current of fungus could be developed that could be harvested. That could lead to a virtually infinite supply – solving much of the food problem of the planet.

Of course, there were cautions. We didn't want to pollute the Jupiter atmosphere. It was uncertain whether fungus could propagate in the atmosphere, or whether such a strain would be edible, or whether such a harvest was feasible. So we let Yonner study it. For three years he and his team researched and experimented and struggled, trying strain after strain in special capsules of Jupiter atmosphere at different pressures. The expense mounted. But this was Jupiter Bubble; we knew the atmosphere could be harvested for inorganic material, so we were more tolerant of a notion about organic material than his original company was.

And suddenly he had it. He found a strain that would flourish at the conditions extant in the cloud layer just above the inhabited zone. Water, pressure, temperature – the lab tests proved that it was feasible, and it was an edible variety. Its tolerance was limited; it could not survive beyond that fairly narrow range, so could not spread out of control. It looked very good.

Now, in an ordinary government it would have required decades of bureaucratic consideration before such an experiment was permitted. But I studied the data, consulted with the experts available to the Tyrancy, and concluded that the potential benefit outweighed the potential risk. So when Yonner put in his petition for approval, it was granted immediately by the supposedly distant Tyrant.

It worked. The strain of fungus propagated phenomenally well, suffusing the swirling clouds, and in a matter of months the first harvest was possible. It didn't amount to much, for as yet the spores were spread very thinly, but it proved it could be done. Within a year there were commercially viable harvests, and thereafter it became something very like a cornucopia: seemingly unlimited protein from the clouds. We had solved the problem of food for the hungry masses of the System.

I think this would be about as nice a note on my place in history as any. True I was a tyrant; true, I authorized the demise of many old folk, facilitated the suicide of those of any age, and prevented the birth of many babies. But true, also, that the system I set up, and the specific company I reorganized, may have done more good for humanity than any other. If this doesn't justify me, then I don't know what does.

But meanwhile the Tyrant was not exactly idle. We had had continuing trouble with the importation of illicit drugs, despite the clinics. There were some that were simply too dangerous to tolerate, so were not provided by our clinics, and these were becoming big business. Unable to persuade a certain Latin government to take serious steps against the producers and exporters of the most serious drugs, we took firmer action: we invaded.

It was an almost surgical measure. The other Latin governments, in debt to us and dependent on us for much of their food and other key supplies, sat tight. In a month the target nation was ours.

Using the enormous leverage of our external farming expertise, we prevailed on other governments to make increasingly binding commitments to us, until all of Jupiter represented a sphere of cooperation. Officially all the original separate nations remained, but in practice they had become vassal states. But their poor were no longer starving, and their populations were under control. Certainly there was muttering about the Tyrant of Jupiter, but I think there was also an underlying acquiescence because, of course, the Tyrant was Hispanic. Competent and honest administrators replaced the corrupt ones who had governed before, and the lot of the average citizen improved.

Of course, I may not be objective about this. It will be for history to say whether my realm was benign, like that of Asoka. But I did the best I could. So though my madness was developing like hidden cancer within me, the Tyrancy itself, organized by more stable minds, was good.

12

Madness

But even in my hour of success the end was approaching. I am trying to be objective about this, to present it fairly, but this is difficult because it becomes unflattering to me. You see, I lost my reason, and not just when the wind was north-northwest, and great was the mischief thereof.

I suppose it got serious with the iron industry. Iron is critical to interplanetary operation, because it is the avenue to most of the energy civilization uses. Laboratory black holes fashioned and controlled by special gee-shields change the iron to its contra-terrene state, and this is handled magnetically so that it can be combined in controlled fashion with terrene iron to generate the power of total conversion of its mass to energy. Ultimately it is gravity that is the source of our energy, but iron, because it can be handled without direct and destructive contact, is the major instrument. We need the energy where we need it, and iron enables us to have it precisely where we need it. That makes iron important.

Naturally the suppliers of iron are in an advantageous position. Jupiter is actually one of the major processors of iron, for it is among the trace elements thrown up in the bubblene layer, and so is Saturn. But refining it from atmosphere is tedious. While there are some pure nuggets, most of it is in the form of dust and is combined with other substances, so that it must be refined. As more is harvested the returns diminish, until it becomes too expensive to make it economically feasible. All the major users and refiners have been searching for centuries to develop more efficient methods of refinement, so as to be able to tap the immense potential resources of the major planets, but so far they have not been successful.

The gas giants, however, are not the only objects in the System. Politically the solid inner planets are inconsequential, but they do have ready access to some critical substances. Earth and Mercury have gems, which retain their value because of their rarity, beauty, and hardness. Venus and Mars have iron. In fact, the proven accessible iron reserves of the Red Planet are greater than those of the rest of the System combined. In addition, it is relatively easy to obtain. It is on the surface of a solid planet, so that it can be picked up in solid state and refined virtually on-site. This makes it relatively cheap to produce.

Mars, in fact, has long enjoyed an interplanetary economic leverage quite out of proportion to its planetary population. Mars has got rich by raising the price of its iron as high as the market will bear, with seeming indifference to the hardships worked on poor planets sorely in need of energy. But it has long been suspected that Mars is not the only culprit. The Jupiter iron companies also profited considerably by their handling of Martian iron, because they simply raised their prices to accommodate the higher Mars prices and added a generous margin for profit. But no one was able to catch them at profiteering because their accounting policies were concealed, and not even the Jupiter government had the means to verify the correct figures. More billionaires have been made from iron in the past century than from any other trade.

But the Tyrancy nationalized one of the iron processors, the Planetary Iron Company, or Planico. It took our accountants some time to fathom the records in detail – key files were mysteriously missing – but in due course we verified that this company, in its prior freedom, had defrauded the Jupiter public of monstrous value.

317

Apparently this was standard practice; indeed, there were memos verifying collusion on pricing. We put a good man in charge, and he did approximately what I did with Jupiter Bubble, rendering it into an efficient, innovative, and militantly competitive organization that provided iron at a fraction of the former price. Naturally the other companies had to drop their prices to match, and the cost of living for the average Jupiter citizen declined. Our effort, when it became successful, was widely lauded and became the model for other planets. The power of the Big Iron had been broken.

The public was pleased, but the free iron companies were not. No billionaires were being generated by this industry now. Accustomed to having their own way with the various planets, Big Iron set out to reclaim its own. It determined to eliminate the apparent cause of its malaise: the Tyrant of Jupiter.

I hope I have presented this objectively enough. It is no easy task. Had I known the nature and consequence of their drive, I would have nationalized them all at the outset and shipped their executives to space. Even now I shake with anger. But hindsight is pointless.

I should clarify that this was not the Resistance. The Resistance remained passive, merely building a subtle network among concerned citizens, doing nothing to attract the ire of the Tyrancy. No, the Iron Fist was a private, ultimately selfish effort ungoverned by ethical scruples. That kind is dangerous, too, especially when backed by substantial resources. But because it was canted towards action, it was likely to expend itself rapidly. The moment action occurred, the hounds of the Tyrancy were on it, rooting out the source. Thus an action-opposition had to be effective early, or it was soon out of business.

The iron companies approached the Tyrant forthrightly: they believed I misunderstood their position, and they wanted to clarify it. I did not trust this, but it behooved me to listen, so I agreed to a meeting. This was not a physical meeting, of course; I had learned my lesson with the senators. We set it up with holo: an image of each iron exec was to be projected to the White Bubble, while the actual execs remained in New Wash, close enough so that transmission of the images was virtually instantaneous. This was really just about as good for such meetings as physical presence was, and far safer for me.

Thus I was physically present in the Oval Office, along with Shelia and Coral, who confined themselves to the background. There were seats around the table for six iron execs, and another for Gerald Phist, who also projected in for the occasion. He was the one in charge of industry, including the iron industry, and I wanted him to backstop me. I knew the iron magnates would be hurling statistics at me, and I wanted competent refutation at hand.

They appeared on schedule. Abruptly the seats were filled, and certainly if I had not known that the visitors were non-physical, I would not have guessed. The leaders of Energiron, Spacirco, Rediron, Jupico, Standard Iron, and Abyss Metals. Of course, they sat at similar tables in their own offices, so that when their hands touched the surface, they did not hover above it or penetrate it; they were precisely zeroed in. The days of such inadequacies were long past.

'What gentlemen, is your concern?' I inquired evenly. I suspected that this whole business was a waste of time, but I had to maintain the forms of reasonableness, and it also showed that I remained in the White Bubble and actively on the job. That was important, since, of course, most of my time was spent elsewhere, while Spirit handled

319

the job. Reba's ploy to maintain my safety had been working excellently, and in fact, I liked my active life as Jose Garcia better than my standby life as Tyrant.

'We feel that you have underestimated the importance of the profit system,' the exec from Standard Iron said. 'By forcing us to cut down our margins, you reduce our competitive viability on the System scale. We can no longer expend the same resources for iron exploration that Mars can, and that is not only bad for us, it is bad for Jupiter.'

'What's good for Standard Iron is good for Jupiter,' Phist murmured sardonically. He was old now and getting crusty, but his mind remained sharp.

The exec grimaced. 'Laugh if you will, but there is some truth in that. The strength of Jupiter's business *is* the strength of Jupiter, and we are in great danger of losing it. The greatest advantage Jupiter has had over Saturn is our appeal to the industrious person; to the one who labours most effectively go the greatest rewards. Naturally the elephant consumes more than do the smaller creatures, but the elephant also accomplishes more. If you insist on punishing those who generate the real strength of the planet – '

'You forget that we nationalized Planico,' I cut in, stung by the reference to the elephant. I had elected to save the one in our zoo despite its enormous consumption of food, and I didn't like this not-too-subtle reference. 'That we finally got to the bottom of the iron industry finances. You have been defrauding the public for centuries.'

He reddened. 'That is purely a matter of interpretation! If you insist on defining a reasonable return on investment as – '

'What you call reason, I'd call piracy,' Phist said.

'Only if you do not take into consideration the risk

entailed! Prospecting for iron is an expensive matter, and ninety-eight per cent of the sites prove barren. Therefore some allowance must be made for – '

'Only sixty per cent of Planico's exploratory sites proved barren,' Phist retorted. 'And I believe that you yourself, sir, have castigated that government company as "Saturnistically inefficient".'

'Of course, there is great variance in strikes. The fact that Planico was lucky does not alter the overall – '

He broke off, because something strange was happening. The household garbage disposal unit was trundling in on its wheels, unattended.

These units are mobile, because there are many kinds of refuse, and it is often easier to bring the unit to the garbage than vice versa. But normally ours remained in the kitchen. Though it was self-propelled, it normally did not travel unattended, because the refuse had to be fed to it by hand.

All eyes followed the somewhat lurching progress of the machine. 'A late arrival?' Energiron inquired, smiling.

'From the garbage industry!' Jupico responded, and they all laughed. Naturally they found it hilarious that such a foul-up should occur at this moment, as though the Tyrant could not keep his own house in order. I knew that the media would have a field day with this one; naturally they had a camera present.

The disposer rolled slowly around the table, outside the ring of chairs, working its way towards me. I saw Shelia wheeling to intercept it, simultaneously murmuring into her mike. She was summoning the kitchen staff to come and recover their errant equipment, but meanwhile she would deactivate it herself.

Then several things happened in rapid order. A flicker of motion caught my eye; I turned to spy a man backing away from me. But I hadn't seen or heard him come near, which was strange – and he looked exactly like me, which was stranger yet. I glanced down at my torso as if to verify that I remained me – and was startled to discover that I *wasn't* me. I was invisible.

And the actual disposer suddenly clanked and lurched at me, its incinerative laser coming into play. 'It's remote-controlled!' an exec cried. 'Assassination!' another exclaimed.

Coral leapt towards it, her arm moving. 'No!' Shelia screamed, jamming her chair right at me. But Coral's grenade was already in the air, bound accurately for the disposer, which had now overlapped my space. I felt no contact, no laser-heat; it was merely a holo image.

And the grenade, which was quite real, was coming at me. Still seated in my chair, I could not get away from it in time.

Shelia's chair crossed before me, crashing into the table. Her right hand reached up and plucked the grenade from the air. She hauled it down to her bosom and hunched over it.

The grenade detonated.

Pieces of Shelia and her chair flew outward. Blood spattered floor, table, chairs, and ceiling – and me. I was half stunned by the concussion, and half blinded by blood, but I was alive. Shelia . . .

I looked up and saw Coral standing there, totally appalled. Then the madness closed in.

I must clarify, as objectively as I can, what had happened, though the tears of grief and rage well up from my eyes as I write this. It was, of course, an assassination plot – but far more sophisticated than I had deemed at the time. The iron execs had set it up, acting much as had the senators who sought to kill Caesar, but with a fiendishly clever twist.

There had been no runaway garbage disposer, and no remote control. It was only a holo image. The execs had rehearsed their reactions carefully, to contribute to the illusion that the machine was literal. The image was crafted to resemble the White Bubble disposer exactly, and it was possible for that unit to enter the Oval Office; that aided the verisimilitude. So we had had no reason to doubt the obvious: that the machine had gone haywire – or that it had been preempted for a remote-control assassination attempt.

Coral, catching on, had acted in her typical manner, hurling a grenade to destroy the machine before it could reach me. But Shelia had caught on to the truth: that my person had been covered by a holo image of the machine. A holo image of me had been crafted to retreat from my place, while I had been blanked out. A properly manipulated holo can do that, by projecting an image of an empty chair to replace what is actually there. It is tricky and cannot be perfect, but this was only for a moment, while the image of the disposer rolled forward to overlap that same place. Thus, to the observer I was retreating from an assassination-bent machine.

Shelia had penetrated the ruse but too late to stop Coral from throwing the grenade. So Shelia, already moving forward, had goosed her chair and intercepted the grenade, making a spectacular catch. Her legs were paralysed, but her arms made up for it by being highly coordinated. Knowing that the grenade would go off in a second, she had brought it in towards her body, so that the explosion would be muffled.

Shelia had quite literally given her life to save mine. She had foiled the assassination attempt. It does not surprise me that she did that; she loved me. But it appalled me that she should have had to sacrifice herself like that.

So the iron magnates had plotted to cause my own bodyguard to kill me but had killed my loyal secretary instead.

As I recovered consciousness, being attended by the White Bubble medics, a scene from history was running through my mind. Back in the twentieth century, before Earth had expanded to space, there had been a dictator of Germany, a man named Hitler. There had been a plot to assassinate him, in which a bomb was left in a case beside him, at a meeting. But the case had been inadvertently moved, so that though it exploded, Hitler survived. Even as I had survived.

Hitler had seen to the complete extirpation of the plotters. I intended to do no less.

But first there were matters to attend to. Coral was setting up for seppuku, the Saturnian ritual suicide of the warrior class. I felt this was not warranted.

She was adamant. 'Had I fathomed the plot, I would not have hurled that grenade,' she said. 'I failed you – and killed my friend.'

'It was a most sinister plot, intricately planned,' I reminded her. 'We could not judge in seconds what was crafted for months. I was deceived too.'

'It is not your business to foil plots. It is mine.' She gazed at the short sword she had laid out before her. She was kneeling, bare-breasted, on a tarpaulin; she intended to have no blood soil the floor of her room.

'It is your business to safeguard my life. You have not failed.'

She turned to me. 'Sir, I love you, as she did. Please do me the great honour of acting as my second in this.'

That would mean taking the large sword she had, waiting while she used the short sword to disembowel herself, then severing her head with one swing. This was the honourable and less agonizing way to go, once the guts had been spilled.

'But your job is unfinished,' I said. 'If you do this now, you leave me undefended.'

'There are other bodyguards,' she reminded me.

'You are the one I require.'

'I ask you to release me.'

'I refuse.'

Again she turned to me. 'Sir, do you not see the pain I am in? *I failed in my duty and I killed my friend.*'

I knelt before her, straddling her sword. 'Woman, do you not see the pain *I* am in?' I gazed into her eyes and let my feeling show. It was the north-northwest wind.

Slowly her gaze clarified. 'I apologize for my selfishness. What would you have me do?'

'I would have you join me in vengeance.'

She nodded. 'We shall wash their bodies.'

'We shall wash their bodies,' I repeated.

Then I opened my arms to her. She leaned into me, we hugged each other, and I felt in her body the mirror of the agony in mine.

We washed their bodies. All of the top executives of all of the independent iron companies were arrested and interrogated by chemical means, their guilt spilling out of them. They were put on trial, found guilty of conspiracy to assassinate the Tyrant, and condemned to death. In a public ceremony the leaders were hanged; that is to say, suspended by the neck by means of ropes, in the ancient style, until dead, and then left hanging for twenty-four hours in public view in New Wash. The lesser conspirators were beheaded, and their heads hurled into deep space to drift forever. Those merely guilty of complicity were permitted to take the euthanasia pill.

Coral supervised it, and I approved it, and we both

watched every execution. There were several hundred in all. Then the Tyrancy nationalized their companies. Big Iron was dead.

But it wasn't enough. Shelia, my loyal secretary, my right hand, my friend and my lover, remained dead, and the void of her absence refused to heal in me.

I caused a memorial to be erected in her name, and in her name also I allocated the sum of one billion dollars for the treatment of all who were crippled in the legs. The Shelia Foundation was instituted, dedicated to the study of nerve and limb regeneration, that the crippled of the future might walk again.

Still, it wasn't enough. I ached for the loss of her, and I could find no way to alleviate it. It was not that I loved her, though certainly I cared for her; it was that she had been close and loyal and reliable, and I had no substitute for her. I needed her, her competence and support, and without her I lacked proper anchorage. Megan helped me select her when Shelia was still a teen; thus she represented one of my intimate links with Megan.

I strode about my room, alone, trying to abate the void that would not be abated. Then I went to the vision port of the White Bubble and gazed out into the murky atmosphere. 'Damn!' I cried, and smote the panel with my fist. 'Where are you now, Shelia?'

My fist passed through it. Off-balanced, I fell after it, stumbling through the panel and out into the Jupiter air. I flapped my arms and ascended to the layer of cloud above. There was a stair cut into the cloud bank. I set foot on it and climbed, and the stair wound up in a spiral through the layer until at last it emerged on the cloud surface.

There, parked at the top, was a wheelchair. I got into it and wheeled it forward along the path that showed.

This coursed along the mounds and declivities of the bank and to the shining gates of a mighty, walled city.

This was heaven, I knew. I wheeled on into it, and there were people, and all of them were in wheelchairs. One approached me. 'For whom are you questing, sir?' he inquired.

'For Shelia,' I replied.

'Why, she arrived last month,' he said. 'She has been lonely.'

'She loves me,' I explained.

'Of course. I will locate her for you.'

I followed his wheelchair through the bypaths of the shining city, and soon we came to a small chamber. I entered, and she was there. 'Hope!' she said, brightening.

'I have come to take you back,' I said.

'I don't think I can do that.'

I took her hand. 'You must do it.'

'I mean that Helse would not approve.'

So I searched for Helse. She was in a wheelchair, too, but it was just a formality, as it was with me. 'I want to take Shelia back with me,' I said.

'Of course, Hope,' she agreed. 'You know I want only what is best for you.'

'But if she can return,' I asked, 'why can't you?'

'I am already with you,' she said. 'I was with you the first time you used her body; don't you remember?'

I remembered. 'But that isn't physical!' I protested.

'It is when it needs to be.'

Then I understood. I wheeled on out of the city of Heaven, alone, and back along the path. I parked the wheelchair at the head of the stairs and walked down. I swam through the atmosphere at the base and into the White Bubble.

I caused the crippled women of the region to be brought before me, and when I found one that resembled

Shelia, I brought her to the White Bubble and to my room, and I lifted her to the bed and undressed her and made love to her. 'Shelia!' I whispered in her ear as I climaxed. 'Hope!' she responded raptly.

I dressed her and returned her to the wheelchair and brought her out to meet the others. 'This is Shelia,' I informed them. 'Take her home.' Then I departed the bubble, returning to my alternate identity as Jose Garcia.

The madness was upon the Tyrant but not on Garcia. Not so that it showed.

In the tenth year of the Tyrancy Jupiter was prospering, but the people were restive. As Garcia I knew the cause: it was the madness of the Tyrant, who was given to odd habits, such as summoning some woman in a wheelchair at random, taking her to the White Bubble, forcing her to commit sex with him, and returning her to her home. The women involved did not seem to object, but other members of the Jupiter society did. 'He's loco!' I heard men of the company exclaim. 'One of these days he's going to go all the way off the deep end!' But there were also women who took to going around in wheelchairs, though they were not crippled. There were even scattered reports of pregnancies in these women, for now the birthrate had been restored, limited to zero population growth, but these were not confirmed. It was known that the Tyrant had spent fifteen years in space before coming to Jupiter. 'But he did sire a daughter,' the gossipers would murmur.

Of deeper concern were the continued executions. Early in the Tyrancy no one was executed; all were sent to space. But gradually that changed, first for a few capital cases, then for lesser crimes, like conspiring against the Tyrancy. It was as though the Tyrant had become more callous as he aged. Also, the manner of execution changed, so that now men could be hanged in public, instead of taking the euthanasia pill in private. It seemed that the Tyrant's anger over the assassination attempt that took the life of his secretary had never faded. Yet there had been no such reaction when his sister had died. (I suspect, in retrospect, that there had been that reaction for Faith, but it was hidden. The first blow had weakened my sanity; the second had shattered it.)

As Garcia, I shared the doubts of the common man. I was now high in the councils of the Resistance and knew things about it that most did not. Its leader was a woman – a highly intelligent, educated, experienced older woman who knew the political process inside and out and guided the Resistance unerringly to greater influence. But I did not yet know her identity.

In private, as the Tyrant, I speculated on that. Paranoia surged in me: had Reba, the head of QYV, betrayed me? Did her aspiration for power go beyond her present position? Should I have her liquidated? I was uncertain on all counts, so did not act – and this, too, was perhaps a sign of my madness. I was no longer doing what I knew it was advisable to do.

But as the behaviour of the Tyrant became more bizarre, the Resistance gained strength. It was not that Jupiter chafed under the policies of the Tyrancy; it was that Jupiter feared that too many of the successful policies would be eroded or dismantled, in the manner of the criminal code. The Tyrant was becoming a loose cannon: a thing without proper anchorage whose random blunderings were a threat to all around him.

As Jose Garcia, I had to agree. It would be best to depose the Tyrant, before he betrayed the Tyrancy. Jupiter could not afford madness.

But how was that to be accomplished?

The Resistance had an answer. It sponsored a general

strike. It had been years since anything like this had been tried, and it took some courage, because the Tyrant had acted swiftly and effectively in the past to squelch such efforts. But this one was extremely broadly based; in fact, nearly half of all the employed citizens of North Jupiter participated in it, and a quarter of those in the Latin provinces. As Jose Garcia, I led Jupiter Bubble on strike, granting all workers a holiday for the duration.

This was a significant surprise. The Resistance had developed so quietly and peacefully that few people realized the proportions to which it had grown. Probably not all the strikers were members, but this demonstration was enough to paralyse the vital planetary services and too widespread to be amenable to wholesale discipline. It was peaceful but impressive.

Something had to be done, and because this demonstration was obviously well meant, Spirit concluded that it should be met with appropriate restraint. Violent methods, in this case, would alienate a far greater segment of the population than we could afford. What would be both gentle yet effective?

As Tyrant I made the decision: I would challenge the leader of the Resistance to a contest of some kind, winner take all. If I won, the Resistance would be dismantled; if she won, I would retire from the Tyrancy. Spirit was against this, but I think she was getting tired of governing, so she did not object strenuously. Or perhaps she was wary of my madness and thought in her secret heart that it would be better if I did step down. Maybe I was looking for a pretext to do that. Then I could retire to my life as Garcia, which was more productive. Though even that was not a perfect solution, because Amber was now twenty-three years old, was able to function competently in Spanish, and not needed in other languages. I felt it was time for her to go forward into her own life, but she would not do so as long as I was there. I think eight years of being my mistress had finally abated her fascination with me, but she felt she owed me, so duty kept her with me. We both needed a good excuse to separate amicably.

So the mad Tyrant made the challenge, and the public attention focused on this, for this was indeed the kind of madness he was noted for. Wagers were made: would the Resistance leader answer?

The leader answered: Yes, she would meet me in a contest. The terms were acceptable. To the winner would go the management of Jupiter, and to the loser, exile.

This really wasn't as crazy as it sounds. All parties knew that the Tyrant, now almost sixty years old, would not live forever, even if his sanity recovered. It was best to arrange for an orderly transfer of power before his condition worsened. Probably the Tyrant would overcome the Resistance leader – wagers were being made on that too, of course – but even so, it would establish the principle of a peaceful change of government.

It was necessary to have an intermediary, to arrange the details of the contest. The Resistance leader designated Jose Garcia.

Now, this made sense. Garcia was a highly respected figure and a solid member of the Resistance. He had been appointed to his post by the Tyrant. The Tyrancy could hardly object.

But it put me in a most interesting position. How could I negotiate when I was actually the Tyrant?

Spirit was elated. 'They have played into our hands!' she exclaimed. 'They don't know who you are!'

Perhaps not. But what bothered me was that I wasn't quite sure who I was either. The positions of the Resistance were generally good, and I agreed with them. A return to democracy, with elections within two years. Release of the client nations. A considered restoration of

331

medical benefits for those in serious need, so that no one would be required to die when he could be saved. Curtailment of the euthanasia programme. Abolition of capital punishment. As Garcia, I supported these principles – and perhaps as Hope Hubris too. The machinery of the Tyrancy was such that I could not simply change existing policies, but the urge to do so was growing in me.

Was I to set up an encounter that could result in the destruction of the Resistance? It seemed to be a conflict of interest.

On the other hand, if by this mechanism I could finally meet the Resistance leader personally and identify her, there would be no need for the contest. The Tyrant could arrest her and root out the leaders of the organization.

It seemed I had no choice about this office. The public approved, widely and emphatically. Thus, as Garcia, I travelled formally to New Wash and was received at the White Bubble. I consulted with Spirit privately, then emerged to say that the Tyrant had suggested a number of possible types of contests, ranging from chance to a game of chess, and had suggested that the leader of the Resistance come to the White Bubble herself to participate.

Now, this was a bit more than the average man could swallow. Obviously the head of the Resistance was not about to place herself in the power of the Tyrant. So next I travelled to Ston, where a representative of the Resistance was to pick me up in a private vessel and take me to the secret residence of the leader. There I would present the Tyrant's offers and listen to her counter-offers.

The process of negotiation promised to be convoluted, but meanwhile the strike was suspended. Jupiter was operating again, and all attention was on the progress of the meetings.

I boarded the Resistance vessel in Ston, in the Old Colony State, and was taken to the unknown destination. This was going smoothly; no one suspected my nature. But still I wrestled with myself. As Hope Hubris I could use my bare hands to kill the woman and free the Tyrancy of this challenge. As Jose Garcia, I was honour-bound to carry the negotiations through. Yet if I did, what would I do when I had to meet her formally for the contest, in my other identity? Then my duplicity would be revealed, and all would fall apart. So I might as well act as the Tyrant. But if I killed her, then I would be trapped in the heart of the Resistance and would be killed myself. So I should complete the negotiations as Garcia, then return to the White Bubble and use the information to strike against the Resistance most effectively. Yet if I did that, where was honour? The Tyrant might suffer the touch of madness, but he had always acted honourably by his definition.

I still had not resolved my internal conflict when the ship docked. I did not know the city and was ushered into a closed car. I realized with a kind of relief that I might not be able to betray the location of the Resistance, and if the leader masked herself or addressed me via another intermediary, I would not know her, either. Still, she would know me – when I showed up for the contest as the Tyrant. Well, would that be a disaster? I wasn't sure.

As I was guided into a building I made my decision: if I met the woman face-to-face and she was Reba, I would leap at her and kill her, for she would otherwise recognize me and kill me. If she were a stranger, I would talk with her and use my talent to judge her nature, then decide.

I entered the apartment, and my guide retreated,

leaving me alone. I saw a chair that faced away from me, and the back of a head. Now was the point of decision.

'I am here,' I said, stepping forward.

The chair swung around, bringing the woman into view. I froze, stunned. 'Hello, Hope,' she said.

It was Megan.

Editorial Epilogue

Apparently Hope Hubris was unable to write beyond that point. He had encountered, to his total surprise, the one woman he could not deny. His wife had finally called him to account. He had forgotten the Beautiful Dreamer's warning. He had in the end allowed the means to become the end and his namesake to overtake his common sense: the hubris of power. 'I caused a memorial to be erected . . .' he writes, as if he is a deific figure. Megan was correct: it was time for sane people to set things right. The rest followed: his voluntary abdication from power and acceptance of exile, together with Spirit Hubris.

The identity of Jose Garcia was never revealed. He announced his retirement, feeling that after negotiating the conclusion of the Tyrancy he had no further need for public life, and he disappeared. Amber returned to New Wash, alone, where she worked as a translator of recorded transmissions, using the helmet to communicate her renditions. She never commented publicly on her private relationship with the Tyrant.

The various officers and staff members of the Tyrancy were allowed to retire with due respect. There was no pogrom, no forced elimination, just a demotion to subservience to the new order. A number of them continued in their existing offices, for they were all excellent administrators. It seems fair to say that the quality and dedication of the personnel of the Tyrancy were the best ever seen on Jupiter, and their influence hardly faded with the demise of the Tyrancy itself.

Hope Hubris may have suffered some problem of sanity

after some of those close to him were lost; that remains in question. But the reforms he wrought in only one decade were enough to establish his place in history beyond question.

Megan headed a brief caretaker government, setting up a framework for restored elections and public representation. She had no interest in power for herself and stepped down the moment the elections produced a new president and Congress. She was called a great woman. She was.

It turned out that a number of planets were interested in providing sanctuary for the exiled former Tyrant of Jupiter. He accepted the most challenging offer. Thus it was that Hope and Spirit Hubris travelled to Saturn to commence what turned out to be perhaps the most remarkable stage of their careers.

Coral, unable to go to that planet, accepted a position as a physical therapist with the Shelia Foundation. Ebony joined her there.

And I, the daughter of the Tyrant, now twenty-five, took my eleven-year-old adopted brother, Robertico, and retired to a paid position within the restored Department of Education. It was, after all, what I understood best.

Of course, I must answer the obvious question: how did I feel about Amber? I can only say that the process of education can be trying at times but that I learned to understand and appreciate my father for what he was, and he was a man who needed women. Age was irrelevant, and Amber was hardly to blame for being captivated by him. All women who knew him were. I have asked myself whether I am able to forgive her, and I have answered that forgiveness is unnecessary, for there was no fault. How could I forgive without admitting injury or jealousy – jealousy for what? And so we remain, in our fashion, sisters.

– Hopie Megan Hubris